WILD

HANDS

TOWARD

THE

SKY

A Novel By

RAY ELLIOTT

Tales Press
Urbana, Illinois
2002

Address inquiries to Tales Press, 2609 North High Cross Road, Urbana, IL 61802.
Visit our Web site at *www.talespress.com*.

First Edition, 2002 by Tales Press, Urbana, Illinois

Library of Congress Cataloging-in-Publication Data
Elliott, Ray, 1940-
Wild hands toward the sky : a novel / Ray Elliott.-- 1st ed.
p. cm.
ISBN 0-9641423-7-6
1. Boys--Fiction. 2. Illinois--Fiction. 3. Farm life--Fiction
4. Rural families--Fiction. 5. Fatherless families--Fiction
6. World War, 1939-1945--Veterans--Fiction. I. Title.
PS3605.L457 W55 2002
813'.6--dc21   2002011207

Printed in the United States of America

Book design by Vanessa Faurie   Cover design by Carlton Bruett

For my parents,
for all the people who endured and survived
the Depression and World War II
and for those who never made it back

WAR IS KIND

Do not weep, maiden, for war is kind.
Because the lover threw wild hands toward the sky
And the affrighted steed ran on alone,
Do not weep.
War is kind.

> *Hoarse, booming drums of the regiment,*
> *Little souls who thirst for fight,*
> *These men were born to drill and die.*
> *The unexplained glory flies above them,*
> *Great is the Battle-God, great, and his Kingdom —*
> *A field where a thousand corpses lie.*

Do not weep, babe, for war is kind.
Because your father tumbled in the yellow trenches,
Raged at his breast, gulped and died,
Do not weep.
War is kind.

> *Swift blazing flag of the regiment,*
> *Eagle with crest of red and gold,*
> *These men were born to drill and die.*
> *Point for them the virtue of slaughter,*
> *And a field where a thousand corpses lie.*

Mother whose heart hung humble as a button
On the bright splendid shroud of your son,
Do not weep.
War is kind.

— Stephen Crane, 1899

PASS IN REVIEW

How many times they had heard the old, long-drawn-out, faint command pass down the long length of vast parade grounds, fading, as the guidons moved out front.

So slowly it faded, leaving behind it a whole generation of men who would walk into history looking backwards, with their backs to the sun, peering forever over their shoulders behind them, at their own lengthening shadows trailing across the earth. None of them would ever really get over it.

— James Jones
from *WWII*,
a nonfiction, soldier's view of the war

Prologue

Nobody had mentioned that it was the anniversary of the D-Day invasion on the morning in 1956 when Sam stuck the Mauser in his mouth and blew the back of his head up against the side of his house. And I hadn't said anything about it, either. I was so shocked at the time that I couldn't talk much; but I knew that he'd taken the rifle from the German soldier he'd killed in the breakout on the drive from St. Lô, and I knew what day it was when he killed himself. Sam and I had talked about things like that too many times for me not to have known the day. Maybe other people really didn't know or just didn't think about things like that, I thought now, standing in the cemetery and fishing a cigarette from the package tucked away in the top of my sock.

The echo of the long-ago rifle salute at Sam's funeral service that was rolling through my mind reluctantly gave way to the sound of a tractor crawling through the field a half-mile away. I looked off in the distance and stared at the tractor for a few seconds, then turned back to Sam's grave marker, a piece of blackened bronze that said: Samuel A. McElligott, August 10, 1920 - June 6, 1956, S/Sgt. A Co., 741st Tank Bn., United States Army, World War II.

It's probably more likely that most folks just don't think about things like that, I thought, lighting the cigarette and staring quietly at the name on the marker. I didn't remember anything about the Invasion itself, just that Sam had been there. And that'd been twenty years ago now. I was only sixteen years old when he'd killed himself, but I had spent hours and hours with him from the time he came back from the war until just before he died. When I could catch him right, Sam'd talk about the war some. So I figured he had to have known the date he decided to die. I inhaled deeply and watched the smoke drift lazily through the pristine country air in the small rural cemetery and then fade slowly into the sky.

Sam'd been gone for a long time now, killed like my daddy and so many others who'd gone away to war back through the years. I stood under an old pine tree, smoking quietly and looking out over the cemetery, while I thought back to the days of the war when I could first remember. My daddy was already dead then, Sam was already in the Army and lots of others were on their way somewhere. ...

1

"By god, Sedwick, you want to smoke them cigarettes?" Barney Ford asked that morning when he'd caught me picking up his cigarette butts for the second time after he'd flipped them away. "I'll give you a goddamn cigarette to smoke."

He was a tall, skinny kid with sandy-colored hair and a freckled face who worked for my uncle but was getting ready to go away to the service. Daddy'd already been dead for going on two years. All I knew of him was through some old pictures and what my mother and the rest of the family had told me. That was just enough to keep him in my mind. A picture of him holding me with his arm around Mother the last time he was home stuck in my head as I stood looking helplessly at Barney, my face flushing hotly.

He walked down the decking-board walkway to the truck parked in the circle drive in the lot between the house and the barn. Stepping up on the running board, he leaned in the open window of the passenger's door and got a package of cigarettes. As he walked back toward the porch, he ripped the cellophane from the package, tore open the stamp sealing the cigarettes in and shook one out for me.

"I'm goin' to let you smoke this whole friggin' pack," he said, grinning slightly as he held the pack of Marvels and handed me the cigarette he had just lit, "one after the other. You take this one out on that lumber pile in front of the truck. Sit your ass down. Smoke. When you're done with that one, come on back to the porch, an' I'll give you another one 'til you smoke the whole goddamn package an' get green around the gills."

I took the cigarette and traced his steps down the wood planks to the truck. I grinned and took a drag as I walked, letting the smoke trail out the corner of my mouth the way Barney had done earlier. He thought he'd break me of smoking by letting me smoke so much I'd get sick. I grinned and took another drag.

At the end of the pile of lumber to replace the rotten porch Barney was working on that morning, I sat down with my elbows on my knees and puffed away. Everybody smoked. Although I was only four, I didn't see why I shouldn't smoke, too. Smoking was normal, I figured. I'd even seen my mother sneak a Kool out of a package she kept hidden in her pocketbook. She looked funny when I'd catch her smoking, letting the smoke drift out of her mouth and up into her eyes. Then she'd lean back and fan the smoke with one hand.

"What's going on here?" Mother said, standing in the door with her sister Aunt Helen when I walked back for another cigarette. Through the screen door, I could hardly tell one from the other. Both of them had light hair and the dense screen wire just let me see their shapes in the morning light and the darkness of the house. I thought they looked real pretty.

Barney lit a cigarette and handed it to me as he explained that he was going to break me of picking up butts and smoking them. I hurried back to the lumber pile, puffing away before somebody decided I couldn't smoke anymore.

"Bob'll have a fit," Aunt Helen said.

I wondered what she thought my uncle would say, but by then I was out of earshot and just watched them all standing there talking. Before I finished the cigarette, I heard Barney laugh and Mother and Aunt Helen went away from the door and back into the house, and he went back to work. So I smoked one Marvel after another, grinding each butt out with my heel before walking to the porch for another one. By the time I'd reached the last cigarette in the package, I could feel my head getting lighter and knew I wobbled when I walked.

"My god, boy," Barney said, "you look like a ghost. Somethin' get you out there? I got to take your mother out to the store an' help Big get his outfit ready to take a load to Indianapolis tonight. Don't you go gettin' sick on me."

But that's just what I did. Sitting on my mother's lap while Barney headed the long nose of the old Dodge toward Bellair, I felt the Cheerios I'd shoveled down to get outside with Barney a couple of hours earlier churning in my stomach. Less than a mile down the road, I got real dizzy and leaned out the window and puked the whole bowl full and more awful-tasting stuff.

"Oh, John Walter," Mother said. "Are you all right, honey?"

I could only nod and wipe my watery eyes. I felt better right off, but my face felt drained and I was tired.

"Hey, Sedwick, don't go to sleep," Barney said. "We've got to help Big get the other truck ready for a load of hogs."

"I'm not sure that was the right thing to do, Barney," Mother said, holding me close to her and stroking my throbbing head. "You think that'll break him of smoking?"

"He won't smoke no more, Lorene."

Right then I wouldn't have smoked a cigarette for anything. But even as sick as I felt, I knew nothing made me feel more like a big feller than to have a cigarette in my hand, smoke curling from my mouth or nose while I watched the cigarette burn and the smoke trailing off into the air.

We topped the hill just outside of town, and the houses popped up like Big said mushrooms do after a warm spring rain. One minute there was nothing, the next minute, there was a whole sleepy little town painted against a background of trees. Bellair was just a square with houses all around, some with barns and chicken houses, some with only a garage, and a general store on the southwest corner of the little town. Barney drove around the north side of the square and let the truck roll to a stop at the store so my mother could get out and then drove away. At the abandoned old schoolhouse where my uncle kept things for his trucks, we stopped and got out. I was still wobbly on my feet and knew my face was whiter than a sheet.

"What 'n the devil's wrong with you?" my Uncle Big asked me as we walked to the back of the truck and looked up at him. He looked pretty big to me, so I just called him Big — instead of uncle and his given name of Robert or Bob — like most everybody did after they said my daddy told somebody he wasn't the "big un," that was his brother and Big stuck with my uncle as a nickname. He was sliding eight-by-ten-foot decking boards, two inches thick, into a slot halfway up the stock rack for the load of hogs he'd take to Indianapolis more than a hundred miles north and east of Bellair on Route 40.

Charlie Kline, who had drove and worked for Big before going away to the Army, was home on leave and was handing the boards up to him. Old Joe Marshall, the feller who owned the place and helped out, put another board up against the back of the truck and stood back smiling at me. "You look like the last rose of summer."

"I caught him pickin' up my butts, Big," Barney said, laughing. "So I gave him a fresh pack to smoke out on the lumber pile. He's a little green about the gills."

"Now, shit, Barney," Big said, slamming a decking board to the front part of the truck bed. "You oughten to let that boy smoke."

"I was tryin' to break him."

"Break him, my ass," Big said, flipping a half-smoked Lucky Strike away as he did. "Just make him sick. Help the boys get them deckin' boards up here. I want to get loaded up 'fore dark."

Charlie reached over and pulled my cap down over my eyes. When I pulled it back up and looked up at him, he winked and grinned real big. He looked handsome in his Army uniform just like everybody said he did. "You watch them old cigarettes, Sedwick," he said, putting a decking board on the back of the truck. "They're goin' to do you in."

I grinned back. He always made me feel good when he came to our house. And he had been coming to wherever we had lived ever since I could remember, driving a truck or working for Big or just coming to visit. Charlie had a cigarette dangling from his mouth. Yet half sick, I eyed the long butt Big had just flipped away and wondered how I could get it without being seen and knew I probably couldn't, unless I could grab it real quick and get up in front of the truck. With everybody around so close, it'd be a hard job. One of them would see me sure. Big didn't always seem to notice what I was doing, but he had a way of always seeing things whether he seemed to know what was going on around him or whether he had a faraway look in his eyes that you had to say his name a couple of times before he heard you. That's the way he looked now, like there was other things on his mind.

And I reckon there was other things for him to think about. He had a little farm where he raised hogs and fed a few cattle and had a bunch of trucks that he hauled livestock with and whatever else the other farmers had to haul. Big said he had "to work his ass off to make a dime." Him and my daddy had started working together before the war, but both of them couldn't make a living right away. One day they said Daddy flipped a half dollar in the air and told Big to call it.

"You call it right," I'd heard my daddy had said, "an' you stay here an' keep this outfit together an' I join the Marines; you call it wrong, an' you join the Marines or whatever else you want to."

Big had called heads and stayed home. Daddy had joined the Marines. They said he had planned to do his hitch and come back, marry my mother like Big married Mother's sister Helen, drive trucks, get some more ground and farm with Big. 'Course that never happened. But it was something I thought about through the years. They wasn't twin brothers, but they may as well have been. From pictures I've seen, Daddy was a real handsome feller, with high cheekbones and a little twinkle in his eyes that I saw in my own when I looked in the mirror. Big was a bit thicker through the chest, an inch or two taller and a couple of years older but looked almost identical. Both of them was strong, like young bulls. Everybody'd told me they'd wrassle around all the time when they was together, first one throwing the other but neither ever able to pin the other's shoulders to the ground. I sure wished I'd been able to see them together.

After Daddy was in the Corps for a couple of years, the Japs bombed Pearl Harbor and he shipped back out to somewhere in the South Pacific where he'd already been. Him and my mother had got married when he came home on his first leave before he went overseas the first time. But I didn't remember ever laying eyes on him, except in pictures. The second time out, he went to a place I'd heard a man down the road call the 'Canal and got killed somehow. I always wondered how, but nobody seemed to know. Big said he didn't reckon it really mattered because it wouldn't change nothing. I reckoned that was right, but I still wondered.

Him and Aunt Helen took me and Mother in and let us have the upstairs bedroom after a while. They had two kids, two girls younger than me. Gave me a ready-made family. Big was just like my daddy, the only one I'd ever known. I guess all that had something to do with him not going away to war. He got called up. And I remember taking him to Robinson to the train station so he could go up to Chicago for his physical. Aunt Helen drove Mother, my cousins Nancy and Mary Beth and me home from the train where we'd waved goodbye to him in the early-morning dark. He'd passed his physical and had come back home to get things about his trucking and farming in order when somebody had gotten a petition together for the draft board that said he was needed too much around Bellair to let him go. That had made Big madder than an old wet hen. He said he wasn't no different than anybody else, even though he'd lost a brother and they was taking care of me. He had four other half-brothers who was much older than him. I'd heard them say one or two of them had been in the First World War. And they all had boys about Big's age. Most of them was already in the Army. Everybody went and done their part, he said. Big allowed he ought to do his part but didn't go and wouldn't talk about it when I asked him years later.

Even Barney was going. And I knew I'd be going some day, too, and played Marine more than I did cowboys and Indians. Over in Terre Haute one day while Big went into a store for something, Aunt Helen and I stayed in the truck parked along the street. I had a little toy rifle and was keeping watch on the truck to keep all the Germans and Japs away from it. As people walked along the street, I picked them off one by one when they looked suspicious. A colored feller I was just about to pick off put up his hands, walked up to the truck window and said, "Oh, please don't shoot me, mister. Please don't shoot me."

He was right up to the window before I could pull the rifle back in the truck and start rolling up the window. I'd never been that close to a full-colored feller before and was scared to death. His eyes was open wide with big old yeller-white color showing all around, but they was smiling at me. He just didn't look like the people I was used to being around. Aunt Helen laughed a little and told me that's what I got for trying to shoot people through the window.

As I watched the stock rack change inside to haul hogs, I heard Johnnie Larson's old Model T come chugging down the road. He stopped at the back of the truck, right in the middle of the road, and got out. Johnnie was an old man, I thought, although looking back, I don't guess he was more than sixty years old or so. He was a little man, wore bib overalls, and always seemed to have a long-stemmed pipe clenched between his teeth unless he was adding Prince Albert from the can with a real prince on the front or taking a swing of his

"Pepsi Colee." If it was cold or just a damp, chilly day, Johnnie would wear an old suit coat over his overalls and blue work shirt, buttoned at the collar, and an old dress hat on top of his nearly bald head. I only knew that from times I'd watched him play forty-two up at the store when he'd lay down his dominoes and take his hat off to wipe his forehead in the middle of trying to figure out how to make a bid he'd known at the time was way too much. He'd plop the hat back on his head and cover the few strands of hair, pick up the dominoes and throw one out, giggling between clenched teeth and say, "There she is, boys. You're goin' to have to take a trick 'r two here, 'r I'm goin' t' make forty-two."

Holding up his right hand with his other fingers curled and the first finger and the thumb held out together like to grab something, he looked at me as he got out of his car and said, "Want me to peench you, boy?"

"No," I said as I backed away from him, eyeing the blue smoke still trailing away from the cigarette at the side of the truck. As I backed away, everybody but Big was looking at Johnnie and talking. Big had his back to them while he took another decking board to the front of the truck. That made things easy. Lots of times I felt kind of like nobody could see me, and this was one of them. All I had to do was bend over like I had found an old Indian bead for my match box down there among the rocks and get that Lucky before it burned out. So I did. By ducking in under the truck, just in front of the back wheels, I took two quick drags and flipped the butt away like I'd watched Big do.

"Know what one belly button said to the other, Robert?" I heard Johnnie ask as I come out from under the truck and saw Big through the stock rack bending over to get another decking board.

"No," Big said.

"Every time we get together, somebody always comes," Johnnie said, snatching his pipe from his mouth and slapping his leg with the other hand, all the while giggling and sucking wind through his teeth with a hissing sound.

I could hear the rest of the men laughing as I walked to the back of the truck, trying to see the two belly buttons together in my mind like I did the first time I heard Johnnie ask about the belly buttons getting together. Reaching inside my overalls, I felt mine. At night,

I sometimes picked at it and sucked my bottom lip to help me go to sleep. But I couldn't imagine another belly button up against mine. How could that happen, I wondered again.

"Heard from Morris, Johnnie?" Charlie asked. He was shipping out to go overseas the first of the week, I'd heard Mother say, and was riding along with Big to Indianapolis like he used to when he worked for him. They was about like brothers everybody said and wrassled like Big and Daddy used to do before the war. And everybody said Charlie was stout as a bull, just like Daddy and Big. I'd wanted to go to Indianapolis, but Charlie's leave was over in a couple of days. They wanted to talk over old times, Big said. I could go any old time.

"No," Johnnie said, quiet like. "Ain't heard nothin' from him in more 'n a month 'n a half. Mertie gets mighty worried 'bout 'im bein' over there in the thick of things, 'specially when we don't hear. Whatever'll be, 'll be, I reckon."

That sort of quieted things down. Besides Charlie shipping out someplace overseas right away, almost every feller around was in the Army or the Navy somewhere and now Barney was going to the Marines. He was barely eighteen years old. It was all a little confusing to me. I didn't know much about what was going on, just that all the young fellers was leaving for the war. Most of what I knew came from talk I'd overhear or from the newsreels. We'd go to the free shows over at The Corners and see the war news on those reels. And that was old news. All I could remember was hearing about Tojo, Hitler and Mussolini being the bad guys and Roosevelt and Churchill being the good guys. You could tell that by the tone of voice the news fellers had when they told what was going on.

Up above the store, a record of sorts was kept of how things was going. There was a big board with the names of all the boys from around Bellair who was in the service. Ones who'd been killed got a gold star after their name. My daddy's was the first one. When they had a supper a few days earlier for Charlie, Barney and a couple of other boys who was shipping out, I saw there was four gold stars all together. The board hung on the side of the room, just above the piano and off to the left of the stage. On another board nearby, pictures the boys sent back from wherever they was stationed was arranged for everyone to see. My daddy's had hung there for as long as I could remember.

He had a cigarette dangling from the side of his mouth and a grin on his face as he looked out at me. I imagined I looked like that when I found a cigarette. My mother had a few more pictures in her dresser drawer and a big picture of him setting on top. He looked like a movie star, I thought. But the one I liked best was of them together when they got married. They sure looked good together, standing there with their arms around each other. Every once in a while, I'd slip upstairs at home and take the pictures out and look at them. One time I caught my mother doing the same thing. She looked like she'd been crying when I walked into the room. I went up to the bed, and she took me in her arms and held me for a long time. She never said nothing, just held me real tight.

At the supper up at the store, she picked me up as I stood looking at my daddy on the board and looked with me. Neither one of us said a word. When she sat me down, I walked on to the back of the store, stopping to look back at her. She was still looking at me, and our eyes locked together for a long look. Then I walked behind the chimney.

When I looked back through the railing, Charlie had walked up behind her and put his arms on her shoulders and turned her around to him. She looked around like she was startled, saw who it was and smiled as she stepped back. I liked Charlie, but him and Mother together where everybody could see made my face get red. I was glad she pulled away, but I stepped back behind the chimney again where nobody could see me and waited until my face wasn't so hot anymore before coming out.

After that, I went down the stairs to play with the kids. I'd been around these kinds of crowds enough to know that after I ate it was time to get outside. Every now and then, somebody'd see me walking through the crowd and pat me on the head or on the shoulder or say something meant to be nice or to make me feel better. They didn't say much usually, but just patted me like I was some little dog, wagging his tail and wanting to be petted. I didn't. And I didn't feel better. Probably felt worse that people felt sorry for me.

So I wandered around to the front of the store, looking for something to do. The kids just a little older than me was playing tag in the street east of the store. I'd tried that a couple of times and didn't like to play. Everybody could catch me when I'd run across the road. I watched them for a minute, then walked up on the porch where five or six older boys stood talking and laughing and striking matches and flipping them off the porch as the fire went out and blue smoke trailed the match to the ground. I watched awhile and didn't reckon anybody noticed me. Then the boys laughed pretty loud, and one of them turned to me with a long screw between his fingers.

"Here, John Walter," a chubby kid named Jackie Wallace said, "take this old screw, will you?"

I reached out right away to take it, feeling good that I was included in what was going on. Jackie let go of the screw, and I clamped down on it so I wouldn't drop it.

I felt the sear of hot metal on my fingers and heard the other boys holler and laugh before I could move my hand back. The screw dropped to the concrete floor as I opened my thumb and finger. Tears flooded out of my eyes like old North Fork Crick after a spring rain, and I cried out once. Then I stuck my fingers in my mouth and turned away. Off to the side of the store, I looked at what the screw had done to my finger and could see the print of the screw burned into the flesh.

Sonsabitches, I thought. Wiping the tears out of my eyes, I walked back toward the door upstairs. Big and Charlie was going to box on the stage, but I didn't want to go back up there for that the way I was feeling or for any more pats on the head or looks of Charlie trying to hug Mother. The burn hurt, too. A couple of tears still rolled down my cheeks. I fanned my finger in the air and saw a burning cigarette laying in the grass in the early evening light. Five or six men sat or stood smoking and talking around the step leading to the stairs going upstairs. I walked slowly, bent down, picked up the butt and kept walking.

At the back of the feed and coal shed, I stopped and leaned on the wall, smoked and let the cigarette dangle from the corner of my mouth while the sun slipped quietly behind the trees down towards the bottoms. In my mind's eye, I saw two belly buttons, each with eyes, nose and mouth, laying close together on my bed. The belly buttons was connected to people I couldn't see, almost floating in the air and looking out of the corner of their eyes while they lay there. Then I saw the doorknob start turning and the door

begin to open. But nobody was there to see the belly buttons together. They kept looking and looking but didn't see a thing.

Barney took me back home after the decking and the bedding was
fixed for the load of stock going to Indianapolis. He was leaving for
Chicago the next morning and was going to Martinsville to see his
girlfriend Wilma Jean Foxx before he left.

"Stay away from them cigarettes, Sedwick," he said after he'd
cranked up his old Model A and was ready to leave. "An' don't take
no wooden nickels."

I nodded and waved as he drove off. I still wasn't feelin' too good
and took a little nap. Later that afternoon, Aunt Helen took the old
truck and we went to the store to do the trading. Big and Charlie was
parked at the gas pump with a load of hogs. I listened to them squealing and wondered what they thought about going off to market to be
butchered so somebody could eat them. Maybe they'd even end up in
the meat case at the back of the store for old Horsey to sell back to us.
The storekeeper was a chunky, dark-skinned man with a few strands
of black hair combed back over his bald head. His name was Howard
Matthews, but everybody called him Horsey because of the horse's-
assy way he run the store, Aunt Helen said. Mother worked for him
once in a while when he needed extra help. He breathed through his
mouth and stood with his hands on his hips, watching while Aunt Helen
told Mother what she wanted and put her list on the counter. After a
minute, he walked away. Big and Charlie came in from the gas pump
and both of them got a bottle of Pepsi out of the case filled with pop of
all kinds, the bottles sticking their necks up out of the cold water where
they stood in neat rows like soldiers waiting to be taken away.

"You want a bottle of pop, Sedwick?" Charlie asked.

"I reckon I do," I said, smiling up at him. "I'll take me a grape pop."

Charlie smiled back and got a grape for me.

The radio was on in a little cubbyhole at the back of the store.
I figured a ball game was on. They headed back there to drink
their pop, and I followed them. I didn't know much about baseball,
but I knew Big would want to know what the Cardinals was doing.
He told Charlie they'd been doing real good, which made him happy.
I just liked hearing the people's voices coming out of the radio.

We had one by Big's chair at home, but that old radio didn't get played much. It'd break off, couldn't get anything, anyway, and wasn't hardly ever on. Whenever it was or I was up at the store, which was about the only other place I ever heard a radio, I'd look around and try to see where the voice came from. That puzzled me. Now, some man was talking from a long way off about the war and some place overseas. That seemed like another world to me, like the 'Canal did when I first heard where my daddy got killed. I'd hardly been any place except around the square and at Big's or at other relative's, that I could remember. Oh, I'd been to Indianapolis and the little towns around Bellair once in a while. Even if I did go any place in the truck, I usually ended up going to sleep. One day, I was in the truck by myself, standing on my knees, looking out over the steering wheel and thinking I could drive that truck off. I slipped down under the wheel and put my foot on the starter with all my weight behind me. The truck jumped a little bit at a time until I saw the gate to the barn yard move. That scared me, and I got back up under the wheel. Mother snatched me out of the truck and told me to stay in the house where she could watch me.

"Cardinals winnin', Howard?" Big asked while him and Charlie walked toward the storekeeper at the back of the store.

"They didn't play," the storekeeper said, his ear glued to the radio. "They wasn't scheduled, but it just came over 'while ago that it's Invasion Day. Even the two scheduled games between the Dodgers and the Phillies and the Pirates and the Reds tonight have been put off. Don't know much more about the invasion yet."

"This is it," Charlie said, taking a swig on his bottle of pop and looking up at the clock hanging over the meat case. "We better get that truck headed for Indianapolis, Big, if I'm goin' to go with you. Won't be much more time for me."

Big and the storekeeper just looked at Charlie. Nobody said anything for a minute. I wondered what "it" was and looked at the clock and around the store for some idea.

"Think you'll have to go over there?" Big asked.

"I 'magine that's where I'm headed."

"Can I go to Indi'nap'lis with you, Big?" I asked, wanting to know more about where Charlie was headed.

"Not tonight, Sedwick," he said, looking up to the cash register

Cristo, or Crisco as I liked to call him, who dashed around the country getting in and out of trouble and having the girls fall all over him. The music gave me the feeling I had in my head when I thought about the belly buttons getting together, anyway.

But I didn't see any in the shows or anywhere else. After a while, I forgot about belly buttons except when I'd pick mine and suck my lip to help me get to sleep at night when everybody finally went to bed, and I still couldn't sleep. From belly buttons, I went to worrying about socks. One night I tried to figure out which sock went on which foot to keep from going to bed. I'd learned which shoe went on which foot pretty easy but figured that socks was a bit harder. Bertha Chapman, one of the neighbors, was there that night helping get us to bed. She was quite a bit older than Mother or Aunt Helen. So I figured she could tell me about the socks.

"Why there's no difference in socks," she said in answer to my question. "Socks are the same."

"How come shoes are different then?" I asked. "Socks go on your feet, too."

"But socks are soft and fit your feet no matter how you put them on. With shoes, they're harder and are made to fit your foot only one way. So there's a left and a right. Put your socks on either foot and see. Then put your shoes on."

I couldn't believe it was so easy.

That night I couldn't sleep, though, because of an earache that had been hurting off and on all evening. Mother and a bunch of others sat around the card table playing rummy. I didn't see much sense in mixing cards around on the table, then throwing them back down again, hollering rummy and laughing and talking all together. But it kept me out of bed. I had to lay down in the room and try to go to sleep on the old daybed off in the corner. Every time I laid down, the ear ached more. I complained and stopped the card game more than once when I'd get up and walk to Mother's side.

"Here, let me fix that earache up, boy," Gene Shaw said, a pipe clenched between his teeth and a sweet-smelling smoke drifting from his mouth and up toward the ceiling. He was Pete's brother and was in the Army and home on leave. "I got just the thing to take care of it. You got a piece of cotton, Helen?"

Germans coming down the field behind the house. Now every tree and hill to the north and off to the east had a German soldier or a tank behind it. Blowing the bridge sure sounded like a good plan to me.

"Let's put the charges here," Jimmy said.

"Looks good," Albert said. "Then we can leave John Walter here behind to set the charges off when they start across the bridge."

But I never got to blow that bridge. Just about the time they were going to set the charges, Jimmy's dad pulled up at the edge of the field and waved for the boys to come to him. While we were walking to the tractor, Orville got things ready to go back to Bellair and his farm on the little hill at the edge of town.

"You guys come back," I said in a soft cry.

They said they would. Jimmy told me his dad said to have my mother bring me out sometime. That made me feel real good.

"But tell her you have to wear long pants," Jimmy said like he had out at the store. "You can't wear them short pants."

That didn't make me feel quite so good.

"I ain't wearin' no short pants today, am I?" I asked, hooking my thumbs in the galluses of my favorite overalls like I'd seen my Uncle Billie Peterson do. "I don't wear them shorts no more an' don't aim to ever wear 'em again."

When Jimmy had brought up the short pants Mother had made me wear to the store one time, I'd been more embarrassed than I could ever remember. I'd tried to talk her out of ever wearing them again. Until he came out to our place earlier in the day, I'd felt like hiding every time I saw him walk into the store. His invitation to come to his house and what he'd told me earlier had stayed in my mind. I'd fought harder against wearing the short pants than I ever had before, too. "'Bout all I've got is bib overalls," I'd told him another time about wearing the short pants. "She's trying to get me to wear these short pants instead of them."

"Well, you just tell her you can't wear shorts," he said.

So I did.

"Jimmy Barker said to tell you that I have to wear long pants to come to his house," I'd told her. "I can't wear them short pants."

"James Barker is not dressing you, young man," she'd said. "You look so cute in that outfit."

"I don't like 'em," I'd said. "They make me look like a sissy. My daddy wouldn't want me lookin' like no sissy an' dressin' in a dumb old sailor suit. I just hate it an' them old short pants, an' I just can't wear 'em no more."

So far I hadn't worn the outfit again. But I hadn't been out to Jimmy's yet, either. As I watched the tractor drive slowly away, I was purt near in tears and decided I would take Jimmy up on his invite right then. I knew my favorite overalls, hole and all, was okay to wear for the trip. The tractor turned the corner at the end of the lane and headed down the narrow road for the wide gravel road that led into Bellair, a mile and a half or so away. I started walking down the lane. When I turned the corner and got on the road, I saw the tractor turning the corner a quarter of a mile away. Determined to keep them in sight, I ran for a minute or two, then settled down for the walk to town when I figured the tractor was going too fast for me to keep up with it.

At the corner down the road where Dempsey O'Neal lived, I turned south and walked toward Bellair. By the time I got to Johnnie Larson's house, not far past Dempsey's, I was plumb tuckered out and wanted a bite to eat. So I turned into the driveway and walked up to the side door where I knew I'd find Mertie. She was at the door when I got there.

"Could I have a cookie, Mertie?" I asked. "I'm hungry."

"I think I can find a cookie," she said, smiling and leading me back into the kitchen. "Where are you goin', John Walter? You a bit far from home, ain't you?"

"Oh, no. Jimmy an' Albert was out to our house with Jimmy's daddy. Then they left. Jimmy, he asked me at the store to come to his house, not to wear short pants, an' play with him one day. He's got a big, big yard an' lots of kids to play with all the time. That's where him an' Albert are goin' now. An' they asked me to come on out. That's where I'm headed."

"Does your mother know where you're goin'?"

"Oh, yeah. Her an' Aunt Helen are goin' to the store pretty soon, but I couldn't wait on them."

She smiled and sat two oatmeal cookies like Grandma Mary Elizabeth made on the table before me. "Would you like some milk?" she asked. "Cookies an' milk go together."

I nodded, looking up at her and shoving a piece of the cookie in with the flat of my hand. Her eyes looked big through her thick glasses. They made the smile in her eyes have a kindness like I saw in Grandma's just about all the time. I poked another bit of cookie in my mouth as Mertie sat the milk in front of me.

"You don't have to hurry so, John Walter."

"I've got to go," I said, taking a gulp of the cold milk. It didn't taste quite like ours, which came from an old Jersey Big bought at a sale over by The Corners. That cow sure gave good milk, he said, and lots of it.

"Where'd this milk come from, Mertie?" I asked. "It don't taste like ours."

"From Orville and Alma. We buy milk from them."

"They've got Holsteins. That's why the milk tastes different. We got an old Jersey cow. Her milk is real rich, 'bout half cream, I reckon. Makes good butter."

Mertie smiled. She didn't seem to want me to leave, but I told her I had to get on down the road. She didn't say nothing, just smiled more and told me to be careful and to come back.

"I'll stop again some time," I said at the bottom of the steps, turning to look back at her. "Thank you for the cookies, Mertie. You make real good cookies."

"Thank you, John Walter," she said and smiled again.

I started to ask her about her boy Morris that was over yonder someplace in the war, but I remembered that Johnnie had said she was mighty worried about him and decided it wouldn't be good to ask her anything about him. Big always said there wasn't no use of worrying the women about things they couldn't do anything about. Which I reckon was about right. So I didn't say anymore.

Back on the road, I walked faster until I got past Borax, the little crick that ran under the road just beyond Johnnie and Mertie's small house. The bridge that went across the crick only had a short rail of concrete between the road and open air. I had a funny feeling as I walked across the bridge. Once, I looked down over the rail and then back on the road. It was a long ways down to the trickle of water that ran under the road over to Floyd Springer's pasture.

Nothing was coming from either way on the road, so I edged away from the side of the road and walked in the track between the rows of gravel ridged up by the tires passing over the road. The track was hard and smooth, which made it better for walking. I could walk as fast as I could and look at the ridges on both sides to see if I could find any Indian beads. My old match box was about half full, but not many of them had holes in the middle of the spool-shaped beads you could find in the gravel. I wanted to put a bunch of them together on a string for a necklace of the Indian beads I knew the Indians wore when they lived around Bellair. A couple of times when I'd played cowboys and Indians, I'd seen the Indians with beads on as they ran towards me when I tried to keep them away from the house. They'd never get close enough for me to see the beads with my eyes, but I could see them in my mind, for sure. Just before I got to the road on into Bellair, I found a pretty little bead that had almost perfect spirals around the spool from top to bottom. I was real tickled with the find.

The last half mile into Bellair seemed to take forever. Borax, the little crick I'd heard was called that for the oily and scummy stuff that the oil company workers dumped in it after they swabbed and treated an oil well, curved around from Johnnie Larson's and crossed the road just east of town and ran toward the North Fork, leaving an oily film on the banks when the water got low. Another little bridge covered the crick here, too, and I pumped my legs faster and faster to get across. At the top of the hill, I saw the houses and buildings of Bellair spread out before my eyes. A warm, good feeling swept over me.

Jimmy lived just at the edge of town. I could see his house sitting up on the hill, barns and sheds strung out behind it. The closer I got the more excited I got. Orville's garage sat out in the corner of their yard in an area cut off from the long yard by neatly trimmed shrubs. The shrubs run around the yard on two sides. I could hear kids playing, hollering and laughing. But I couldn't see anyone. At the road ditch, which was mowed all the way out to the road, I jumped across and skipped up to the entrance to the yard through the shrubs. Jimmy and Albert and Ronal Crucell, all two or three years older than me, and a couple of other kids I didn't know was under one of the two pine trees just inside the yard. Tall, willowy poplar trees lined the side of the yard that separated it from the orchard on that side. The house stood at the top of the little raise. I'd never seen the back yard. The front just about took my breath away. What a place to live, I thought, as I ran up to the other boys.

"What're you doin' here, John Walter?" Jimmy asked.

"You told me to come to your house sometime an' not wear them short pants my mother makes me wear sometimes. I 'llowed as how today would be a good day to come to your house."

"Does your mother know you're here?"

"Oh, yes," I said, knowing that if I told him the truth I'd probably have to go back home. "She said I could come out here. Just as soon as you left, I went in the house an' asked Mother an' Aunt Helen both. Mother's going to come out an' get me when they go to the store to do their tradin' this afternoon."

"How'd you get here?" Albert asked.

"I walked. Stopped at Mertie's an' got me some cookies."

"That's a long way out here," Ronal said.

"Sure is," I said. And it was a long way. The boys looked at me a little different, too, I reckoned, and that made me feel good. They let me play hide-and-go-seek and other games with them for a long time. Jimmy's mother Alma backed their old car out of the garage and headed back out towards home where Orville was still farming on another piece of ground. Before she drove away, she stopped in the middle of the road and said, "John Walter, I'm going out toward your house. Do you want a ride?"

"Don't reckon I do," I said, running away from the road and hollering back at her. "I'm playin'."

And we started playing war and soldiers and played about as hard as I'd ever played anything. We killed so many Japs and so many Germans that I got tired of killing them. But it felt good a right smart to have boys to play with. Nancy and Mary Beth was okay as long as we played in the house, but that wasn't like playing with boys like I had been at Jimmy's. All my cousins wanted to do was play house and have me hold their old rag dolls while they cooked supper. I was tired of that. I thought about having the brother I reckoned I'd never have. That's what my mother said one morning, anyhow. She'd been talking with Aunt Helen while they sat at the kitchen table and smoked cigarettes when nobody else was around to see them. They sure looked funny holding their cigarettes out in front of them while the smoke curled up and into their eyes, I'd thought, when I'd come down from upstairs to eat breakfast and saw them smoking.

"I'm tired of being alone, Helen," I heard my mother say. "We can't stay here with you and Bob forever. But I don't know what to do. I don't know what in the world to do."

"Charlie'd make a good man for you, Lorene. He seems pretty sweet on you. There's not many other fellers around anymore."

"Charlie's not around, either," my mother said, beginning to cry a little. "And he's got a girlfriend, anyway."

"Him and Liz broke up, Bob said."

"They've done that before. Besides, Charlie's gone now and may not come back, either."

I hurried over to Mother and held out my arms to get up on her lap. I'd heard her cry in the night sometimes, but when I'd ask her what she was crying about, she'd just say, "Oh, I'm not crying. I've just got the sniffles."

Now I could see she was crying.

"What's the matter, Mommy?" I asked. "Somebody hurt you?"

"Yes, somebody hurt me, John Walter," she said, taking me in her arms and squeezing me so tight it nearly took my breath away. "Very much. By taking your daddy away from me. From us. They say God has a plan for every life. Maybe He even has one for mine. But I can't imagine what it'd be. You're not ever goin' to have a little brother or a little sister. And your daddy is gone forever. What are we going to do? What can we do? That's the matter with me."

Being with the other boys nearly made me forget all about that part of my life. But then I saw the long nose of one of Big's old red trucks pop up over the hill and knew Mother and Aunt Helen was coming after me. "Uh-oh," I hollered out, although I didn't mean to. The boys looked down the road to where the truck was picking up speed.

"Attack, attack," Jimmy said. "It's a Jap truck. We can ambush it as it comes along the road."

I wasn't so sure about getting involved in the "ambush." I knew who was in the truck and what was going to happen. And it wasn't the Japs, nor was there any ambush going to take place. More than likely there was going to be nothing take place except me getting my butt paddled. But I still laid down at the side of the road with the others and took aim at the truck's front tire. I remembered Big saying something about one of the drivers having a blowout on the front tire and it throwing the truck off in the ditch. That was about the best I figured I could hope for. I guess we all missed because the truck turned in the driveway and stopped on that dime I'd heard fellers talk about. I could hear Mother before I could see her.

"Now you get over here, young man," she said, each word a little louder that the last one, as she came around the front of the truck and stood waiting for me to come to her.

I looked around for the other soldiers. They stayed out of sight behind the trees or in the ditch. I couldn't see any of them. But I wasn't going to give up that easy.

"You're under arrest, Jap," I said, looking around the tree I was hiding behind. "The rest of you just got ambushed out there on the road. Get your hands up."

"I'll get my hands on you, John Walter, and blister your little butt 'til you can't sit down for a week. You'll think Jap. Now you get over here this minute. Just wait until your Uncle Robert hears about this."

Wasn't no other choice, I reckoned, and stepped out behind the tree and surrendered. I knew it was going to be a long ride back home. I don't remember much of what Mother said, except that it went on for the whole ride. "What in the world did you mean?" she said. "We didn't have any idea where you were and was out looking for you. Mertie tried to call, but there wasn't anybody in the house then. It wasn't until later when Alma came out to bring Orville's dinner that she stopped and told us where you were. And Mertie finally got us and told us you'd been there."

When Mother wasn't talking, Aunt Helen lit in on me.

"Your mother was worried sick," she said. "We both was. We didn't know what in the world had happened to you. She'd ought to blister you good for pulling a trick like that."

And she did. Only it wasn't good from my way of thinking. Aunt Helen turned in the lane and hit the bridge faster than I'd ever been over it before. I hoped it fell through this time. That'd save me, I thought. But the bridge held up, and Mother almost drug me out of the truck and through the gate. Neither one of us stayed on the boards as she pulled me along the path to the house. There was only a narrow walkway to the door on the porch. The other new boards still hadn't been put on yet, and the bare ground lay open beneath the floor joists.

If I could just get through one of those boards, I thought, I could get under the new part of the porch and hide for a little bit. Sooner or later, I knew I was going to get it. It was sooner.

At the porch step, Mother stopped, turned around and sat down. She pulled me across her lap and started whipping me with a little peach switch. She'd whipped me before, but never like this. It hurt more this time and lasted longer. I don't know how long she kept it up. I was crying wildly and she was shouting, "Don't you ever do that again! You hear me? You stay right in this yard!"

Then she stopped and took me up in her arms. Her breath came in short spurts, almost in pants, the way I was breathing when I ran on the way out to Bellair that morning. I was still crying my eyes out and screaming bloody murder, as a feller says, but I had started slowing down some when she quit whipping me. I was plumb wore out. When I'd stopped and she'd caught her breath, she stood up and sat me down on the porch.

"You sit here and think about what you did and why you shouldn't do it again. I'm going inside and talk to your Aunt Helen. Don't you go any place, except right here. You got that?"

I nodded, feeling the tears streaming down my cheeks. Fingering my belly button inside my overalls for the first time in a while, I thought about the two being next to each other and wished mine could have one to get together with right now. And like Mother said she felt about being alone, I was tired of it. I was still sitting there thinking about being alone and wishing I could go away when she came back outside. She picked me up and hugged me hard. I saw a couple of tears rolling down her cheeks and hugged her hard back.

"Please, John Walter," she said, starting to sob and holding me harder that she ever had. "I don't want to lose you, too."

2

Just before I was going to turn five years old, Big and Aunt Helen decided to move to Bellair. She'd been wanting to move off the farm every since thcy got there, she said. They'd been able to buy a house on the square that she liked, and my mother was able to take the full-time job at the store that Horsey had offered her and walk to work. The house was on the cast side of the square, just up the street from the old abandoned school where Big kept his truck beds, decking boards and other trucking stuff. The new school was just across the street, and one of the churches set in the next lot south. Another church was just around the corner. Next to it was the old Bellair Hotel, Jake's restaurant and an old barn, all empty or no longer used for what they used to be in the old days. The store, a long, two-story building with a false front covering the top story, set on the southwest corner of the square. Another old store, a bank and a post office, all long closed, sat east of the store. Ross Childers' house sat catty-cornered from the store on the hill on the west side of the square.

Now I could play with Jimmy and Albert and the kids around town all the time and not have to run away. Everybody except Big seemed happy about the move. One day I heard him say that he hated to move off the Bowman place where he could have hogs and cattle and a little room for his trucks. But he said the women wanted to move into town so my mother could work and Aunt Helen would be close to the store and have some neighbors. Wasn't anything else he could do but move, he'd said.

The house wasn't much like the one out on the farm. Tony Williams had built the one in Bellair for his wife when he divorced her, Aunt Helen said. The rooms was bigger and had tall ceilings that I had to look almost straight up to be able to see the top. Like the house out on the farm, there wasn't any indoor toilet, but there was a little room off to the back of the house that I heard Mother and Aunt Helen talking about that could be used as an indoor toilet. That'd be funny, I thought. There didn't seem to be any place to have any holes in the floor to poop through, and I didn't see how you could sit down on a hole in the floor and do like you could on a pot or in the toilet out at the side of the garden. I'd never seen anything like that in a house.

The kitchen had a swinging batwing door like I saw in a cowboy movie one time. Other doors to other rooms covered the whole doorway. This one to the kitchen swung open from the middle with each half able to go either way. Or one could go one way and one the other way. With them closed, the kitchen was set off a little bit from everything else. It was in the kitchen that Mother gave me a bath after Aunt Helen gave Nancy and Mary Beth theirs every Saturday night. The water was only lukewarm and looked milky white when I got in the wash tub. I didn't like to use the same water the girls had used. That's the way I'd always taken a bath, though.

"It'd take too much time to heat fresh water," Mother said. "Nancy and Mary Beth wasn't that dirty, anyway."

"Just get some water out of that pump," I said, pointing to the small hand pump on the side of the sink. "That's not hard."

"But then we'd have to heat the water. That's cold water. And it takes a long time to heat enough to fill that wash tub."

The bath water wasn't really cold, but it sure wasn't hot, either. The weather was still pretty chilly when we moved in, and there was no fire in the kitchen except the old gas cooking stove. With the batwing doors shut, the heat from the coal stove in the dining room didn't come drifting through enough to keep the goose pimples from standing out all over my body. More than once when I was standing there shivering, I wished we was back out on the farm. We took a bath there in the little kitchen that was warm as toast. The longer we was there, though, the better I liked living in Bellair. I could get up in the morning and have something to eat with Nancy and Mary Beth, then play in the toy room where Aunt Helen kept saying the toilet was going to be or go outside and play with somebody else.

But moving to Bellair wasn't everything. Some things didn't

work out better. Charlie got killed sometime in the winter just before we moved. We didn't hear about it until after we'd already moved and got settled in some. Big came home one evening and told us about it. He'd stopped over at The Corners to have a tire fixed and heard the news from the fellers at the garage.

"Charlie got killed over yonder about six weeks ago," he said real quiet just as soon as he walked in the door. "Some place in Germany. Up north."

I couldn't believe it. How could Charlie get killed? He was alive and strong. I figured Big'd just heard wrong at first, or there'd been some kind of mistake. But the way Big talked and the way everybody else acted, I figured he was right.

Mother's face got awful white, and she went to the back bedroom. I ran after her and threw my arms around her like she did to me when I was hurt. She pulled me up on her lap, and we sat on the bed, crying together. I tried to say something to make her feel better. But each time I opened my mouth and tried to talk, I'd start crying again. That'd make her cry more. She held me tight and stroked my hair until we could speak.

"There's nothing we can do, John Walter," she finally said. "Daddy's gone, and now Charlie's gone. So are lots of others. We're here, though, and we must go on. That's what your daddy'd have wanted us to do. I'm glad I told him I'd marry him when he asked me right after he got home that first time. I've got you, and I think he wanted to have a few days of happiness together as man and wife before he went overseas. I don't know why he felt that way, though. We didn't even have a home of our own, but he said he didn't care, even if we'd have had to sleep on the floor.

"We didn't, but we'd have to now, if it wasn't for your Uncle Bob and Aunt Helen. They help us so much. I think — Oh, John Walter, I don't know what I think, anymore. Now that your daddy's gone, I don't know what to do or where to go. Not 'til this awful war is over, anyway. No telling what it'll be like then. Whatever'll be will be, I guess. There ain't much we can do about it but to just keep on living and keep on trying."

I'd never heard Mother talk quite like she was, and I didn't know what to say. So I hugged her again and patted her back. "We'll go on, Mother," I said. "We'll go on. I'll help you go on."

She pulled back and looked at me with tears still rolling down her cheeks. Then she pulled me back to her shoulder and said, "I know you will, sweetie. We'll go on together."

We sat there on the bed awhile longer before she went over to her chest of drawers and got a picture of Charlie and her together and the last letter she'd got from him nearly a month earlier. First she looked at the picture a long time, then she opened the letter and was reading it.

"Can you read it to me, Mother?" I asked. "I want to know what Charlie said. Is that okay?"

"Sure it's okay," she said, smiling slightly and holding up a little piece of paper with some writing on it. "He says, '*Dearest Lorene.*

"'*Hello, pal! How are you? Fine I hope. I'm just fine myself. But I'm better when I get a letter from you. You know there's nothing like a letter from home to pick my spirits up.*

"'*Have you been working lately? I suppose you have. Don't work too hard Lorene. It's not good for you. Ha!*

"'*Well there isn't much I can write about here. So goodbye pal and be good. I can hardly wait to get back home again and see you all. I'll see you sometime, somewhere.*

"'*Worlds of love,*

"'*Charlie.*'"

She started crying again and hugged me hard. But then she asked me if I'd go back to the kitchen. "I need to be alone for a couple of minutes. Then I'll be okay."

I nodded and left.

When Mother came back to the kitchen, she started washing dishes and never said a word. I always thought she was so pretty with her blonde hair all wavy and fixed to set off her round face and smiling blue eyes. I knew she liked Charlie, and I'd heard him say before he left that she "was about as pretty a girl as there was in the country." And she still was pretty, but now she looked sad. She still got that way every once in a while about Daddy and would look at his picture and letters. But that didn't happen as much anymore, not that I saw, anyway. She even seemed to be happy at times before Charlie got killed. Afterwards she hardly ever looked happy and seemed tired all the time. Every place we went somebody told us how sorry they was that he'd been killed. She'd smile, say thank you and her eyes looked like she was about to cry. When the people wasn't around and sometimes at night, she would cry. I'd hear her and put my arms around her and hold her real tight until I went to sleep. She was gone to the store by the time I woke up, so I didn't know how long she cried in the night. But it was about every night and for a long time. She hardly ever looked like she enjoyed her life.

I missed seeing her happy, and I missed her during the day. The toys that took up more than half of the little room kept Nancy and Mary Beth and me busy for a while, but I'd soon want to go outside and talked them into going with me. The little room made me feel like I was caught in a trap after so long.

"You stay in the yard," Aunt Helen would tell us.

And we usually did. There were two big old tree stumps in the yard left from where somebody had cut the shade trees on either side of the decking boards leading from the sidewalk at the road to the wooden steps to the porch. I liked to play on the stumps and imagine what the yard would have looked like before the trees were cut down. Houses on either side and across the street all had trees in the front yards. Ours was the only one that didn't. The stumps stood there only as reminders. And it didn't seem right that they was gone anymore than it did that Daddy, and now Charlie, was gone. On my fifth birthday, Big decided that the stumps had to go, too.

Mother and Aunt Helen was having a birthday party for me with some of the kids my age there. Richard and Jerry Owens, who lived on the other side of the square, Ronnie Cooper, who lived next to them, Cheryl Matthews, Horsey and Arletta's girl who lived across the street, and a couple of kids visiting their grandma, Miz Hancock, across the street the other way was all there. Mother wouldn't let me invite Jimmy and Albert and Ronal because she told me they was too old. We was having fun, anyway, and I'd just tried and failed to blow out the candles. I'd tried so hard because for my birthday wish I'd wished my mother wouldn't be so sad. I thought she wouldn't be if I could just blow them out. That was still on my mind when Aunt Helen told us there was going to be a big old boom outside but not to be scared because Uncle Big and Old Joe Marshall was "settin' off dynamite" to blow the stumps out of the ground. She always called Big Uncle Robert to me and thought I was disrespectful to call him Big like everybody else did. I didn't see nothing disrespectful about it, and it made me feel pretty big myself to be able to call him that.

All of us, including Mother and Aunt Helen gathered around the big front window to watch the dynamiting. It was my birthday, so I claimed the spot in the center of the window where I could have a clear look. Big was down on his hands and knees at the side of the biggest stump on the south side of the yard, next to the driveway. I saw him reach into his pocket, then turn back to the bottom of the stump where him and Joe had dug out around to get to the roots. One minute Big was hunched over and the next minute he was up and running for the ditch on the other side of the road. He hadn't anymore than dove into the ditch than a big kaboom shook the window in front of me so much that it rattled and dirt flew out of the hole and came down all over everywhere. Some dirt smacked against the window just as we all jumped back and nearly knocked each other down.

I wanted to go outside and see up close how Big was blowing the stumps out of the ground. Both Mother and Aunt Helen said no and wouldn't let us stand near the window for the next time Big set the dynamite off. He set off another stick or two on the big stump before it got blown loose and then went to the smaller stump on the north side of the boardwalk of decking planks. When both stumps was loose and out of the hole, we all went outside and stood on the porch. Mother and Aunt Helen sat on the seat on the north side with honeysuckle growing up and covering the opening behind the seat. The scent of honeysuckle and dynamite mingled together, giving the air a curious odor of sweet-smelling flowers and explosive powder that made me feel good and strong inside. The holes the stumps left when they was loose and out of the ground was deep and wide. I wanted to get in them, but one of Big's trucks was there with a load of dirt to fill in the hole just after the stumps was loaded on another truck to haul them to the junk pile south of town. The rest of my party wasn't nearly as much fun after we went back inside. Even the cake and ice cream didn't taste as good as I thought it would.

Later that summer, Big and Lawrence Lindley came in early one morning from taking a load of stock to Indianapolis. Lawrence was a boy from a place down the road He had just got out of high school and was farming with his dad, waiting to be drafted. I was awake but still in bed and could hear the excitement in their voices. Nobody would pay any attention to my calls for them, so I just listened. Big didn't say much. Lawrence was doing most of the talking about what they'd heard about the war with Japan being over.

"Everybody was hollerin' and laughin'," Lawrence said, "now that Japan has surrendered, too. When we stopped at the truck stop there at Derby Hill to get supper, they said they'd heard they was tearin' the sides off of trucks over in Terre Haute. Big got pretty excited about that. 'Course they wasn't. But everybody was real happy. The stockyards was a mad house. Then all the way home, trucks and cars was honkin' their horns an' flashin' their lights."

"Do you think you'll still have to go, Lawrence?" Mother asked quietly after he'd finished. "I hope not."

"Oh, I imagine I'll have to go. I just won't have to go to the war like a lot of 'em."

My mother's face was paler than usual, but she didn't say anything. She turned and came to pick me up and held me in her arms. She held me tight and for a long time.

"I hope you never have to go away to war," she said softly in my ear. "I couldn't stand that."

I hugged her back but kept quiet. I could see myself in a Marine uniform like Daddy, standing proud and tall, but didn't say anything. She probably wouldn't like to hear that.

That fall and winter after the Japs surrendered, the boys started coming home from the war. One of them was my cousin Sam. I didn't remember him from when he left, but I figured that's who he was when Big brought him home for supper one evening.

"Are you Sam?" I asked to make sure it was him, walking close to the man with the Army clothes and a big grin on his face and keeping my eyes on him. With him being a soldier and in our house, I figured it had to be him.

"Yes, I'm Sam, you little dickens, you," he said, grabbing me before I could move back, tossing me up in the air and then sitting me down on his lap. "Don't you remember me?"

"Just from your picture, I reckon," I said, knowing I knew him and knowing his name from being in the war. But I didn't remember much about what he looked like or when I'd even ever seen him. "I reckon I seen you up to Granddad's or someplace, but that was a long time ago. Real long. 'Bout ten years, I reckon."

"Don't reckon it could've been that long," he said, smiling some but looking a little sad in his eyes, "But it was a long time ago, John Walter. We got a lot of catchin' up to do."

I smiled, feeling like I'd known him all my life, and said, "I reckon we do."

Everybody stayed around the supper table for a long time that night doing some of the catching up. I listened awhile, then went off to play with Nancy and Mary Beth. But they was playing with dolls, so I went back to the kitchen. After Mother and Aunt Helen had finished the dishes, everybody went to the front room to play cards. The card table was set up in the middle of the room, just under the single light that hung from a cord attached to the ceiling. The bulb was pretty dim but lit the room enough so you could play cards and talk.

The four of them sat around the card table with Mother and Aunt Helen facing each other. Big sat across from Sam. He was a tall, rangy feller like some of the movie cowboys and wore a cap that sat crookedly on his head. He had a big old grin that spread across his face when he was telling a story or took a trick in the card game. By this time, the girls and me had our pajamas on and was supposed to be going to bed. But we just kept out of sight and hadn't gone to bed yet. From my lookout point in the hallway, I could hear the table talk as they dealt the cards and played gin rummy.

"Gin," somebody would say and snap down the hand.

"Now, you get to bed," Mother said when she saw me peeking around the corner. "Santa Claus is going to miss you all together when Christmas comes, if you don't get to bed right now."

Nancy and Mary Beth started to bed right away without much fuss. But I tried everything I could think of to stay up. Mother took me to bed, tucked me in, told me to stay there and went back to the card game. Just as soon as she left the bedroom, I got up and went in through Big and Aunt Helen's bedroom and stood in the darkness by the door, looking out at the card players. Sam hadn't been home long and said he still wore his Army clothes about everywhere he went.

His cap wasn't like anything I'd ever seen before. It didn't have a bill and fit his head like a glove. Part of the cap was pulled up from each side and buckled together at the top. I looked at it from the bedroom door, then walked around through the dining room to look at him and the cap from another angle.

Everybody was laughing and throwing cards on the table and didn't notice me at first when I walked around to Sam's side of the table to see his cap up close. He had a big smile on his face as he slammed his cards down on the table and hollered, "Gin."

"What kind of a cap is that, Sam?" I asked, watching him take a drag on his cigarette and rub the smoke out of his eyes. "I ain't never seen nothin' like it before. Is it an Army cap?"

"I reckon you could call it an Army cap," Sam said, looking over at Mother. "It's to wear under your helmet when you're in a dang old tank. I was in a tank outfit."

"You're going to be in a tank outfit," Mother said, "if you don't get to bed and get to sleep right now like I told you."

Sam laughed and tousled my hair with one of his big hands. I'd never seen hands so big. They were like big old hams with a bunch of fingers sticking out that clamped around my head like it was a little ball. "Better get to bed, John Walter. But wait. I'll give you somethin' first."

He took his shirt off, leaving a brown tee shirt on that showed his big, thick arms sticking through the arm holes. I know my eyes got real big, and I reached over and took ahold of one of his muscles. He just grinned and took a pocket knife out of his pocket and started cutting his stripes off the arms of the shirt and a three-sided patch of red, blue and yellow with tracks and a big gun in the center with a red streak running through it that was just above the stripes.

"Here," he said, taking the cigarette from his lips and laying it down in the ash tray in front of him, "these are for you. My stripes an' my tanker patch."

"For me? What do they mean?"

"Well, the stripes show my rank, staff sergeant, an' the patch is the tank outfit I was in."

"Thank you, Sam."

"You're welcome, you little monkey," he said and tousled my hair again. "I ain't ever goin' to need 'em anymore. I was goin' to give them to you later when I give the girls a couple of necklaces I picked up somewhere in Romania. But I'll give these to you now, if you'll go to bed."

"Okay, Sam," I said, taking the stripes and the patch and looking at them up close. That was something to have stripes and patches from a real soldier's uniform, one that'd been off fighting in the war like my daddy had been. I clutched the stripes and the patch in my hand as I finally took Mother's outstretched hand and headed for bed again, feeling real special and thinking about putting them in an old cigar box where I kept my favorite things. But I still didn't want to go to bed. I didn't like to go to sleep when there was somebody around, especially Sam, the way he made me feel. "Can't I just stay up for six-five more minutes? I can't get to sleep 'cause I hear everybody talkin' out here. I want to talk to Sam. How 'bout that?"

"How about this?" Mother said. "You go to sleep now and talk to Sam later. He'll be around. It's time for little boys to be in bed."

"I'm not a little boy. I'm a little man, I reckon. An' I'm going to be as big as Big an' Sam when I grow up — how do you know he'll be around? I ain't got to see him very much before."

"You will. He'll soon be driving for your Uncle Robert."

"Really? You're not kiddin' me?"

"No, I'm not kidding you. It won't be for a while. But Gus Trout is not very good and probably won't be driving much longer. When he quits, Sam's going to start driving that truck."

That was the best thing I'd heard all day. Maybe Sam would let me go with him in the truck and talk to me then. I went to bed, clutching the stripes and the patch, and the things we'd talk about and places we'd go was racing through my head. Mother kissed me good night and left me in the dark room. I could still see the light peeking around the corner of the front room when I opened my eyes. To help me go to sleep, I started sucking my lip and picking my belly button. Two belly buttons floated close together in my mind, then fluttered together in the air like a couple of butterflies coming together over the garden on a hot summer afternoon. I never saw anybody coming but heard the laughter drift in through the door.

A couple of Saturday nights later, there was a shivaree for Chris and Elsie Matthews. They got married while Chris was in the Army, and he went overseas before everybody could get together to shivaree them. Charlie Kline and Chris had gone overseas about the same time. Only Chris went out somewhere in the South Pacific and came back after the war was over. Out at the store one day I heard Elsie tell Mother that she went to a fortune teller in Robinson who told her that Chris would come back but Charlie wouldn't. Mother never said anything while Elsie told her and stared straight ahead when she left.

"I don't believe in fortune tellers," Mother said, still staring out through space, her eyes a little watery and looking like they wasn't seeing anything. "The good die young."

Mother had come with us to the shivaree, but she looked sad. I'd never seen a shivaree and was excited. Old cars and pickups drove up to the house just after dark. Everybody got out and walked down the short lane to the house. Chris came out on the porch where somebody grabbed him and straddled him on a fence rail that two fellers held and raised up and down with him hanging on and hollering, "You sonsabitches, I'll get you for this."

"You ain't gettin' us fer nothin'," somebody said. "We'd ought to dump you in the dang old horse tank right now."

A big shiver went up my back. It was cold out. I could feel the first snow of winter against my cheeks as they was talking and wondered what it would feel like to be dumped in the horse tank.

Everybody gathered around Chris and the rail, and they started hollering and walking out of the yard into the barn lot towards the horse tank with Chris high about their heads. A cow and a calf came running out of the barn and ran to the back of the lot.

"No, you sonsabitches, you —," Chris said.

"You just shut up, Chris," somebody hollered as they lowered him and the rail. "We ain't goin' to put your sorry ass in the tank tonight. As tender as you are, it'd probably kill you."

On the way back to the little house that sat just off the road, fellers slapped Chris on the back and hollered out how sorry they felt for Elsie. He'd just laugh, shake his head every once in a while and say, "I'll get you sonsabitches for this."

I don't know what the women did with Elsie, but pretty soon we all went in the house to warm up and see what there was to eat and drink.

"Now, boys, they ain't much here," Chris said, "but you're welcome to whatever you can find."

"That's right neighborly of you, Chris," somebody said, "since we're goin' to take whatever we find, anyway."

Chris was a big red-headed old boy with freckles all over his face and arms. His face was so red, though, that I couldn't see the freckles most of the time we was there in the kitchen.

"Looks like you don't have much laid up here, Chris," somebody said as some apples, a couple of loaves of bread and a few other things was set out on the table. "You're goin' to have to lay in a little for the winter or you'll starve to death. Don't care much about you, but that woman deserves better 'n that."

Laughter and words of advice to both Chris and Elsie filled the house. People was standing and sitting everywhere. Arthur and Fern Hamilton's older boy, Pearl, who had just got home from the war and was living with them out on the hill east of Bellair, was sitting in a chair in the corner, the stub of a cigar in the corner of his mouth, a hat cocked off on the side of his head and an old Army coat in his hands in front of him. He was wearing cowboy boots with his Army uniform and was taking the stripes and patches from the coat with a little pocket knife. I watched as a bunch of kids gathered around with me.

"I'm not goin' to need these anymore," he said, clenching the cigar stub between his teeth. "They don't have sergeants out here."

I already had my hands out for the stripes. Pearl lay them in my hands and went back to taking the patches off the coat. "What's a sergeant?" I asked. "What's he do?"

"That's an old boy who's got them three stripes," he said, holding one of the patches out to Richard Owens. "In my outfit, he was a crew chief who was in charge of keepin' an airplane in the air. That patch is the 8th Air Force patch. That was my outfit."

Pearl didn't have anything else to take off of his uniform but talked and kidded with us for a little longer. Then he put his jacket and coat back on and got ready to leave with everybody else. I went to the car with Mother, Aunt Helen, Big and the girls. Nobody said anything until we pulled away with all the other cars. Then I pulled the stripes out of my pocket.

"Look what Pearl gave me, Mother," I said, extending the sergeant stripes for her to see. "He was in the 8th Air Force."

Mother looked away.

"He got these while he was in the war."

"He wasn't in the war much," Mother said, sounding a little like
she was choking. "Fern told me in the store one day that he asked her
and Arthur to send him some cowboy boots where he was overseas,
that he could wear them on base. And he wanted some cigars. Pearl
wasn't in the war like some of the others."

It was quiet in the car for the rest of the way home. Mary Beth was
sitting on Mother's lap. She hugged her and let out a deep breath. I
thought I could hear her crying softly. But I wasn't sure. By the time
we walked into the house and turned on the lights, she wasn't crying.
But her eyes was a little red.

When bad weather was over and things was starting to turn green
again that spring, I turned six years old. By now, I was leaving our
yard and running all over town. While I was up at the store playing
with the kids one evening, I'd seen Mother leave and walk up the
street and knew it was time to go home. I kept thinking I'd leave in
just a minute. But before I did, I heard her calling for me. Her voice
was not normally loud or very strong. When she hollered, though, I
could hear her from just about anywhere around the square. For a
while, I pretended I didn't.

"Jooohhhnnnnn-Waaalllllttter!" she called out several times.

After about the fifth time, I slipped away from the kids playing
tag at the side of the store and headed down the road with my head
down. She was still hollering as I walked along, watching the dust
puff up between my toes with each step I took. I kicked at the gravel at
the side of the road and wished I could have kept playing. In front of
the old hotel where Fannie Boone and her son George lived, I saw a
long row of gray ashes where he'd been burning last fall's leaves.
With the row long since burned and no smoke coming from the leaves,
I thought I'd just walk through the ashes and watch them puff up
through my toes just like the dust did on the road. The powdery soft
gray ashes felt good to my feet. For the first few steps, I thought of the
difference the ashes made compared to the dust. The ashes poofed up

like the brownish road dust, but the leaves had little pieces in them that fluttered through my toes and broke up as they settled back among the ashes. Then I stepped in hot coals and felt them sear into my feet, burning more and more every time I took a step. I remembered the hot screw Jackie Wallace had held out for me to grab and how much that had burned and hurt. But this time both feet were burning all over more than I could stand.

Jumping and screaming, I hopped three or four times through the red-hot coals before I could get out of them and to the edge of the road and fell down in the ditch in front of the Church of Christ, crying out louder with each breath as my feet sent screams of pain to my head. I felt the hot tears streaming down my face and tasted their saltiness as they made their way into my mouth. Ronnie Cooper came running down to me from the store. Between screams I somehow managed to tell him what had happened. "Don't cry, don't cry," he kept saying. "It'll be all right."

"Go get my mommy," I said, hollering and crying louder as I rolled around in the grass. "I want my mommy."

Ronnie ran off toward home to get Mother. He'd run a little ways, then turn around and come back to tell me not to cry. I'd only cry more. He finally saw one of Big's trucks coming from the south with a load of livestock on the way to Indianapolis and waved wildly at the truck and ran to meet it at the corner. The truck slowed to a stop, and I saw Big step out. He seemed to be listening to Ronnie, then looked down the street and started running towards me. I was still crying and hollering at the top of my lungs when he got there. He looked down at my feet, then scooped me up in his arms and started walking fast toward the house. I felt better in his arms, but the pain and hurt didn't stop. I kept crying while he held me in his arms real tight.

"Just hold on, Sedwick," he said. "We'll be home in just a minute, an' your mother can look after them feet."

At the house, Mother and Aunt Helen took me and laid me out on the daybed in the dining room. Big told me they'd take care of me now because he had a load of stock and was headed for Indianapolis. They bathed my feet gently in cold water before drying them off and putting lard on them like old Doc Bates had told them to do before he got there. "There, there, honey, this'll keep your little feet from hurting so much," first one, then the other one would say. I could hardly tell who was talking, but the pain stayed. And I kept crying all the while and kept it up after Doc Bates got there and took a look. All he did was look at the burns on the bottoms of my feet, told me to shut up and wrapped both feet in gauze.

"I think we'd better call Henry Pierce," Aunt Helen said after the doctor left and started to the phone just inside the front door. "He can blow the fire out of the burn."

"Does that work?" Mother asked. "I don't know what to do."

"It worked when Vern Samuels got burned real bad last year. And we called Henry the other night when Mary Elizabeth's nose wouldn't stop bleeding. It stopped right away."

I didn't know anything about Grandma's nose bleeding or anybody else's feet getting burned, but mine was burned and they was hurting like nothing I'd ever had hurt.

Mother sat down on the edge of the daybed, tears filling her eyes, too. She took me in her arms and held me, muffling my tears and sobbing while Aunt Helen called for Henry. I heard her talking to someone, but I couldn't make out what she was saying. Just a minute or two later, she came to the side of the bed and stood there explaining to Mother what she'd found out.

"Henry's in the field," she said. "But Flossie is going to go get him. He'll be here as soon as Flossie can find him."

Then she turned to me and said, "He'll blow the fire out, John Walter. Then it'll quit hurting."

"You hear that, John Walter?" Mother asked. "It'll quit hurting when Henry gets here to blow the fire out."

I heard what they had said but kept on crying and hollering. That was the only thing I could do. "Tell him to hurry," I said through my crying and sobbing. "It hurts, it hurts."

"It won't hurt anymore when Henry gets here and blows the fire out," both of them said over and over. No amount of talk or anything else helped much, but that promise was all I had to hang onto. I was still crying and hollering when Henry got there quite a bit later. The lard hadn't done anything for the pain. And when Henry did get there, I heard him tell Aunt Helen that he wasn't sure he could blow through the lard and do any good. My heart seemed to race, then skipped while he carefully unwound the gauze and set it aside. I couldn't believe what I was hearing.

"But they said you'd make it quit hurtin'," I said, crying louder. "Can't you make it quit hurtin'?"

"I'll try, son," he said. "An' I think I can."

My eyes was riveted to Henry's as he kneeled down in front of me to get to work. I was still crying, but I watched his kind face and steady eyes with hope as he took his cap off and laid it on the floor, uncovering a few strands of hair that only partly covered the white baldness of his head. He unwrapped the gauze from my feet, took first one foot then the other in his big hand and held two thick fingers, one missing everything back to the knuckle, and blew lightly threw them on the bottom of my foot. His eyes never left his work. As he blew, I never felt his breath on my burning feet. But something made them cool down. The pain seemed to go away a little. I could even feel it leaving, I thought. I kept my eyes glued to his and knew what Aunt Helen had said about him blowing the fire out of the burn was working. At least my feet wasn't hurting as much, and I wasn't crying as much. He kept right on blowing through his fingers for a long time. My eyes would feel heavy, and I'd almost drop off to sleep, still blubbering. Then I'd feel a sharp pain and open my eyes. He'd keep blowing steady and never say a word. After a while, he quit and stood up.

"How much do I owe you, Henry?" I heard Mother ask while he stood there talking to her and Aunt Helen.

"You don't owe me a thing," he said. "It's something a feller can't charge for. Wouldn't work, if I charged. Wouldn't charge, anyway. I'll come back after I do the feedin' an' the milkin'."

After he left to go do his chores, I was still crying some, but heard Aunt Helen explaining to Mother how somebody could blow the fire from a burn. Listening to her took my mind away from the pain. And that helped me quit crying a little more.

"Henry says it don't take any special ability to do it," she said, her eyes taking on a look of wonderment that I didn't always see there. She wasn't smiling, but she looked relaxed and peaceful. "Like you saw him do, he just blows over his fingers at the burn without letting his breath touch the burn and keeps repeating words over and over and over in his mind.

"Now I don't know what the words are or where they come from. I think they're from the Bible. Henry said he'd tell me someday. That's the only way you can find out. Somebody like him who knows the words can tell a woman, never a man. Then a woman can tell a man, never a woman. And you can't tell your relation."

"I've heard Dad and Mom talk about it," Mother said. "But I never took much stock in it until now. It sure seemed to take the fire out of John Walter's burn."

"That's all it does, they say," Aunt Helen said. "They don't claim that they can cure the burn, do anything so it don't leave scars from bad burns or take away the pain while the burn's healing. They just blow the fire out of the burn, I guess you'd say, so it don't hurt so."

That was all I cared about.

Henry came back in an hour or so and blew on my feet again. After he'd been there awhile the second time, even my blubbering had quit. My feet still hurt a little, but I could feel my eyelids getting heavier and heavier as I drifted off to sleep with Henry still blowing through his fingers toward my feet. His steady eyes and soft breath was the last things I remembered seeing and hearing until the next morning.

When I woke up, Mother was sitting by the daybed holding my hand. "How's my little angel?" she asked.

"I got to pee," I said, starting to get up.

Mother picked me up and told me she'd take me to the pot. "You're not going to be able to walk for a while," she said. "I've got to go to the store, but Aunt Helen is going to borrow a wagon from Arthur and Fern to pull you around in. She'll bring you up to the store later today."

That tickled me. I liked their boy Jeremy's little red wagon and had wanted one myself. Now I had one to ride in. And that's the way I got around for the next couple of months. In a few days, Mother drained the water from the big blisters on the bottoms of my feet. I got so I liked to be pulled around in the little red wagon and have everybody fuss over me, reading books to me, bringing me ice cream and carrying me everywhere I went.

By the time I could walk on my own again and was out of the wagon, school was about to start. I'd been driving everybody crazy with questions about school. When the morning finally came to go, I got up earlier than usual, pulled a pair of bib overalls over my underwear and fastened the galluses over a blue chambray shirt. Then I went to the kitchen for a bowl of Wheaties with sliced bananas, a dash of sugar sprinkled over each slice, and thick cream.

I'd wanted to start school the year before but wasn't old enough. Now I was having mixed feelings about the whole thing. One minute I couldn't wait for school to start; the next I'd try to think of how to put it off. For days I'd been asking Mother, Aunt Helen, Big, Madge Lewis, our next-door neighbor, Carolyn Matthews, who was Horsey and Arletta's older daughter and lived across the street — anybody who'd listen — to tell me what it was like to go to school. Somehow I thought they could tell me enough so I'd know. But the day had arrived for me to find out for myself. I shoveled the Wheaties down like a starving pig, occasionally chewing a banana before swallowing it. At the kitchen sink, I slowed down enough to pump some water into a wash pan and splash a little on my face to erase the milk mustache with one hand and to slick down a cowlick with the other one.

Then I ran out the door as Carolyn walked out of her front door. She was three or four years older than me and in the fifth grade.

"What'll I have to do today, Carolyn?" I asked as we walked down the dusty road toward the school.

She didn't tell me anything right then that she hadn't already told me and had been telling me for days, but I kept asking. And she kept answering like she had been for days. She might as well have told me that Miz Ryan carried a blacksnake whip like Lash LaRue and would pop one of your eyes out if you ever crossed her, though. I was too nervous for anything to have made any difference.

"But what'll I do today?" I asked again, looking at the school with one eye and watching Carolyn's face with the other.

She answered again. I asked if the teacher would whip anyone.

"Of course she will," Carolyn said. "She's the teacher. But you don't have to worry about it. All you have to do is mind what she says and do your work. She only whips you, if you're bad."

"What if I have to go to the toilet?" I asked as we walked into the schoolyard, feeling much more like going to the toilet than going to school.

She smiled, held up one finger and said, "Hold up one finger, if you have to do number one, and two fingers, if you have to do number two. That's all there is to it."

It all seemed pretty simple.

"Is school hard?" I asked, firing off another question as the school-house threatened to swallow us before I could learn the answer. "I don't know how to write."

Carolyn sighed and took a long breath before she patiently explained that that was why I was going to school. "You won't have to do anything but play with your crayons," she said. "You'll get some books, and you'll color in your coloring books. Maybe read a little. Nothing hard. First grade is easy."

"Heck, I can't read," I said.

"That's why you're going to school, I just told you," she said. "Don't worry about it."

But I did worry about it. My knees knocked together as we made the final assault and started through the schoolhouse door. Miz Ryan looked up and said hello to several kids at the same time. School started right on time at eight o'clock. From there on, one day blended into the next. I learned to read by reading about Dick and Jane and Sally and Spot all running and playing and having a good time. At home, I read to Mother or Aunt Helen every day and had trouble remembering the word run. Mother told me so many times that every time I'd hesitate, Nancy would say, "Run." That made me so mad that I finally refused to read when she was any place close.

Other than that, school pretty much went by without any problems. Carolyn had been right. School wasn't too hard. It was really pretty easy and fun most of the time. Miz Ryan was a pretty nice woman, too. Most of the time, I liked school. When I'd see one of Big's trucks pass by the school, though, or hear him or one of his drivers across the road at the old schoolhouse getting a truck ready to take a load of stock to Indianapolis, I'd want to get up and walk out of the door and get away from school. I'd wonder if I'd ever grow up and get out of Bellair. The only world I knew was just outside the window. And I wanted to see what was going on beyond where I could see. I knew the only chance I had to do that for a long time was to go with Big in the truck and listen to the stories I always heard when I was around him and the fellers that worked for him or the ones we'd run into while we was trucking around the country.

3

Not long after he'd been down to our house after he first came home from the Army, Sam started riding with Big to Indianapolis every week or so and coming to Bellair for dinner on the days he went or rode with him to help haul something else. Now and then he'd drive by himself. Even though I hadn't turned six yet when he'd come home and he was a big person who'd been away in the Army and fought in the war, it was almost like Sam was the big brother I wanted so bad. At first I thought he was more like Big's little brother because they was together so much, but I thought more about it and saw that Big was really his uncle just like he was mine.

On Sunday when the whole family went to Granddad J.W. and Grandma McElligott's for dinner, I always managed to sit by Sam at the table and eat whatever he did. I couldn't eat as much as he could, though, no matter how hard I tried. He always took second helpings and sometimes even thirds because he never ate deserts or sweets of any kind. Grandma started making iced tea without sugar because Sam didn't drink sweetened tea. That took me awhile to get used to since I liked sugar so much. But I finally got to the point where I liked it just fine after I asked Sam why he didn't like his sweetened like everybody else did. Even Big would put a couple of teaspoons of sugar in his tea. In coffee, he'd add cream and sugar until it was nearly white.

"We didn't have no sugar over yonder," Sam said. "So I just got used to not havin' it, I reckon."

He really seemed to like Grandma's coffee, too. She boiled it in a pot on top of the cook stove and made it so strong and thick that Aunt Helen said you could stand a spoon straight up and it wouldn't fall over and was only fit to drink when you put enough cream and sugar in it to cut the bitterness. Sam would drink the coffee black and still be at the table finishing his after the rest of the men had gone outside and the women started cleaning off the table and doing the dishes. I'd stay with him and go outside when he went out to smoke.

Everybody else would sit on the porch or stand around smoking or chewing or just talking. Granddad would have someone bring his rocking chair and coal bucket he used as a spittoon out on the porch so he could be with the men. He'd lean pretty heavy on the big old cane with a knob on top that he kept by his chair inside. He had a hard time getting in and out of the chair. Somebody had to help him most of the time. Then everybody'd talk about the weather or the crops or something else I didn't care much about. Sam usually stood off at the end of the porch and smoked, looking out across the garden and the pasture into the woods where Granddad's place ended. I tried to see what he was looking at, but I never saw anything except what was always there. When I'd go up and try to talk to Sam, it'd take me a minute to get his attention and then he'd just say, "Huh?" and look down at me, then keep on looking out at the woods. The look in his eyes was sad, and he didn't grin and talk to me like he did at home.

At other times, he'd just go off in the barn lot and smoke and stare off across the pasture to the south. He was looking for something he couldn't find, I reckoned. Nobody bothered him, and I was almost afraid to go out to him. The look in his eyes scared me. He looked like he was someplace else and even like he was somebody else some of the time. I didn't quite know what to make of him. But I was drawn to him for some reason and wanted to be around him when I could.

Not long after school had taken up in the fall of '46, Gus Trout had a heart attack one hot night when he was sleeping on the front porch at his house and rolled out of the daybed dead and down off of the porch where they said he came to a stop when he hit the tree. Sam went to work full time driving a truck for Big after that and was in Bellair nearly every day. I started going with one or the other of them every time I could that I wasn't in school. One day just as school was let out, Big, Sam and Joe was in the old schoolhouse barn lot taking the stock rack off and putting another kind of bed on to haul gravel. I'd never seen them change beds and ran across the road to watch.

"Now you stand back out of the way, Sedwick," Big said, growling like he always did when he was working and I was anywhere close by. "I don't want you to get hurt."

"I won't get in the way," I said. "I just want to watch."

Sam pointed to an overturned five-gallon bucket sitting against the wall of the old schoolhouse and told me that'd be a good place to watch from. They had backed Sam's truck in between four big iron pipe joints set in the ground. Two long iron pipes with chains welded to them in three places on each side was fastened to the stock rack. When the chains was in place, a wheel had been welded to the pipes at the front of the changing outfit so they could be turned and the stock rack lifted out of the truck bed and tied in place with another chain fastened to the wheel and held in place with baling wire. The bed itself was held in place by long clamps around the bed and the truck frame. I'd only seen a truck without a bed of some kind once when Big bought a new truck. I was plumb amazed to watch the stock rack taken away and a naked truck left there when Sam drove it out from under the stock rack so they could lift the bed off and start putting the gravel bed on.

"I hope Clyde Cottrell has enough gravel for you to haul this fall so we don't have to change this sonuvabitch back right away," Big said as Sam started backing the long-nosed red truck back under the gravel bed at the side of the stock rack and held in place by the pipes and chains the same way. "This could get old."

"Is old," Sam said, backing and looking in the mirrors and at Big as the truck inched back under the gravel bed that looked a little like a tank to me. The bed was all metal and narrowed in from near the top to make a hopper-like look at the bottom where the gravel come out to spread on the road. Two sections of decking board was bolted into the bed on both sides of the hopper so you could walk from the front of the bed to the back on both sides. The truck sure looked different with the smaller bed on it when they lowered the bed on the truck frame. It didn't look like the same truck.

After Big and Joe had lowered the bed on the frame and it wasn't sitting straight, Big went to the back of the truck and stooped down under the bed. With both hands on the underneath side of the gravel bed, he jerked it to him in short, hard jerks until the bed rested squarely on the truck frame. Then the three men put the clamps on and tightened them to the frame in no time. That they had changed from the stock rack to the gravel bed in such a short time was something to see. Sam drove the truck out from between the poles and was ready to haul gravel.

"The pit will be closed by the time you could get over there an' get a load this evenin'," Big said, lifting on the gravel bed and shaking it. "Get her filled up with gas an' get an early start in the mornin'. Somebody is usually there ready to load you by seven or a little after. Start there on the Porterville Road where it angles off past Jim Richards' place. Probably take a week or better to get it all hauled. Just spread it out there the best you can. The maintainer'll come along an' spread it out after you get it all hauled."

"Can I go with Sam, Big?" I asked. "Tomorrow's Saturday."

Sam and Joe grinned and looked at Big. He'd just flipped a Lucky Strike off towards the gate and turned around waving the truck through the gate. "Too early for the first load or two," he said, smoke coming in spurts from both his nose and mouth as he talked. "He can come by here an' pick you up after the first load, if it's all right with your mother."

I knew most she'd let me and watched the smoke spill out and drift into the air. I'd never noticed anyone smoking a cigarette and having the smoke come out that way before. How in the world did he do it? I wondered. All I'd ever done was just take a drag and blow it out. I couldn't wait until I could try to make the smoke come out of both my mouth and nose at the same time. I wondered if Sam could do it, too. He let me ride to the house with him where he was going to gas up but didn't smoke a cigarette until he was checking the oil. When he was finished with the truck, he went in the house to talk to Mother and Aunt Helen. On the way in, he flipped his cigarette off the porch as he walked in the house. I waited until he was inside and ran out in the grass to find the smoking cigarette. He'd only half smoked it and left a good part of it for me to try to get smoke to come out both my mouth and my nose when I talked. I ran around back of the house and out alongside the garden to the toilet where I could smoke without being seen and where the smell didn't stay.

The toilet was one of my secret places to get away from everybody. I sat down between the holes where you sat to do your business and took my first drag off the Lucky Strike, thinking of something to say.

Looking to my right and down into the hole I said, "What a pile of shit that is down there! Looks like an old hard rock candy mountain with chocolate sticking out through the white stuff. Don't smell much like candy, though."

I thought that was funny and laughed at what I'd said. A cloud of smoke drifted out of my mouth and hung all around my face with the first word. I kept talking but no more smoke came out of my mouth and none ever came out of my nose. I tried it over and over until the butt was so short that I had to throw it down on top of the mountain of my family's poop and watch the butt roll down the hill side and stop at a torn piece of an old Montgomery Wards catalog. Maybe Big is the only one who could make the smoke come out of his mouth and nose when he talks, I thought. It was sort of like the smoke rings that Gene Shaw blew for us kids sometimes when he sat around smoking his pipe, strumming a guitar and singing to us. He'd stop strumming and singing to take a puff on the pipe, then tilt his head up and blow perfect smoke rings until all the smoke was gone from his mouth. I'd tried that, too, and hadn't been able to blow the first ring. All the smoke came out at once unless I closed my mouth and blew a little out at a time. That's pretty much the way I'd seen everybody but Mother blow their smoke out. She'd take a drag on an old Kool and let the smoke drift up from the corner of her mouth and into her eye. It'd water and she'd rub it. I didn't try that.

The next day I watched Sam smoke and listened to him talk as we drove along the road between the gravel pit and the angling Porterville Road. He laughed and grinned like he always did down home. Even his eyes laughed. He told me stories and kidded with me while I looked out over the dashboard at the country as it rolled by. I noticed right off that he could do the same thing Big did when he smoked and talked. I couldn't wait to try it again.

Sam had picked me up after his first load of the morning. With the gravel pit closing at noon, he said we'd have to hustle to get the three more loads by noon that Big had wanted him to get. On the first load we got, he stopped and backed up to the end of the pile of gravel where he'd stopped off at the last load. "You stay right here, Sedwick," he said. When he came back a minute or so later, he jumped in the truck and said, "Now we'll spread some gravel."

He pushed the gear shift up with the stick down, give her the gas and the truck jumped off down the road. I could hear the gravel sliding down the bed and hitting the underneath side of the truck on the way to the road, making a pinging sound. Sam shifted gears once, the truck lunged forward faster and then the noise of the gravel stopped. He wheeled the truck around and into a little dirt road off to the side and got out again to close the bed for another load. Then he backed out into the road the other way to head back to the gravel pit.

"Watch this now, Sedwick," Sam said, a grin breaking out on his face as he gunned the truck and kept one hand on the steering wheel and one on the gear shift and hit the long narrow pile of gravel we'd just spread with the front wheel on the driver's side, making the truck set up at an angle and Sam higher than me in a scary way. "I'll show you how to spread some gravel."

I looked up at him and held onto the window and the back of the dash as we bounced and weaved like I'd seen Joe Louis do in the newsreels at the free shows over at The Corners. Sam looked over at me and grinned while he was shifting again. "How'd you like that?" he asked. "That's how you spread gravel."

"It was fun," I said, happy to see Sam grinning. It'd scared me a little, the way the truck kept rolling and jerking while it was on the gravel ridge, but I wasn't about to tell him. I didn't want him to know I was scared even a little bit. And it was fun. When we went to Casey for the Fourth of July, I always wanted to ride the Ferris wheel and some of the other rides, but Mother always said I was too little and would only let me ride the kiddy cars. I wished I'd hurry up and grow up so she'd never try to have me wear short pants again and I could ride anything I wanted to ride. The ride in the truck wasn't exactly the Ferris wheel, but it was more fun than I usually had any place else.

On the way to the pit for the last load, I asked Sam about being in the Army like I'd been wanting to for a long time. He still sometimes wore his old uniforms when he was trucking but then had started wearing a dark-green shirt, trousers and cap with a high-topped pair of work boots almost all the time. It almost looked like his old Army uniform, except it was green. Big wore the tan, Army-looking outfits like Sam's. The only difference was the color of the clothes, and the boots Big wore laced down to the toes.

"Was you ever in a fight when you was in the Army, Sam?" I asked, wondering what it would be like to fight in the Army.

He looked over at me and smiled slightly. Then he grinned a little and said, "Oh, I guess I was. I reckon you could say that."

It wasn't until a long time later that he told me he'd landed on Normandy at Omaha Beach on D-Day in a tank and had it shot up right away. And he was lucky at that, he said, when I asked him about it. Only five tanks in his whole outfit of fifty-seven had made it to the top of the hill that morning. The other companies in his outfit had tanks with the new-fangled flotation contraptions that was supposed to let the tanks float, he said. But the "thingamajigs," Sam called them, didn't work, and the tanks went right to the bottom of the English Channel, drowning many of the crews, when they was put out into the water a half a mile from shore. He said only a few of the fellers in the other companies had made it out of their tanks and swum to shore. Then I was older and had been around Sam for a long time. He'd talk to me about the way it was when I asked him and seemed not to mind my questions. His tank had been stopped on the beach, and he was getting out when the hatch banged down on his head and jammed his neck into his body. For a long time afterwards he said he couldn't move his head or look either way without his neck hurting like the dickens. He went on up the beach and up the hill with the infantry without a tank before him and his crew finally got one. He said he was wounded a couple of months later but was only in a field hospital ten days before being sent back to the front. Then he spent part of the winter at the Battle of the Bulge. But it wouldn't have made much difference to me, if I'd known all that at the time, anyway. All I thought the Army was about was fighting somebody and being overseas. I never knew anything about all that stuff or understood much about it until I was quite a bit older.

With the war over and work to do everywhere, Big kept four of his five trucks running almost all the time. Gene Shaw and Barney Ford, who'd both not been home from the service long, drove the other two. I didn't get to ride with either of them. Mother wanted me to stay with Big or Sam. Gene kept his truck up at his folks' house where he lived and just came by for gas. He'd stayed in California

while he was in the Army and was a happy-go-lucky, easy-going man
who still smoked a pipe and usually had a smile on his face. Barney
was not anything like I remembered him. He looked a lot older than
he did when he tried to break me of smoking. His cheeks was hollow,
and his eyes had a blank look in them that wouldn't let you in. Sometimes he'd laugh and I'd think he was going to be like he used to, but
most of the time he was just quiet and mean looking. The first time I
saw him when he come back, he grinned at me real big, tousled my
hair with a big hand and said, "Still smokin' them old cigarettes,
Sedwick?" But after that he never said much to me and spent most of
the time he wasn't driving a truck in the taverns in Robinson. Big
didn't like that and said he was going to have to let Barney go, if he
didn't quit drinking so much.

"How come Barney's not friendly like he used to be?" I asked
Sam one day when I was riding with him. "I don't think he even likes
me anymore."

"Oh, he likes you, Sedwick," Sam said, looking over at me with a
sad, kind look in his eyes like I saw a dog give a boy in a Hollywood
movie I saw down in Oblong one Saturday night the week before.
"That's probably not changed."

"What's changed?"

"Barney has."

"How'd he change?"

"You ask a lot of questions for a little feller. That's hard for me to
explain to you."

"You can try. I'll listen."

"This is just between you an' me then. Okay?"

"Okay."

"Well, Barney had a girlfriend when he left."

"Yeah, I remember. He was goin' over to see her the day before he
left for the Marines. That was the day he let me smoke a package of
Marvels 'cause he wanted to break me of smokin'. I got sicker 'n a dog."

Sam grinned. "Didn't help much, did it?" he said.

"Don't reckon it did," I said and grinned back. "What about Barney?"

"Well, Wilma Jean sent him a Dear John letter while he was still
in basic training. He —"

"What's a Dear John letter?"

"It's a letter a woman sends a man when she breaks off with him. Lots of fellers got them back then."

"Did you ever get one, Sam?"

"I thought you wanted to know about Barney."

"I did."

"Well, I reckon that thing with Wilma Jean an' what he went through on Okinawa is what's got him to where he is now. He got hit real bad just before the island was secured, an' he spent quite awhile in the hospital. Don't have his strength back yet."

Later, I was riding with Big and asked him about Barney and why he was so much different now. We was coming back from Indianapolis and had stopped at the coal mine in Brazil for a load of coal. Big had slept a little in the cab, and I'd sat out on the running board of the truck to wake him up when they started loading and the line moved. He hadn't had much sleep and would nod off out on the road after we got loaded and started for home. Just south of Marshall, he started drifting across the line, heading right for a car coming from the other direction, and I waited as long as I could before I reached over and took ahold of his arm. "Wake up, Big," I said. "We're goin' to —"

"I'm awake," he said and turned the steering wheel to the right like he was just driving any old time.

I didn't quite believe him but was too scared to say anything. He still looked asleep to me, so I asked him about Barney to make conversation, hoping that would help get us home. Big just shook his head and mumbled something about the drinking and went back to nodding off, then woke up to scoop the load of coal off when we got to The Corners. He never talked when he was tired, and he didn't tell me anything about Barney that helped me understand.

Helping keep Big and Sam awake was part of the deal for me to go with them as much as I did. And I went with whichever one I could and knew it'd be a different kind of day, according to which one I rode with. They was a lot the same, but they was a lot different, too. Big punched the punch boards and won big, long candy bars that had nuts on the outside and chewy stuff on the inside. Sam never played the punch boards or did anything like that. Most of the time he just drove the truck and hauled his loads and talked to me when I could get him to talk. I always opened the glove compartment in Big's truck

the first chance I got to see if there was any candy in there. I usually
only found a package of the Red Man chewing tobacco that he chewed
or tape or lights and things he used on the truck. But when I did find a
candy bar, I'd take a bite off if it'd been opened. Once in a while Big
would open one and break off a piece for me.

The best thing about going with him was that he stopped in a lot
of places Sam didn't stop with me. I hadn't stayed in the hotel at the
stockyards like Big and Sam did sometimes and like I wanted to. But
Big had let me go with him when he was going to sleep in the truck
while waiting in a line somewhere to unload a load of wheat or get a
load of coal. And Big took me to cafes and pool halls, too. Mother
didn't like for me to go there, either. But I liked to watch the men play
and watch the old men sitting on the benches, spitting tobacco juice in
the spittoons and talking and laughing about the game or anything
else that came up.

We stopped in the pool room and tavern in Porterville for a sandwich one night on the way home from taking a load of cattle from Oat
Davis' place to a cattle feeder over on the Wabash River. Pappy Foote
owned the tavern and pool hall and made the best hamburgers around,
Big said. Pappy was a little feller who wore little wire-rimmed spec-
tacles that kept slipping down on his nose. I'd jumped in the truck
with Big after school when he was filling up with gas, so it'd been a
long day. And I was hungry. But the big hamburger, which was as
good as Big said they always was, and the little Coke filled me up
pretty quick, and I turned to look at the pool table behind us while
Big finished his second hamburger and took the last swig out of
his beer. Jim Richards, the big old raw-boned feller who lived just
down the road, and another feller named Fred Campbell was playing pool, and there'd been a lot of talking and laughing going on
while we was eating. They'd had two more bottles of beer while
we'd been there, and they got a little louder with each beer. Jim had
waved at us when we came in and said, "Hey, Big, who's that old boy
you got with you there?"

"This here is Sedwick," Big said as we walked to the counter
and ordered our sandwiches, calling me the nickname he'd given me
because I liked the livestock commission house named Sedwick's at
the stockyards in Indianapolis. "He's my right-hand man."

"He's a good-lookin' old boy," Jim said, winked at me and went back to playing pool.

I stood a little straighter and felt my face flush as they talked about me. It made a feller feel good to be kidded like that, especially by somebody like Jim. I knew he'd been in the Army and in the war like Daddy and Sam had been. He had a load of cattle sitting in his truck on the road outside. He was a truck driver like Big and looked big, too. Maybe Jim wasn't quite as thick through the chest, but he was a couple of inches taller than Big and wore the same khaki outfits. Jim always wore his cap tipped around to the left and looked at you with a crooked grin on his face. As I watched him, he stretched his long frame out across the pool table to shoot the eight ball into the far corner pocket. His big left hand made a bridge for the pool cue, and he took slow, measured strokes while Fred kept talking to him about something I couldn't hear.

"If you don't dry up, you old peckerwood," Jim said, stroking the cue ball softly toward the eight ball, "I'm goin' to stuff your sorry ass in that corner pocket, too."

As the cue ball hit the eight ball and started it towards the corner pocket, Fred turned his pool cue around so he could hold it like a club or a baseball bat, drew it back and said, "You ain't goin' to stuff nobody nowhere, Jim Richards."

The big end of the pool cue hit Jim up side the head about the same time the eight ball rolled into the corner pocket. His tan cap fell off and his head sort of slumped down on the green table for a little bit. His right hand dropped the cue to the table and grabbed his head where Fred's cue had hit him. "Why you silly sonuvabitch, you," he said, bellowing like the bull Big and Sam had loaded over at Oat Davis' earlier in the day. "I ought t' kill your fuckin' ass."

"Now boys, now boys," Pappy Foote said, still standing behind the bar. "Watch your language an' let's not quarrel."

If Jim heard him, he didn't show it or pay any attention. He pushed himself up with both hands and brought his right hand around as he stood and backhanded Fred, knocking him into the table a little ways away. His glasses flew off and went under the next table, and he slid to the floor. He was about the same age as Big and Jim, right at thirty years old, I reckon. Fred wasn't a tall man like them, and although he looked big through the arms and shoulders, he was thicker in the belly than anyplace else. He always wore a flannel shirt with the top button buttoned and wore suspenders instead of a belt. The top button had popped open and one suspender came off his shoulder and halfway down his arm when Jim hit him.

While Fred was struggling to get back on his feet, Jim took two big steps towards him, kicked a chair out of his way, and grabbed Fred by the front of the shirt with one hand and hit him with a cocked right hand that knocked him over the table. Blood spurted from his nose as he flew through the air. Jim knocked the table aside and grabbed another handful of Fred's shirt and pulled him to his feet.

"I oughta kill you, you silly sonuvabitch," Jim said, his big right hand cocked again. "But I'm not goin' to this time. I'm just goin' to slap you sillier 'n you already are."

And he backhanded Fred three or four times, making a loud smack each time his hand hit his cheek and his head snapped that way, dropped him in a heap and said, "You silly sonuvabitch."

He picked up his cap off the pool table and put it on, tipped off to the left. But he didn't have that grin that I usually saw. His face had no look on it at all that I could tell. His eyes weren't wide open like I'd always seen them, and they looked cold and hard. "Silly sonuvabitch," Jim said again, tipping his beer bottle back for the last drink. His Adam's apple bobbled back and forth a couple of times before he finished the beer. He sat the bottle on the rack hanging on the wall, picked up his pool stick from the table to put in the rack and turned to leave. Fred lay on the floor and back under a table. Pappy stood wringing his hands, still standing behind the counter. Nobody said anything as Jim walked out. But I watched him real close to see what he was going to do. He just squeezed my shoulder as he walked past and said, "Watch out for old Big there, Sedwick."

I could only nod and swallow, but I also felt about ten feet tall. The scared feeling I had when the fight was going on went away, even though I kept thinking about it. All the fights I'd ever seen had been the fellers who worked for Big wrassling in our yard and a boxing match or two up at the store that I never paid much attention to or kids getting into fights around the store or at school. And I'd walked around when all the men gathered at the store to listen to Joe Louis fight somebody.

But I'd never seen anybody bleed or get knocked out. I heard Jim's truck pull away and shift a couple of times to pick up speed while I kept my eyes on Fred. A couple of fellers had gotten a wet rag and a towel to help get things and him cleaned up. When Big hollered at me to come on, Fred was sitting up on the floor, moaning and holding the rag to his nose.

Big opened the door of his red truck and hoisted me up to crawl over on the other side. It wasn't quite dark yet, but he turned the lights on and pulled the truck out into the road to head for home. I was tired but still thinking about seeing the fight. It wasn't like the fights at school that was mostly just wrassling around and where the teacher always broke them up before they got too far along or like the ones in the cowboy shows where they knocked each other all over the saloon for a long time but never showed anybody bleeding.

Big hadn't said anything since we left the tavern. He was like that sometimes, even when nothing was happening. He'd just get quiet and seem to be lost in his thoughts about something he'd never talk about.

"How come nobody stopped the fight?" I asked, looking at him for an answer as we drove along. When he was still quiet for what seemed like a long time, I asked him again. "How come nobody stopped Jim from hurtin' Fred, Big? He was bleedin' on the floor."

"If a feller ain't got no better sense than to hit Jim Richards over the head with a danged pool cue, ain't nobody goin' to stop him from gettin' his plow cleaned," Big said, flipping a Lucky Strike out the window and talking with the smoke coming from his nose and mouth, "Wonder Jim didn't kill the dumb sonuvabitch."

And that was about all that needed to be said about the matter.

"Better not say anything to the women about what happened over there," Big added as he turned the corner for home. "Wouldn't set well with them, I don't 'magine."

I knew what he was talking about and didn't want to do anything that might keep me from being able to go with Big and Sam. As it was, Mother said she didn't like that place when I told her where we'd had a sandwich. Aunt Helen frowned at Big when she heard me talking to Mother.

"That place ain't fit for you to take John Walter," she said.

Big never answered. He just pulled off his shoes and picked up a western book to read a little before he went to bed like he did most nights when he wasn't too tired. I tried to catch his eye, but he wouldn't look at me.

He was gone the next morning when I got up. Since it was a teachers' institute day, we didn't have school, and I'd wanted to go with him. With the day after being Armistice Day, I thought I could ride with Sam or him for both days. I figured Mother would let me go, if it was all right with them. She was just leaving for the store when I sat down for breakfast with Nancy and Mary Beth, and I didn't ask her. I'd do that later, if Big said I could go. Horsey had been to Terre Haute the day before and brought back a stock of fresh bananas he hung on a hanger behind the meat counter. Mother had brought a bunch home, and we was having some Cheerios with sliced bananas and fresh cream Aunt Helen had got from Orville and Alma Barker and their Holstein milk cows. That made one of the best breakfasts I could think of, even better than buckwheat pancakes and fresh sausage at butchering time.

"Your Uncle Robert play pool over there last night?" Aunt Helen asked after she'd got us all sitting at the table and eating. "Big, Bob, Bert or whatever you call him now."

"Nope," I said, ignoring her comment that I figured she made just to aggravate me. None of them other names sounded as good as Big. "We just had our sandwiches an' left."

I didn't like it when she asked me what we did when I was with Big or Sam. Sometimes I'd say the wrong thing, and she'd tell Mother it wasn't good for me to be around the kinds of things I had been. So I tried to say as little as possible.

"They was real good sandwiches," I said. "I reckon they was about as good as them pork sandwiches Frog McCabe makes down there at Joe's Tavern in Oblong that you like so well."

"I've had Pappy Foote's hamburgers," she said. "They're not a bit better than they make down at Rich's, and you don't have to go into a pool hall or a tavern to get them."

"I reckon not."

Nancy and Mary Beth started fussing about who had the most bananas, and I buried my head in my bowl. The rest of the morning, we played in the toy room. Big came home for dinner and allowed since there wasn't any school for two days, I could go to Indianapolis with him and Sam if it was all right with Mother. I ran out of the house and never stopped running until I was on the store porch.

"Big says I can go to Indianapolis," I said, panting and stopping to catch my breath, "if it's okay with you. Can I? Can I? Please, Mother."

She smiled at me and put me up on one of the benches to hug me. She'd been telling me that I was getting too big for her to pick up anymore. And I reckon she was right. I was nearly as tall as she was and weighed about eighty pounds.

"You be good and mind Robert," she said, holding me against her shoulder. "I wish you'd call him Uncle Robert instead of Big, John Walter. Even Uncle Bob or Bert would be better than Big. You just don't sound respectful when you call him Big."

"That's what other fellers call him, an' they respect him."

"I know, but that's other fellers. They're not his nephew."

"Can I call him Uncle Big?"

Mother laughed and pulled back to look at me.

"You're your daddy's boy, no doubt about that. He'd love you to pieces. Just be a good boy and make him proud of you."

"I will, Mother," I said, noticing the tears in her eyes. I wiped one that was running down her cheek and gave her a kiss. "Thank you, Mother. You're the best mother in the world."

"I wish I could be," I heard her say as I ran out the door.

She had called Aunt Helen by the time I got back home and told her it was all right for me to go to Indianapolis. Later that afternoon, Sam met Big and me out at Wes Davis' place. Wes had a little farm just east of Oat's and was a feller who could sure tell stories. He chewed tobacco and laughed and spit, his eyes smiling and laughing all the time when he told one. He had two double-deck loads of hogs to go to Indianapolis where I couldn't go most of the time because of school. Big and the other fellers would load up in the late afternoon and evening when they took a load to Indianapolis so they could do some other hauling in the morning and haul the stock in the cooler part of the day so the hogs or cattle wouldn't have to wait too long for the market the next morning. But it was cold weather now and hunting season started the next day, so they planned to load up a bit earlier. Big and Sam had been talking about going rabbit hunting ever since Sam started working part time in the spring. They'd talked about a time when Sam was in the Army just before he went overseas that he'd helped Big run his traps. He didn't trap anymore, but then he'd had traps set for mink, muskrat and 'coons and had places set from the bridge on the North Fork just west of Bellair around to just west of Hoguetown where he'd walk out and take the road back to Nash Bowman's place where we lived then. The whole trip to reset the traps and pack what he'd caught, Big said, would take him about six hours during trapping season. He'd taken Sam with him that day because it was the last day of the season and the traps had to be picked up, too. With gunny sacks full of traps and animals to gut and skin back on the farm, it was well after noon when they walked back into town. Big said Sam's eyes looked "like a kid's in a candy store" when they topped the last hill and saw town. That's sort of like I looked when I got to go to Indianapolis, I reckon.

Sam was backed up to the barn, setting up the loading chutes with Wes when we pulled in the barnyard. I was pretty excited. Wes was going today, too, I'd heard Big tell Aunt Helen at dinner. "You don't need to be taking John Walter in them taverns and pool halls," Aunt Helen had said. I figured they'd talked about stopping for a sandwich at the tavern over in Porterville. She hadn't said anything more to me about being there other than about Big playing pool and what I'd seen. I'd just told her about the big old hamburger and little bottle of Coca-Cola and fellers playing pool and others just sitting around. So I didn't say anything. Big didn't say anything, either. Pretty soon, he just tipped back his head, drained the coffee cup and pushed back his chair as he sat the cup on the table. We left right away to load up.

"Well, good afternoon, there, Big Un," Wes said, coming up from under the loading chute. "I heard old Richards put on a show over at Porterville last night. Think Fred'll live?"

"He'll live," Big said. "But I doubt that he'll want to hit old Jim Richards over the head with a pool cue anymore. Old Fred looked like he'd been run through a meat grinder, but I don't think he was hurt bad."

"Naw, I don't think so," Wes said, turning a little and sending a stream of tobacco juice toward the barn. "I was over at the store awhile ago, an' they say he's got a broken nose, both eyes are swolled shut an' he's got a couple of cuts that'll leave nice scars. Sounds like he was pretty lucky at that."

"I don't know if lucky's the right word. Hittin' Jim like that was about the dumbest thing I ever seen a feller do. I don't know what 'n the devil he was thinkin'."

"Wasn't thinkin' atall, Big. Wasn't thinkin' atall. Fellers like Fred don't think. And old Jim don't think. He just fights."

Sam set his chute and took baling wire from the back of the truck to tie the back of the chute to the barn. Big and Wes kept talking while Sam finished setting up the loading chute. With a couple of quick twists, he had the chute tied down and was ready to load hogs. Wes was still talking and spitting and laughing.

"Mac here knows what I'm atalkin' about," Wes said when Sam walked back to us. "When we got to Paris an' them fuckin' Krauts had pulled out, they was people everywhere. On the streets, hangin' out the windows. Everywhere. Somebody'd hand you a bottle for you to take a drink, an' you didn't know what 'n the hell it was. An' you didn't care. I took a big slug out of a bottle an old French gal handed me that I thought was wine, an' it was cognac. Cleaned the shit out of my pipes an' burned all the way down. Old Kelly, some French gal grabbed him an' gave him a big kiss. A lot of them French women was whores an' put out to anybody that come along, but I had a lot more respect for them than I did them goddamn French men, the kind of bastards that'd go whichever way the wind blowed. But we didn't see Kelly until just five minutes before we was to pull out two days later. Captain wanted to write him up fer bein' AWOL, but the old first sergeant said to wait until we pulled out. When old Kelly showed up agrinnin' like a possum eatin' shit, First Sergeant said he's here an' we need him. That's all they was to that. Kelly kept his tank arunnin' an' always done his part when it counted. That's all we cared about.

"But Old Slim Carpenter down at Oblong was in an infantry outfit an' said him an' a buddy was walkin' along one of them main drags there in Paris when we was all camped out there, an' they saw a couple of them French policemen fightin' with an old boy up ahead of them, an' a couple more of them *gendarmes* arunnin' towards them. Slim says they walked a little faster when he seen it was Jim Richards. 'That's an old boy from back home,' Slim says to his buddy. 'We better go help him out. Looks like they're agangin' up on him.'

"So old Slim an' his buddy waded in with both fists aflyin' an' evened things out a little. Then it was only four of them goddamn Frenchie *gendarmes* to three Americans. Them French don't like them odds. An' after goin' at it fer a while, Slim an' his buddy was able to get Jim untangled an' things settled down a little. Old Richards was tanked up an' belligerent as hell, Slim says, an' looked around and says, 'Any of the rest of you sonsabitches want any of this?'

"Well, Slim an' Richards talked for a couple of minutes, then he went on down the street. After he'd left an' Slim an' his buddy walked on, too, his buddy said, 'If you see any more of them sonsabitches you know from back home, let's keep on awalkin'.'

"Old Richards' a fightin' sonuvabitch," Wes said, laughed and slapped his leg. "He'll fight at the drop of a hat. He'll hurt a feller, too, if that's what it comes to. He can be meaner 'n hell when he's tanked up. An' that's ever so often. But let's get these goddamn hogs loaded an' get 'em to Indianapolis before dark."

Both Big and Sam grinned and walked in the barn. Hogs started running up the chute with one or the other of them coming along behind with the hotshot and hollering, "Suuueeey, suuueeey up there, you sonsabitches. Get on up there." When they got the upper deck full, they stopped and wired the walk-up board to the stock rack to keep the hogs in place. Then they ran the rest of the load in on the lower deck, pulled the pin for the end gate to slam down and pulled the truck out in the barnyard, and Big backed his truck to the barn door. They had the hogs loaded in no time. Big sat in the truck and wrote out what he'd told me earlier was a "bill of lading" and gave it to Wes. "Don't take long when you got things fixed like you got 'em here, Wes," Big said, sweat dripping off of him even though I thought it was kind of chilly. "Wish everybody had a place like this."

Wes smiled and nodded, then went over to get the bill for Sam's load. I went over to get in Sam's truck. Wes was riding with Big on the way over, so I got to ride with Sam. When he pulled out of the barnyard and turned away from the afternoon sun, it was still high over the treetops.

He stopped and went back to close the gate. Big crawled around us with just an inch or two between mirrors. I was looking out the driver's window and thought for sure he was going to knock our mirror off. Wes had his window down and winked at me as they passed. I tried to wink back but closed both eyes instead.

I kept them wide open from then on and sat on the edge of the seat watching the country I was beginning to know like the back of my hand. Joe Randle's place where we used to live was coming up on Sam's side. I saw the gate I'd almost driven a truck through when I was three years old and stepped down on the starter like I'd seen Big do. And I remembered everybody standing on the porch while Jake Wilson roared off down the road on his big old motorsickle, the one that had an Indian mounted on the front end looking out at everything in front of him there like he was getting ready to lead a charge. That was the kind of motorsickle I wanted when I got big, I knew. And I remembered the huckster's truck that used to stop on the road out in front of the house ever so often. Mother and Aunt Helen would hurry out with their eggs or whatever they had to trade and get in the back of the truck and walk down the aisle to see what they wanted. I got in once and followed them along. Things was hanging or stuffed everywhere.

Just over the next rise we started down the hill and over the little bridge across the crick. I was always scared that the bridge would fall in when I crossed it. The truck looked like it was too big to fit through. And when it did, you could hear the bridge planks creak and groan. Sam had geared down and crossed the bridge pretty slow, then began picking up speed to get a run at the long hill that led to the tree-lined road into The Corners.

Sam pulled in behind Big and Wes at Charlie Franklin's garage just past the stop at the four corners of the roads. Wes had climbed up the stock rack and was punching at some hogs on the top deck so they wouldn't be smothered. Big had his foot back under the truck, kicking the front of the tires. Sam checked his truck the same way. I walked to the back of the truck and reached in and kicked the back tires on one side. Pain shot through my foot after the second kick. My heel had bounced off the big tires like a little rubber ball. I must have hollered out because Wes laughed and said, "Them tires got plenty of air in 'em, Sedwick?"

"Think they do," I said, pleased that he asked me.

By the time we got headed out of The Corners, I had pretty well decided that I would be a truck driver when I grew up. At one time, I had wanted to be a Marine like my daddy, but then the war got over and being a Marine wasn't as important to me without a war to fight. I liked going to Indianapolis. I'd only been there a few times, once when Aunt Helen went along. She was supposed to help keep Big awake and then drive when he slept a little. I told them I could help. Big'd smiled and said, "Let him go." I woke up when Aunt Helen turned off at the Busy Bee Farm and headed toward The Corners. It was real dark out. Big was leaning on a folded-up coat up against the window. I put my head over on his lap and went back to sleep. I barely got to sleep when I felt the truck veering off to the side of the road, dip down and stop with a loud snap and pop, rolling me off on the floor.

"There's where Aunt Helen went to sleep and ran off the road, Sam," I said, pointing to the tree in the hedge row where she hit. The truck had the front end knocked back under it a little and had to be hauled in the next morning. Aunt Helen had hit the bottom of the dash with her knees and had big welts across both of them. She cried out when we first hit, then cried a little later. Big and me was okay. We'd waited until first light before he went to the house down the road to call Gene to come and get us.

"What'd Big say?" Sam asked, grinning over at me.

"'Sonuvabitch, Helen. Why in the devil didn't you wake me up, if you couldn't stay awake?'"

Sam nodded and said, "Sounds like what he'd say."

The tree still had a big skinned place where the truck had banged into it. I wondered if the bark would grow back like the skin on my knee did when I fell down running on the gravel road out in front of the store. If it did grow back, I wondered how I'd ever be able to tell where Aunt Helen hit the tree. The trees that lined the wide gravel road looked pretty much the same to me on both sides of the road from almost back to The Corners all the way out to the Busy Bee Farm. I'd always wondered why it was called the Busy Bee Farm. Only bees I ever saw there was the two giant ones painted on the barn with the letters telling the name.

"Why'd they call that the Busy Bee Farm?" I'd asked Big on the way over to Indianapolis before Aunt Helen had plowed into the tree. "They've got cows and hogs and chickens just like other fellers. I don't see no bees."

"'Cause they think they work like bees, I reckon," Big had said, turning the truck out onto the slab and picking up speed. The long ribbon-looking highway unfurled through the trees and hills as far as I could see. I got over on Aunt Helen's lap that day so I could set up higher and see everything.

I was bigger but still scooted up on the edge of the seat or sat on a rolled-up coat to see better. Sam shifted down and slowed as we passed the barn with the bees standing on their hind legs and sort of facing each other at an angle. They looked kind of happy, like they was playing and having fun the way I felt when I was playing with Jimmy and Albert and Ronal or Richard and Jerry. The bees didn't look any busier than the cows that was milling around in the barnyard or the hogs rooting and walking around in the pen on the other side of the barn.

Sam edged out to the slab and leaned out to look down the road past me. After two cars passed, he pulled out on the road and headed up that stretch of road leading to wherever I imagined you could want to go. I'd barely been able to see Big and Wes right behind us through the side mirror for the sun shining on the mirror as long as we was headed east. But after we got out on the slab the sun wasn't at our back any longer, and I could see them clear. Wes was talking and waving his hands. I couldn't see Big's face, but I knew that he'd be smiling now and then and grinning or laughing a little at Wes' stories.

Sam and me didn't say much while the truck headed up the road, slowing only to go through West Union and past The Silver Moon Tavern where Big'd stopped one time for some catfish and beer. Fellers said it was the best catfish in the country. And I reckon it was good, although I didn't think they was as good as what Mother and Aunt Helen cooked up for breakfast one morning. Big had brought a big mess from the river when he was hauling gravel and asked Uncle Billy and Aunt Annie to come up for breakfast. I'd never had fish for breakfast and asked Mother to wake me up so I could eat fish, too.

"That's too early for you to get up," she'd said. "I don't know why anybody'd want to eat fish for breakfast, anyway."

Aunt Helen had agreed, but Big told me if I was awake I could eat. Nobody woke me up that morning. I'd been dreaming that I was falling from a tree and woke up with a jerk just before I hit the ground. I could see the light shining faintly out through the kitchen door and smell the catfish frying and coffee cooking. Quick as I could I put on my shirt and overalls and went to the kitchen. Sam was sitting at the table, too. He grinned at me when I came through the door rubbing my eyes and grinning back at him.

Them old fish that we had that morning had been the best I'd ever tasted. They was crispy on the outside and dry white flakes of river catfish on the inside. With bread and butter and hot black coffee, Big said there wasn't "any better eatin' anywhere." I reckon he was right. Aunt Helen wanted to give me something else to go with the fish, but I wouldn't have it.

"Don't want nothin' besides bread an' butter an' coffee an' fish," I'd said, echoing what I'd heard Big say a lot of times when we had fish.

Thinking about that breakfast made me wonder what we'd have for supper at the truck stop in Brazil. Big always got a plate, but I just wanted a sandwich. Maybe a cheeseburger like Mother and Aunt Helen liked so much, I thought. By the time we'd passed through Marshall and Terre Haute and turned towards Brazil at the old minor league ball park where people were headed to a night baseball game, I was so hungry I didn't know whether I could last any longer. I'd started to ask Sam again about fighting in the Army, but the people going to the baseball game got my attention. I'd never been inside or seen anything like that ball park. It wasn't anything like the old baseball fields over at The Corners or at Yale. You couldn't see the field for the big building and fences all around. Even Sam hadn't been to a baseball game there.

"It's one of the Phillies' minor league farm clubs," he said, turning off the truck route and going alongside of the whole stadium as he headed out east of Terre Haute. "That's where the good players start as kids an' learn the game an' grow up a little. Gets 'em ready for the big leagues."

That sounded a bit like what Miz Finley, the new teacher, said about school, that it was to help get you ready for life as a big person. And it sounded a little like what Sam had told me about what he did in the Army before he went overseas. "The Army was getting you ready for the war, I reckon," I said, "when you trained down South."

Sam jerked his head around, a funny look on his face, and looked at me a minute. "I reckon they tried," he said and looked back down the road. "I reckon they tried. But a feller can't get enough trainin' to get him ready. Nothing can do that."

When we got back out on the open road, Sam looked over at me and grinned. He didn't say nothing, just grinned. I grinned back. "Did old Jim Richards do any fighting in the Army 'sides what Wes told about this morning?"

"I 'magine. He was with a glider outfit, crash landed in a field behind German lines early in the mornin' on D-Day. I 'magine he did a little fightin' 'fore he got to Paris. Probably done a little afterwards, too."

"Was you ever in any fightin' when you was in the Army?" I asked, still thinking of the fight in the tavern the night before.

"Oh, I reckon," Sam said, grinning a bit more. "I already told you that."

"I know, but you never told me anything about it."

He turned and looked back down the road again.

"Nothin' much I'd want to tell you 'bout that, Sedwick. But the kind of fightin' you're talking' about, I was just in one fight of that kind. There was an old boy from New York named Franklin Elliott, Elit. He pestered everybody a little like Fred Campbell was doin' to Jim last night. Only Elit was big an' mean. An' he was a bully. He wore glasses thick as bottle caps. But he'd pick on somebody 'til they couldn't take it no more an' start after him. He'd grab his glasses with his left hand an' take a big old haymaker swing with his right. Broke three men's jaws that way. One punch an' the fight was over. If it hadn't been over, he couldn't see to go on. He was purt near blind without his glasses.

"I told him when we got into it, I said, 'Now you big four-eyed sonuvabitch, it ain't goin' to be like it was with them other fellers. You ain't goin' to hit me with one punch an' break my goddamn jaw. I'm goin' to get in a lick or two.' He just laughed and pulled his glasses and swung. I knew where the punch was coming from, ducked under it an' hit him with my shoulder an' drove him back into the tank tread. We wrassled around a minute, then got back up. I hit him with a couple of good left jabs an' had his nose an' mouth bleedin'. He couldn't see a thing, so I finally said, 'Now Elit, if you'll quit messin' with me, you can get your glasses an' go on about your business.'

"He said okay an' that was it. He left me alone after that. Only feller I ever saw him leave alone all together or back down from was old Merv Gallagher from down there west of Oblong. Elit wouldn't mess with Merv after he'd cleaned three old boys' plows all together after they kept mockin' his way of talkin' at the slop chute where they was drinkin' one night. But at the chow hall one morning, Elit kept teasin' Wes who was sittin' across from him, then would take the pepper shaker an' shake a little pepper on the feller's bread. Wes asked him not to, but Elit didn't pay no attention to him. Old Wes only weighed about a hundred and twenty pounds soaking wet back then. About the third time he started to pepper the bread, Merv reached over an' took ahold of Elit's wrist an' brought his arm down on the table. 'I wouldn't do that no more, Elit,' Merv said. Big Frank Elit never said a word, just let go of the pepper shaker. Just like a bully. He got killed before we got off the beach on the first day."

"Who killed him?" I asked. "A German?"

"I don't know. I wasn't with him. Didn't even know he'd got hit until later on. Could've been anybody."

I wanted to hear more and ask some questions, but Sam pulled in the truck stop. I'd have to wait until we got back in the truck after we ate supper. By the time we'd eaten and Big and Sam had filled out the papers they had to have at the stockyards and we got back in the truck, it was totally dark and I was tired. On the other side of Brazil, I lay down on the coat in the seat and went to sleep. I woke up when Sam backed up to unload and I heard squealing hogs. After we got unloaded, we went over to the commission houses to turn in the tickets for the hogs. Wes sold his through Producers, but I told him I figured Sedwick's, which was just down the hall, was the best place to sell anything and when I had hogs and cattle, that's where I was goin' to sell mine. Big liked Sedwick's, too.

"Is that right, Sedwick?" Wes said and grinned as we got back into the trucks to head home.

"It sure is," I said and nodded.

Everybody grinned and Big said, "You better find some other way to make a livin' than raising' stock, Sedwick. Now you hop up in the truck with Sam. We'll stop over at Derby Hill so you can ride with us, an' Sam won't have to come over to Bellair until in the mornin' when we go rabbit huntin'."

Sam was in a quiet mood as we pulled out of the stockyards and didn't seem like he wanted to talk, so I went back to sleep. Everybody but me was wide awake when we stopped at Derby Hill. Sam carried me over to Big's truck, and we headed on home. I never really woke up completely, but I could hear Big and Wes talking whenever I was more awake than asleep.

"Poor little feller," Big said. "He's had it pretty rough with Bill gettin' killed over yonder."

I didn't like to think of myself as a "poor little feller," but I didn't let on that I heard and just kept my head on Wes' leg for a pillow. He patted my shoulder and kept his arm laying right along my back. That felt good, and I started to go off to sleep again. But he started talking and I listened.

"Lots of 'em had it pretty bad, Big," Wes said quietly. "Lorene had a pretty rough way to go with Bill gettin' killed an' leavin' this boy for her to raise by herself. She's pretty lucky to have you an' Helen to help her out. I 'xpect there's a good many women an' little kids out there that don't have that."

Big didn't answer, but I heard him take a deep breath and then light a cigarette. He did that sometimes when he didn't know what else to do. One time when he caught me smoking, he told me he'd started smoking to keep awake when all his drivers was going off to the Army and he needed something to keep him awake with all the trips to Indianapolis he had to make. And then he said he smoked when he didn't know what else to do. I figured if that's how Big got along, it was good enough for me. I wished I had one myself, thinking about my daddy and mother and smelling Big's cigarette. Instead of having one, I just lay still and felt tears well up in my eyes and roll down my nose onto Wes' overalls.

"An' I 'xpect old Sam is havin' a pretty rough time, Big," Wes said. "He don't talk about it none, but he's got a helluva temper an' he's as nervous as an old whore in church. Always was. He lost his goddamn tank right after we got on the beach an' had to go along with the fuckin' infantry until he got another one. That hatch'd slammed down on his head an' liked to broke his fuckin' neck. He took it for quite a while, but then along in the summer just before we hit Paris, that smack on his head an' his nerves got to him. Got hit, too — a little shrapnel wound that didn't amount to much. But he was back in a field hospital for about ten days with what they called battle fatigue. Lot of 'em in our outfit was like that. They sent a bunch of green-ass troops in there on D-Day because they knowed anybody who'd been there before would have better fuckin' sense than to think they could get through the landin' an' up that fuckin' hill in one piece an' would have been scared shitless. More 'n we was, anyway. An' we was scared shitless, I can tell you for shore. Lot of 'em that got their tanks knocked out like Sam's crew got 'em arunnin' again or got new ones by the time we got to St. Lô, but some of 'em stayed on the ground 'til they got stuffed in a body bag or dozed into a fuckin' hole."

I lay real still, afraid Wes wouldn't keep talking if he knew I was awake. While he talked, I listened real careful, going back and forth in my mind trying to see Sam and him like he was talking about them being and then trying to see Daddy in the war.

"You seem to get along okay, Wes," Big said. "How do you do it? You was there, too."

Wes chuckled a little before he said anything.

"Well, seemin' to get along an' gettin' along is two different things, Big. I reckon I get along as well as any of 'em. But a lot of 'em went to the rubber room after the war, an' I probably ought to have been in one my damn self. After movin' around like we did for four years, not knowin' whether you was goin' to live or die an' drinkin' like a fuckin' fish, none of us is goin' to get along very good for a long time. A real long time, I 'xpect. I decided I was goin' to quit drinkin' for one thing, though. That helped a lot because that drinkin' makes you crazy, anyways. I just quit it. An' then being with the wife helps a lot. She lets me be when she sees I need to be left alone. An' her folks let us move into the old place, an' them an' my folks helped us get started farmin'. Lot of 'em didn't have that kind of help. They took us in the fuckin' Army an' trained us to be soldiers an' how to kill, stuck us in the middle of the worst goddamn war in the history of this sorry fuckin' world an' then them that made it through got throwed back out where they came from to flop around like a goddamn fish out of water. We didn't count for nothin' then, an' we don't count for nothin' now. We was always what they call 'expendable.' Sometimes I think the ones that didn't come back like Bill is the lucky ones."

I couldn't believe what he was saying. It didn't make any sense to me that Daddy was lucky for not coming back and getting to live and be my daddy and Mother's husband. I thought about sitting up and telling Wes he was full of shit and crazier than a goddamn loon. My whole body was as stiff as a board, and I had to fight as hard as I'd ever fought anything to keep laying there on his lap.

"Been better off if I'd have lost that coin toss," Big said real quiet. "Bill'd have been here to take care of this boy."

"Aw, hell, Big," Wes said and tossed his chaw of tobacco out the window before going on, "it's all just one big fuckin' coin toss. Don't go blamin' yourself for nothin'. Luck's about all they is to it. You do the best you can an' the cards fall where they do. You don't have much to do with what happens. Look at old Wick Hardway. He went in the Marine Corps with Bill back in '38. Wick made it back, but he's a mess. Don't know whether he'll ever come out of it. He's meaner 'n hell, if you cross him, an' is havin' a helluva time settlin' down an' tryin' to be a civilian.

"Him an' Bill both went overseas before the war ever started, an' they was back in Hawaii headin' fer the States when them fuckin' Japs pulled that sneaky-ass attack on Pearl Harbor to start the war. Old Wick said he was Sergeant of the Guard out there on Ford Island that mornin', right there in the middle of Pearl Harbor, just gettin' ready to get off duty at eight o'clock an' was out relievin' the old guard an' puttin' the new one on when he looked back an' seen these planes acomin' around the big island an' right in around this mountain range an' right over Barber's Point where he was stationed an' another bunch of 'em come down through a place he called Iao, down the middle depression right onto Pearl Harbor. He was right in the middle of it an' said he stood right there an' watched it.

"He said he thought it was the fuckin' Army on manuevers," Wes said and laughed quietly, but I could feel his stomach shaking.

"He said he stood there an' watched them for a bit an' finally thought they didn't look like any Army planes he'd ever seen. 'Bout that time he said they was close enough that he could see them red meatballs on the wings. He says he was so goddamn dumb that he even wondered why they painted over the stars on the wings. He seen the rounds hit the runway before he realized what was agoin' on. An' then he heard the rounds start hittin' closer an' one ricocheted an' hit him in the shoulder an' knocked him end over end. They patched him up, an' he went right back to duty that mornin'. Him an' a whole bunch of the others that got hit.

"Instead of comin' home an' lettin' somebody else do the fightin', they was sent right back out into the thick of things. That was the kind of luck them fellers had. Wasn't nothin' they could do about it. Wick an' Bill was both there on Guadalcanal. Bill didn't make it back. An' Wick didn't for a long time. He damn near got killed on Saipan, I think it was, an' a couple of other places an' was in the hospital a long time before they ever sent him back to the States. Then they kept him for more 'n a goddamn year before they let him out."

"Guess old Ott called the sheriff out on him the other day," Big said, lighting another cigarette. "I was picking up a couple of veal calves up there the other day when he come out."

"Oh, yeah," Wes said. "That crazy fuckin' Ott Kincaid rented Wick that place when the Marine Corps finally let him go last year, then comes out there all the time an' tells him what to do an' how he wants things done. That don't go over with old Wick Hardway. It wouldn't have before the war. He had a temper back then. Now he's got a helluva temper an' ain't nobody to fuck with, I can tell you. He's big an' he's hard. Like old Richards over there the other night. It's a goddamn wonder he didn't kill that fuckin' Fred Campbell."

"That's what Wick told Ott he was goin' to do if he ever set foot on that place again while he was arentin' it," Big said. "Old Dutch Leonard stopped out at the road an' walked back to the barn where we was loadin' the calves like he didn't want to be there an' asked Wick about whether he'd threatened to kill Ott or not. Wick said, 'Well, I reckon I might have said that, but I didn't exactly mean that I'd kill the sonuvabitch. He rented me this place, then come back here all the time, tellin' me how he wanted this or that done. I told him as long as I was arentin' the goddamn place for him to keep his fuckin' ass away 'cause the next time he stepped foot on the place I'd kill him. Now I really didn't mean I'd kill him, I don't suppose, but I meant for him to stay away from the goddamn place.'"

Wes laughed kind of quiet again I reckon so's not to wake me up. "What'd old Dutch say?" he asked. "I'll bet he didn't know whether to shit or go blind."

"Well, he hemmed an' hawed around for a little bit," Big said, laughing a little himself. "Then he finally said, 'Now, Wick, I know you didn't mean to kill Ott, but you just can't go around sayin' things like that to fellers out here. I ain't goin' to take you in, but I'll have to, if you say anything like that again.' Old Wick looked at him for a minute and said, 'I reckon you'll have to try. But I want to tell you one goddamn thing, as long as I'm arentin' this fuckin' old place, I don't want Ott Kincaid steppin' a goddamn foot on it. That's what I was atryin' to tell him so he could understand it.' Dutch kinda grinned and said, 'I'll tell him, Wick. But you don't go tellin' him you'll kill him, either.'"

"What a lot of fellers out here don't realize," Wes said, "is that we was in that fuckin' Army or Marines or whatever for a long time where things was a helluva lot different than they are out here. Oh, there was that usual chickenshit stateside stuff. But it was different overseas where we was. You just didn't fuck around with anybody like Kincaid was adoin' with Wick an' not get your plow cleaned real good one way or the other. Old boy named Franklin Elit never got off the beach on D-Day. He was a big old bully who was always pickin' on everybody. I don't know for sure, but I've always thought that somebody put a round in his sorry ass when they had the chance. If they did, nobody said a word about it. That's just the way it was. That's what happened to fellers like Ott Kincaid an' that fuckin' Elit back then."

I'd heard Sam talk about that feller earlier and didn't like him, but a little chill went down my back while Wes was talking. After that I drifted off to sleep and never woke up until Big was carrying me back in the house sometime later. I didn't even know when Big stopped at Wes' place to let him out.

"Was you ever in any fights, Big?" I asked sleepily.

"You go back to sleep," he said, "or I'm goin' to have to fight your mother an' Helen for keepin' you out all night. An' then I wouldn't get to go rabbit huntin'."

4

Big and Sam was out hunting rabbits the next morning before I got up. By noon, they was back with a gunny sack full of rabbits to clean. Cleaning rabbits wasn't something I really liked to do, but I helped by keeping the guts and skins cleaned up. They sold some of the rabbits for fifty cents a piece and then had Mother and Aunt Helen fry up the rest of them for supper that evening. Big said fried rabbit and gravy and bread was about as good a meal as a feller could find. Sam agreed. The rest of us didn't say much, but I knew Mother and Aunt Helen didn't like any kind of game. I got a couple of pieces of shot in a bite of my rabbit and like to broke a tooth.

"Be careful, there, Sedwick," Big said. "I told you fellers you'd find some shot in these rabbits, the way we was shootin'. Old Sam an' me got into some rabbit thickets today. They was jumpin' everywhere, an' we was shootin' first left, then right."

"More rabbits than I ever seen in a month of huntin'," Sam said, his eyes laughing. "Makes some good eatin', too."

Big and Sam both sounded real happy about the rabbit hunting. Just being with them made me real happy. I was in either Big or Sam's truck so much in the next few years that I felt pretty much like a trucker. Sometimes I thought the other fellers thought I was, too. I couldn't drive yet, but when we hauled lime, I could scoop a little back into the spreader. Each truck had to have a driver and a scooper, so I got to help with the scooping. The lime quarry broke down late one evening when we'd all been waiting for the last load of the day. It'd already been the hardest day I'd ever had. Everybody was covered with lime dust, was hot and thirsty and short-tempered.

Sam stepped off the back of the spreader when he was setting things up to spread a load early in the afternoon, hit his head and arm on the back of the truck as he fell and came up cussing and hitting the truck with the scoop until it broke.

"Goddamnsonuvabitchincocksuckinbastard," he said and threw the broken handle of the scoop down at the truck. "I'll break your fuckin' ass an' leave your sorry ass in this fuckin' field."

I didn't know what he was going to break besides the scoop and didn't know what it had to do with him falling off the truck. But I'd never seen anything like the way he was doing and was scared to death. Everybody just stood back and never said a word. Big came over from his truck and got Sam settled down.

"Here, now, Sam," he said, much calmer than I expected him to be when I saw him hurrying over to where we all stood. "Take it easy, take it easy. No use to get all riled up. You all right?"

"Yes, goddamnit, I'm all right," he said, tears rolling down his cheek. "I don't know what the hell happened to me."

He walked off to the edge of the field, wiped his eyes with a big red handkerchief and smoked a cigarette before he came back to spread the load. Nobody said anything, and we went back to work. I started to say something to Bernie Bartlow, a cousin about sixteen who was helping us, but he shook his head and held his finger up to his mouth and said, "Sh-hh." So I didn't say anything and went back to work. Even Barney Ford was quiet. But he'd been quiet for the last few weeks since he was on the way to Indianapolis one night and he hit a hitchhiker walking along the road in the dark somehow and killed him. Barney said he hadn't seen him but heard something hit the truck. He pulled off the road to see what had happened. When he didn't see any damage to the truck except that the side mirror had been pushed in, he went on down the road. At the next town, he stopped and told the police what had happened and then went on to the stockyards.

On the way back home, the police flagged him down in Putnamville and told him what he'd hit. By the time he pulled into Bellair the next morning, his face was drawn and haggard, and Mother said he looked much older than he did when he came back from the service, much older than his twenty-two or twenty-three years. He sat at the kitchen table with Big who was eating breakfast when he got there and talked to him. I was eating breakfast, too, and Mother and Aunt Helen was still sitting at the table. But it was almost like we wasn't there. Barney wouldn't eat but drank coffee and smoked cigarette after cigarette and went over and over what had happened like that would make it go away.

"Goddamnit, I just didn't see him, Big," Barney said, his hands trembling as he talked and raised the coffee cup or a cigarette to his mouth. "He must've been walkin' just off the slab when the mirror hit him an' knocked him back into the bed, spun him around an' rolled him off in the ditch. I didn't see anything when I went back an' went on. Goddamn, I didn't never want to kill nobody else again as long as I live. You don't know what it's like."

"It wasn't your fault, Barney," Big said, lighting a Lucky and blowing smoke out across the table where I was sitting. "I almost hit a hitchhiker right there this side of Putnamville awhile back, too. They walk along the dang slab at night, an' you can't see 'em. I don't know what they mean, walkin' along the slab like that, but you can't blame yourself."

"Maybe not, but I can't help feelin' like hell. I didn't just about hit him. I killed the poor sonuvabitch sure's I would've if I'd lined him up in my sights an' blowed his ass away. I need a drink, bad."

"That won't help a thing, Barney. Just make things worse. Ain't helped nothing before, has it?"

"Nope, but it sure's hell helps you forget."

Mother pulled me away from the table, leaving Barney, Big and Aunt Helen still sitting there. She had to go to work and asked me to walk to the store with her. I guess she didn't want me hearing any more about what had happened. I couldn't help but remember that when we all went to the tavern in Casey another day after the lime quarry was closed while they fixed the loader. Jim Richards was ahead of Big's three trucks in line and came walking back to us when we found out that we wouldn't get loaded that evening.

"I've got a pint, boys," he said, holding up a brown bottle of Seagram's whiskey. "Might as well take a drink an' forget about haulin' this fuckin' lime 'til tomorrow."

He unscrewed the cap and took a big drink, then held it out, still holding the cap in his big hand. Barney grabbed the bottle first and tilted it up, his pointy Adam's apple bobbing up and down like a bobber with a big catfish on the line. Sam and everybody but Bernie and me took a drink. Even Big drank right from the bottle. By the time it got back to Jim Richards, there wasn't much left. He finished it off, tossed the bottle over in the weeds and wiped his mouth with the back of his hand.

"Let's go to Casey an' have another drink, boys," he said.

Big looked like he had started to say something, but everybody had wheeled and headed for their trucks before he had much of a chance to open his mouth. Bernie crawled in the truck with us, and we followed everybody to Casey. By the time Big had parked his truck and we all walked in the back door of the tavern, the rest of them was bellied up to the bar and had ordered drinks. They was hooting and hollering like a bunch of kids when school let out at the end of the year. Barney was laughing and grinning like I hadn't seen him in a long time.

Jim Richards stuck a bottle of beer in Big's hand and said, "Give us another round here, bartender. An' give these boys here a Pepsi Cola an' whatever else they want. How about some peanuts, boys? You fellers hungry?"

Bernie nodded and edged his way toward a table at the end of the bar. He grabbed my hand and pulled me along with him. His mother was one of Daddy and Big's older sisters. Big had told me Bernie's daddy was in the First War, and he was an oil field driller. Bernie worked with him sometimes and told me about going to the taverns with him when they was working.

"Them boys ain't supposed to be in here," the bartender said. He was a heavy-set feller with a puffy face and beady eyes and a cigar clenched between his teeth, standing behind the bar and leaning forward with both hands on the bar. "I can't serve you with them in here. They've got to go."

"Them boys are with us, mister," Jim Richards said. "They ain't goin' no place 'til we do."

"Just give the boys a Pepsi," Sam said, "an' us a drink."

"There's a city ord —"

"You heard what the man said," Barney said. "Give us a drink, an' give them boys a Pepsi."

I couldn't see Barney's face then, but his voice sounded cold and hard, much different that it had a few minutes ago when he was laughing and hollering with everybody else. Gene and his brother Pete, who hadn't been out of the Army too long and who was helping haul lime, stood at the bar with Sam, Barney and Jim. A couple of other fellers picked up their drinks and moved down the bar.

"Here, I'll get this round, boys," Big said, elbowing in to the bar. "We ain't goin' to be here long, Garland."

"It's against the law, Big," he said, taking the cigar out of his mouth. "It'll cause me trouble."

"Looks to me like you've got trouble," Pete said, cackling like he did when something was funny to him. "Ain't no law here now. It's just us chickens."

Everybody had crowded in around Big, waiting to see what was going to happen. The noise in the bar that had been real loud when we walked in had fallen away to near complete silence. Nobody moved until Garland opened the cooler in front of him and reached in and started pulling out bottles of beer.

"Better give us a shot of Seagram's to go with them beers," Jim Richards said. "If we ain't goin' to be here long."

"Nah, we don't need no whiskey," Big said.

"Loosen up, Big," Barney said. "We're just havin' a little fun. You've worked us to death these last few days. An' you'll be doin' it again tomorrow when they get things goin' down at the quarry. Drink an' be merry for tomorrow you may be dead."

I could see that Big was getting madder by the minute. But he didn't say anything else. He just tilted back his head and drank his beer down like the rest of the boys and tossed the shot of whiskey down like it was water. Sam was grinning and laughing like I hadn't seen him do before. Everybody but Big looked liked they was having the time of their lives. Bernie shook his head and laughed right along with them.

"I ain't never seen anything like this, Uncle Robert," he said to Big when he sat down with us for a minute. "They're worse than a bunch of oil johnnies. Them boys are sure puttin' the booze away, ain't they?"

"Why, it's like sloppin' a bunch of hogs," Big said. "I ain't never seen anything like it, either. We're goin' to get out of here pretty quick. I ain't goin' to have a bunch of dang drunks drivin' my trucks home."

And we did leave pretty quick, but not as quick as Big wanted to leave. Sam bought another round of drinks for everybody, including another Pepsi Cola for Bernie and me.

"Now that's it, boys," Big said when Garland set the drinks in front of us. "We're gettin' out of here or you can give me the keys to them trucks an' get home the best way you can."

Garland poured another shot of whiskey that somebody had ordered. I didn't see who it was, but there was more hooting and hollering and kidding Big when he started railing at them.

"Now dang it, boys," Big said, stopping to toss down the shot of whiskey, "this is it. I'm taking these boys and gettin' out of here, an' you'd better come along. Garland don't need no trouble here, an' you've had enough."

He stood up, picked up his bottle of beer and drained it off faster than Bernie and me could drink our Pepsi Cola. Jim Richards stood with his elbow on the bar with a crooked grin on his face while the rest of the boys was finishing their drinks and ordering beer and whiskey to take with them.

"Let's go," Big said to no one in particular and started walking towards the back door. "Time for us to get out of here."

"That's right, Big," Garland said, the cigar clenched tightly between his teeth. "I know you follow the law."

Big never said another word. I hurried behind him, running to keep up with him with Bernie right behind me. At his truck, Big told us to get in and stood waiting for the rest of the boys. When they came out ten minutes or so later, Big was pacing back and forth and was about as mad as I'd ever seen him. Barney was stumbling along with a sack under his arm, a silly grin on his face and his cap pushed back on his head.

"You can ride with me, Barney," Big said. "Can you drive his truck, Pete?"

"I can drive that sonuvabitch anywhere you want me to, Big Mac," Pete said. "You just tell me where you want me to drive her, an' that's where she'll go."

"I want you to take it to Bellair an' park it."

"Gotcha."

Sam and Gene was quieter than the others, but they had sacks of beer under their arms, too. Jim Richards had two sacks, one smaller that I figured was more whiskey.

"I'll meet you fellers down there at Joe's old schoolhouse," he said, "an' we can have another drink."

"Now we've got to haul lime tomorrow, Jim," Big said. "They don't need no more dang booze."

"Come on, boys," Jim said and laughed. "Let's get these trucks out of town 'fore the law gets us. Big don't want us to get in no trouble."

Bernie rode with Sam, and I sat between Big and Barney. We hadn't anymore than got on the road heading south out of town before I heard Barney open a beer, spraying it all over me and the windshield.

"Now shit, Barney, you don't need any more," Big said. "You've had enough. An' you're goin' to have this boy smellin' like a brewery."

"This is for you, Big Mac," Barney said, handing the beer across my head and spilling it on my leg. "Sorry about that, Sedwick."

Big took the beer and said, "Now you leave the rest of them in the sack. The way you fellers drink this stuff is like sloppin' a bunch o' dang hogs."

"We are hogs, Big," Barney said softly. "We're just big old fuckin' hogs, wallowin' around in our own shit. The world's shit. Everybody's shit. That's all there is to it. Shit. And more shit."

Big didn't say anything. He just turned the beer can up to his mouth and drank it all before throwing the can out the window. For a while, all I heard was the sound of the truck engine as we drove down the slab. At the six-mile curve south of Casey, Big drove off into the grass and stopped the truck real quick. He opened the door and jumped out. I heard him puking in the grass and saw the other trucks pull in behind us.

By the time Big was done puking, the whole bunch was gathered in front of his truck. They was still laughing and carrying on, now about "old Big gettin' drunk an' pukin' over in the grass." Pete was cackling in his high-pitched voice while the rest was just laughing and shaking their heads.

"We probably ought to get out of here before he gets back," Sam said. "He's goin' to be madder 'n anything, if we're standin' here laughin' at him."

"That's right, boys," Jim Richards said. "I don't know about the rest of you, but I've seen Big Mac mad a time or two. He's like a ragin' bull. I don't feel like gettin' into that tonight."

"Sounds like he's got the dry heaves," Barney said. "He'll be over there awhile. Let's go on down to the old schoolhouse, like Jim said, an' drink some beer."

Bernie looked at Sam. He shrugged and jerked his head toward the truck. Everybody disappeared just as quick as they'd showed up. The trucks motors roared, the lights came on and I was left alone in Big's truck with him still out in the grass a ways off. I looked out through the darkness until I finally saw him walking towards the truck.

"Where'd them fellers go?" he asked as he crawled in the truck.

"I reckon they went to Joe's old schoolhouse."

"Sonuvabitch," he said, shifted into gear and pushed the foot feed to the floor. "They've had all of that stuff they need. We got lime to haul. They won't be worth a dang."

I started to ask him how he felt but decided that wouldn't be a good idea. Neither of us said another word as we drove to Bellair. Then Big drove to the schoolhouse and saw the little fire out in the barn lot between the old school and the church.

"Sonuvabitch," Big said and got out of the truck.

I jumped out and ran to his side to go with him.

"Feel better, Big?" Barney asked before we got to the fire. "You sounded like you might up an' die out there in the grass 'while ago. I thought you'd given up the ship."

Snickers filled the night air. Even I had to laugh. I just hoped Big didn't hear me. Nobody else seemed to care now. I saw Bernie put his head down to hide his face.

"I'll live," Big said, ignoring the snickering. "I'm not so sure about you fellers. Leave these trucks where they are tonight an' be ready to leave here at six in the mornin'. I want to be there when the quarry opens. You come on with me, Bernie."

Big turned and walked back to the truck. I waited for Bernie and walked along with him, glad to have some company. The door was already opened, and we hopped up in the truck as it rolled along. I leaned up and looked out at the fire and the fellers just as they went out of sight.

Mother and Aunt Helen met us at the door when we got on up to the house. They'd seen us drive by on the way to the quarry for the last load and figured we'd be there for supper much earlier. Supper was cold and waiting for us. I was starved and couldn't wait to start digging in.

"Where in the world have you been, Robert?" Aunt Helen said before Big hardly had the door open. "You smell like a brewery."

"I 'xpect I do," he said and headed for the kitchen to wash up. "Get these boys fed an' off to bed. We lost a load today when the loader broke down, an' I want to be there when the quarry opens in the mornin'."

"You ought to stay out of the taverns then."

Big acted like he didn't hear and began washing up to eat. Mother shook her head at Aunt Helen and pulled me close and hugged me. Bernie just stood in the door of the kitchen and waited. I knew Big well enough that there wouldn't be any talk about where we'd been or what we'd been doing. Maybe him and Aunt Helen would talk about it later, but not now.

After we'd washed up, the five of us sat down at the table. Nancy and Mary Beth was already in bed, but they came out in their pajamas and went over to give Big a goodnight hug and kiss. His eyes lit up when they came through the door. I figured the girls being there broke things up enough so we'd get off to bed without any more talk about where we'd been. Before they even got to say goodnight, though, Big shoved his plate back and tore out of the kitchen. I couldn't figure out what was going on.

Aunt Helen followed Big. We could hear them arguing in their bedroom. Then it sounded like he was puking again. I didn't feel like eating anymore and nudged my plate away. Bernie kept eating and scraped my plate off when he'd finished his. I reckoned he was hungry. He was a big old boy, taller than Big or Sam either one and quite a bit heavier. Everybody said he was going to be bigger than Granddad.

I couldn't believe Bernie could keep eating with the sounds coming from the bedroom. Big must have been real sick. Mother held her finger to her lips when I started to ask about that and told us all to go on to bed. When I walked by the bedroom door, Big was sitting on the pot on his side of the bed, and Aunt Helen was holding another one up in front of him. It was a funny-looking sight, but I kept real quiet and went on to bed.

The next morning I woke to the smell of frying bacon. Bernie had slept with me and was already up and dressed when he took ahold of my foot and gave it a shake.

"Better be rollin' out, if you plan to haul any lime today, mister," he said. "Uncle Robert is already eatin' breakfast."

I jumped out of bed and into the same dirty clothes I had on the day before. Bernie was just sitting down at the table when I ran through the door still wiping the sleepy dirt out of my eyes. Mother was holding a wash rag out for me to wash my face. Big looked a lot better and had a big grin on his face when he saw me.

"You're just like your daddy," he said. "Not goin' to miss a thing, if you can help it. But I figured you'd lay in bed an' sleep this mornin'."

"No way," I said, grinning back at him. It made me feel like a million dollars when he told me I did something like Daddy. Mother had a little smile on her face, but I knew she also got a little sad anytime somebody mentioned his name.

"Fix them fellers a bacon-and-egg sandwich while I go get them up," Big said as he pushed back from the table and started for the door. "Better get them a jug of coffee, too."

"We've already got the coffee," Aunt Helen said.

Big was backing the truck out into the road when me and Bernie got outside. He beat me to the truck and had the door open for me to jump in. The truck was moving down the road when he slammed the door behind him.

"Reckon them fellers'll be up?" I asked.

Big never answered me, and Bernie just smiled. It looked like a cyclone had come through the south side of the old schoolhouse when Big turned in the barn lot and nosed the truck up to where the fire had been. I could see Sam and Jim Richards laying on the ground when Big started blowing the horn. They both rolled over and looked up right away. Gene and Pete Shaw jumped out of the two trucks that was closest to the fire. And Barney rolled out from under one of them and was on his feet before Big stopped the truck. Beer cans, whiskey bottles and paper sacks was scattered wherever they had been tossed.

"You fellers are a sight," Big said. "Get this mess cleaned up an' get ready to get these trucks on the road. Helen an' Lorene have got some sandwiches an' coffee for you when you go by."

I was so surprised I didn't know what to think. I figured Big would be real mad at the fellers and raise the devil with them. But it was just like nothing had ever happened. Before I knew it, everything was cleaned up and we was ready to go. The cows was waiting at the gate when Joe Marshall came around from the back of the old schoolhouse ready to do the milking.

"There's a couple of beers there we missed last night looks like, Joe," Jim said. "We don't need them this mornin'."

Joe grinned and shook his head. The fellers looked pretty rough to me. They'd slept in their clothes, and their bloodshot eyes looked sunk back in their heads. Old Joe said they looked like "they was rode hard an' put away wet." I reckoned that was right. Big was backing the truck out, and I ran to it to ride with him. We hauled lime all day, just like we had the day before, only we got an extra load by being first in line and getting back for the last load right before the quarry shut down for the day. When I tried to talk to anybody, they'd just look at me and grin a little but not say much like they usually did. Barney did kid me a little about smoking, but I didn't understand the kidding.

"Your mouth tasted like mine does today," he said when he flipped a half-smoked cigarettes off in the weeds, "you'd never want another friggin' cigarette. Somethin' must've crawled up in there an' died."

A couple of weeks later, I was riding with Big again and him and Barney was hauling gravel for the township. Because there was a bridge out south of The Corners, we came around through Oblong to save time from making all the turns on little roads. Big and me was following Barney west of Robinson in the middle of the afternoon, headed up Firebaugh Hill on the way back to the gravel pit when a car started to pass a semi-truck coming down the hill. We was just crossing the bridge quite a ways back when I saw the car in our lane headed right for Barney's truck.

"Sonuvabitch," Big said and started braking and gearing down. "Get that fuckin' car back in there — look out, Barney. Look out!"

But the car kept coming. I saw Barney's brake lights come on as the truck slowed, then it swerved to the right off of the road as the car cut in front of the semi that had hit its brakes, too, and sort of hunkered down as it slowed. Barney's truck run up the ditch and onto the side of the hill before it scraped by a tree and flipped back over on the side and skidded down the road. Barney flew out of the truck and disappeared under the side as it scooted along and stopped about half way up the hill. I couldn't see where he was, and my heart was beating so fast I thought it was going to jump out of my chest.

Big got pulled partly off the road, stopped just behind Barney's truck and jumped out and ran towards the truck. I followed him, falling into the ditch when I jumped out of the truck. The semi was stopped on the other side of the road, and the car had gone off the side of the road on the other side and flipped over on its top and came to a rest in the ditch.

"Get back out of the way, John Walter," Big said as he ran. "Get clear off the road and out of the way. Don't come up here."

"Is Barney okay?" I asked, scared and near tears. "I hope he ain't hurt."

"Get out of here," Big said, down on his hands and knees, crawling under the back of the gravel bed. "Now."

Big's tone of voice stopped me in my tracks. I turned and ran up the bank and could see the semi driver running up to us, flagging down cars from both ways as he ran. For the next hour or so, things was kind of blurry. I was dazed, I reckon is what I was, and just sat on the bank of the hill top and watched. The two boys in the car was hurt bad and was taken away in the ambulance that'd come right pretty quick after the wreck. I couldn't see Barney and wondered why he wasn't coming out or getting taken away in the ambulance. Big had walked up to me before the sheriff got there and stood in front of me.

"Where's Barney, Big?" I asked.

He looked away a minute, then said, "He's dead, John Walter."

"Dead. He can't be dead."

"Yeah, he's dead. Deader 'n anything."

"But we just spread that load of gravel, an' he was kiddin' me an' told me he'd take me to the free show over to The Corners Saturday night."

Big didn't say anything. His eyes looked like he might cry, but I knew he wouldn't. Big never cried. He sat down on the bank and put his head down in his hand for a minute. Then we heard the siren from the sheriff's car, and Big stood up. He put his hand down on my shoulder and told me to stay there.

"Let me go with you, Big," I said. "I'm scared to stay here by myself."

He nodded and we walked down the hill toward the sheriff's car with Big's arm around me. I felt the tears running down my cheeks and wiped them off, not wanting anybody to see me crying.

"What happened, Big?" Dutch Leonard, the county sheriff, asked. He was from up north of Porterville and was up in The Corners a couple of times when I was there with Big or Sam.

Big told him what had happened, pretty much the way I remembered. He said something about a blind spot in the road that I didn't understand.

"Yeah, this is a bad spot," Dutch said. "We've had a couple of other bad ones here. There's a blind spot that'll hide a vehicle, even a truck, for two or three seconds. Enough to give a driver a false sense of security. Them boys probably didn't see old Barney until they was right on him."

"He tried to get off the road so they could get by," Big said. "They'd both been killed, if they'd hit that truck head-on."

"I'm sorry as hell, Big," Dutch said. "Barney was a good old boy. Had a few bad breaks in his young life an' went through a helluva lot on Okinawa, I've heard. That's the kind of thing that eats on a feller, an' you don't know much about it, less you been there."

Big just nodded.

After the wrecker came and set the truck up, Barney was put in an ambulance to be taken away. Big made me go back to the truck and wait. His face was nearly white as a sheet when he walked back to the truck and the ambulance pulled away. I'd never seen him look so scared or sad. We got in the truck and followed the ambulance away from the wreck.

"How'd Barney look, Big?" I asked as we turned off on the Portersville wide gravel and headed for home.

"Real bad. Real bad. I couldn't even tell it was him. He was all tore up. I don't think they can even open the casket."

"What'd the sheriff mean he'd had all them 'bad breaks' and 'been through a helluva lot on Okinawa'?"

"I reckon about bein' in the Marines an' what he went through over yonder an' losin' his woman back here. He carried all them things around with him. Couldn't let go."

"Lettin' go might be hard to do, Big," I said.

"I 'magine," Big said, his voice cracking a little.

We was quiet the rest of the way to The Corners. There, Big stopped in front of Luke and Bess Ford's and told me to stay in the truck again. He walked real slow to the house, his head down. Luke answered the door and Big walked in. I couldn't see anything after the screen door was shut, but I heard a loud scream and then wailing and crying for a long time. It was nearly an hour before Big walked out the door and back to the truck. His face was real white again. I didn't say anything.

"A feller never knows what's goin' to happen, Sedwick," Big said, calling me my favorite nickname again when we started to turn in at Bellair. "All you can do is watch the other feller an' do the best you can to watch out for yourself. Sometimes it's luck that you make it, sometimes it's just that your time has come when you don't make it. I reckon Barney's luck ran out an' his time had come."

I swallowed hard and nodded.

"What in the world's the matter with you, Robert?" Aunt Helen asked when she met us at the door. "You look like you've seen a ghost."

"I wish that's all I'd seen."

He tossed his hat on the floor and took Aunt Helen in his arms. I hadn't seen him do that before. She started to say something, but he shhhed her and just stood there with his arms around her. I went over to Mother and she hugged me. After a while, we all went into the front room and sat down. Big told them what had happened, and they started crying. That set me off, too. Nancy and Mary Beth came in and sat on the davenport and watched for a minute, then started crying with us.

Big told the story two or three more times that night and several more times when anybody came the next day. Sam and Gene and Pete all was there early the next morning. They looked grim.

"Sounds like Barney," Sam said, the muscles in his jaws working back and forth when he closed his mouth after Big finished telling them what had happened. "That's the way he was."

"He was a good man," Gene and Pete said almost together.

He sure as hell was, I thought, tearing up a little and walking out of the room. Not dead, though, not goddamn dead and gone. He can't be. This is a sonuvabitch. Hell, my daddy was a good man, everybody said. But he's dead and goddamn gone, too. How come good men like him and Barney got killed? What the hell's that? Mother said the good die young. What if that's true? What if all the rest of the good people I know leave me like Daddy and Charlie and Barney did? I couldn't stand not having Mother and Aunt Helen and Big and Sam and all the rest of the fellers I'm around all the time. What would I do without them?

Thoughts and questions like that kept running through my head as I heard fellers talk about Barney and say what a good man he was. His closed casket set in the front room of his folks' house, and cars lined both sides of the road as people came by to pay their last respects. Granddad and Grandma McElligott, Bill and Lela Kline, Charlie's folks, and a bunch of older folks like Johnnie and Mertie Larson, Russ and Eunice Taylor and Arthur and Fern Hamilton who had boys in the war passed through the house and held Luke's and Bess' hands a little longer than others did.

A picture of a much younger Barney in a Marine dress blue uniform sat on top of the casket beside a more recent photograph of an older, more mature Barney in a baseball uniform and that was taken at the ball diamond south of The Corners. The front room was crowded all the time, and the men stood out in the yard, smoking and talking while the women carried food into the kitchen and piled it on the table. I heard Big tell the story over and over again when fellers stopped to tell him what had happened "was just one of them things."

The little church down the street was crowded at the funeral the next day and people stood outside during the sermon. At the graveyard, the fellers in the American Legion fired shots in the air and Sam and bunch of other fellers saluted while the shots was being fired. And then it was over. We left Barney there to be lowered into his grave and walked away.

As we headed for the car, I promised him I'd never pick up another cigarette butt again. That wasn't much, but it was something he'd asked me not to do, and I meant to do what he asked. I figured that was the least I could do for him.

5

Big only had three trucks after Barney's wreck, and they was always going somewhere, day or night, all through the week. After I got a bicycle for my eighth birthday in '48, I acted like Big hired me to take Barney's place driving and the bike was another truck for me to drive. It was a Montgomery Wards special. It was about as different from the bikes the other kids had as Big's Dodge trucks was from Matt McIntyre's Fords or Harvey Burkett's Chevys. The bike had a curved handle bar and a horn and a cover fit in the frame just under it. On days when I couldn't go in the truck, I'd gas up the old Monkey Wards at home and fix the decking boards up for whatever kind of a load I was picking up. I'd have Nancy and Mary Beth and Cheryl set up truck stops at some places along the way to Indianapolis.

Driveways up and down the street served as the farms where I had to pick up cattle or hogs. I'd wheel in the drive, slide around and back up to the garage door to load up. After I got loaded, I'd stand up as I pedaled the bike towards where the girls had a table set up. Most of the time that'd be in Miz Hancock's driveway across the street. One day it was hot out, and Cheryl wanted Nancy and Mary Beth to set up under the grape arbor at the back of Matthews' smokehouse. I liked the idea of stopping at different truck stops. Big and Sam always stopped for supper and to fill out their tickets at Marvin Drake's truck stop just outside of Brazil. I knew there was a couple of other places where stock trucks parked and asked Sam one night why we didn't stop at one of them places.

"Because Big wants to stop at Marvin's place," Sam said, looking over at me and grinning. "They play checkers an' talk about the markets. But we stop at Derby Hill on this side of Terre Haute sometimes or other truck stops on the way. It's just accordin' to how things are goin' that day."

They usually went okay when I was along. And I had seen Big play checkers. I didn't know nothing about it, though. One night I'd sat there long after I'd finished my hamburger and Pepsi while Big and Marvin played. They'd sit there staring at the checkerboard with their chins in their hands for the longest time, then make a move. Big'd put his finger down on a checker and keep it there for another long time before he actually made the move. I couldn't find a thing to do while they played and finally went to the window of the side room of the truck stop where Marvin always sat at his desk. The window looked out over the gas pumps and out to the road. I counted eight stock trucks parked on both sides and in front of the truck stop. A man came running out from the other side of one of the trucks with another man following him, hollering and waving his arms. I couldn't hear what he was saying, but the other man was coming to the door as fast as he could get there.

"That feller's crazy," the man who had been running said as he ran inside and closed the door behind him. "Says he's goin' to kill somebody in the name of God. I can't understand much of what he said, but I got that."

"Who is he?" somebody asked.

"Don't know. He just come from behind a truck an' started hollerin' like a ravin' maniac."

Everybody had peeled off from the counter and jumped out of the booths to look out the windows. Marvin went to the door.

"I wouldn't go out there, Marvin," somebody said. "He looks like a mad man."

I was still back at the office window and could see what he meant. The feller outside was tall and dirty looking. His hair didn't look like it'd been combed for a week, and he lurched back and forth under the lights over the gas pumps and hollered all the time about something I couldn't hear. When Marvin opened the door, the feller hollered, "The wrath of God shall take us all. I am an instrument of His wrath and will help Him take you all. I will kill you in the name of the Lord. ..."

Marvin shut the door and came back into the small office to call the sheriff. While we all waited for him to come, everybody milled around at the front of the small truck stop and looked out the window. Nobody would go outside. I got tired just watching the feller. He kept walking back and forth, hollering and waving his arms in the air while he kept us treed like Ralph Crucell's dogs treed a 'coon. Quite a bit of time had passed while all this was going on, but the sheriff hadn't come yet. Finally Big said we had to go. I moved over closer to him.

"Aw, now, Robert, a crazy man can be stronger than you can imagine," Marvin said. "You'd better wait."

"A scared feller can be pretty strong, too," Big said, taking ahold of my hand. "That feller ain't going to hurt nobody. I know he ain't with this boy along."

I wasn't so sure of that. But when Big opened the door, we started walking for the truck right past the crazy feller. Maybe Big was looking at the feller. I don't know. Big'd told me to just walk along like there wasn't nothing going on and keep my eyes on the truck. That's what I did, my head up and my shoulders back even though my legs was a little shaky. When we got to the truck, Big peeked in the through the end gate at the hogs on the lower deck. I looked back at the feller then. He was staring at us, and I looked away so he wouldn't see me looking at him.

Big took me around to the driver's side door to put me in the truck. I scrambled over to my side and looked out at the truck stop. I felt like I was looking at something from a play like they had on the stage upstairs at the store or at the school. The little match-box-looking truck stop was the back of the stage with two gas pumps and a couple of lights bringing the focus to the drive lined with big stock trucks filled with hogs and cattle that was squealing and mooing. At the center of all that with the smell of hog and cattle manure hanging in the summer air was the crazy man. He'd gone back to walking up and down in front of the truck stop, hollering and waving his arms, when we got in the truck.

I felt really close to Big when he headed the truck out on the road towards Indianapolis. Looking over at him in the darkness of the truck, I almost felt like he was my daddy or they was one and the same. They looked alike. Even sounded alike, people said. Maybe my daddy was out there in the sky, I thought. Everybody said he was in heaven. I looked out through the windshield and up into the night sky. All I could see was the clouds and stars in the sky. The moon sat off to my side of the truck.

"Reckon Daddy's out there in heaven, Big?" I asked, pointing out through the windshield to the big sky before us. "Reckon he can see us?"

"I reckon he's out there, Sedwick," Big said, lots quieter than he usually talked. "An' I reckon he can see us all right. Wish he was here to be with us, though."

"Yeah. Me too."

I liked talking to Big like that. And feeling so close to him made me feel good the rest of the evening, and I slept like a newborn baby on the way back from Indianapolis. Times that made me feel so good like that didn't happen when I was just driving my bike around town and acting like I was a truck driver, and I'd get tired of only pretending after a while and look for something else to do. So I'd hang around up at the store and listen to fellers talk. Burns Larue and a bunch of old men was always up there telling stories from a long time ago, chewing and spitting, or playing dominoes. They was even there on Sunday mornings when other people went to one of the two churches just down the street. One Sunday I heard a story that was hard to imagine. Arthur Hamilton and Foxie Lyman was sitting over on the church side talking. Everybody else was over on the far side talking louder and laughing.

"Now Granddad Hamilton told me when I was just knee high to a grasshopper that one of the Snearley boys killed the last Indian in these parts down here in the woods south of town just before the War Between the States," Arthur said. "That would have been '58 or '59. Said he just shot him and buried him on the spot."

They went on talking while I walked off the porch and looked down past Belle Brandywine's house to the woods. I could see the old Indian walking along in the woods down there, and one of the Snearleys standing behind a tree taking aim on the old man. Shooting him. Burying him. That sounded like a Snearley, I thought. Arthur told his story so I could see it that way. I just couldn't see any Indians around here and anybody killing them like that. But hearing them stories made me want to be at the store.

I especially like being around there on Monday when all the delivery trucks started coming in pretty early. The store was a lively place as they came and went, mixing with the old men and the regular traders.

"You Bill McElligott's young 'un?" the Chesty potato chip man asked me one day when I stood on the porch watching him get the store's week's supply of chips out of his truck.

"I reckon I am," I said, eyeing him suspiciously. People didn't talk about my daddy to me. Not even Big or Aunt Helen, not even hardly when I asked them over and over. How'd this feller know who my daddy was? I wondered.

"Name's Irons," he said, sitting the box of potato chips on the bench to the side of the door and held out his hand. "Brad Irons. I didn't know your daddy, son. But I know where he was. I'm proud to know you."

"Well, I reckon I'm proud to know you, too," I said, not knowing what else to say. His hands felt like steel grips but comfortable to the touch. He smiled down at me just a bit and then took the box on into the store where my mother was working. I put my arm around the corner pole and swung around and around until I was nearly too dizzy to stand by myself. When I could, I wobbled out back of the store to see if I could reach any mulberries.

That day stayed with me for a long time. I couldn't get that Irons feller out of my mind. But I hadn't said anything to Mother because anytime anybody mentioned my daddy's name, she got all sad. So I figured it was better not to say anything. The next time I was with Sam I asked him if he knew the Chesty man.

"Yeah, I know who he is," Sam said, looking out through the windshield at the darkening sky. "Looks like a storm's comin' up. But what about Irons? Where'd you see him?"

I told him about the Chesty man talking to me at the store and asking if Bill McElligott was my daddy. "Chesty said he didn't know my daddy, but he knew where he was," I said. "What'd he mean that he knew where he was, Sam?"

"Your daddy got killed in the war," Sam said, staring out through the windshield, his hands gripping the steering wheel hard. "Irons was there, too."

"Was he where Daddy was?"

"Nope. Your daddy was on Guadalcanal in the early part of the war with the Japs. Irons was fightin' the Dagos and the Krauts in Italy on the other side of the world."

"Was you there?"

"Nope. I was all over Europe but not Italy."

"What'd the Chesty man do?"

"I've never talked to him, but fellers said he had a helluva rough time. He went in at Anzio with a Ranger battalion an' fought through Italy. Couple of them battalions had more 'n a thousand men killed there in a four-hour battle one mornin'. An' more 'n nine hundred of 'em was captured. The Krauts trapped the two battalions an' Iron's outfit got wiped out. He was one of fifty-eight men from his battalion who walked out after the Army quit on 'em. They survived. Feller told me Irons thinks they was deserted an' left to die. He's probably right. We wasn't very high on the totem pole back then.

"Then they was goin' through Italy an' come to the town where old Mussolini was hung upside down from a tree in the town center. Irons saw the old bastard hangin' there, I guess."

"Who's Mussolini?" I asked, remembering the name from the newsreels at the free shows over at The Corners during the war.

"He was the Italian dictator. Crazy bastard like Hitler."

"Did Irons hang Mussolini?"

"No," Sam said, smiling more than usual. "But I 'xpect he would have. He's been through a lot. Feller told me he can get pretty mean when he's been drinkin'. Best to stay away from him then."

"You been through anything, Sam?"

"A little," he said, smiling again. "Enough that I wouldn't take a million dollars to go through it again. But I wouldn't take a million dollars for what I've been through and what I've seen, either."

"What was it like?"

"You don't want to know."

"I told Dad Garner I reckoned by the time I got old enough to get in a war an' see what it's like, there wouldn't be any. He said not to worry, there'd probably be plenty for me to get in. You think he's right about that?"

"I 'magine he is, Sedwick," Sam said, the smile gone from his face. "But I hope you never have to go. I hope you grow up an' never have to know what it's like to catch a few winks when you can an' never know from minute to minute whether you'll ever have another one or not. War's ugly an' people get hurt an' die all around you. You don't want to have to go through all that."

He was quiet after that and looked out over the steering wheel at the lightning that had started flashing in the sky. We was headed for Indianapolis and had one more stop before we was loaded up. It had just started to rain a little when we pulled into Burlson Williams' barnyard. He had the gate open and pointed to the door at the corner of the barn.

"Let's get this calf loaded an' out of here before it really starts rainin', Burl," Sam said as he drove past. Then to me he said, "Don't let him get started on a story while I'm loadin' or we'll get our asses wet."

Burlson always had a story when you stopped there. He wasn't quite as old as my granddads, but he seemed pretty old to me. Every time I ever saw him, he had a pipe clenched between his teeth and wore faded old bib overalls and a blue shirt with the sleeves rolled up to just above the elbow unless it was Saturday and he was going to town. Then he wore a new pair of overalls and a new blue shirt with the sleeves rolled up to just above the elbows. I'd never seen him with a cap on, but his forehead was much lighter than the rest of his face.

His eyes would light up when he told a story. He'd take the pipe from his mouth and hold it in his hand, waving it like a wand as the story unfolded. One day, he'd got Big cornered and was telling him about the foxes getting into his chickens every night for a week and dragging off a chicken just before morning. Burlson said he had been "bound and determined" to catch that old fox before he ate up all of the hens that was laying eggs.

"Well, sir," he said, cackling a little as he got to the end of the story. "Long 'bout four in the morning, I woke up an' heard this commotion out in the hen house. The dogs hadn't raised no ruckus, but I figured it was that old fox up to his tricks again. I figured on puttin' an end to them tricks an' took my old double barrel an' headed out to the hen house. It was just startin' to get light in the east, but I couldn't see much. I walked out through the chicken lot with both barrels ready for that rascal.

"When I got to the hen house, I slipped the pin out of the door an' opened it quiet like so's not to make any noise. The ruckus had stopped, but I figured that old fox might still be in there. So I started creepin' in there with my old double barrel at the ready. I reckon I'd taken about three steps when I felt somethin' wet up against my behind, right through the openin' in my night shirt. I jumped forward, hollerin' out an' pulled the trigger on both barrels. Old hens flew everywhere. An' I turned an' headed out the door. I'd dropped the double barrel on the floor an' dang near tripped over Old Blue who'd been followin' me into the hen house, unbeknownst to me, an' run his nose right into my behind an' scared the bejesus out of me. Maude an' I cleaned old hens until noon."

Burlson had slapped his leg and nearly bent over double when he finished the story. I believed every word and could see every thing he'd been telling Big. It seemed like it happened right before my eyes. I wanted to know for sure.

"Did that really happen, Burlson?" I asked when he had settled down some. "Did you really shoot a bunch of hens?"

"It's true even if it's not, isn't it?" he said, laughing again. "Didn't you see it happenin'?"

That one stumped me. So I ask Big when we left if Burlson's story was true. Big allowed as how it might be. "But Burlson's a storyteller," he said. "He stretches things a little. An' he tells you lots of things that's true but didn't really happen. He just imagines whatever he has to to fit his story an' makes them to be whatever he wants them to be."

That sort of stumped me, too. But Burlson was a storyteller all right. The shock of white hair on his head blew in the wind as we passed him standing with the opened gate. By the time he had it closed, Sam had backed up to the barn door and had the loading chute pulled out from under the truck and ready for the sideboards. He'd left room for the door to swing open to load the calf without backing all the way to the door. Burlson got one sideboard off the side of the truck and put it in the chute while Sam got the other. Just as Sam started to open the door, a bolt of lightning flashed across the sky and a clap of thunder boomed and rolled across the countryside. I jumped. Sam turned real quick and dove under the loading chute and the back of the truck, grasping his hands over his head when he hit the ground. The rain started coming down harder, and Sam crawled out from under the truck. He never looked at us but opened the door and led the skittish calf from the barn and up the chute.

Burlson and I stood next to the barn to shield us from the rain a little while Sam loaded the veal calf. "He was in the war," Burlson said, a lot more solemn and quiet that I'd ever heard him. "Him and my boy was there at Normandy on Invasion Day. They're awful techy sometimes 'cause of what they went through. Don't say nothin' to him 'bout what you seen. He's embarrassed, I 'xpect."

Sam let the end gate down and put the loading chute back and side boards back on the truck without looking at us or saying a word. While he was writing out the bill of lading for the calf and handing it out the window looking straight ahead, I crawled in the truck on the other side and done what Burlson'd told me and never said a word after we pulled out of the barn lot. He waved to us as we pulled away. Sam waved, and I started talking about baseball like nothing ever happened. He was a Cardinal fan like Daddy had been and like me and Big and Granddad J.W.

"Sam Hill, boy, I been a Cardinal fan every since they been around," Granddad had told me once. "Might have made it to the big leagues myself if I hadn't hurt my arm gettin' throwed off a horse when he was feelin' his oats when I was a young'un."

Granddad was more than six feet tall by quite a lot and was pretty big. I could almost see him playing baseball when he told me the story. He was left-handed, and although they tried to change him to be right-handed when he was little like they did my mother, he only used a fork and wrote with his right hand, he said. He still threw left-handed and figured left-handed. "They couldn't hit me atall," he said. "I sailed 'em in there."

He was Sam's granddad, too, so I expected Sam'd heard the story a time or two himself. Granddad'd chew tobacco and spit in the coal bucket at his side, his eyes shinning more than I'd ever seen them, when he talked about baseball way back in the old days.

"When did you get to be a Cardinal fan, Sam?" I asked, not long after he turned out on the gravel road and headed off toward Indianapolis with the wind and the rain to our back.

"Huh?" he said, then looked at me and smiled slightly. "I guess I've been a Cardinal fan for about as long as I can remember."

"Me too," I said. Trouble was I couldn't even remember much about the World Series a couple of years before when the Cardinals won. I'd heard the story about Enos Slaughter, one of my favorite players, racing from first to home on a single to left field by Harry Walker. And I could just imagine old Harry Caray announcing

to Cardinal fans that "Slaughter's roundin' third, he's the winnin' run —
he's headin' for home, he's gonna try to score ... the Red Sox don't
believe it ... Pesky is holdin' the ball ... there's the throw to the
plate ... he's safe, Slaughter's safe ... the Red Birds go ahead 4-3
... it's up to Brecheen to hold 'em in the ninth for the Red Birds to
win the World Series ... Hooollllyyy Cowwww! What daring base
running! Enos Slaughter raced from first base to score on Walker's
little blooper to left-center field. ..." I wondered if Sam remembered that.

"How'd Slaughter get from first to home on a little old single in
that World Series?" I asked.

Sam's face lit up like a Christmas tree. I reckoned old Burlson
was right in telling me not to say anything to Sam about what he'd
done. And he seemed glad to talk about baseball.

"Well, sir," he said, "That was quite an exhibition of base runnin'.
Slaughter was one of the last of the Gas House Gang from the thirties.
He always gave it everything he had. When Walker got that 'little old
bloop double,' Slaughter put his head down an' started runnin' like
the dickens. Boston's left fielder took his time an' never thought about
old Eno going all the way home. Neither did anybody else. Pesky, the
Sox's shortstop, held the ball just a split-second too long on the relay
throw home, an' Eno rounded third with his head still down, them old
legs churnin' an' him headin' for the plate. I was listenin' to the game
with Big over at Charlie's there in 'Napolis. The crowd just went wild.
Harry Caray was callin' the game. He just kept gettin' more an' more
excited. When Slaughter rounded third, Harry began shouting, 'He's
headin' for home, he's heading for home.' I couldn't believe it. I thought
for sure they'd throw him out at the plate.

"But that's the way the old Gas House Gang played. Pepper Martin was like a locomotive when he was runnin' the bases. Old Dizzy
Dean throwed little aspirins past hitters until his arm give out. They
was all like that. I saw old Pepper stop a ball with his chest down there
one day, get up an' throw the runner out at first. The whole team of
them fellers just flat out played their hearts out every day."

I got pretty excited just hearing Sam tell the story. It helped us
think about something besides the storm and the rain that stayed
with us all the way to Indianapolis. We talked about baseball and

playing baseball most of the rest of the way to the stockyards. It was good to hear Sam talk about the old Cardinals. He knew a lot about them. I liked them, too. But I liked the ones I knew best. Slaughter was one of my favorites. I really liked old Stan Musial, too. Stan the Man. I'd take an old tree limb or broom handle and crouch over the plate, batting left-handed like Musial, stare out at Big Don Newcomb in Ebbets Field in Brooklyn where Stan had got his nickname from the fans who'd say, 'Here comes that Man' after he'd hit the hide off the ball, and I'd take a swing and pull the ball high over the fence in straightway right field. It was awkward at first to swing from the left side. But the more swings I took, the more natural it seemed.

"You think the Cardinals'll win the pennant this year?" I asked. "Stan the Man is leading the league in hitting, he's got twenty-three home runs already an' a whole bunch of RBIs. Slaughter was the Star of the Game when Big an' me went down to St. Louis with them fellers from The Corners the other day."

"Nah, I don't think they'll win the pennant this year," Sam said, shifting down again to make the top of a long hill and grinning like he always did at me calling 'Napolis The Corners. "Brecheen an' Brazle are the only two pitchers they've got. Pollet sort of fizzled out when they needed him. I think his arm's hurt. An' they need more hittin' than Musial an' Slaughter."

I didn't want to believe he was right, but that's the way things seemed to turn out for me. The war was over before I had a chance to go off to fight, the Cardinals hadn't won a pennant since I had been paying much attention and life just wasn't as exciting as it used to be in other people's lives. I figured I just missed out on the good times. But then when I found out I was going to my first big-league game, I again believed the Cardinals could go all the way. I felt pretty lucky to be going and just knew the Cardinals was going to win the pennant. They was playing the Redlegs, who was in sixth place. I didn't even know their players' names as I looked at the scorecard. The Cardinals was in second place, and Harry "The Cat" Brecheen, quick like a cat, was pitching against some old boy named Blackwell. I figured it'd be a cinch for the Cardinals to win that game and go all the way.

Big had told Mousy Gordon and the fellers from The Corners that I was going when somebody couldn't go for one reason or another.

Mousy ran one of the filling stations in The Corners and had got the tickets. He wanted somebody else to go and was telling Big that while he was settling up for his gas bill. Mousy's top front teeth stuck out over his bottom ones and make him look a little like a rat or a mouse. His legs were crippled somehow and he wobbled along on them when he walked.

"This boy wants to see a ball game, Mousy," Big said, putting his billfold back in his hip pocket and his hand on my shoulder. "This'd be a good time for him to see one. I don't get to do much for him like this."

That made me feel real good inside. I almost felt like his boy sometimes, even though I hung back around home when Nancy and Mary Beth crawled up on his lap and called him Daddy. I knew he wasn't mine then. It was different with Mother and Aunt Helen. They was who they was and treated me regular like. But when I heard Big talking about taking me to a Cardinal game, I felt like I had another daddy. Not one to take the place of my real one, but one that was there for me like my real one. Getting to go to a big-league game was something I'd only been able to dream about.

Claude Cottrell, the road commissioner that Big hauled gravel for, Mousy and an eighteen-year-old feller named Burton Shook, who was Mousy's nephew and who had wanted to bring a friend of his along and looked at me like he didn't like me, Big and me got there for batting practice. I could hardly believe I was in old Sportsman's Park, the place I'd heard Harry Caray talk about so much when I listened to the games on the radio with Big or Sam. On the radio though, the ball park seemed so far away and kind of like a fantasy world. About the only thing I couldn't see that Harry talked about was the Ford place on the other side of Grand Avenue that Stan the Man could reach with a home run out of the park. But I knew it was over there and hoped to see Stan break a window with a home run and win a new car from the Ford people. With that thought and all the fancy pepper games, running, catching and hitting, I felt good about the game and still had high hopes for the year. Then this Blackwell pitcher started throwing for Cincinnati. He was six feet, six inches tall and threw hard.

"They call him 'Ewell the Whip,'" Big said. "He comes around with that sidearm fast ball, an' it looks like it's comin' from third base, in on a right-handed hitter and right dead at a left-hander.

An' Brecheen is a tough little southpaw who throws a lot of ins and outs. He's got good control an' puts the ball where he wants it. You're goin' to see some pitchin' today."

And I did see some pitching. It just wasn't always by who I wanted to see doing it. Ewell the Whip shut down all the Cardinals except Slaughter. He went four for five, hitting the cycle, a single, a double, a triple and a home run and was the Star of the Game for the Cardinals. They'd still lost 6-2. Musial struck out twice, flied out once and hit a dribbler to the first baseman. That was just my luck, I'd thought after the game, to see the Cardinals lose, and I started thinking that they couldn't make it this year. Maybe next year.

"You think they can do it next year, Sam?" I asked. "I want them to go to the World Series."

"Me too," Sam said, turning out wide in front of the cattle pens at the stockyards and starting to back to an empty spot in the row of trucks already unloading in the rain. "Right now we've got to get this stock unloaded. It's rainin' like the devil. You just stay in the truck. No use you gettin' wet, too."

"I don't care," I said, thinking about how I could play trucker in the rain back home when I couldn't be with Big or Sam. It was hard for me to imagine, though, Nancy and Mary Beth sitting at their truck stop out in the rain. The Matthewses had a long porch that might work unless the rain was blowing all over like it was now. Then I reckoned we might have to get up on our little porch and use the seat for a counter. The honeysuckle vines would keep the rain from blowing in on us. "Can I watch you unload? Or help? I want to see."

Sam turned over to look out of the mirror on my door as he backed between two trucks. "Okay, Sedwick," he said. "You crawl over the seat this way when I get out, an' I'll pack you back an' put you up on dock. Climb up on the pen an' stay back out of the way. You'll stay dry there."

I crawled over the seat right behind Sam and jumped into his arms hardly before he was ready for me. He turned and ran toward the back of the truck, shielding me from the driving rain. We both scrambled up for the shelter of the cattle pens. By the time I was perched on the top board of the pen, Sam was reaching down to lift the end gate. About that time a bolt of lightning flashed across the sky, lighting up the stockyards like day time, and a sudden boom of thunder followed right behind that and rolled across the night and through the driving rain. I flinched so hard I nearly fell off the board backward into the pen. Sam dropped the end gate and dove off the back of the unloading dock and under the next truck over. I thought maybe he'd been hit by lightning, but I hadn't seen it that close and that was the second time that day that I'd watched Sam dive under a truck when it lightning and thundered. So I figured it was from the war, like Burlson said and wondered if Sam was okay. Just then he stuck his head up over the back of the dock and began pulling himself up between the stock rack and the hog dock. His face had a couple of pieces of mud hanging on one cheek and muddy streaks of water ran down his face and dripped off. He was caked all over with mud and straw.

"You okay over there, feller?" the trucker from the truck next to us asked, hollering over the sound of squealing hogs, cussing truckers and the blowing rain.

"Yeah, I'm okay," Sam said, wiping his face with a red bandanna and leaning down to lift the end gate.

I didn't know if he was okay, but he started unloading Burlson's veal calf and a couple of heifers and an old cow like nothing had happened. The rain kept on falling. Sam never looked at me, and I never said anything to him. He looked like he'd gone swimming down in North Fork when it was needing a good rain. The mud was dripping off of his hands as he made out the ticket to leave with the cow and calves. All the time, he hadn't said a word except, "Suuuueeey, you sonsabitches, suuuuueeey. Get on back there," several times as he was unloading the cattle and the hogs lunged forward and squealed like they did when Sam put the hotshot to them.

The rain kept on falling while we backed up to the unloading dock at the hog alley. Sam never said anything to me while we unloaded the hogs, either. He never offered to take me to watch him unload the hogs, and I never asked. I could see his feet and the hogs leave the truck through the little back window and the slats of the stock rack. When he finished unloading and we headed for the commission house to turn in the tickets, he said, "You okay?"

I nodded.

"I'm going to have to stop in the toilet an' clean up a little," he said. "I'm a mess."

He smiled a little, a tired look in his eyes. I felt we was both okay now and smiled back. "Which commission house we going to tonight, Sam?" I asked. I didn't know them all yet, but I knew there was Producers', Shannon Graves' and Sedwick's. Of all the ones that I'd been to, I still liked Sedwick's best. I didn't know anything about any of them, really, except that Big liked Sedwick, I thought, because he'd always talk about Budd Scholtz at Sedwick's who'd get the top money for your stock. I just liked the name.

"How about Sedwick's, Sedwick?" Sam said, grinning widely.

"Yeah, Sedwick's," I said, grinning back.

When we got back to the truck to head for home, the rain had stopped. I could see dark clouds rolling across the sky as we walked across the parking lot. Sam was still wet but a little cleaner. I was wide awake. Usually about this time of the trip to the stockyards, I was tired and ready to roll up a coat for a pillow and sleep until we got back to Bellair. Tonight, I planned to stay awake all the way home.

Everything looked wet and damp under the street lights as we turned out on Kentucky Avenue. Water was across the street in a couple of places and got pretty deep under a viaduct. Sam had to gear down, double clutching like he always did when he shifted down, and go slow through the water.

"Gotta be careful here, Sedwick," he said, "or I'll drown this sonuvabitch out."

"An' you don't want to do that, like Big an' Gene did down there on Willow Crick awhile back," I said, remembering being stuck in the truck when Gene'd tried to cross the bottoms north of Oblong rather than go back and go all the way around the wide gravel. Big and me went down to pull him out and got drowned out, too. We was there for about two hours before Earl Lyman came along with his big six-by-six Army truck and come in to hitch on to us and pull the trucks out backwards until we was back on dry road and able to dry things out. I'd stayed in the truck all the time while the rest of them waded around in water up to their waists. Being there like that gave me a funny feeling. Everywhere I looked around us was just water.

On my side of the truck, I could just see out to the brush. In the other directions, I could see water stretching out to the top of the hills where the road came up out of the bottoms. "I didn't like having all that water around me."

"You wouldn't want to be in the Navy then, would you?" Sam said, shifting up as we left the water. "Them Navy boys are always surrounded by water. They're never very far from land, though."

"Sure they are. It's a long way overseas, ain't it? You told me yourself that it took you ten or eleven days to go from New York to England when you was in the war. You'd have to be a long way from land on a boat trip like that."

"Never over a few miles."

"That can't be, Sam. There ain't no islands or nothin' between New York 'n' England where you'd be that close to land," I said and thought back to when he'd told me about going overseas. They'd sailed out of New York, he told me. And he told me how all the soldiers stood out on the deck and looked at the Statue of Liberty as they passed and stayed out for a long time, looking back until they couldn't see New York or land at all. Then he said they had sailed in a big convoy of ships, carrying soldiers an' airplanes an' everything else a feller'd need for war. An' everything like that was put in the middle of the convoy an' surrounded by destroyers for protection from the German submarines. I couldn't see how he could have even seen any land or have been close to it. "How'd you figure you'd only be a little ways from land?"

"Straight down," Sam said and laughed at his joke on me, "it's only a few miles to land no matter where you are."

I laughed, too. What he had said was true, I guess. And it made me even more sure that I didn't want to go in the Navy. Not that I ever had, anyway. Matt McIntyre had been in the Navy and didn't like it, I'd heard him tell Big one night at the truck stop while we was eating supper. "Why'd you go in the Navy then?" I asked him. "Well, sir," he said and laughed, "I didn't want to go to the Army, an' when I got to the head of the line in Chicago an' the feller asked me where I wanted to go. I said, 'Any place but the damn Navy.' 'The Navy it is,' he said. 'Next.' I guess they didn't want anybody to be happy."

I'd always thought I'd probably join the Marines because that's what Daddy had been in. They was the ones that went in first and didn't have to stay in ships that just floated around the ocean and didn't see land for days at a time.

"I know I don't want to go to the Navy," I said.

"I hope you don't have to go any place," Sam said. "That'd be the best deal all the way around."

"But I want to go."

"You just think you do."

"I want to join the Marines like my daddy."

"I wish he hadn't. Maybe he'd still be here, if he hadn't."

"Who else was in the Marines that you know?" I asked, trying to ignore what he was saying but wishing Daddy was still around, too.

"Oh, there's a few of them around. Barney was. Smokey Cottrell, the barber down at Oblong, was on Iwo Jima. Wick Hardway out there on the Kincaid place was everywhere out in the South Pacific. He was on Guadalcanal with your daddy and went on up through the Solomons. Jack Vaught was on Iwo, too. Still out there with a bunch of 'em they buried on Saipan where they went to a hospital before they died. They's some others around. Like Shorty Bennett down south of Oblong where we was haulin' cattle out when the water was so high down there last spring 'n' they thought the levee was goin' to break. Shorty lost a leg on Tinian, I think it was. And there's Tops Calvert up here north of Annapolis. He lost a leg, too."

"I like them fellers, Sam," I said.

"I do, too. That's not the point."

"I saw that old Shorty climbin' on the barn when we was loadin' cattle," I said. "Looked like he climbed right along with the others.

"I 'magine. Probably had to. Tops does the same thing. They don't let it slow them down too much. A feller does what he has to, I reckon. But ask Shorty or Smokey or Wick or Tops about you joinin' the Marines. They been there. They'll tell you things you won't hear from the recruiter. What you hear a lot of fellers talk about their time in the service is the good times they had. They don't talk about the bad times because they want to forget 'em."

"Did you have any bad times, Sam?" I asked.

"More 'n I wanted. Just bein' there was bad sometimes."

"Didn't you get wounded or hurt bad?"

"Not bad, I reckon, but bad enough for me."

"What happened?"

He didn't say anything for a minute, just looked out over the steering wheel and gripped it. His knuckles stood out in the dim light of the truck cab for quite a while before he started talking.

"We started takin' fire one day when we was workin' on the tank," he finally said and let go of the wheel with one hand. "Goddamn German come chargin' at us when we was tryin' to get inside. I was bringin' up the rear an' shot him with my .45 before he shot me. I picked up his rifle an' jumped up on the tank.

"Then an artillery round hit close enough that I got some shrapnel in my back an' legs as I scrambled up the side. Bein' the last man in, I pulled the hatch with me an' didn't get out of the way when I fell inside the tank. The hatch came down on my head like a ton of bricks an' knocked me clear to the bottom. That was the second time that'd happened. My neck felt like it'd been shoved down into my shoulders. After things was over, I was sent to the field hospital. They picked some of the shrapnel out, left some, gave me a neck brace an' a few days rest. I needed that. Then I went back to my outfit."

The rest of the way home Sam talked more than usual. If he was quiet for a while, I'd ask him something. He never mentioned the two times that day that he'd dove under the truck when it thundered. And I didn't ask. I just listened and tried to get him to talk about the war. I really wanted to know about the tanks he'd landed in during the Invasion that he'd told me about before.

"How'd you tell me them tanks sunk?" I asked, not quite sure I'd understood what he'd said when he mentioned it the first time.

"They was the ones they'd rigged up a flotation device for that was supposed to let the tank out a half a mile out an' move to the beach in the water. Them boys hit the water an' went straight to the bottom like a rock. They never had a chance to get out. A DD tank weighs five tons an' no little old flotation gizmo like they rigged up is goin' to keep a tank like that afloat. They had figured out them things at the last minute an' never tried 'em out in the ocean. We had water-proofed Sherman tanks an' got in okay. A couple of them left the LCTs too early an' sank, though."

"How come you wasn't in one of them that sunk?"

"I was lucky. That's all they was to it. Lot of us didn't think the tank'd float, but the crews with the DDs got them an' didn't get no choice about the matter. The rest of us had regular tractors an' got out farther in to the beach in the shallow water where we all should've been. But we took a hit not long after we hit the beach that knocked both tracks off an' disabled us. We left her there an' went on in with infantry."

He usually told me about what I asked without a lot of detail or comment. This time he talked as we drove along. Other than telling about the fellers that drowned, he never said nothing about the soldiers getting wounded or killed until I asked. And then he painted a picture for me of what he saw on the beach that would probably stay with me forever.

"We didn't see much comin' in from where we was in the tanks an' the LCTs. An' you don't worry too much about what's goin' on anywhere except right around you. After we got out of the tank an' headed out, I didn't gawk around much, either. But I looked back out to sea. All you could see in either direction was ships of one kind or another. Beach was filled with men an' equipment as far as I could see in either direction."

Our truck kept rumbling along in the night as we talked, the lights cutting a path through the darkness. I was quiet for a while when Sam finished. I thought about Daddy in the war like that and wondered about if Sam'd seen fellers get killed.

"Was there fellers gettin' killed an' wounded then, Sam? When you was there on the beach? Did you see anybody get killed like Daddy got killed on the 'Canal?"

"They was plenty that got killed or wounded there on Omaha an' later on, too. It ain't a pretty sight."

"How come my daddy got killed an' you didn't?"

"Luck," Sam said and reached over and put his big hand on my shoulder. "Pure luck, Sedwick. An' I guess it just wasn't my time."

That sounded the best I could figure after thinking about it most of the night. At Bellair, Sam said he thought he'd go in and sleep on the couch as late as it was and as early as he had to be back. Both of us was quiet as we walked across the yard to the house. He stopped at the porch to pull off his shoes.

"Thanks for lettin' me go with you, Sam," I said before I went inside. He said something about being glad to have the company that I couldn't quite make out, but I was already in the house headed for Mother's bedroom. She wasn't awake when I sat down on the bed beside her, so I didn't say anything. I stared at her in the darkness and began crying softly. One of the old fellers up to the store told Ross Childers awhile back about all his aches and pains. Ross listened awhile and then laughed and said, "Gettin' old ain't fer sissies, Harmon."

I hadn't been quite sure what that meant at the time. But that's the way I was beginning to feel about growing up. Sissies'd have a hard time of it, I thought, as I was making my way to the daybed where I slept most nights.

6

Big and Sam and all the other drivers got their hair cut wherever they happened to be that they had the time. Sometimes they'd stop over in Marshall where Big said "there's a good darkie barber" they liked having cut their hair. Big and Gene had stopped there on the way back from Indianapolis earlier in the week. My hair was getting long down on my neck and nearly over my ears. Dad Garner had cut it with his old hand clippers a couple of times and offered to again. I told him I wanted to get a haircut in town. Truth was, his clippers was old and dull, and they pulled at my hair, hurting a lot, particularly down on the lower part of my neck where the clipper had to get the hair close. And it didn't look as good as a town barber would make it look.

So when Big said he was going to Oblong to get the truck greased and the oil changed, I jumped at the chance to go. I knew I could get a haircut while he played pool and then go there to hang out awhile. Saturday morning was the best time to get a haircut. You had to wait for a long time sometimes, but everybody was talking and telling stories. When Big let me out at the corner and gave me the fifty cents I needed, I ran to the door leading down to the barber shop and down the steps.

Ned Cottrell, or Smokey as Sam called him, had the first chair as you walked in the door. Jap Parker, the guy who owned the barber shop and had slanted eyes that made him look like a Japanese feller, had the chair next to the other wall. Both of them wore a cap-like thing with a green-colored visor to keep the light from the ceiling out of their eyes. Jap had cut my hair a couple of times because it'd worked out that way with the line. I liked Smokey best from the beginning. But after Sam had told me Smokey was a Marine, I started waiting for him.

I'd sit in one of the chairs lining the walls of the small shop, pick up an old copy of *Argosy* magazine and peek out over the top to count it out and see whether I went to Smokey or Jap. If my turn came with Jap, I'd keep looking at the magazine and say, "I'm waitin' for Smokey."

I particularly wanted him to cut my hair this time. Albert Matthews, who lived with his mother on the corner three houses north of us, had gotten a Mohawk haircut. He had red hair and had an inch and a half wide stripe an inch or so long at the front that narrowed back to a point at the nape of his neck. The rest of his head was shaved. I thought it was about the neatest looking haircut I'd ever seen and asked my mother if I could get one.

"Absolutely not," she'd said. "I'll disown you if you do something like that. It looks ridiculous."

No amount of arguing would change her mind. But she finally did say I could get it cut short. I had to pass on Jap again to wait for Smokey. When I finally got in his chair, he twirled the apron out in front of me like a Mexican bullfighter and brought the strings together behind my neck while the apron was straight out in front of me, still even with the floor, and tied it behind my neck while the apron settled down over me.

"How'd you want her cut today, Sedwick?" he asked

"I want a GI haircut," I said.

"A GI? You goin' to boot camp?"

"Not yet. But I want her like they did yours in boot camp."

"Your mother say that was okay?"

"Yep. She said I could get it cut short," I said, looking directly at Smokey's eyes through his thick glasses. The tinted visor shaded his eyes from the glare of the lights I was looking into so I couldn't much see the look in his eyes. But I could tell they was shining and laughing.

He looked at me for a bit with a little grin on his face, then said softly, almost under his breath, "Your daddy'd kick my ass."

"Why'd he kick your ass?"

"Well, he'd try," Smokey said and laughed, "for what I'm goin' to do."

He'd never said much to me about Daddy. Nobody did. But Smokey always had a soft look in his eyes when he saw me. I hoped it was because he liked me, not because he felt sorry for me.

I didn't want anybody feeling sorry for me for not having a daddy. Sometimes when I felt a little sorry for myself, I'd go in the back bedroom and close the door to look through Daddy's seabag they'd sent home with his personal things. There wasn't much there to look at, a stack of letters from Mother, a smashed box of Marine Corps PX stationery with a sheet dated "12 October 1942" and "Dear Lorene" written on it, a cigarette case with a tarnished Marine Corps emblem stuck in the front of it, a little Bull Durham sack with some change, a pocket-sized copy of the New Testament and a couple of western books by Zane Gray. And there was a photograph album with the Hawaiian Islands painted on the cover. The first page had pictures of Mother and him before he went to the Marines. Then, there was pictures of him and some other feller who was in the Marines with him and some more of Mother and him when they got married. There was a baby picture of me and some other snapshots Mother'd sent to him now and then. I'd lay all the things out on the bed, looking at them or just holding them in my hands like I figured my daddy had back then.

With his thumb and forefinger lightly holding my head at the temple, Smokey tilted me back so I was looking in the mirror that lined the opposite wall a little more than half way to the ceiling. He had a little gleam in his eyes when he held the clippers in the crook of his hand like he was throwing a paper airplane and turned me around so I could see what he was going to do. The first swipe he took was right down the middle of my head. By the time I got my breath back, he'd taken both sides off with the same quickness and was going back over it to get what he'd missed. I didn't quite feel like old Sampson did in the picture show, but I knew better what he felt than I did when they cut his hair. I felt naked, looked rather naked, I thought, as this kid with an egg-shaped, shaved head looked out at me with a silly grin on his face.

"There you go," Smokey said, shaking the rest of my hair to the floor to mix with all the other hair of the day. "You're ready for boot camp."

"He'll think boot camp when his mother gets ahold of him," somebody said and everybody laughed. "Wonder what Big'll say?"

Everybody laughed again.

Smokey gave me a pat on the shoulder when he gave me back the dime change from the half dollar I'd given him. "Have a double dip on me today," he said, adding a nickel to the nickel he usually give kids when he cut their hair. "You deserve a little extra this time."

"Thanks," I said and looked in the mirror again. I guess I really didn't like the way I looked. Seeing that old bald head kind of shocked me, but I knew having a boot-camp haircut was something a feller had to do. I ran out the door and bounded up the stairs to the street to go for my ice cream. The pool hall had moved from right above the barber shop to just down the street where Rich's Cafe sold big scoops of ice cream in a cone for a nickel, doubles for a dime, and Joe's Tavern where old Frog the bartender made what everybody said was the best and biggest pork or ham sandwiches around. I wasn't supposed to be in the tavern, but Big had taken me in there one day during the winter when it was too cold for me to go anyplace else. Frog looked at me but brought us both a sandwich. Big got a mug of beer, and I got a little Coke. Joe came over later and said, "Far as I'm concerned, he's always welcome, Bob. But the law here says different." We never went back in again until I was a few years older. Then I heard Joe talking about being overseas in the Army and having "to police up cigarette butts when MacArthur came to Guadalcanal." That must've been after Daddy got killed, I thought. I didn't think they was policing up cigarette butts for nobody when he was there, but I didn't say anything.

I had part of the ice cream wolfed down by the time I got to the pool room. Big was just hanging up his cue when I walked in the door. He glanced at me but didn't say anything. I wasn't sure he noticed my haircut. "Ready to go, Sedwick?" he said.

"Yep."

I'd finished the ice cream cone before we got to the truck down at Jones Brothers filling station. Big still hadn't looked at my haircut like he gave it any thought, I didn't think. He paid his bill and we started home. But out on the wide gravel north of town, he turned to look at me and said, "You look like a striped-ass ape. Your mother is goin' to throw a fit. Do you know that?"

"She said I could get it cut short."

"I reckon that's short. If it was any shorter, you'd be scalped."

Mother did throw a fit. She hollered at Big when we walked into the house. "My god, Robert," she said, nearly screaming, "why'd you let him get his hair cut like that?"

"Now, Lorene, you know I didn't let him do anything. He goes to get his hair cut by himself. I didn't know he was going to get it cut like that. He said you said he could get it cut short."

"I didn't say he could get it cut off like he was some criminal. He looks just awful, like a convict. He's got to wear a hat until that grows out. That's all there is to it."

I'd never seen my mother quite like this. She went and got an old boy's broad-rimmed dress hat I'd had for a couple of years and smashed it down to my ears. "Now you wear this or another hat, and don't you ever do anything like that again."

"Yes, ma'am," I said, bringing my right hand up to the hat brim in a salute. I thought she was being silly. The hair would grow out in no time. I'd wanted to see how I looked with a boot-camp haircut and saw that it made me look pretty goofy.

I was still wearing the hat when Sam took Nancy and me to stay all night with Uncle Billie and Aunt Annie the next week. Mother had some different ideas about the clothes I wore than I had. The hat was bad enough. It made me look like Ross Childers or one of them gangsters in the movies. But with the gabardine coat that was somewhere between a suit coat and a jacket, silk-like shirt that she insisted that I keep buttoned at the neck and matching pants, I felt I looked more like Little Boy Blue than I did a salesman like Ross or a gangster. Little Boy Blue, come blow your horn, I thought, sheep's in the meadow, cows in the corn, Little Boy Blue's gotta dress like an idiot and wish that he was never born.

Staying with my favorite uncle and aunt like Uncle Billie and Aunt Annie was made me forget about it some. They didn't have any kids and had their nieces and nephews down to stay for a night or two, showed us a big time and took us home. Uncle Billie said it was "better 'n havin' your own kids." He had an old .22 single-shot rifle with the firing pin taken out that he always let me play with when I was there. He kept it down in the basement in a little cellar kind of room for canned goods. I opened the door and edged in until I could reach the string hanging from the light in the ceiling. The dull light showed rows of canned fruits and vegetables on shelves at the back of the damp room and rusty old guns on two other walls. I grabbed the old rifle off a nail and the string for the light and let the string slide through my fingers as I started to shut it off. I never stayed longer than I had to. The place sort of gave me the creeps. Besides being damp and musty, it always had a cobweb or two somewhere, letting me know there was spiders around.

It was even a little more spooky with the old German rifle Sam had brought from the war and given to Uncle Billie. Sam'd taken the rifle from the German soldier he'd killed. Even with the old damp smell in the little room, I could pick out the smell of the rifle. It gave me a funny feeling. It wasn't the same feeling I had when I smelled the other things Sam had brought back with him. Then I just saw things and smelled something that was different and made me feel the difference. But I was drawn to the rifle in another way and looked at it before pulling the string for the light. The rifle looked so out of place on the wall with the old musket loading rifles and shotguns. I wanted to take it off the rack and get it out of there. The strange smell and look of the old rifle gave me the creeps even more and made it seem downright evil. The necklace Sam got from a house back in the war and had given Nancy had that different smell and look that I thought was the Germans and was bad because they was the ones who'd started the war and got so many people killed. And like the rifle, the necklace had that smell even after she'd let it lay out for a while. I could always pick it up and get a whiff of that old foreign smell I'd know anywhere. I could still see the rifle after I'd pulled the string and the little room was dark again.

Nancy didn't like guns and looked away when I walked out of the basement door into the back yard. I spied a German peeking out at us up behind the chicken house and put the barrel in the crook of my hand to take aim at him before he got away. I eased the hammer back and pulled the trigger. "Bang," I said. "Got 'im. Got that dirty sonuvabitchin' Kraut bastard."

"I don't like guns," Nancy said. "And I don't like that kind of talk."

"I know that," I said. "You're a girl. You're not supposed to. Come with me, I'll take care of you. An' I won't cuss in front of you no more. Come on."

I walked off towards the other chicken house. It was an old bus Uncle Billie had set up on blocks and used to raise baby chickens. One time when we was there he had the whole bus filled with fluffy little yellow biddies, cheep-cheeping from one end to the other so much that you couldn't hear anybody talk. The young pullets had grown out of that stage. They was almost ready for the locker and walked around the hard, almost bare ground with their head down looking for something to eat. They clucked and moved away when we walked through them. Nancy stayed close to me until we passed by and got over to the far fence. I'd seen some people over on the next hill and wanted to see what was going on. Nancy didn't and fussed at me until I took her back to the gate.

"You monkeys stay around here," Uncle Billie said. "We're goin' down to Carl King's an' get that other bus later. Annie's gonna take us, so we've all got to go."

Billie and Annie was Sam's aunt and uncle, too. It seemed funny to me that we could have the same aunt and uncle as Sam. He said he'd been visiting them since he was a little kid, and he said he still liked to come visit with them. So I reckoned I'd still like to come visit when I got big, too.

Nancy headed over to the garage where Sam and Uncle Billie was looking through things he'd picked up at auctions. I'd looked through things a couple of times and didn't see much of interest. The two boys and the ponies on the other hill was another matter. I climbed over the fence and started zigzagging through the pasture toward them. I was right on them before the boys saw me. They looked about my age. The one that spoke first was skinny and kind of scrawny, I thought, and had a little squint to his eyes that made me think of old Jap Parker.

"You got a gun?" he asked.

"Yep," I said.

"A real gun?"

"Yep. My Uncle Billie lets me use it when we come down here. There's Japs an' Germans an' Indians an' all kinds of things lurkin' around in these hills an' hollers. I shoot 'em when I see 'em. Got me a goddamn German just awhile ago."

"Where you from?" the squinty-eyed one asked, looking at me like I looked at fellers sometimes when I wasn't quite sure if they was playing with a full deck. "You sure dress funny. Sound a little funny, too."

"Why, I'm from Bellair," I said, taking my hat off and wiping my forehead with my sleeve. "I don't reckon I sound any funnier 'n you. An' my mother is thc one that dresses me '*funny*.' If I was to dress myself, I'd sure dress different. But you don't dress so goddamn good yourself, I reckon."

I really thought he dressed good, much too nice to be out playing with ponies. He even had a pair of loafers that had the little cutout on each shoe where you could put a dime and have the liberty head shinning out at anyone who looked. He had a new Roosevelt dime in both of his. I didn't even have any clothes like that for school, let alone two dimes I didn't have. The boy stood away from the pony and eyed me with his squinty eyes. "What's the matter with your hair?" he asked. "Looks like you don't have any."

"I reckon I don't. Got it cut off to go to boot camp."

"Boot camp?"

"Yep. I'm joinin' the Marines."

"You're goin' to do what?"

"Join the Marines. What's the matter? Did I stutter? You gonna ride them ponies 'r talk all day?"

"I don't know how to saddle them. Do you?"

"Why sure, I can saddle 'em. Ain't nothin' to saddlin' a pony. Anybody can saddle a pony."

I'd never saddled a pony, but I didn't figure it'd be any job to saddle one. And hell, I was eight years old, going on nine. I figured it was high time I learned to saddle a horse. I'd watched Jimmy Barker saddle his old red horse a few times. He just slipped the bit in the horse's mouth and the halter over his head and tied the horse with the reins. Then he tossed the blanket and saddle over its back, put the stirrup up over the saddle horn, pulled the cinch strap under the horse's belly and tied it tight. After he got the strap tied, he'd always poke the horse in the belly to get it to let out its breath so he could tie the strap tighter to keep the saddle from slipping. I figured I could get the job done on two little ponies.

"You don't say?" the squinty-eyed one said. "My dad or Uncle Bronk always saddles them for Dale an' me."

"That's right," the one called Dale said. He was a little bigger than the other boy and had thick, rust-colored hair. "They don't let us, do they, Lonnie?"

"'Course they don't let you," I said, wondering why they didn't watch the saddling and learn that way. "You don't know how. Let's get these ponies saddlcd. You fellers lead 'em over, an' I'll do the rest."

I followed them towards the barn where Lonnie handed the reins to Dale and looked at me. "You sure you know how to saddle a pony?" he said. "I'm not sure we ought to do this."

"Don't want to ride 'em bareback, do you?"

Lonnie walked to the saddles and pointed to them. One was black leather with all kinds of designs carved in and strips of white leather laced in around the edge of the saddle, giving it a black-and-white trim. The other saddle was brown and had a simpler design stamped into the leather. I grabbed it and a little blanket that was nearby. Lonnie took the black saddle and the blanket with it, and we headed back out the door.

The little palomino with the golden white mane should get the brown saddle, I decided. The black one went with the pinto. One of us could be Roy Rogers and the other could be Gene Autry. I wanted to be Roy and started saddling Trigger. I put the blanket on just like I'd watched Jimmy do, then tossed the saddle over the pony's back, the far stirrup flying high before the saddle settled on the pony's back. Next I took the blanket and saddle from Lonnie and did the same thing. I'd just reached under the pony's belly for the cinch strap when Lonnie's dad walked into the barn lot.

"Heeerrrreee," he said, stretching the word out as he walked, "what're you fellers adoin'? You can't saddle them ponies."

"This boy knows how," Lonnie said. "He's doin' it. An' he's showin' us how."

"That gun over there loaded?" Lonnie's dad asked, pointing to the old rifle I'd leaned against the fence with his finger but looking me right in the eyes.

"No, sir, it ain't. Don't have no firin' pin, anyway."

"What's your name, young man?"

"John Walter," I said, not going into detail about not liking the whole thing together but not knowing exactly what I wanted to be called by everybody yet. But then I said, "Some of 'em call me Sedwick, though. What d' they call you?"

"My name's Nelson Dailey," he said, sticking out his hand to take the one I was offering. I took his meaty hand, pumped it a couple of times and pulled back to tighten the cinch. "An' you know how to saddle ponies?"

"Yes, sir, I do."

"Well, that's good, but these boys don't have time to ride this mornin'. We're not goin' to stay that long. So get the saddles put back. Maybe you can come back sometime an' saddle the ponies for us an' you an' the boys can ride around a little. How'd that be?"

"That'd be good, I reckon. When d' we do that?"

"Next time you're here."

That wouldn't be very soon, I knew. But I'd sure keep it in mind for when I did come back. Now I had a picture in my mind's eye of me riding one of the ponies across the hills of the pasture with the boys. Those little ponies could fly across the hills. Maybe Uncle Billie would buy one so we could all three have a pony, and I could ride like I always wanted to. The only time I'd ever ridden a horse of any kind was up behind Jimmy or Ronal and that wasn't often. They didn't like to ride double. They'd let Albert ride alone, but they wouldn't let Richard and Jerry or me. Getting my own horse and having one to ride down at Uncle Billie's would change that.

When I got back over to Uncle Billie's, everybody was outside and ready to get in his old Chevy. "Where've you been, you little monkey? Nancy said you went over to Bronk's."

"I did. Them boys was goin' to let me ride their pony, but their daddy come along an' wouldn't let us ride. He said I could come back sometime, though. If you had a pony here, we could all ride."

"Think a little old pony could hold me?" he said, laughing.

I guess I'd never thought about that. Uncle Billie must have weighed a ton and was as strong as an ox. He wasn't very tall, but he had big arms and was thick through the shoulders. Uncle Chris Bryan, my Aunt Christine's man, was taller and looked like his muscles was bigger and that he was stronger than Uncle Bille, but had had his hip shattered in an accident over in France in World War I when this feller that was driving some kind of Army truck tried to beat a train at the crossing and didn't make it. One of Uncle Chris' legs was quite a bit shorter than the other, and he wore one shoe with a thick sole and heel.

But he was strong as anything. I felt the strength in his hands and arms when he'd pinch me on the shoulder or take ahold of me, but I'd never seen him lift anything other than to throw one of us kids in the air. He limped real bad and always put the knee of his broken leg on the floor when he sat down. I didn't figure he could squat down and lift like Uncle Billie. He'd lifted the front end of an old Model A Barney and Tilda, Grandma's sister, had driven over to visit her one time. And the tires was nearly a foot off the ground, I'd bet. Uncle Billie just squatted down and stood up with the bumper in his thick, stubby arms. Uncle Chris didn't try. And none of the rest of the men, including Big, could get the car to budge much. He just got it up so it was barely off the ground.

"Get it for us kids," I said. "Not for you."

"Right now, we've got to go down an' get the bus."

This bus was just about like the one out in the back chicken lot, I'd heard him tell Sam earlier. Uncle Billie said he'd bought it at a sale for a little of nothing like he did everything else. It was an old city bus that was total wore out. The motor still run, but everything was about to fall off, clear quit or blow out. He said the tires was smooth and the brakes shot. It'd been parked down at Carl's since they'd brought it home from the sale. Now Uncle Billie was going to block it up next to the other one and raise chickens to sell as fryers while the market was good.

Aunt Annie drove us over to Carl's down over the railroad track, past the oil field tool and power houses and around a sharp turn and up the steep Ziegler's Hill through the trees and out onto a stretch of level ground. This part of the country wasn't much different than it was around Bellair. Just wasn't no railroad up home. I liked to watch the trains run along the tracks just outside Uncle Billie's pasture and hear the engine's lonesome whistle. "I could hear that looonnne-sommme whistle blowww," I'd sing in my best Hank Williams voice. Dopey, Uncle Billie's old Collie that'd been around since I could remember, didn't seem to like the trains the way I did. It didn't matter whether it was four in the morning or four in the afternoon, he'd start howling the minute he heard that whistle and keep it up until the train passed. I'd laid there a couple of nights long after everyone else was probably asleep, thinking about things and picking at my belly button a little and sucking at my lip but feeling a little guilty because I was getting too old to be doing things like that, and listened to the midnight train come rolling down the track and heard Dopey howl. I reckon the sound of the whistle hurt his ears. That's what Uncle Billie thought, too.

While him and the others stood around talking with Carl and his daughter, a big old girl not much older than me but bigger, I went out in the barn lot to take a closer look at the old bus. It'd been painted a flat green with a silver band around the bus just under the windows a long time ago and had a faded look to it now. I pushed on the upright door that let you in past the driver, and it folded back from the middle to each side. I hopped up the three steps to the driver's seat and sat down behind the wheel. Driving a bus never interested me, but I had a picture of me with a bus full of people going someplace. The bus was sort of wobbling down the street while I tried to figure out how to drive the thing. The dash panel looked much like the dash of Big's trucks. This panel had REO written in the speedometer and had a flatter steering wheel that let the driver rest his arms on it as he guided. That's the way I did when I got up on my knees and pretended to drive the bus through the city.

"I think Sam'd better drive," Uncle Billie said to me from outside. "You can't see over the steerin' wheel."

"Can too," I said, getting down and going outside. "You goin' to drive, Sam?"

He smiled and went back to helping Uncle Billie get the bus running. When they finally got it started, it rumbled and shook almost like a summer storm. Uncle Billie sat in the first seat right behind the door. Nancy and me sat in the seat right behind Sam. He started the bus with a jump when he let out on the clutch and pulled through the gate Carl and Mary Jo stood holding open for us. For the first mile or so, we jumped along every time Sam shifted gears or tried to speed up. By the time we crossed the wide gravel and was headed for Ziegler's Hill, the motor seemed to smooth out and was running fairly good. Nancy and I looked out over each of Sam's shoulders as the roadside flashed by and hung on to his shoulders as we started down the long hill that turned a sharp left right at the bottom. He'd geared down and was trying to slow down, but it seemed like we was going a hundred miles an hour at least.

I'd heard Uncle Billie tell Sam that the brakes wasn't very good, that he'd have to be careful taking the hill. The faster we went, the harder I griped Sam's shoulder and the shiny frame right behind the driver's seat. Nancy grabbed my arm.

"You'll have to pump the brakes, Sam," Uncle Billie said louder than I usually heard him talk, his eyes bulging out a little more and a little more the faster we went. "You've got the pedal all the way to the floor. Pump 'em, pump 'em."

My heart was racing so fast that I don't know whether Sam pumped 'em, but he took that corner in a big wide curve and didn't get the wheels straightened out to stay on the road. Instead, we went almost in a U-shape and jumped the ditch and stopped in the hill bank, up against a little tree. I banged my head against the window. Nancy flew out of her side of the seat over towards Uncle Billie who caught her just before she was headed to the steps and the outside door which had flown open.

"Well, you got her stopped, Sam," Uncle Billie said. "Not exactly in the place I wanted her, but you got her stopped."

"Is everybody okay?" Sam asked, then seeing that Nancy was crying, turned to her. "You okay, hon?"

"I think she's just shook up," Uncle Billie said. "I caught her before she hit anything."

A big Army truck pulled up and stopped as we was standing looking at the damage. Nothing was hurt much. The only problem was getting back across the ditch and the rest of the way home.

"What happened, boys?" a tall, slope-shouldered man I thought looked a little like Abraham Lincoln that I'd seen before but couldn't remember his name asked, nodding to Sam and me as he walked up to us. "Looks like she got away from you, Billie."

"Got away from Sam," Uncle Billie said, the redness of his face gone now. "We was tryin' to get her from Carl King's up to my chicken lot. Brakes are shot an' Sam U-turned her off the hill."

"I think I can pull you back in the road, if she still runs."

"She's runnin', Wick," Sam said. "Let's get the sonuvabitch back on the road."

The big feller smiled.

"This Bill's boy, Mac?" he asked.

"That's him. His name is John Walter, but we all call him Sedwick. Sedwick, this here is Wick Hardway."

"Well, I'm a right smart pleased to meet you, Sedwick," he said, holding out his hand for me to shake. "I've seen you around with your uncle. An' I knowed you daddy real well. He was a good old boy. One of the best."

"I reckon he was, sir," I said, a good feeling running through me as I heard the words and saw old Wick Hardway smile down at me. "That's what fellers have told me. I'm pleased to meet you, too."

I hadn't been around him much, but I'd never seen him smile before. When he'd lived out on the Kincaid place up by Bellair, he'd kept pretty much to himself and wasn't often smiling when I saw him. After I'd heard Big telling Wes Davis about the sheriff coming out when Wick'd threatened to kill old Ott Kincaid because he kept coming out to the place and telling Wick what to do not long after he came home from the Marines, I looked at him different than I looked at a lot of other fellers. And Wes said Wick and my daddy had joined about the same time and that they was both on Guadalcanal, but Wick had gone on to other islands later on. On New Guinea, him and some of his outfit got cut off from everybody else and took ninety days to get across the island through the Japs and the head hunters and find some other Marines. That sure sounded exciting, and I wished Wick could tell me about it sometime. I'd been kind of scared of him from the stories I'd heard about him, but he seemed like a good feller up close, kind of friendly and willing to help. Even when we passed him on the road, he'd stick his arm out the window and fly his hand and arm like an airplane the way I did all the time when I rode with the window down and played like I was in a dogfight with a Jap Zero.

"You still stickin' your arm out the truck window an' flying them planes?" he asked, the smile bigger than ever.

"I reckon so," I said, real surprised that he remembered that.

He nodded and swung up in his old six-by-six Army truck and backed it in behind Uncle Billie's bus at an angle, leaving both back wheels on the road. One chain wouldn't quite reach the bus, so Wick took a piece of cable from his truck and got down under the bus and tied it down underneath and brought both sides out to a point where the chain could tie on.

"You kids stay clear away from here now," Wick said, stopping by Nancy and me after he'd finished and was ready to start pulling on the old bus. "I don't think this cable'll snap or the chain'll break, but you never know."

Uncle Billie motioned us back up the road and started walking with us. Sam stayed back with Wick to guide the bus out. As we walked off Sam said, "Like these old six-bys, do you, Wick?"

"Why, hell yes, Mac. I like 'em. They ought to give us all one when we got out. They gave the darkies forty acres an' a mule when they let them go back durin' Reconstruction. I didn't get jack shit when I got out. All I got was out. An' it took me a helluva long time to even get out. When I finally did, I didn't get nothin' 'xcept a lecture about how much they was goin' to help us now that we'd won the war. Old boy in front of me turned around and said, 'I think they're sellin' us an empty bucket, Abe.' I didn't think so at the time, but I 'xpect he was right.

"You know it's taken me a long time to settle down to be a civilian, Mac. I 'xpect you know what I'm atalkin' about. An' I ain't settled down yet. Not by a long shot. I'd been in the Marine Corps for right onto nine years when I got out, an' I'd been overseas the biggest part of them. An' I got to where I didn't have no respect for anybody. Might made right as far as I was concerned. It was kill, kill, kill.

"These old six-bys wouldn't have helped that part of the deal much, but they're like a mule. These old boys'll go about anywhere. They oughta given us one to them that could've used one. You can drive 'em into the ground without hurtin' 'em, an' they're easy to work on when something does go wrong. Nothin' much ever does. Mine'll pull that old bus back on the road, if you'll git in there an' guide the sonuvabitch out, Mac."

Other than a little rocking from side to side, the bus came out without a hitch. That old Army truck sort of hunkered down, Wick tightened the chain real slow, then just kept moving only a little faster with the bus right behind it. When it was all back out on the road, Wick stopped and backed up a little to put some slack in the chain.

"Do you fellers think you can get this outfit on up to Billie's place?" Wick asked after they'd gotten the chain and cable unhooked and back on the Army truck. "I can follow you back up."

"Nah," Uncle Billie said, "we can get her on in. Them brakes are shot, but there's a little there when you pump 'em."

"There ain't much," Sam said. "I was pumpin' the devil out of them, an' there wasn't enough there to slow me down so I could take the corner. But we'll make 'er."

Nancy and I walked up the road. I was looking through the gravel for Indian beads and found a couple. They looked about the same as the ones I found up around Bellair. They were little barrel-shaped rocks with string-like circles all up and down the outer part. Neither of these had a hole through the center so I could string them on a necklace, but I stuck them in my pocket for the match box at home.

"Say, Mac, you was with old Merv Gallagher over yonder, wasn't you?" Wick was saying when Nancy and I got back between the bus and the Army truck.

"Was in the States. He went to the Pacific an' ended up on Okinawa. I went the other way."

"Well, you know old Merv, anyway."

"Oh, yeah, I know Merv. He's a helluva man. Good feller to have on your side, whatever you're doin'."

"You got that right," Wick said. "Him an' old Poke Winfield — you know he sort of raised Merv after his daddy died — was doin' some dozin' over towards Louisville here 'while back an' stopped at a tavern in Olney on the way home one night. Well, you know how them things go when you're adrinkin'. Poke'd been arguing with Old Jake Samuels, the old boy who owns the joint, about how many times Babe Ruth struck out in his career an' shit like that. They'd bet on somethin', an' Jake reneged, said Poke'd set him up, an' the check he'd wrote wasn't no good. An' they kept at it. First thing you know, it's closing time, you ain't had nothin' to eat an' you'd like to have another drink. That's about where Merv an' Poke was, Marty Delp told me — an' he was there — when Jake an' the bartender wouldn't sell them another beer 'n' told them it was time to leave.

"They didn't argue. Old Poke just nodded to Merv an' said, 'I'll be right back.' He went out an' backed the winch truck up to the door an' let the line out for Merv to pull it back through the bar an' wrap it around the coal stove. Nobody said a goddamn word to Merv. 'Course they wouldn't. He's big as a bear, nearly as strong an' can be real mean when he gets riled. An' Poke's about the same, maybe only a little over six feet, but still a pretty good man even though he's gotta be better 'n fifty. Marty said old Jake went back in the back room. Marty figured he was calling the cops or gettin' a gun. Had to be one or t'other. But when Merv got the winch line tied fast, Marty said Old Merv hollered, 'Take her outta here, Poke.' An' by god, he took her out, right through the front door an' pulled her right out in the street, spreadin' hot coals, glass, wood an' what have you, spreadin' it all everywhere. 'It's closin' time!' Merv hollered. 'It's time for the goddamn fire to go out. Time to go home.'

"The fire was still going when the cops got there. One of them marched right up to old Merv an' told him he was under arrest. Merv smiled at the old boy an' walked away from him. The place was in shambles. Pieces of stove pipe, coal soot, ashes, some still burning, turned-over bar stools an' the front door hanging by a thread where it'd been knocked off by the stove. The cop followed Merv an' is going to cuff an' haul him over to the jail. 'Let me tell you something, son,' Marty said Merv told the cop while the three or four fellers still left stood back and watched, 'Poke an' me'll go over to the goddamn calaboose with you. But you ain't goin' to put them cuffs on me an' take me no place without one helluva fight.'

"Well, the cops decided not to try an' cuff 'em an' just let 'em walk over to the jail. Damnedest thing he'd ever seen, Marty said. They was under arrest, you understand, but the cops decided it'd be better not to try an' cuff them an' just walked along with 'em on the way to jail like they was goin' over to the restaurant for a cup of coffee."

"That sounds like Merv," Sam said. "Three old boys from New Jersey decided they could take him at the EM club one night. Sorta come up behind him an' told him they was there to whip his ass. A couple of us just sat across the table an' listened. Then we watched. We knowed what was goin' to happen. Merv sort of shrugged his shoulders an' hit the middle feller with a right hand as he came out of the chair, knockin' him down an' then jabbed the one on his left right in the nose with a short left. The blood spurted out of that nose like a gusher. When Merv turned back, the other feller had swung a sweepin' long right hand that Merv blocked with his right forearm an' knocked the feller back across the table behind him with a sharp left hook.

"He was pretty good with his hands. We tried to get him to see about boxin' Joe Louis when he came through camp one time. Merv wouldn't have anything to do with it. Said a feller that likes to fight ain't right. He was as gentle as a lamb unless you crossed him. Then you'd better watch out."

"Well, the cops didn't rile him," Wick said. "Marty said it was downright comical watchin' them cops pussyfoot around Merv an' Poke when they was takin' them to jail. Guess they spent the night an' went to court the next mornin'. Judge fined them an' ordered them to pay for the damages over at the tavern. Old Merv laughs about it. Just gives you that big old grin an' chuckles a little."

"I can see him," Sam said. "Probably had that old bashful kind of look in his eyes, too."

"I 'magine, an' kind of proud that things turned out like they did," Wick said and swung up into the truck. "You fellers take care of yourselves."

"That's hard to do nowdays," Uncle Billie said. "What d' I owe you, Wick?"

"You don't owe me a goddamn thing, Billie. You know that. But I'd take some of them young fryers you're goin' to raise in that old bus. When they're ready. I'll pay for 'em, though."

Billie nodded.

"An' you watch out for 'em, Sedwick," Wick said as he drove off. "You've got your work cut out for you with this crew."

I nodded and waved. Old Wick had made me feel real good about myself. I was right glad to meet him and get to hear him talk. He was another one I figured was a lot like Daddy would have been if he'd lived through the war. Tears started to well up in my eyes, and I turned away to stop them before we got back in the bus.

Sam still drove, but this time he went slower and shifted down more. At the railroad crossing, he pumped the brakes and shifted down into first gear. The brake pedal slapped against the floor board with a bang each time his foot hit the floor.

"This dang thing ain't got no brakes atall," Sam said, hunched over the steering wheel with both hands holding the wheel like he was afraid it might get away. "Good damn thing there ain't no train comin'."

Billie chuckled without making much of a sound. But his belly shook and his eyes had a gleam in them. Nothing much ever seemed to bother him. He was always laughing and joking with us kids, letting us stay down at his house, taking us swimming in the summer time, playing Santa Claus for us at Christmas and doing all the other kinds of things my daddy couldn't do for me and Big didn't have the time to do. My mother said Uncle Billie was like he was because him and Aunt Annie never had any kids. I didn't know about that because some of the rest of my aunts and uncles and others that never had any kids wasn't like Billie and Annie.

"Just bring her to a stop right there by that big oak in the front yard," Uncle Billie said at the railroad crossing. "We can roll her down the hill to get that motor pulled an' the bus on over in the chicken yard. Tree'll stop her."

He laughed a deep belly laugh this time and looked over at me and said as we started across the track, "Railroad crossing, watch out for cars, can you spell that without any Rs?"

"R-a-i-l-r-o-a-d c-r-o-s-s-i-n-g," I said right away.

"T-h-a-t," he said back right away. "Listen, you monkey you. I said, 'Can you spell *that* without any Rs?'"

"You tricked me."

"No, you didn't listen to what I said."

Uncle Billie had one of those little puzzles or riddles for all kinds of things. So I should have known enough to think before I blurted out the wrong answer. We passed the graveyard on the way into Oblong one other time Nancy and I stayed with Uncle Billie and Aunt Annie. That time he'd asked me if I knew how many people was dead in the graveyard. 'Course I had no idea and didn't know how he could, either. .

"Do you?" I'd asked.

"Of course," he'd said.

"How many?"

"All of them," he'd said, winking at Nancy.

She'd laughed and said, "Fooled you, didn't he? You're not so smart."

That'd tickled her, and she was tickled again that I didn't have the right answer to Uncle Billie's question. Sam laughed, too, and slowed to a crawl when we got close to the tree where he was going to park the bus. I jumped off the bus and ran around back to the basement door to get the rifle and play a little before supper time. We was going back to Bellair the next morning, and there wasn't any rifle there.

I didn't have much time before going in to eat fried chicken and gravy. Only time I ever had fried chicken was on Sunday unless Nancy and me stayed with Uncle Billie and Aunt Annie. She could sure cook good fried chicken. The gravy wasn't quite so good. It had a good taste, but it was real thick and sometimes a little lumpy. Mother called it paste. But it was still good gravy, kind of like Grandma Mary Elizabeth's. I piled the potatoes and gravy on my plate and pulled the wishbone off the chicken plate. That was my favorite piece of the chicken. Sometimes there wasn't much meat on one. Then sometimes you'd get one that was all plump and full of white meat. But I liked to have the wishbone to make a wish with after I'd eaten the chicken.

"I see you found that old pulley bone, mister," Aunt Annie said, smiling at me, then frowning. "But now you get you some of those green beans and hominy. You can't just eat mashed potatoes and gravy and chicken."

Well, I could, but I knew Aunt Annie wouldn't let me get away with it and took a little of both green beans and hominy. It wasn't that I didn't like them. I just wasn't used to having fried chicken with gravy through the week. Not having chickens like Aunt Annie did, we didn't even have it on Sunday all the time at Big and Aunt Helen's. I ate fast because I knew Uncle Billie and Sam was going over to visit Mr. Martin in the little house next door after supper. When I finished, I held out the wishbone to Uncle Billie. He took ahold of the other side of the V-shaped bone and looked at me a little bit. "Ready?" he asked.

"Yep," I said, wishing that I could have a horse for my birthday. For a long time, I used to wish for my daddy back or for a little brother. After a while, I knew that I was just wasting a wish to wish for something that could never come true and started wishing for something I thought was possible. A horse might just be possible, I thought, and jerked my side of the V. I heard the crack and saw the bone give way on Uncle Billie's side. The big part came loose in my hand. My wish would come true, I figured, and smiled at him.

"Let's go to Mr. Martin's," Uncle Billie said, chuckling.

We all got up to go, but Aunt Annie wouldn't let Nancy go until she'd cleaned up her plate. All she had left was her gravy and a little mashed potatoes. I knew she didn't like the gravy. Mother's and Aunt Helen's was much thinner and not as lumpy. "I don't want the gravy," Nancy said, watching us leave the kitchen.

"Well, now, you're going to clean your plate up or you ain't going to go over to Mr. Martin's," Aunt Annie said, not laughing like Uncle Billie did when he told us the same thing. She got real stern with us when we didn't do as she said.

I sort of hung back to wait for Nancy. She had started shoveling the gravy in her mouth. Between bites she said, "Wait for me, John Walter."

"Hurry up, then."

She had a mouth full of gravy, just holding it there when we walked out the door. Uncle Billie and Sam were about halfway up the hill when I saw Sam flip a cigarette off in the ditch. I took Nancy's hand and started pulling her along towards Mr. Martin's house. We hadn't got to the cigarette yet when I saw she wasn't going to make it much farther. Her face was white and she was starting to gag. She pulled her hand out of mine and bent over just as she began puking all the gravy and other stuff she had just had for supper. I went on down the road a few feet to get the cigarette, then remembered my promise to Barney about never picking up butts again and went back to where Nancy kept puking.

"I'm never going to eat gravy again," she said, tears in her eyes and gravy running down her chin. "I hate it. I hate it. I hate it. I hate it."

I gagged a little when I looked at the puke and turned away. But I knew I had to help her and took my old blue handkerchief from my pocket and held it out for her to wipe her mouth and dry her eyes. I gagged again when she started to hand it to me and pointed to the weeds. I could come back and get it tomorrow. After she spit a couple of times to try and get the taste out of her mouth, we went on over to Mr. Martin's.

The next morning, Sam took us home after we had biscuits and gravy with some side meat for breakfast. I grinned at Nancy and took a bite of gravy when nobody was looking. She raised her head just a little and looked away. Aunt Annie didn't make Nancy take any gravy. Neither did Aunt Helen after Nancy told her what had happened.

7

Mom Garner had been sick and in bed all winter. We didn't go up there much because of that. But Mother or Aunt Helen or their sister, Aunt Millie Workman, was there all the time. Dad Garner was there, too, but he needed help from his girls. Aunt Millie couldn't help out much because of her son Valmore Lee. I just thought he was a little goofy, but I reckon somebody had to keep an eye on him all the time. He'd never been able to learn to read much but would talk all the time about things like he knew what he was talking about, hemming and hawing for as long as anybody'd listen. It didn't matter who was talking or what they was saying, he'd butt in and tell a story about something that didn't have anything to do with anything. And he always pestered the girls and wanted to be with them all the time. That made them uncomfortable. Mother said she'd been there the night he was born and "they had to use forceps to get him" was the reason "he wasn't quite right."

"Squeezed his head too hard," she'd said.

Mother would go up to look after Mom a day or two through the week after she got off at the store and from Saturday night until Monday morning. Aunt Helen was there the rest of the time. With neither of them around much and Big only home to sleep most of the time, Nancy and me looked after ourselves and took care of Mary Beth. Madge Lewis, who lived next door to the south, came over about every morning to see that we were getting along okay and to help out. Most of the time she brought a loaf of bread she'd just baked or some oatmeal cookies or something to eat. Other neighbors helped out, too. Miz Hancock across the street did our washing and ironing a couple of times. Russ and Eunice Taylor, who lived next door north, brought a gooseberry pie and chicken and noodles one day. Big liked the way she cooked the chicken and it strung out in broth instead of in hunks like it was with Aunt Helen's.

"How's Eunice do that?" Big asked one evening when he'd come in long after dark and sat at the table with his big arms spread out, shoveling chicken and noodles and mashed potatoes straight into his mouth like he was unloading a load of coal. "You have them big chunks in your chicken an' noodles."

"She cooks it to death, that's all she does, to make it stringy like this," Aunt Helen said, ruffling up a little, I thought. "You don't ever get a piece of chicken. Just these little strings. You like these strings?"

Big winked at me and never said a word. He just kept chewing and shoveling. I liked them, too, and winked back.

Right after the first of February, Mother and Aunt Helen both went up to stay with Mom. Arletta worked Mother's days at the store instead of just helping out when Horsey needed her. Nancy and Mary Beth and me went to one of Mother's and Aunt Helen's cousins to stay for the weekend. We was still there on Monday when Big stopped by in the truck on his way back from Indianapolis to pick us up before we had finished breakfast. Orville Phillips had already gone to work. Martha went out to talk to Big while Leslie, a high school girl who was real pretty like I figured all high school girls was, stayed with us to see that we ate. I cut the hard-fried egg in half, folded each one in half and took them a bite at a time like Big did all the time. Then I gulped the rest of my milk and took the piece of toast and hurried out of the kitchen before Leslie could stop me. She was nice to us and all, but I wanted to see Big.

I might as well have not hurried so much. He was taking us with him. Martha was on her way back to the kitchen with a sack of our clothes in her hand. She handed it to me and told me to go outside with Big. Nancy and Mary Beth came right away, and we all piled in the truck. Nothing was said on the way to Bellair. It was cold in the truck, even with the heater on. I couldn't wait until we got there to get in by the stove, forgetting that nobody had been there in the night to keep the fire going. It was freezing cold in the house. I blew my breath out and saw a stream of smoke-like air leave my mouth like when Big took a drag on a cigarette and blew the smoke out.

I did it a couple of more times while I stood there shaking from the cold. Nancy and Mary Beth had gone in on the couch in the front room and wrapped a big, heavy comforter around them.

I watched Big wad up a newspaper and put some kindling and a corn cob soaked in kerosene in the stove. He took three or four pieces of coal from the bucket in front of the stove and put them in the stove. Then he poured a little kerosene on the coal and lit a match and threw it inside. It was a dark and dreary morning outside and was even more so inside the cold house. Big stood in front of the stove and watched the fire blaze up, giving off some light in the darkness of the winter morning. I could see him staring into the flames and the outline of his thick nose and square chin against them.

"Your grandma died this mornin'," he said finally. "Your mom an' Helen are goin' to help Selva until after the funeral. Then he'll probably come down here for a while. Madge's going to stay with you today while I get this load of coal scooped off, then I'm going to go by an' pick your Aunt Harriet up to help out here."

I stood still. The only sound in the house was the crackling of the kindling as it burned hotly and the coal caught fire. I didn't know what to think. Mom Garner had been sick for a long time. We always went in and said hello to her in the front bedroom where she lay all the time. She was part of the family that was just there. It seemed like I should be sad that she died, but when I thought about how tired she looked all the time, I felt kind of happy for her. She wouldn't be tired no more. But nobody in the family, except a great-grandmother I'd never seen in real life, had died since I could remember. And Mom's dying started me thinking about death and dying. My daddy had been killed long before I was old enough to know about it. There was just a hole in my life that Big and Sam and the fellers around Bellair didn't quite fill. I thought most every day about having Daddy alive and around all the time. That's how I filled the hole. It didn't really do the job, but I'd never known anything else. Then Charlie Kline had gone away and got killed, too. Neither him nor Daddy came home to be buried like Mom'd be buried up to Kickapoo. They was buried way off from Bellair in either direction.

"Did Mom go to heaven?" I asked, mostly to break the silence and quit feeling sorry for myself. Every time I got to feeling like that,

I went to Mother and ended up making her sad and causing her to cry. She had enough on her hands without me adding something else for her to worry about.

"I guess she did," Big said kind of slow. "That's what they say."

He didn't sound too sure, but I reckoned it didn't matter where Mom went. She was gone. Like Daddy. Like Charlie. Like everybody would be someday.

"You fellers are goin' to have to behave yourselves an' help out around here," Big said, standing still now, just staring into the fire as the coal chunks started burning. "Think you can do that?"

I nodded.

We didn't behave or help out after Aunt Harriet got there later that day, though. Nancy, Mary Beth and me stayed in the kitchen with her while she cooked our meals. She was my daddy's twin sister, wasn't married and worked for a judge and his wife in their big house in Casey. She was kind of nervous and wasn't used to being around kids at all, let alone around the three of us and Big, who could be like a kid, too. He looked out after things and wasn't always patient with what happened that didn't go the way he'd had set in his mind.

At supper, Nancy had set the table and run into the front room and told Big it was ready before Aunt Harriet had started making the gravy. Mary Beth and me was already sitting at our places with spoons and forks in our hands. Big took his place at the head of the table and looked over at Aunt Harriet stirring the gravy. "I thought you said it was ready, Nancy," Big said, growling at her a little.

I tapped my fork on the plate the way Aunt Helen said Granddad McElligott did when dinner wasn't ready at 11:30 on the dot the way he wanted it. The ringing sound made Aunt Harriet jump. Nancy and Mary Beth started tapping their forks on the plates in time together. I joined them and started chanting, "When's it goin' to be ready? When's it goin' to be ready?" over and over.

"Oh, please stop that," Aunt Harriet said, smiling kind of weak and looking like she might cry.

We kept it up. Big smiled and picked up his fork. It was the first real smile I'd seen on his face for a while. He didn't look mad or sad or anything like that most of the time. He just didn't smile. He smiled more and bounced his fork off of his plate along with us.

"That's enough," he said after a little bit, laying his fork on his plate and smiling again. "Now you fellers are goin' to have to behave better than this. Your Aunt Harriet can't take a bunch of wild Indians in here while she's cookin' supper. She's techy. One time when we was just little kids up home, Mom told her an' your daddy to help me carry the milk up to the house."

Big looked over at me when he said Daddy, and I sat up straight. Nancy and Mary Beth looked over at me as he came alive in my eyes.

"They had a full bucket of milk between 'em," Big said. "About halfway across the barnyard, he held a little toad he'd caught that evenin' an' held it up in front of her face. She like to jumped to the moon, dropped her side of the milk pail an' lit out arunnin' for the house like somethin' was after her. Mom was mad at us for spillin' the milk. That was too bad, but old Bill an' me laughed an' laughed 'bout the way old Harriet took off. Jesse Owens couldn't have caught her 'fore she got to the house."

We'd stopped the rattling on the plates when Big told us to and he started telling the story. I never got tired of hearing stories about my daddy. This one was one I hadn't heard before. I looked over at Aunt Harriet as she was pouring the gravy into the dish. Tears was streaming down her face. By the time she brought the gravy to the table, she was really crying. I didn't know what to do. We'd just been playing. I hadn't meant to bother her that much.

"What'n the devil is the matter with you?" Big asked. "These kids are just bein' kids. They don't mean nothin'."

"I'm not used to that," Aunt Harriet said, down to a little sniffle. "I'm used to more quiet."

"Well, it ain't quiet around here. You better get used to it or go on back to Casey, if you can't do better 'n that."

"That's not the only thing, either," Aunt Harriet said, starting to cry again. This time she was sobbing and ran out of the kitchen.

Big followed her out. He was gone for a few minutes. When he came back, his face looked tired and he wasn't smiling. "You fellers calm down a little. Harriet's upset with things, the way we've been actin' an' hearin' that story about her an' your daddy. She's always been a little flighty. But it's worse 'n it was when we was up home."

She came back in the kitchen after a bit, sat down and picked at her food while the rest of us talked. She didn't say much for the rest of the night, but she later walked me to my bed and tucked me in. When she bent over to kiss me on the forehead, I felt a tear splash down on my face. "Your daddy would be a right smart proud of you, John Walter," she said as another tear hit me.

I thought of Daddy for a long time before I went to sleep. Laying there awake, just thinking, I never thought about picking my belly button and sucking my lip. And I never did much after that night. Never even thought of the belly buttons like I did most nights. I had more of an idea about the belly buttons getting together and somebody coming and what was going on, but none of that mattered right then. I missed Daddy and thought how it'd have been having him here in our own house and having a brother.

After a while, I started to think my little prayer, "Now I lay me down to sleep," but I stopped short and started whispering, "Barney Ford was right: 'We're just big old fuckin' hogs, wallowin' around in our own shit. The world's shit. Everybody's shit. That's all there is to it.' What kind of a fuckin' world an' what kind of a fuckin' god would take a boy's daddy away from him like they done me an' let me grow up like I'm agrowin' up?"

"Oh, I don't mean that, honest I don't," I said, backing off from the way I was feeling. "I mean a good god. How could a good god let a boy's daddy get killed an' let the boy never know what it's like to have a daddy? I miss him so much I don't know what to do sometimes. An' I never even knowed him. I need him, God, I need him. Please, please, God, please, please. ..."

Mother and the rest of her family went off to the funeral home to make the arrangements. They had to pick out some clothes, the casket and all that stuff I'd never thought about before. The only funeral I'd been to was for my daddy's grandma, Grandma Mary Elizabeth's mother, died right after the war. I didn't know a thing about her. She lived with one of Daddy's aunts over in Indiana, and I'd never seen her that I remember. But we all piled in Big's old Ford coupe and followed a whole bunch of the rest of the family over south of Terre Haute. I reckon we went to that aunt's — Aunt Polly I think it was — house and met everybody to follow the hearse back to Wesley Chapel where they had the funeral and buried her. The only thing I remember is the real good sandwiches Aunt Helen made and that we ate on the slow ride through the windy hills in that part of Indiana.

"It's sure pretty country," Big said while we ate.

Mother had brought some spiced ham from the store. We'd never had anything like it before. All we usually had when we had lunch meat was baloney. It was okay with some cheese and crackers like Big got us up at the store sometimes. But it wasn't nothing like that spiced ham. Aunt Helen had got store-bought bread, put mayonnaise, lettuce from the garden and a couple of pieces of the meat on each sandwich. That's what I remembered most about my great-grandma dying.

It was different with Mom Garner. The last time I'd seen her she'd laid there in bed with hardly enough strength to raise her hand to say hello. "I'm tired," she said and smiled a little. She looked a lot better when they brought her back to Dad's place from the funeral home and brought her in through the front door and into the living room. I knew she was dead. But she looked better. She didn't look tired anymore. She just looked like she was asleep. And everybody else looked better, too. They was pretty dressed up for everyday and just looked tired and a little sad, except Valmore Lee. He was dressed in a little suit and pranced through the living room around through the kitchen and completed the circle through the dining room and back to the casket, laughing and talking to anybody who'd listen.

At the funeral up to Kickapoo, it'd been pretty somber until after the preacher had finished his preaching. Then everybody started crying and sobbing. One woman I hadn't been around only once or twice started crying and carrying on like I'd never seen anybody do. Well, maybe a kid. But not a grown up. She cried out, "Oh, Jesus," sobbed and let out a high-pitched yell and done the same things over again in various ways and at different times. She was Uncle Homer's sister, Audrey Ralston. She put me in the mind of Valmore Lee the way she looked, but not the way she acted. He was a good kid when anybody'd pay attention to him. And I'd never seen him act like his old aunt, crying and carrying on. I couldn't cry, though. I tried but I couldn't even get tears to come to save my life. Mom looked real peaceful up there in front of us, and I didn't see any reason to cry about that.

I only felt a little sad for Mother and the rest of them that was crying. I knew how much Mother loved Mom and how hard things was what with Daddy gone and all. Besides that, Dad was going to be there on his place all alone. That bothered all his girls. I'd heard Mother and them talking about where he was going to stay after the funeral.

"Why, I'm goin' to stay right here," he'd said. "It's where my home is, it's where I live."

His girls didn't like that idea, I knew. They didn't think he could take care of himself. He seemed pretty good to me, still kept horses and worked like he always did. I told them that when I got a little older I could stay with him and help him take care of things. Nancy and Mary Beth, and even Valmore Lee, could come up and stay to help out at times. Nobody seemed to hear what I'd said, I remembered, as we walked behind the casket to the graveyard.

That hole in the ground bothered me more than anything. I didn't know what else they could do with a feller when he died, but putting someone down in a hole and covering him up didn't sound right. Albert Matthews, whose father wasn't dead but might as well have been, was always talking about dying and getting buried down in the "cold, cold ground" and having "the worms crawl in and the worms crawl out" when we was out playing. The whole idea was kind of spooky to me. And it was just the beginning of the funerals I'd be going to. Got so I marked time with people dying and their funerals. "That was the winter Mom died," I'd say or something like that, the way Mother did all the way back to her grandparents when she was a little girl.

Big had decided to take his big old grain-hauling truck with tandem wheels under the back out West to follow the wheat harvest. Ralph Barber, whose wife was from Kansas wheat country, had gone out the year before. Ralph was taking two trucks and Gene Shaw, who used to drive for Big, to the Texas Panhandle at the end of May and would go on at least to the Canadian line through the first of September. I wanted to go in the worst way. And I wasn't alone.

"I thought I might get to go," Sam told Matt McIntyre in the Highway Cafe in Oblong one morning when we was eating breakfast. "But Big says he's goin'."

And he did. He left early one morning before we left for school. Nancy and Mary Beth and Aunt Helen was all crying when he pulled away. Mother even looked a little sad. I had some tears in my eyes that I turned away so nobody could see. I was crying because I had thought right up until the night before that I still had a chance of going.

"Now I've told you before, Sedwick," Big said at the supper table, "that you can't go. You've got to stay here an' take care of the women. I want you to keep the yard mowed an' help Helen an' your mother. You're big enough to start helpin' out around here. Sam can keep the truckin' going, but he ain't goin' to mow the yard or burn the trash."

I knew I could go with Sam a lot. But I hated to mow the yard. It was boring. We had an old mower that I could hardly push through the grass unless it was mowed every week and then I got tired right away. I always planned to be up and ready to go by the time Sam stopped by to gas up so I'd get out of all the other little piddly jobs besides mowing Aunt Helen had for me to do. With the big saddle tank Big always had made and added to his trucks, Sam didn't always stop by regularly each day. So Aunt Helen kept me busy burning the trash, taking tin cans out to the junk, going to the store for a loaf of bread and whatever came up. She even tried to get me to help Nancy dust and work in the house. That's when I'd run out and grab the old mower and take off on a tear through the yard. I never got the yard all the way mowed the whole summer. The front part was just two little squares on each side of the sidewalk and was easy to keep mowed. The sides and back always needed mowing somewhere. It wasn't that I wanted it that way. I wanted Big to be proud of me and felt obligated to him to keep the yard mowed. With everything else, it was a big job.

One morning when I thought I might mow until I got the job done, I saw Sam turn the corner up by Albert Matthews' house. By the time he'd passed Andy Utley's and Russ Taylor's houses, I'd already left the mower with the handle bouncing up and down and was around to the gas tank.

"Where you goin' this mornin', Sam?" I asked before he stepped down off the running board. "I'm ready to do some truckin'."

"You are?" he said, grinning at me through the smoke drifting up from the Lucky Strike in the corner of his mouth. He flipped it off in the grass a good truck's length away. "I got a couple of loads of corn to scoop out of a corn crib over across the river at Hutsonville. You can come along an' help a little."

I could hardly wait to jump up in the truck and get started. Sam had already had a tire fixed at The Corners and cleaned the truck bed out to haul the corn. He hadn't had breakfast so Aunt Helen was fixing him bacon and eggs. I wanted a smoke real bad and decided Barney wouldn't care if I smoked Sam's cigarette. So I waited outside to take a couple of drags off his cigarette, then went inside and washed my mouth out so Aunt Helen wouldn't smell the smoke. And I had another piece of bacon and an egg fried in hot grease splashed up on it like Sam and Big both liked their eggs fixed. I didn't feel good about picking up butts, though, when I'd promised at Barney's funeral I never would again. I had to figure a way to keep my own smokes around so I could get at them and not go around thinking about picking up somebody else's butts.

"Can I have a little coffee, Aunt Helen?" I asked when she had the food on the table. "Just a little."

"I reckon," she said, "but just a little."

She started to fill the cup up with milk. I knew she'd put in a little sugar, too. That's the way they all drank coffee.

"I don't want anything in it," I said. "Sam don't drink nothin' in his, do you?"

"Nope," he said, taking a third of an egg in a bite.

"Don't you like cream and sugar?"

"Used to. Got used to not havin' it, though. But you'd better start eatin' that egg if you're goin' with me, Sedwick."

I folded a big piece of my egg like Sam had done and shoved it in my mouth like I thought any other truck driver would. Aunt Helen said she could fix us sandwiches or something else if we'd come by.

"No," Sam said before we walked out to the truck, "we'll get somethin' in Hutsonville between loads. I'll be back by here about supper time."

We'd just turned out on the Bellair-Corners Road when he looked over at me and said, "Well, Sedwick, I finally got that car I've been waitin' for. Going to go pick it up Saturday."

Sam had told me about the car before. He'd signed up for a new Dodge right after he came home from the war and thought he'd get it a long time ago. I didn't quite understand why it took so long.

"Did you have to save the money before you got the car?"

"No, I've had the money in the bank, drawin' interest since I got home from the Army. They wasn't geared up to make enough cars. Them things take awhile. They're gettin' caught up now."

"How'd you get the money saved up?" I asked, remembering Big saying he couldn't afford a new car. "Takes a lot of money to buy a new car, don't it?"

"Reckon so."

"How'd you save the money?"

"That's a long story," Sam said, smiling a little.

"Tell me."

"Well, I'll make it short. Just don't go tellin' what I tell you. This old boy, Kentuck, down to Robinson, was in my outfit. He was what you call a card shark and gambler. Didn't make no difference whether it was cards or dice or some kind of bet, old Kentuck was always right there in the thick of things. I'd loaned him money since we'd started trainin' together, an' he'd always paid me back an' then some. After the war was over an' we started for home, everybody had a lot of money in back pay. Wasn't no place to spend it, either.

"'There's goin' to be some good games from here on all the way back to the States,' Kentuck told me one day awhile before we boarded ship. 'An' I plan to take some of it back to Robinson, Illinois. You keep backin' me, Mac, an' hold some money for me, an' you'll do okay.' I knew that was right. I just didn't know how much he'd win. Or how much I'd get. He'd clean up in one place an' then go to the next. Winners in the companies would go to the battalion games; winners there would go up to regiment an' so on. Kentuck'd win a bunch an' drop some off for me to hang onto an' then take off for the next game. They'd go on for days before the winners would go off lookin' for more. Sometimes he'd come back an' get a thousand dollars or so. But mostly he'd just drop it off for me an' a couple of others to hold an' help out if he needed any. By the time we hit New York, I 'magine old Kentuck had better 'n thirty grand stashed away. That's where I got the money to buy the car. Couple people asked him how much he brought home, but he'd never say. Never say how much he gave to the fellers that helped him, either. He'd just say, 'They was glad they knowed me.' An' that was right. I was sure glad."

Neither one of us said anything for a while. I didn't know why Sam didn't say anything, but I couldn't say anything. The story he told me was more exciting than anything I could imagine. Even the poker games in the saloons in the western books I started reading where the rancher lost his spread or somebody lost a herd of cattle at the poker table wasn't as exciting. That was in a book. Sam was telling me real stories that he'd lived, and he made them clear in my mind. Pictures of a bunch of men sitting around on the floor or wherever they could find a place to play, dealing cards on a blanket and holding handfuls of money, ran through my head. My daddy's face flashed across my mind. I wondered if he'd had stories like that to tell.

I didn't ever remember crossing the Hutsonville Bridge before. Anytime I'd been in Hutsonville, we'd turn south and go down the west bank of the Wabash to the gravel pit. When we'd stop at the stop sign right at the foot of the bridge and start to turn, I'd look to the center of the bridge where it started heading down to Indiana and wish the gravel pit was on the other side. Now we was crossing it. And it was like the Golden Gate Bridge in San Francisco to me. I sat up on the edge of the seat and looked both ways. The water was bank high and rising.

"Looks like we'll about have time to get them two loads hauled before the river gets clear out of the banks," Sam said. "Wish you could scoop some corn."

"I reckon I can," I said. "Got another scoop?"

Sam shook his head and grinned great big. I reckoned I could help him out somehow and told him so at the crib. It was one of them old-time corn cribs that was made in horse-and-wagon days. Big told me he'd shucked a lot of corn with a team of horses, then drove it into one of these cribs and scooped it off in the cribs on either side. That worked fine, he said, because all the wagons had to do was fit in the crib drive. It was a lot different with big old trucks. They barely fit in the drive, and the doors would hardly open. And three two-inch, two-foot-by-ten-foot rafters or cross beams stretched just at the top of the side boards on the grain bed. Sam squeezed his way out of the truck and made his way up the side of the crib to get in the bed for the scoop. He climbed out of the bed and over into the top of the corn in the crib and smacked his head on the sill as he ducked under it.

"Goddamnsonuvabitch," he said real loud and rubbed his head. "Watch them sonuvabitchin' things. They'll knock you out."

I tried to crawl up the side of the crib, but my toes wouldn't fit between the slats. So I went up the front of the grain bed and followed Sam into the crib on his side. I got in the crib and went on my hands and knees to the other end. While he tried to get a shovel full, I threw ears with both hands. For a while I reckon I was throwing about as much corn in the truck as him. He couldn't get his scoop shovel down in the ear corn and finally had to fill the scoop with his hand. When he got to where the corn filled the scoop a little easier, the corn started flying. I'd kick the corn a little to roll it down and fill his scoop each time.

"Thataboy," he said when I got it figured out just how hard to kick and he got a rhythm going. "We'll get this sonuvabitch goin' yet."

The sweat was beginning to roll down his cheeks, and his green shirt started getting darker in spots. Each time he moved forward or backward in the crib he had to dodge the cross beams that supported the crib. After hitting his head first off, Sam had stayed away from the beams. It wasn't until we started the second load that he hit his head again. This time he grabbed his scoop from where it'd fallen, swung around on one leg while leaning on the scoop and kicked the beam a couple of times. "Goddamnsonuvabitchinfuckin' bastard," he'd say, hollering and crying, then say the same thing or something like it over again so fast I couldn't tell for sure what he said. His eyes was opened wide and kind of desperate looking. They was glazed over a little, but there was tears in them, too. I couldn't tell if the tears was from the hurt or something else. I could just tell they was there. "I'll kick the goddamn dog shit out of you, you cocksuckinsonuvabitch, you."

Then he stopped kicking and took a swing at the beam with the scoop. I didn't see that he was hurting the beam much. But it must have made him feel better. After a while he leaned on the shovel like a cane, fished a Lucky Strike from his shirt pocket and took a matchbook from his pocket. He stood there smoking, taking long, slow drags on the cigarette and staring down into the corn in the crib. The matchbook was from Wilson's Truck Stop in Seelyville, Indiana. Sam had showed me this one earlier. He'd been bringing me matchbooks from wherever he picked them up and others from all around the country he'd find. Big and others saved them for me, too. But Sam was the one who was always bringing me a new one, sometimes from as far away as New York or Florida.

"Here, Sedwick," he said after a minute, "here's you another matchbook. We better get this corn scooped an' hauled away before I get knocked out or kill myself. Don't never make a livin' like this."

I nodded, but I reckoned I would someday when I grew up. That was taking longer than I wanted, but I knew I wanted to go a lot of places and do a lot of things before I came back to drive Big's trucks. While I helped Sam as much as I could, I thought about things I wanted to do. The way Daddy and Sam and lots of others I knew had done in the war was what I wanted to do. I didn't want to die and hoped if I did that I didn't leave a little boy behind to grow up without me. I turned my head so Sam wouldn't see my eyes watering like I'd seen his doing.

By the time we got the second load unloaded and was headed home, it was getting along towards supper time. We'd stopped at a little store just before we crossed the river and got a Pepsi Cola. I was hungry then and wanted a candy bar but didn't ask. On the way home my stomach started growling like an old bear. I hoped Aunt Helen had supper ready like I figured she would. But when Sam and me walked through the door, I didn't smell anything cooking. Nancy and Mary Beth was real quiet while they played in the front room. Mother and Aunt Helen was sitting at the kitchen table. I couldn't hear a sound from them either and ran on into the kitchen. Both of them looked around at me. I stopped short at the door. They'd both been crying.

"What's wrong?" I asked.

"Oh, John Walter," Mother said, holding out her arms to me and holding me real tight when I'd gone to her, and sobbing. "They're sending your daddy home to us. That's what I wanted and now it's going to happen."

A picture of Daddy walking through the front door flashed through my mind before it registered what Mother meant. Sam stood behind us at the doorway. I saw his jaw muscles moving back and forth when I looked around at him. His face looked pretty grim. Aunt Helen stayed sitting at the table. I could see her looking at me and reached out for her hand. She started crying and squeezed my hand real tight.

Nobody ever said much about Daddy, but I knew everybody thought about him. I did every day and got the big picture in his uniform out of the picture album to look at all the time. One day when Mother caught me looking, she took me in her arms just like she was now and told me she thought about him all the time, too. It was then that she showed me the telegram she got when he got killed. It was short and to the point:

Mrs. Lorene McElligott
Route 2 Bellair Illinois

Deeply regret to inform you that your husband, Sgt. William S. McElligott was killed in action on 25 October 1942 while engaged in fierce fighting with Japanese forces in the Lunga area on Guadalcanal in the Solomon Islands. You have my deepest sympathy for your loss but must know that Sgt. McElligott gave his life in the performance of his duty and service of his country.

Thomas Holcomb General USMC Commandant of the Marine Corps

I felt real proud when I read the telegram. Mother probably was proud, too, but she was hurt, angry and proud all rolled into one. She said at first she sat alone and just cried. Then for a while she would see other people who had family in the war and get bitter towards them because Daddy was killed and their boy or husband was still living.

"Your Aunt Helen and me begged Bob not to go in," she said, crying and hugging me harder when she'd showed me the telegram. "He was bound and determined that he was going out and enlist. When they finally called him and he went and took his physical in Chicago, I prayed he didn't have to go. Thank God he didn't. I couldn't stand for Helen and the girls to have to go through what I have and what you have. My whole life changed forever when I got that telegram. Bill and you was my life. Part of it was gone forever."

And now they was sending him home to us, I thought.

"When?" I heard Sam say and backed out of Mother's arms.

"He gets into Robinson next Wednesday."

"That's not quite a week. What about Big?"

"I just got a letter from him today," Aunt Helen said. "He had a wreck out in Sharon Springs, Kansas, last week and his truck won't be fixed for another week."

My heart began beating faster right away, and I felt weak in the knees. I couldn't imagine anything happening to Big. What would we all do if he got hurt bad or even killed? I wondered.

"Get ahold of him," Sam said. "He'll want to be here. What happened?"

"He didn't say much. Just that he'd had a wreck, wasn't hurt but the truck would be in the garage for a couple of weeks. He's staying in Sharon Springs."

Big caught a bus home minutes after Aunt Helen got ahold of him, he said later. We picked him up in Casey the next day and filled him in on what we knew. Nobody had told Granddad and Grandma McElligott. We headed straight for their house from the bus station. On the way, Big told us about the wreck.

"It was rainin' to beat the band," he said, "an' I was goin' down a long old hill loaded with five hundred bushels of wheat. You couldn't see more 'n a hundred yards ahead. Right at the bottom of the hill, some feller in a car had run off the road, then jerked it back on the road an' across in front of Ralph an' hit him. The car spun around an' hit Gene, who was right behind Ralph. There was a car between me an' Gene. It banged into the back of his truck. By the time I got there an' saw what was happening, a couple of cars from the other way had smashed whatever was in front of them. I knew I couldn't stop before I crashed into somebody, so I geared her down as much as I could, then headed her out across the ditch an' through a barbed-wire fence. Bunged the front end up pretty bad an' sprung the frame so it'll never be fixed right, I'm afraid. Blew three tires on one side of the tandem."

"Anybody get hurt?" Aunt Helen asked.

"Not right off. But it started rainin' even harder when I walked down to the bottom of the hill where everybody was standin' around. The feller in the car that caused the wreck was standin' out in the middle of the road tellin' us what had happened, an' a semi couldn't stop an' came barrelin' through. It hit the feller before he could get off the road. Knocked him asailin'. He must've flew twenty feet through the air an' landed off in the ditch. Old boy that was a medic in the war got there first an' said his neck was broke."

Big stopped the old Ford in front of the gate, and we walked up the boards in the grass leading up to my grandparents' old house.

It was a simple two-story farm house similar to dozens of others I saw on trips around the country with Big and Sam. Granddad hadn't painted the house in nearly twenty years, and the weather boards and window sills was a paintless dull gray just like the barns and the granary where I went every time I visited to see my daddy's initials carved on the wall on the outside of the wheat bin: "WSM." Big's and George's and Vernon's and even Sam's daddy Vincent's was carved there, too. But seeing my daddy's initials there and knowing that he'd done it himself back when he was a boy growing up here was always a special thing for me. I could just see Daddy, a little old boy in overalls with an old pocket knife, carving his initials in the side of that granary. That picture was etched forever in my mind's eye.

Granddad was sitting in the same old rocking chair he'd had since back then, a bucket of ashes beside him to spit in when he had a chew of tobacco in his mouth, which was most of the time. Grandma was sitting in her rocking chair on the other side of the library stand with the coal oil lamp lighting the room against the fading light of the late evening. She never said a word after Big started telling them what we had come to tell them. I did see her reach up under her glasses once and wipe first one eye, then the other. After Big finished, she just sat there with her hands folded on her lap and stared out the window across the room from her into the darkness.

"What in thundernation they shippin' him back now for?" Granddad said, talking much louder than he had to for everybody to hear. A little tobacco juice dripped at the corners of his mouth and lined his lips. He only had a tooth here and there that you could see when he talked. Except for a few wisps of white hair, he was bald down to his sparse beard. "They ought to 'ave left him over yonder where he was killed. Ain't nothin' left of him but bones."

"I know, John," Mother said quietly, "but something of him's coming home. And I'd like to see him buried here and put to rest."

"Yes," Grandma said. "That's best."

That seemed to settle it for Granddad.

"I reckon we can bury him over at Wesley Chapel with the rest of us that got up here. There's room over on the side there by my folks an' some of the kids that didn't make it long."

"That all right with you, Lorene?" Big asked.

She nodded and squeezed my hand a little harder. I looked around the room at my family. Everybody was quiet for a little bit. The lamp on the library stand between Granddad and Grandma lit up the closest side of their faces. The rest of us sat out in the darker part of the room and looked toward them. This whole day was pretty well stamped in my brain forever. What was happening was happening and nothing would ever change it, I knew. But I wondered if everything just happened and then flew away into the sky right off, never to be seen or heard of again except in the stories told over and over again. In my mind's eye, I could always see Abraham Lincoln giving the "Gettysburg Address" that I'd been hearing about at school. He was standing up on a platform looking out over the battlefield he was dedicating, saying, "Four score and seven years ago, our forefathers brought forth on this continent, a new nation, conceived in liberty and dedicated to the proposition that all men are created equal. Now we are met on a great battlefield of that war, testing whether that nation may long endure. We cannot dedicate, we cannot consecrate, we cannot hallow this ground. The brave men, living and dead, have consecrated it far above our poor power to add or to detract. The world will little note nor long remember what we say here, but it can never forget what they did here. ..."

I couldn't remember anymore of it. We didn't have to memorize it at school, but Mother and Aunt Helen had had to when they went to school. So I was memorizing it, too. That was hard for me. Seemed like there would be some way to bring words back somehow so you could hear them again. When you said them, it seemed that they went off into the air waves just like they did over the radio. And so they was out there somewhere, waiting for somebody to bring them back and play them over the radio. Maybe it'd even be possible to pick up Daddy when he was killed on Guadalcanal. I wanted to ask if anybody thought that was possible to invent some machine to do that, but Big said it was time to go. It was probably just as well, I thought.

"We'll help Lorene get things set up, Pop," Big said and walked over to Grandma. He took her outstretched hand in his and held it. She patted his top hand lightly but kept looking out through the window.

For the next few days, I stayed close to Mother. Arletta worked for her at the store while we all took care of some of the details in getting my daddy buried back on American soil. That seemed to be important to everybody. I wasn't sure what to think. It wouldn't give me a daddy, but I reckoned it would bring mine home to rest like everybody said. They was sending Charlie Klinc's body home from Germany, too, Big said he'd heard in Casey where Charlie's folks had moved after he'd been killed. And Mother had heard that Jack Vaught from over by The Corners who'd been killed on Iwo Jima wasn't coming home. At least he was still in the cemetery on Saipan where he'd been buried after he'd died on the ship hospital just off the island, she said, and she'd heard his folks was not bringing him home.

"I wouldn't want that for Bill," she said to Aunt Helen when they talked about it. "I had to bring him home so some of him is here close by."

I reckoned that was the way I felt, too. It'd be more than I'd ever had of him, even if it seemed like a lot of trouble to go to just to get what was left of Daddy home. But it seemed to make Mother happier. That was worth a whole lot to me.

Somebody at the funeral home in The Corners picked the casket up at the train station in Robinson and took care of the arrangements with Big and Mother. She said it'd be better if I stayed with Aunt Helen while they went to the funeral home. I didn't agree, but I saw the look in her eyes and didn't say anything. For her, I was beginning to think they should have left Daddy's body overseas. It didn't seem to be bringing her anything but misery as far as I could tell. She cried a lot at night.

At the funeral home the night of the visitation, she stood around from the casket first in line and met people coming to pay their respects. She never cried a bit and even managed a smile now and then. I looked down at Grandma, a few of her sons and daughters away from us. She had the same quiet look on her face she always had. I could never tell how she felt by looking at her. She showed that by what she said, how she said it and what she did. I felt comfort from her way of doing things.

I looked around the room at the long line of folks moving towards the casket in the front of the room. It was draped with an American flag and had a picture of Daddy in Marine Corps dress blues and some ribbons resting on the top of the casket. A couple of the men had on Army uniforms that looked like they were a little too small for them.

Both of them had a single ribbon above their breast pocket. I asked Sam about that later because Daddy had five more ribbons than that on the casket.

"It's the Army's Combat Infantryman's Badge," Sam said. "It's the only one a lot of the fellers'll wear that was in the Army."

I remembered him saying something about that when he was telling me about not taking a million dollars for what he'd seen, but he wouldn't take a million dollars to do it again. That's probably what a lot of the fellers I knew who had been in the war and was coming through the line thought, too, I reckoned. Mother and I shook hands with friends and neighbors from all around the community and old soldiers from all over came through and gave us a rough hand and a pat on the shoulder or the arm. I saw Smokey Cottrell, Brad Irons, Merv Gallagher, Wes Davis, Jim Richards, Wick Hardway, Chris Matthews and a whole lot more like the Fords, the Larsons, the Taylors and the Hamiltons, who'd had boys in the war, mixed in with everybody else that came through the line. Just like at Barney's funeral, I thought.

Everybody had pretty grim-looking faces while they stood in line. Their looks softened when they got to talking to us. They was all real kind. The ones that had been in the war looked down at me, and all said more or less the same thing about Daddy, about what a good man he was and how proud they'd been to know him.

"Old Mark Twain," Smokey said when he got to me and took my hand, "had one of his characters say that we should try to live so 'that when we come to die even the undertaker will be sorry.' I reckon that's about the way your daddy lived his life. We're all sorry he's gone."

I'd promised myself I wasn't going to cry, but that brought tears to my eyes. Other fellers'd say a word or two about me making my daddy proud of me and go on down the line.

Sam told me later they meant for me to be honest and true like my daddy had been. "He wouldn't take a nickel from nobody," Sam said. "You could go to the bank on what he said. An' you never had to worry about him doin' his part. He'd do that an' more."

That and what Smokey said made me feel much better than anything I heard the preacher say at the funeral up at Wesley Chapel. He talked about God and his plan for us not being for our understanding, that our reward was in heaven. I didn't know about that. All I knew was that my mother was sad, sitting there with tears streaming down her face. Big was sitting with his face in his hand. Everybody else had long looks on their faces. I'd never known anything else but Daddy being dead. He'd got killed more than six years ago. I was only two years old then and couldn't even remember seeing him when he came home on leave. So I didn't have this feeling everybody else had. I only had a hole in my life that was always there and that would always be there. Neither the preacher nor God nor anybody else could do a thing about that. But I knew I'd always try to do what'd make him proud from now on. I figured I owed him that.

After we all sang *Amazing Grace*, which Mother said was Daddy's favorite gospel song, we all followed six pall bearers, men he'd grown up with, carrying the casket to the cemetery across the road from the church. They placed the casket over the grave and two of them took the flag from the casket and folded it into a neat triangle and gave it to the Marine escort. He brought it over to Mother and me, stopped right in front of her, bent over and said quietly, "On behalf of the United States government, I'd like to present you with the flag of the country that your husband, Sgt. William S. McElligott, served so well. ..."

Tears was running down Mother's cheeks, and I didn't hear the rest of what the Marine was saying. He handed her the flag and marched out to the American Legion squad a few yards away where one of the Legion fellers gave some orders I couldn't understand. The men in the squad pointed their rifles toward the sky and away from the grave. Three different times the rifles fired together. I flinched every time. While the last shots was echoing off across the field, two buglers, one close and one off a ways, started playing *Taps*. The notes floated out slowly, low and mournful like, echoing back and forth across the cemetery and the fields before they faded away, and it was real quiet.

Daddy was back home.

8

Granddad didn't last too long after the funeral. He'd been in bed more and more over the last couple of years. Grandma said he "went down-hill fast" after they shipped what was left of Daddy back home and we buried him. Some days she said Granddad'd be able to sit up and get along "tolable"; other days she said he couldn't sit up and didn't know who anybody was or even where he was. Then one day he just went to bed and never got up again. Big and Aunt Annie and the rest of the family started sitting up with him through the night so Grandma could get some rest until it was over. She called Big a little after midnight one night and told him that Granddad had just died. The phone ringing and Big running through the house to answer it liked to scare me to death. I sat straight up in bed, not sure what was happening.

"Pop passed away," I finally heard Big tell Aunt Helen a couple of minutes later. "I'm goin' to go on up an' sit with 'em 'til mornin' an' get help get things taken care of."

So there was another funeral to go to. Granddad was buried while Daddy's grave was still a bare mound of dirt with no marker there yet. Big sat by Grandma at the funeral and took her by the arm as everybody followed the casket across the road to be buried. Everybody seemed a little teary-eyed, except Big and Grandma. They kept a stony face and never cried a bit.

"I reckon your granddad can rest now, son," Grandma told me later. "He had a hard time of it these last few years. I thought he was going to go when we lost your daddy, but he kept hanging on. Didn't seem like they was anything I could do for him."

"I reckon you done the best you could, Grandma," I said.

She looked down at me and smiled a little. But I saw her eyes was watery. I'd never seen that before. She turned away and took off her glasses, wiping her eyes with the back of her hands. Then she put her glasses back on and nodded.

Charlie Kline's funeral shortly after Granddad's was pretty much the same as Daddy's, except that an Army feller came in for Charlie rather than a Marine. Charlie's body was shipped to the funeral home in Casey rather than to The Corners like they did Daddy's. And the funeral was in Bellair at the Church of Christ. I'd never been in it before. It wasn't the church in town that we went to when we went to church, which wasn't often. We went down to the UB, or United Brethren Church, where most of the women who met every Thursday at the old post office building for a Ladies' Aid meeting attended church. Most of the women was part of the war mothers' bunch that met all through the war and had suppers up above the store when one of their boys was going away to war or coming home from it. Old Horsey Matthews had stopped that right about the time the war was over because he got afraid that so many people in the upstairs of the store was going to cause it to break through and hurt a bunch of people. Some fellers thought he just used that as an excuse not to have the meetings anymore. He went to the Church of Christ but didn't go to Charlie's funeral for some reason. He did shut the store down during the service and stayed inside until it was over. I saw a car drive up while we was all standing outside waiting for the pall bearers to carry the casket out. The feller and his wife stood at the door a minute, then went in just as Charlie was being carried out to the hearse. I reckon old Horsey couldn't turn down a customer.

Everybody stood around outside the church after the funeral, waiting for the casket to come out and watching each other. One of Charlie's aunts came walking out, wearing a bright red coat. Some woman standing behind me whispered loud enough fellers standing right around us could all hear her, "I thought you wore black at funerals." Nobody said anything. Richard and Jerry's Uncle Ted Childers stood back in his old Army uniform that was so tight that the buttons looked like they was about to break anytime and saluted when the casket and the pall bearers came through the double doors.

The church inside had been pretty much the same as the UB. But I saw right off that there wasn't any organ or piano like they had down at the UB for the women to play when everybody sang. Mother said the Church of Christ didn't believe in having a piano for some reason or another. I didn't understand that and didn't see what the idea was about this church being so much better. It was a little newer and had been built new right where it stood. But Russ Taylor told me one day that they had moved the old log school in from the hill out on the angling road to the cemetery and made it into the UB church. How they got it moved and set in place made it a more interesting place to me. Russ said they just lifted the school building up and set it down on skids and a four-horse team of mules pulled it out to where it sits next to the abandoned, old two-story schoolhouse where he went to school and Joe Marshall used as a barn now.

"We watched out the upstairs windows all day," he said, lighting a Chesterfield and blowing the smoke up and away on the first drag.

"Can I have one of them, Russ?" I asked.

"No, you can't have 'one of them,' you little shit," he said, laughing a little. "I see you pickin' up Big's an' Sam's cigarettes."

"I haven't picked up somebody's butt for a long time,"

"I saw you pick one up here while back."

"Yeah, once. That's the first time since Barney Ford got killed."

"Well, that don't matter. You ain't gettin' no cigarette from me. Your mother an' Helen would shoot me."

"No, they wouldn't. They wouldn't know."

"Oh, they'd know," he said and went back to his story. "But we watched them set that old schoolhouse on the skids an' drag her down the road. They took a wide turn at the corner an' brought her on down past us an' set her down on the foundation. It was somethin' to see."

I reckoned it was. It was a bit easier for me to picture what Russ was telling me because Arthur Hamilton had told a bunch of us up on the store porch how they'd built the store on skids, then rolled it in on the foundation. But they never pulled it down the road. That kind of building had some history to it.

And although I couldn't say for sure, there was just as much religion and God going on there in the UB as anywhere. I just couldn't find much. Mother and Aunt Helen had taken me and Nancy and

Mary Beth to the revival meetings down there. Big wasn't home to go, but he wouldn't, anyway. That wasn't his church, he said, and he just didn't ever go to church. I didn't know why. He'd sit home and read western books on Sunday morning. I couldn't imagine him at the revival meetings. I didn't feel quite comfortable. But the last night of the revival when the preacher asked for people to come to the altar and accept Jesus, I wanted to be with everybody else and went down and knelt down with them. There was young and old there, some getting saved like me and some of the already saved women there to help us get the job done. I thought maybe I'd feel something come over me. But I didn't, even when Verlie Matthews cried and wailed in my ear that she felt God in me. I figured she knew something I didn't, because I didn't feel a thing that I thought was even close to being God.

I didn't know if they ever had anything like that in the Church of Christ, but I doubted that they did. It just didn't seem like what would go on in that church, when they didn't even have a piano. The funeral for Charlie had been somber and serious, much like I imagined the church services would be but much like Daddy's had been, too. The preacher just talked lots quieter than preachers usually talk, I thought. And the quiet made it feel kind of eerie.

At the graveyard, the same Legion fellers that fired the rifle salute for my daddy shot from the formation, and the Army feller in charge gave the family an American flag. Then it was over. All at once, a feeling came over me and tears filled my eyes. I wiped them away quick as I could and looked around to see if anybody had seen me. I wished Daddy was buried in the graveyard by Bellair instead of over at Wesley Chapel where I couldn't go very much because it was over north of The Corners. I could've walked out to see his grave every day, if they'd have buried him in Bellair. Charlie Kline's grave wouldn't be the same, but I glanced back at it and knew that it was a place I could come and be by myself sometimes when I needed to get away from home.

I still went to the store every chance I got. Sometimes I'd even run up to the store from school at dinner time so Mother could fix me a baloney sandwich. That way I could get up there every once in a while when Brad Irons was there. He bought me a Royal Crown Cola one day and asked me how I liked school. It wasn't as good as going with Big or Sam, but I told Brad that I liked to read and play softball. I really didn't like much else about school except just being there. I told him I'd started reading a library book called *Adventures of Huckleberry Finn* that made me want to get out and go and get my schooling like Huck had done in the book

"Bein' there an' inside every day gives me the fantods just like it did old Huck," I said. "Seems like a feller learns a lot more outside of school than he does in school."

"That's about right," he said, laughed and nodded. "I got my education long after school was out. Just keep your head screwed on straight, an' you'll be okay."

I followed him out to his truck and watched him go.

"Thanks for the RC," I hollered after him and went back inside to get a package of peanuts to dump into the pop. Mother sort of turned up her nose at me when I put the nickel on the counter. She thought it ruined the taste of the pop to pour peanuts in it. But I thought they tasted real good together and had them every chance I got.

At afternoon recess later that day, Ronal Crucell and me got into a fight after he hit me with a pitch during a softball game. I knew he aimed to do it because I'd got a hit off of him the last time. He didn't like for anybody to get a hit when he pitched, especially us younger kids. Jimmy Barker and Albert Matthews and some of the other older kids wouldn't throw as hard if they was pitching and would give us a better chance. But old Ronal would throw as hard as he could and get mad if we got a hit. I was just about two years younger than him but nearly as big and not a bit scared of him.

When he hit me in the leg, I fell down trying to get out of the way and lost my grip on the bat. Which was probably a good thing because I jumped up and ran at Ronal. "You chickenshit sonuvabitch, you," I said, screaming as I ran toward him.

He held out his glove like a bullfighter and tried to keep me away while he danced around. But I knocked the glove out of the way and went on in to grab him with both arms. We crashed to the ground and rolled around. I flailed away with a loose fist but couldn't get a good punch to his nose. He threw me away from him and jumped up.

"You want to fight, you little bastard," he said, "get up here an' fight. I'll knock the shit out of you."

He didn't quite do that, but I walked into a roundhouse right when I got up and went back down faster than I ever had. The punch caught me on the chin and flipped me backwards and off my feet. I'd never been knocked down before. For just a second or two, I caught sight of the stars I'd always heard people talk about. Then I landed flat on my back and tried to get my breath back. By that time, Miz Finley came running over from the merry-go-round and got between Ronal and me.

"You boys are not to fight," she said, holding both of us by the shoulder. "That is no way to settle anything."

I wasn't so sure of that. It seemed to me that sometimes it got to the point that you was either going to have to fight or people would run over you. And I knew Ronal would keep on running over me, if I didn't fight back. It looked to me like I had two choices: I could either fight and get knocked down once in a while or not fight and get knocked down whenever Ronal or somebody else felt like it. Miz Finley had no more than left us to walk back inside when he said, "I'll get you, you little bastard. You're goin' to hell, anyway. But I'm goin' to get you before you do."

I reckoned he meant I was going to hell because I didn't go to the Church of Christ like he did. I'd heard him say that before to other kids. And that's what Aunt Helen said they believed up there at that church. Made me think there'd only be a few folks who'd get to heaven. Just one little church and the few folks who went there from the whole world would be chosen. That didn't make any sense to me. Later, I found out that there was other churches with the same name that figured their folks would get to heaven, too. But that still made them a lot more special than they seemed.

"If you're goin' to heaven, I don't reckon I'd want to go," I said. "Your goddamn ears are dirty an' you stink. My mother makes me wash my ears."

That wasn't quite fair, I knew, because his mother had died right after he was born. Everybody said his daddy had promised her he'd never marry again and was left to take care of Ronal, his sister and a niece from his sister who'd died after her husband had been killed loading logs. But nobody had ever told me anything about fighting fair. I figured we was at war and the way I figured that, just about anything was fair.

"You live next door to a nigger," Ronal said, stopping me in my tracks. "You're goin' to hell, an' you live next door to a nigger. Hhhhhhhhaaaaaaaaaaaa."

He slapped his leg and laughed that long neighing sound like his daddy, Ralph, always did when he bluffed his way to making his bid in a forty-two game up at the store. Hearing Ronal call Madge a nigger made me mad all over again. I'd never even heard him say nigger before like other fellers did and like they did so easy in *Huck Finn* when that's the way fellers talked. Nobody at home ever used the word. Big and Sam always said darkie when they said anything about a colored feller. I never heard Mother or Aunt Helen say anything either way. But I knew nigger was a bad word like a lot of the ones I heard men say and had picked up from them, words they'd never say in front of women. What I didn't understand was how Madge could be called a nigger, anyway. She looked like my grandmother and almost seemed like a grandmother to me. Both of them was white-headed and had sort of a copper color to their skin like most of the old people I was around every day. What Ronal said stayed on my mind for the rest of the day, though, much more than what Miz Finley had said about not fighting.

When I got home, I ran out the back door and over to Madge's house. Her husband, Hank, had just died not long ago, and we all went over there a little bit more often than before. They was real close and was together all the time. The day he died, I'd been standing out in the yard when they'd left to go to Casey to do their trading and waved at them as they drove by. He'd pulled up to a parking place in front of the bank and slumped over the steering wheel. Madge could hardly talk, she told Mother and Aunt Helen later, but finally got it across to somebody passing by that her husband was having an attack of some kind and needed help. But by the time a doctor got there, Hank was dead. I could imagine him with a Lucky Strike still held between his fingers, a long ash burning away as the smoke curled up over the yellowed part of the fingers from fifty years of smoking. I don't think I could have taken that cigarette, even if I was still picking up butts. Never did smoke his, anyway, because he smoked them short enough that he had to hold them between his thumb and forefinger, yellowing both of them real bad before he put any of them out.

Madge was in the kitchen baking cookies when I walked in her back door. I looked at the ones on the cookie sheet on the stove top. She pointed me to a bowl on the table. "Take one of them, if you want a cookie, John Walter," she said. "And just one. I ain't goin' to be the one to spoil your supper."

I took a cookie and looked her over more careful than I'd ever done before. She didn't look any more like a nigger than any other old woman around town. She wasn't any different than any of them was, either. She didn't go to church. Neither did Russ or a lot of other fellers I knew. Madge went to the store and sat crocheting and talking with the other women while the men played forty-two or sat on the other side of the stove and talked. She caught Aunt Helen and kept her from falling on her head one night when she fainted at the store. And Madge and Hank had kept farming long after he retired from the oil field, milking cows and raising chickens. They delivered fresh milk and eggs to them that needed it. Madge had to quit that after Hank died because she'd never learned to drive. But she still kept busy and had one of the cleanest and neatest houses I'd ever seen. The smell of cookies made her house feel homey to me and gave me a pretty fair idea about how good the cookies was even before I bit into one.

For the next couple of days, I wondered about what Ronal had said and how I would find out how it could be that Madge could be anything but what she seemed. Since Hank had died, she'd been coming over about every Sunday evening and talking and crocheting with Mother and Aunt Helen while Dig read western books and us kids played cards or marbles on the floor or the girls played with dolls. Only I didn't play much this time, and Nancy and Mary Beth was playing together. I looked at Madge in the dim light and from different angles to see if I could see anything. She had a little perky nose, thin lips and eyes that could cut through you like a sharp knife through a chicken's gullet. Her words could be just as sharp and cutting when she was riled.

But she sure didn't look like no nigger I'd ever seen. Maybe she used to be one and somehow wasn't anymore, I thought. It sure didn't make sense that she was one now, and Ronal just didn't know what he was talking about. Finally, I looked over at her and asked, "Madge, did you used to be a nigger?"

Big's head snapped up out of the book he was reading. That was uncommon. When he was taken up with an old western book, you couldn't get him to hear or pay any attention to what you said for anything. But my question somehow got his attention. Madge had her back to him and couldn't see him shaking his head at me and the frown on his face. I saw it but acted like I didn't even see him. Madge acted like she didn't hear me and went on talking to Aunt Helen about the tablecloth she was crocheting.

"Madge," I said again when she didn't answer after a minute or two, "did you used to be a nigger?"

I could see my mother out of the corner of my eye. Her and Big both was shaking their heads at me. Madge and Aunt Helen didn't seem to have heard a word I had said. They was looking down at something and acting like nothing was going on. Nancy and Mary Beth moved away from where they'd been playing with dolls near me. They was pretty quiet, too. All you could hear in the room was Madge or Aunt Helen talking. I guess they was pretty taken up with their crochet talk.

"Madge," I said for the third time, figuring she'd have to answer this time, "did you used to be a nigger?"

"Oh, I reckon," she said, looking at me with a fire in her eyes I'd never seen before, even when she was mad, then back to the tablecloth.

That satisfied me for the time being. I still didn't understand it, but she'd answered what I'd asked. My question had sort of put a damper on the evening, though. She left shortly afterwards. Big looked down at me hardly before she'd left and said, "I don't ever want to hear anything like that again, John Walter. That's not the kind of thing you say to anybody."

"Whatever got into you?" Mother said. "I couldn't believe my ears when I heard you say that."

Everybody was looking at me like I was some kind of criminal. All I'd done was ask a simple question, one I wanted answered.

"Ronal Crucell told me I was goin' to hell an' that I lived next door to a nigger," I said. "I told him I reckoned I didn't want to go to heaven, if he was goin' to be there. But I didn't know about livin' next door to a nigger."

"Don't say that word, John Walter," Mother said, looking sternly at me. "Or talk to Madge like that. I don't ever want to hear that again."

She didn't say any more about it, and I knew that was the end of it. Like a lot of things, it was as if something never happened, so long as you didn't talk about it again. Russ Taylor, who lived on the north side of us, was the only feller I could think of that I could talk to about the whole thing at that point. And I needed to talk about it to find out how it could be that she was a nigger. Russ was the kind of feller I could talk to about almost anything. He fixed things out in his little shop and took any kind of job that came along. That and the garden and chickens kept him and Eunice busy. They was always around to talk to and play with. I really liked it when Russ was out in the shop and I was playing like I was hauling stock. I'd wheel in there and park my bike outside like it was a garage.

"What's the trouble there, buster?" he'd ask. "Got a flat tire or you burn that motor up this time?"

"I think the sonuvabitch is about to throw a rod," I'd say, wiping the sweat from my forehead with the back of my hand like I'd seen Sam do. "Sam is goin' to be here directly to get this load of cattle on his truck. Think you can see what's wrong with the sonuvabitch?"

He'd smile and give me a fake serious look. "Your mother know you talk like that?"

"Yep," I'd say. "She taught me ever danged thing I know."

He'd laugh, then look my bicycle over for anything like he was looking for something wrong with it. A couple of times I'd had flat tires and pulled in to see if he'd fix them. The first time he showed me how to turn the bike upside down so the handlebars and the seat was on the ground and the tires was in the air. Next time he kept on working on the lawn mower he was sharpening and motioned toward the tire repair kit.

"Feller's got to learn to fix his own goddamn tires," he said. "How in hell you goin' to learn anything, if somebody else does the work for you?"

He was sitting out in the swing, smoking a Chesterfield and reading a western book when I went over to talk to him the evening after I'd asked Madge about being a nigger. He'd just started a new book and another one lay on the swing beside him. I picked it up and looked at the cover. It was one that I'd seen Big reading last week. Russ had written "Red" on the cover in his big, scrawling handwriting.

"What's that?" I asked.

"'Red.' Means I 'red' the book."

"That's not read," I said. "You've got, 'red,' the color red."

"I 'red' the goddamn thing," he said, growling a little but with a little twinkle in his eyes. "That's what it says. Don't try to make the language so goddamn complicated. That just makes things harder to understand. What's on your mind today?"

I started right off telling him about Ronal and what all had happened since then. He listened as I told him the story, laughing or chuckling most of the time. When I got to the end, he really laughed and slapped his leg.

"You really asked Madge if she used to be a nigger?"

"'Course I did," I said. "I just told you I did, didn't I? An' she said she reckoned she used to be. How'd she used to be?"

Russ looked at me without saying anything for a minute. "I don't reckon she just used to be," he finally said. "Her daddy, Jeff Williams, was a nigger. He had a blacksmith shop an' a mill down there west of the store on the place she has now. He was what you'd call a leading citizen of Bellair, I reckon you could say. My dad always told me that Mort Williams, Lucy Childers' granddad, found Jeff wanderin' around in the woods down South when he was twelve or fourteen years old an' brought him home with him when he came back from the war and raised him. I don't know 'bout that. But that's what they told. Jeff couldn't or wouldn't tell much about where he come from.

"It was during the War Between the States an' they was niggers around different places after Lincoln freed 'em. Lots of 'em come north one way or the other. Jeff, he growed up an' married Lucy's aunt, Sally Kline. They had Madge an' Morgan. I went to school with 'em down there in the old school Joe Marshall uses as a barn now. Both of 'em was light skinned an' sharp as tacks. Morgan had that kinky hair niggers have an' looked like one. Madge didn't much an' could pass for white, if a feller didn't know. She was the prettiest little thing you ever seen. We was close all the way through school."

"Was she your girlfriend?"

"No, she wasn't my goddamn girlfriend. An' I wasn't her boyfriend. We went to school together in the same grade. An' we didn't know nothin' about how fellers felt about niggers. We just growed up together. Later on, I was workin' for Hank in the oil fields when he first came from Ohio. He didn't know nobody over here an' started goin' with Madge before you knew it. They got serious right away. We was talkin' one day at dinner time, just him an' me. He said he wanted to marry her. Things was different then, an' I told him I didn't think that was a good idea. 'She looks white,' I told him. 'But what if she throws a black baby?' He didn't like what I said, but I told him what I thought. Morgan left this part of the country after his boy drown an' 'cause he looked like a nigger, I reckon. That was agin him around here in them days. He's preachin' somewhere over in Missouri. That's what I was tryin' to tell Hank. Anyway, a little layoff come up later, an' I'm the one that gets laid off. I know Hank had somethin' to do with that."

Russ talked on for a bit longer. He seemed mad when he was talking, then sort of cooled down by the time he had finished. He told me Elizabeth had been born to Madge and Hank about the same time the second of his four kids was born. I knew Elizabeth, but I was more interested in Madge's daddy. She talked about him sometimes, but I'd never heard anything about where he came from or who he was until now.

"Is Jeff Williams still alive?" I asked.

"Land no," Ross said, stopping to light a Chesterfield. "He's been dead for purt near thirty years, I 'xpect. He's buried out there in the Bellair Cemetery. Thomas Jefferson Williams."

It was still light enough to see when I hopped on my bicycle and headed out the angling road to the cemetery. It wasn't a big place, and I walked right to the grave in the corner of the cemetery where Ross had told me it was. I looked down and read, "Thomas Jefferson Williams, 1854 - August 21, 1924." Next to that was "Sally Josephine Williams, February 19, 1860 - February 24, 1925." A strange feeling passed over me. I had never thought about a colored feller being buried there. Before it'd just been a name on the tombstone. Now the name had a story with it. The old men like Burns Larue and Johnnie Larson and Arthur Hamilton had told stories about people and things around town that gave things a face or a time I could see. This was one of the stories I'd never heard, and it made me think about the others.

One of my favorite stories had been about the Bellair Bank robbery back in 1929. Arthur had been running the bank. He'd been alone in the bank at the time and would get a glint in his eyes and tell the story like it'd happened the day before.

"I seen two fellers drive up. One of them went into Fannie Boone's store next door. The other one came in the bank an' asked for change for a five-dollar bill. When I went to get him the change, why, he shoved a .45 in my face an' told me to stand still, that I wouldn't get hurt, if I did what he said.

"Now the other feller that went in Fannie's store, he brought Fannie an' George, Belle Brandywine, Violet Baker an' Elzora Milner in the bank with him. That made six of us in there. The guy that was over at Fannie's store, he sent the guy that was holdin' me out in the street with the shotgun an' took over with the automatic. He made me get the money an' put it in a black bag. I was so excited that I couldn't think what the combination was to the bottom part of the safe. I told him I'd have to go out in front an' get a paper that showed the combination."

I always got excited myself when Arthur told the story. Nothing like that ever happened around Bellair anymore. Back in the old days, it seemed like it was almost the old West when Jesse and Frank James or the Dalton gang and some of the rest of the outlaws was robbing banks and trains. I would sit up on the edge of my seat listening to Arthur, even though I got so I knew what was coming next.

"So he followed me out there," Arthur'd say after he'd hesitated a little and looked around at us boys, the ones he'd tell the story to when we'd ask him. "He thought I was goin' after a gun, boys. He said, 'Let me look in there where you're goin' to get this paper first.' He looked in an' saw there wasn't a gun an' said, 'Okay, get your paper.'"

With the combination, Arthur went in and unlocked the safe where there was half dollars, quarters, dimes, nickels and pennies.

"He took everything but the pennies in the silver line. There was ninety dollars in gold on a shelf where you couldn't see that I forgot to give him. Four twenty-dollar pieces an' two five-dollar pieces. He already had all the paper money out of the drawer an' out of the safe in his bag. He took $925.80 in all. Then he said, 'How much money you got on you?' I said, 'Five dollars.' An' he said, 'Let's see.' I pulled out my pocket book an' showed him. He said, 'Well, just keep it.'"

The part that came next was so exciting that it made me think different about Arthur than I had before he told the story the first time. The feller had thought Arthur was stalling when he went out to get the combination and punched him in the ribs with the automatic.

Then after Arthur got all the money out, the feller waved the pistol at them and told them to get in the vault. Arthur was the last one to go in, and the door was shut behind him.

"When he went to turnin' the handle, why there was a slot like that," Arthur'd say and hold his hands up in an inch or two little rectangle. "I stuck my two fingers right in that slot. But the feller turned the plunger an' thought he had it locked. As soon as I heard the car start, why I got my gun from the shelf an' went out an' went to shootin' at them. I was shootin' at their gas tank. One bullet missed the gas tank about that far.

Arthur would hold up his hands about six inches and laugh.

"I reckon the bullet went between the gas tank an' the tire. Two of them hit the turtle back of the coupe. Two bullets missed the car completely an' went down an' hit Uncle Harm's house at the end of the street. Went through the front wall an' through another wall in the house. Uncle Harm told me, 'You don't know it, but you might have killed somebody.'

"I reckon I could've," Arthur'd say and laugh a little.

"Anyway, they went out past the cemetery an' George Dewey's. Samuel hailed them an' said, 'Now there's a bridge out, boys. You can't go through. You might as well turn around an' go back.' So they came back to Bellair an' went around the square an' headed east, out towards Annapolis. By that time, me an' Elva Warren was out to my house behind the hedge with shotguns. But they turned there on the east side of the square an' went south from town."

That's when Madge saw them, she'd told me one time. She was standing out in the yard when they drove by as fast as the old coupe could go. Arthur and several fellers took in after them, he said, and run them three miles south to where they headed east. But there was a bridge out over that way.

"When they came back, Chet Pfeiffer an' Oscar Morris hid in the fence south of Shorty Perkins' an' shot the tire an' back glass out of the coupe. The tire didn't go down for a while. But when it did, they left the car an' set the shotgun down by a rail fence an' went on. Some of the gang — I wasn't with that bunch — found it but thought it was a trap. Charlie Harmon was with them, an' he'd been overseas in World War I. He said, 'I'm not afraid to get it.' An' he did.

"Well, sir, they got away. But they was sittin' some place over in Indiana when a cop recognized 'em. A feller named Wilson was one of them. He picked up his gun an' she jammed. The cop shot him once right here an' the next one got him right here."

Arthur'd point to the side of his face, then put a finger to the center of the temple and say, "That stopped him. Then the feller named Bender, the cop shot him right here," Arthur'd say and point to his mouth. "The bullet went in his mouth an' came out his neck, just missin' the jugular vein. Took two teeth out in front an' took a jaw tooth when it came out. He served some time in the pen an' got out. Don't know whatever happened to him."

As I walked through the graveyard, I saw what had happened to some of the fellers and the women that Arthur said had been in the bank or had helped chase the bank robbers while they was trying to make their getaway. That was one of the reasons I liked to come out and walk through the tombstones. I could see a bunch of names that went with the stories I heard up on the store porch or in the swing under the trees at Russ' house.

I walked over to Charlie Kline's grave and sat down in the grass in front of the tombstone. It said, "Charles A. Kline, PFC Illinois 417th Inf. 76th Div. World War II, May 30, 1923 - February 23, 1945." I knew what Charlie looked like when he was alive and could picture him in my mind as I talked to him. My daddy's face, I took from a picture. There wasn't even a picture of Jeff Williams for me to fix his face in my mind. He was just a dark-skinned old man with a fuzzy face that floated around in front of my eyes, never a face I could see clear. He was dead and gone, but he was still alive in Madge's and Russ' minds and no telling how many more. He was coming alive for me as I looked around the graveyard.

Bellair was a regular little place where I felt downright at home in most of the houses around the square. It was a place where people lived and died together and carried on through love and memory. I didn't just walk right in everywhere in town. I'd knock sometimes. And there was places I guess that I didn't go, like old Jake and Maggie Brummett's. He was a big feller that worked out in the shop at the side of his house and pretty much kept to himself. She stayed in the house. Aunt Helen said he'd been in the penitentiary in Missouri

for killing a man who'd been paying attention to Maggie before they
was married. From what Aunt Helen said, Jake just stepped out of the
bushes and shot the man dead. Even when I'd go with Mother and
Aunt Helen to Lucy Childers' house, Richard's and Jerry's grandma,
where they lived with her and their mother, Ruby, I'd only look out of
the corner of my eyes to see if I could catch a glimpse of Jake. I wouldn't
look over there straight on in case he'd see me looking at him. Ruby
said he wouldn't hurt anybody, that he was a nice old feller. I didn't
reckon I wanted to find out anytime soon.

Ruby was the only woman I knew who smoked cigarettes out in
the open. She'd brought Richard and Jerry back to live with her mother
from up north. Aunt Helen said, "Her and her man are separated."
That's about all I knew for sure. The boys always told me what a good
father they had and how they was going to go back someplace up in
Indiana to live with him. They never did. But they still made him out
to be more than he seemed to be. 'Course I did that with my daddy, too.
Sometimes I imagined he'd pretty much won the battle for the 'Canal
all by himself. Then after he'd killed a bunch of Jap soldiers and saved
the Marines in his outfit, he got hit with a lucky shot, threw his hands
toward the sky, pitched to the ground and lay dying like John Wayne
or somebody else did in a Hollywood movie about the war and asked
the Marine giving him a sip of water from his canteen to tell his wife
and son that he loved them and not to cry. I never told that to anyone
else and knew that was only the movies, like Sam said. But I still
wondered how Daddy died. Nobody knew a thing about that.

"How'd you reckon my daddy got killed, Sam?" I finally asked
him one day that summer. It wasn't something I wanted to talk to
anybody else about, but I figured Sam would be the feller to ask. "You
reckon he knew what hit him?"

"I don't know. Don't imagine you'll ever know. That's just one of
them things in life that you don't have no control over. You just got to
live with it an' go on."

I was near tears but didn't want Sam to know it and looked away.
"I just wonder how he done," I said. "If he was brave."

"He done what he had to," Sam said, rubbing me on the head.
"An' knowin' your daddy, I 'xpect he done a little more."

Looking down at Charlie's tombstone so I could see him better,

I said, "I don't reckon I know how you got killed, either, Charlie. Maybe it don't matter, but I'd like to know how both of you got killed. Just so I'd know. You tell my daddy when you see him, Charlie, that I'm proud of him, just like I am of you. They say you both died for a good cause an' that you're heroes for givin' your lives for us. That may be. But all I know is that you're dead an' you ain't here. Either one of you. I ain't got no daddy, except an old picture that don't talk back when I talk to it. So I'm proud an' sad at the same time. And that's the truth, as near as I could tell. You just tell my daddy that my mother an' me miss him an' love him. Someday maybe I'll get to see him. You tell him that."

The light was going fast as I walked out to my bike. By the time I started coasting down the hill and crossed the bridge over Borax, the trees on both sides of the road made it look like it was already night. I could see lights in several houses as I rode up the hill into Bellair. Everybody but old Miz Taylor. She didn't have any lights yet. She didn't have any electricity in her house. Russ had wanted to wire the house, but she wouldn't have any of it. It had to be almost pitch black before she'd even light a coal oil lamp. Madge's living room was lit up. She never had a light on in more than one room at a time. Every room except the back bedroom light looked like they was on at our house as I rode across the yard and dropped my bicycle at the steps.

"Where in the world have you been?" Aunt Helen said loud enough so they could have heard her up at the store when I walked through the door. "We've been lookin' all over for you. Your mother's worried sick. We've been hollerin' our heads off. Where've you been?"

"Riding my bike. I was too far away before I noticed it was dark an' just got back."

And that was the truth, too. I didn't tell her what Russ had told me about Madge's daddy or that I'd gone out to the cemetery to find his grave.

9

Mother usually worked the afternoons at the store by herself so Horsey could work nights. She liked to have me there so she could keep an eye on me when I wasn't with Aunt Helen. Most of the time I played outside with Richard and Jerry or the older boys who came around when they weren't working. Big had expected me to mow our yard for a long time. He'd had Russ sharpen the lawn mower in the spring and told me he wanted the yard mowed every week. Russ told me he was getting too old to mow his mother's yard and that she would give me fifty cents a week to mow it. That gave me a little money to get a bottle of pop and some peanuts up at the store. I'd have spent it all in a day or two, but Mother wouldn't let me have more than one bottle of Royal Crown Cola a day. One day a week she had afternoons off, though, and Horsey worked. I'd started eating candy again and was able to get at least two RCs and a couple of candy bars then.

He always looked at us like a hawk when we came in to get something or when we just sat on the benches and watched the men play dominoes or forty-two. I guess he thought we'd steal something. And I thought about it when I'd run out of money or Richard and Jerry didn't have a nickel or a dime for a bottle of pop and a candy bar or a package of peanuts to dump in the pop. But I didn't. Mother and Big had both told me not to go stealing anything from anywhere.

"Your mother works up at that store," Big had said. "An' I don't want her to have to worry about you stealin' anything. What a feller thinks about you is about all you got that lasts in this old world. If you're honest an' your word's good, fellers will trust you an' think good of you; if you're not honest an' your word's no good, fellers will never trust you an' won't think nothin' of you atall.

There ain't been a McElligott I know of that'd take a dime that wasn't his. Your daddy'd roll over in his grave if he knowed you wasn't honest an' stole."

I figured that was right and promised to be honest. I don't reckon I always was, but I tried my best. When I mowed Miz Taylor's yard, I tried to make sure that I never left strips and got up around the flowers and under the grape arbor and even around her old toilet like she wanted. Big had said fellers looked at you for what kind of a worker you was and how good you done your work, too. So I aimed to be a good worker and do a good job. And I aimed to treat other fellers with respect like Big said I had to do to have them respect me.

Riding with Sam to haul wheat was the first time I ever talked with Sam about anything like that. Wes Davis had wagons full of wheat when we got to the field. Sam scooped them into the truck while I played and let the scoops of wheat raining down on me be bombs and artillery shells exploding all around me and burying me in the truck. I felt the wheat start running into my ear and jumped up and shook my head to get the kernels out. A full scoop shovel of wheat hit me in the face. I fell back in the truck, my hands reaching up like I was a goner holding on to the last breath of life, and hollered, "He got me, Sam! I'm done for!"

Sam was leaning on his scoop when I stood back up. Sweat was running down his face. He looked tired. The late evening sun highlighted him to me when I stood back up. "You'll think done for," he said, "if you don't watch out. What if this scoop'd fly out of my hands an' hit you right in the kisser?"

"Tell 'em I done the best I could," I said, ignoring his question. "I want 'em to be proud of me an' respect me."

Sam shook his head and fished a Lucky Strike from a package in his shirt pocket. He lit the cigarette and stood smoking while he looked out across the field. He had that look in his eyes like he wasn't there that I saw sometimes when I'd see him looking out at something I could never figure out what it was he was seeing.

"Reckon I'd do all right in a war, Sam? Think they'd respect me?"

"Huh?" he said, taking another drag from the cigarette and looking down at me.

"You reckon I'd do all right in a war?"

"I hope to God you never have to find out. That's not somethin' I'd wish on my worst enemy."

"But it's good to go off an' fight for your country an' yourself to know how you'd do. Maybe you'd do something that'd help win the war an' you'd be a hero."

"There ain't no heroes. There's only survivors. You do what you have to for the fellers you're with, when you have to do it an' that's it. Ain't much other choice. Some of you live an' some of you die. Them that die like your daddy an' Charlie Kline got dealt a bad hand far's gettin' their lives cut short. An' they get yanked out of them that loved them's lives. But them that live has got to go on. That ain't always so good."

"That ain't the way it is in the war movies. There's heroes in them movies, an' war is good. I—"

"That's bullshit," Sam said pretty loud and real grouchy, cutting me off and snubbing his Lucky out on the wagon sideboard like he was mad at me. "Like I told you before, them shows are about as phony as a three-dollar bill. That's Hollywood. In a real war, you live from minute to minute, hour to hour, day to day an' hope that your luck holds up. Because when you do the best you can an' you all know that you can count on everybody else to do their best, luck is all that keeps you alive. Then if your luck holds up an' you do make it, you got to go on livin' with what you've seen an' done an' think about. Everybody don't hold up very good at that."

He went back to scooping wheat, and I got up on the cab of the truck and watched him scoop. He got into a rhythm that made his scooping look easy. Every now and then he switched and turned around and scooped from the other side. I kept watching him until he was done and we pulled out. He still hadn't said anything, and I hoped he wasn't mad at me. The thought of that scared me.

Out on the road, he shifted gears and worked the gear shift with a kind of rhythm like he did scooping wheat. When he had finally shifted into high gear and we was moving pretty fast, he looked over and grinned at me.

I grinned back.

"Don't take no wooden nickels, Sedwick," he said.

"Why not?"

"You can't buy a bottle of pop with 'em."

At the store a few days later, I'd had an RC Cola with a buffalo nickel and was thinking about a wooden nickel when Albert Matthews came out to the mulberry trees where Richard and Jerry and me was crawling around in the trees eating mulberries. Big Al, as we'd taken to calling him now that he was so much bigger than us, was four or five years older than us and usually worked out on the farm for somebody.

"What you doin' here, Big Al?" I asked. "Why ain't you workin'?"

"Finished up out at Olin's. Nothin' to do, so I got the afternoon off. Come on in the toilet. I want to show you somethin'."

We scrambled down the limbs and swung to the ground.

"You know how to jack off?" he asked after we'd all crowded in the little two-holer. The unchanging smell of all of the crap stayed with you all the time you was inside the toilet. Horsey Matthews didn't keep any lime to hold down the smell of the poop that piled up like a mountain with the peak always moving higher. Wasn't his toilet, he said. Mother said he was too cheap to buy the lime.

"Jack off?" Jerry said. "What's that?"

"Well, here, look at this 'Eight-Page Bible.' See that feller's big old cock. He's goin' to fuck that old whore an' get his nuts off. He's goin' to come. Jackin' off is comin' without fuckin' nobody. You do it with your hand."

I'd heard about that a little one night when I asked Jimmy Barker about the two belly buttons getting together and somebody coming. He'd explained how a man and a woman get together and fuck to have fun, but sometimes it causes a baby. But somebody comes.

"The woman gets knocked up," Jimmy said, explaining further when I asked him what that meant, "like Betsy Smith is right now. Old John put his old cock in her cunt an' knocked her up higher 'n a kite. She's havin' a kid any day now."

I reckon I was about as surprised as I was when he told me there wasn't no Tooth Fairy, that it was my mother who put a dime under my pillow before I woke up in the morning after losing a tooth. But like then, I didn't let on that I was too surprised.

We looked at Big Al's pocket-sized book with cartoon-like drawings of characters screwing and getting their cocks sucked by the women. Big Al unbuckled his belt and took his pants down. His cock was hard and stuck straight out in front of him like a little ball bat.

Curly and shiny short red hairs circled the cock that looked as big around as a silver dollar. Big old balls hung down between his legs. I'd never seen anything like it. I know my eyes was big. So was Richard's and Jerry's.

"Get your cocks out," Big Al said, wrapping his big old freckled hand around his cock. "I'll show you how to jack off."

I was kind of slow getting my pants down, knowing that my pecker was about half the size of Big Al's and didn't have no hair around it. And my little balls was about the size of ripe hickory nuts. Richard's and Jerry's was probably about the same, I figured. I felt pretty funny about getting bare-assed in front of him. But we went ahead and pulled our pants down. All of us had little hard-ons.

Big Al laughed when he saw our peckers. "Them little peckers will grow," he said. "Might not get as big as this old cock, seven inches long an' as big around as your arm, but they'll get a lot bigger than them little peckers you fellers got now. Go ahead an' do like I'm doin'. You won't have no jazz comin' out when you come. It'll just tickle."

He started whipping his big old hand faster back and forth until it was almost a blur. We'd hardly started ourselves when Big Al moaned a little and turned toward one of the open holes, hunched over and a big squirt of jazz flew out of the end of his cock, hitting the back of the hole and dripping down on the pile of crap. He stripped his cock out like Aunt Helen had taught me to milk one of her old cows when you got them about milked out and flipped more jazz out and on the floor.

"That feels good, boys," he said, pulling up his pants and stepping over in the jazz and grinding it under his foot. "You'ns go ahead on. I'm goin' over to the store an' get a bottle of pop."

After Big Al left, we started jacking off the way we'd seen him do it. Not long afterwards, I felt a strange feeling start moving through my pecker. I'd never felt anything like it before. It did kinda tickle. I jerked and looked down and saw a wetness come out of the end of my cock about the same time Richard and Jerry started herking and jerking. When we looked at each other, we laughed and smiled.

"That does feel good," Jerry said, putting his cock back in his pants. "I wonder how long it'll be before we can squirt like Big Al."

"I don't know," I said. "Not long I hope. I reckon we have to have some hair growin' down there an' have bigger peckers. Ours look like little pencils next to Big Al's."

He was sitting on the end of the bench with a Royal Crown and a package of Planter's peanuts dumped in it. He watched us run across the empty lot and stop in front of him at the porch steps. Burns Larue and Jim Miller sat on the other end of the porch talking about something we couldn't hear. That was one time I didn't care much what they were talking about.

"Did you make it tickle?" Big Al asked.

"Sure did," I said and nodded with Richard and Jerry.

Big Al laughed and nodded. "We can do it again some time. Feels good, don't it?"

After that it seemed that every time any of us got together, one of the things we had to do was jack off. Jeremy Hamilton was the only kid around town that hardly ever joined us much. He was the same age as Big Al but was a little more shy than the rest of us seemed to be. When I saw his pecker the one time he did jack off with us down in the school garage when we all went in and stood around in a circle, I saw why he might not feel comfortable with us. His old pecker wasn't much bigger than us younger boys had, and it had a long old squishy covering over the end that made it look like a little banana when it was all covered up.

"What's that funny-lookin' squishy thing on the end of your cock?" I asked. "It looks like a midget banana."

The other boys laughed. Jeremy didn't say much, but I knew he was mad at what I said. All I was trying to do was keep up with everybody else and keep them from outdoing me. Jeremy looked more like a bookworm to me with his horn-rimmed glasses and always seemed to be able to talk about things we didn't know a thing about. He didn't exactly make me feel dumb, but I didn't usually feel like I was as smart as him.

Later, we played football out behind the schoolhouse. Jeremy was on the other team and wasn't very good. So he got me as his man. Big Al and me and Ronal Crucell were standing Jimmy Barker, Jeremy and Richard. Jerry had gone home. Jeremy kept talking to me when we ran plays, telling me I was little and dumb and couldn't play football or anything else. I finally got mad enough that I tried to tackle him and get him down. If I could do that, I knew I'd have won something. The other boys would never let him live it down that I tackled him. He was a big old fat kid nearly twice my size and a lot older.

I did take him down and knocked his glasses off. But I couldn't keep him down. He flipped me off and over on my back while he put his glasses back on. Then he got on top of me with his knees on my arms, pinning them to the ground.

"You give up, you little bastard?" he said. "Are you goin' to behave yourself?"

"Fuck you, you fat sonuvabitch," I said, spitting up at him. "You goddamnsonuvabitchinchickenshitcocksucker, let me up."

"Why, you little bastard, you," Jeremy said, wiping the spit from his shirt with one hand and hitting me in the head with the other one, "you spit on me. I don't believe you spit on me."

I spit at him again, and he hit me again. This time he caught me just above the eye, and I saw stars like I did when Ronal knocked me down. I shook my head a little and looked up through tears to see Jeremy stretched out over me with his fist doubled up and cocked to hit me again.

"You give?"

"Go to hell, Fat Jeremy Hamilton. Kill me, you sonuvabitch. I ain't never givin' up to you. You fat-ass cocksucker."

Jeremy kept hitting me in the face and asking me to give. I kept cussing and hollering at him, calling him every bad name I could think of and using every bad word I'd ever heard anybody say. The other boys had gathered around and started taunting Jeremy that he couldn't even make a little fourth grader give. He kept his fists banging away at my head and face. Sometimes he connected, sometimes I'd move enough that he hit the ground with his fist and made the boys laugh real hard. Finally, he just quit and let me up. We was both pretty well wore out. My eyes was puffy from crying, and there was a few lumps on my head. They wasn't bad because Jeremy didn't hit too hard.

"You just wait until I grow up a little more, you sonuvabitch," I said while I wiped my eyes with one of my daddy's old red bandannas. "I'm goin' to get on you like stink on shit an' kick your fat ass all over hell an' half of Georgia."

174   RAY ELLIOTT

"Get 'em, John Walter," Big Al said.

Jeremy started toward me, and I backed away. I wasn't going to try it again just yet and started up the road for home.

Over the next several months, I spent a lot of the time I used to spend with Big and Sam just being with the boys around town. We jacked off, played cowboys and Indians or war and roamed around the countryside. Jimmy Barker and Ronal Crucell sometimes had their horses with them so we could get a ride now and then. Up at the store one Thursday when Mother was off, Jimmy had his horse. Big Al was working someplace or was at home and Jimmy was the leader that day.

"Can you ride your horse across the porch?" I asked him as he sat on his big rangy sorrel out in front of us. Ronal, Richard and Jerry and me stood on the three-foot-high, concrete porch that went across the whole front of the store and had two big concrete steps on each end. The roof was held up by four metal poles set in the concrete.

"Probably," Jimmy said and neck-reined his horse around to the west end of the porch. "I'll see. Come on, Big Red, let's ride across the porch."

Big Red would get his front feet on the first step, then back off to level ground. He did this a couple of times before Jimmy was able to talk him into taking the second step and then on up onto the porch. Jerry and me had shimmied up the middle two poles and watched from just under the roof. The horse stopped with his front feet on the porch. Jimmy couldn't get him to go farther but was trying when Horsey walked out on the porch.

"Now, Jimmy," Horsey said, a trail of smoke coming out through the long, thick hairs hanging down from each nostril, "you know better than to do somethin' like that. You get that horse down off there right now, or I'm goin' to have to call your mother."

Orville and Alma Barker went to the Church of Christ with Horsey and Arletta, which gave him more help when it came to keeping us kids in line. Jimmy went to the Church of Christ, too. Big had already told me that if I got a whipping at school or got in trouble anyplace around town that I'd get a whipping when I got home. Richard and Jerry had their Uncle Ted to deal with in the same way. Jimmy knew better than to go any farther and backed the horse down off the steps and rode off up the street toward his place without another word.

"An' your mother wouldn't like to hear that you was a part of this, John Walter," Horsey said to me when I slid down the pole and stood with the other boys.

"I didn't do nothin', Howard," I said. Besides what Big said, Mother worked at the store, and I knew I'd have trouble from more places than I could handle.

"I heard you ask Jimmy if he could ride that horse on the porch. You gave him the idea."

"I didn't ride that horse," I said, adding Horsey, what everybody called him behind his back, under my breath. "I just wondered if he could. I didn't even ask him to do it."

"The thought is equal to the deed, the Good Book says," Horsey said. "'Great things are done when men an' mountains meet,' the poet says; 'This is not done by jostling in the streets.' You boys are up to no good, I can tell."

Horsey looked at me long enough to make me feel uncomfortable, snorted through his nose like he did sometimes, making the hairs in his nose come out farther and then walked back into the store.

I thought about what he'd said some and decided none of it made any sense. Wasn't nobody "jostling in the streets." And if I thought about killing somebody and didn't, except in my mind, how could that be as bad as actually killing someone? Lots of things like that bothered me about church. I already knew I was far from being able to be a good Christian. I cussed too much, smoked too much and had too many bad thoughts. And this jacking off was sure to be bad, if "the thought is equal to the deed." After we'd started doing it, I knew what the Bible meant about it being better to cast the seeds of life into the belly of a whore than on the ground. But I still wanted to do both of them, especially into the belly of a whore and have our belly buttons come together. I just knew that'd feel even better than jacking off.

The older boys was casting lots of seeds on the ground. The ones of us that couldn't cast any yet was trying. Every time we got together and had the chance, Big Al or Jimmy got what they got to calling a circle jerk going. When they'd come, they'd squirt out towards the center of the circle and see who could squirt the farthest.

We'd go up in the haymow in the barn across from the store, down in the schoolhouse garage or wherever we could. One time we doubled up on Jimmy's and Ronal's horses and rode and took turns walking down to the crick. There was a little open place a half a mile or so north of the bridge that had a white-sand beach we called Bare-Ass Beach on the east side of the crick with a thick growth of trees and underbrush growing up the bank. We helped get the horses unsaddled and tied to a tree, then took our clothes off along side of the old road and waded across to the beach and got in a circle right away.

"We'd ought to get Carolyn an' Linda down here," Jimmy said.

"They wouldn't come," Big Al said. "They're too churchy."

Everybody started jacking off faster and faster. I could almost see Carolyn and Linda on the beach someday, naked just like us. I played catch and talked about baseball with Carolyn. She wore tight shorts in the summer time and sat sprawdle-legged when we sat down to rest after playing catch for an hour or so. More than once I saw the little dark hairs sticking out of her shorts and crossed my legs so she wouldn't see the bulge my hard little pecker made in my jeans. It'd get that way even when I just saw Linda. She was dark like Carolyn but had a creamy skin the color of Big's coffee after he'd dumped cream and sugar in it. I tried harder to imagine them naked on Bare-Ass Beach and felt something a little different as I was getting ready to tickle. Something was moving through my cock and squirted out on the sand about the same time as Big Al and Jimmy and Ronal and Jerry started squirting.

"I'm squirtin', I'm squirtin'," I said, jumping and shouting as the juice squirted out. "I'm squirtin'."

I turned and ran toward the water. The water had been high when the crick was out the last month so the water wasn't as scummy and oily as it was sometimes when they dumped things in from the oil field and the water was low. I ran a couple of steps into the water and dove out towards the middle. When I came up, everybody else was off the beach and in the water, telling me they was glad I squirted. Jerry couldn't swim and stayed close to the edge of the water just walking back and forth. We played tag for a little bit before Big Al said we'd ought to ride the horses bareback over on the dirt road.

"That'd crush my balls," Jimmy said.

"Not if you ride right," Big Al said. "Hold on with your knees. Come on, let's go."

Richard and Jerry and me watched them ride. We wasn't good enough riders to ride by ourselves, and I sure didn't want to hold onto one of them bigger boys when we were both naked as jaybirds. I could imagine riding bare back behind Carolyn or Linda Springer and holding onto one of them. But not a boy. It looked like a lot of fun. I knew I'd tell Carolyn about Bare-Ass Beach. And I told her about everything except the jacking off. I wasn't sure how she'd take that.

As it turned out, she was pretty interested in what I told her about going skinny dipping and riding naked and bareback. I didn't know about her going herself, but she was sure interested.

"How'd they keep their things from flopping around?" she said. "Didn't that hurt them?"

"I don't reckon it did. All you have to do they said is to hold your knees tight against the horses' shoulders an' up off its back a little. That way your old pecker an' your nuts ain't gettin' squished."

"I'd like to see that."

"I reckon you can," I said, feeling the bulge in my jeans jump. "You an' Linda could come down there with us the next time. Jimmy said we'd ought to get you to come down there."

"Maybe we will."

Of course they never did, but I kept the picture in my mind for a long time and kept my eyes between Carolyn's legs when she gave me a lemonade after we'd played catch and then she'd spraddle out on the porch across from me where I could see the hair sticking out from her shorts in a fluffy line along the inside of both thighs. I'd never seen the real thing and just had to imagine what it looked like from the pictures I'd seen in them Eight-Page Bibles. I'd have done about anything just to see Carolyn naked.

Sometimes we went to the old barn and pond a quarter of a mile up the lane behind Jimmy's house. We'd swim or skate or play hockey with cans and crooked sticks, according to the time of the year. The place was pretty much like the Old Bed and the Old Mill and barns down on Madge's place. The big difference was that Madge had told us to stay away from down there. That didn't mean we would, but we had to sneak in through the woods from the north. At Jimmy's grandpa's old place, we just walked up the lane in plain sight. Going to Madge's place, we walked real quiet through the woods like there was Indians all around us. Up at Jimmy's, we walked down the narrow lane, fenced off on both sides and sunk away from the trees and brush covering much of the wire fences, and played like we was soldiers in the war. Sam and me went up the lane on the way back to the hay field in the bottoms one day. I told him how we played soldier here.

He ducked his head down and looked out over the steering wheel. "Ain't no hedge rows," he said. "But it looks a little like them narrow little roads in France."

"They had roads like this in France?"

"Something like this, I guess. Lot of 'em had hedge rows on both sides. The Germans would set up behind them wherever they was an' fight like hell. They was fightin' sonsabitches. Couldn't even hardly get a tank through a hedge row. Finally an old boy who'd drove a cat back home welded some bars on the front of his tank an' went straight into one of them hedge rows, pushed them trees over an' crawled right up an' over to the other side. That evened things out a little.

"'Nother thing them sonsabitches done was to string piano wire back an' forth across the road between hedge rows. Jeeps come along there an' hit one of them right, I guess it'd take a feller's head right off."

I'd never heard Sam say that much about the war without me asking and asking him over and over. And getting a feller's head cut off was more than he'd ever said about anybody getting hurt. I could just see a soldier's head rolling down the lane in front of us, and the jeep running up the bank and turning over on the headless driver while German rifle and machine gun fire bracketed the road ahead of us.

"Couldn't they see the piano wire?" I asked, shuddering again at the thought of getting my head cut off just driving down the road.

"Nope. But some old boy finally figured out a way to cut the wire. He welded a rod to the bumper that had a hook at the top. Jeep'd be driving along, hit a wire, stretch it out an' snap it when it hit the hook."

"I'd want one of them on my jeep," I said. "Did you have a jeep?"

"Nope. Never did. Didn't always even have a tank like I was supposed to. Lost mine at the beach an' walked with the infantry to St. Lô.

Got a tank there an' kept it until I got hit an' my neck jammed again in August. Didn't have one for a while after I was in a field hospital a couple of days. But somebody was always getting killed 'r wounded. Wasn't many replacements, so I got a tank pretty soon an' kept it until the Bulge. Got another one later."

"Did you get scared when you was over there fightin' in the war?"

"All the time, all the time."

"They have barns like this is France?" I asked as Sam turned for the hay field and we passed Chester Randolph's old barn where we played in the haymow and all around.

"Not just like that. But there's a lot of barns. I've stayed in some of them. Glad to have had a place to get in out of the snow an' cold. Stayed in an old wine cellar one night. That was a night an' a half."

Sam laughed and turned to look at me.

"Did you drink wine there?"

"A little," he said and laughed again. "Good thing we didn't have to fight any Germans that night. Fellers ran around popping corks out of the bottles with bayonets an' drank wine like water. We'd had a hard time just before that. Had a hard time the next morning, too. Different kind, though. Splittin' headaches an' cotton mouths came with this hard time. But a wine cellar or a barn was places you liked to see."

On the way back up out of the bottoms after we'd loaded the truck, he reached over in the glove box and took out a box. He handed it to me and said, "Open it. We'll have us some fun with this."

It was a brand new, authentic, major league baseball. I'd never held one in my hand before. All I'd ever played with was dirty, scuffed balls that I found or somebody gave me. Big got a new one a year or two before. By the time I got to play with it, it was dirty and scuffed, too. I'd catch his sweeping curves, "ins and outs," he called them, in a fielder's glove and double up my handkerchief as extra padding when my hand got so puffed I couldn't catch the ball in the pocket without it hurting bad.

"It's yours," Sam said. "I'll play with it when we play catch."

I could hardly believe my ears and just barely squeaked out a "thank you." I'd wanted a new baseball for a long time. Carolyn hadn't even ever had an official major league baseball. For a minute,

I could see us playing catch with the new ball, getting all sweaty and tired, then going swimming naked together down on Bare-Ass Beach and rolling around in the sand together. I didn't see the other boys in the picture.

The next time us boys went up to the barn we gathered in the front part of the barn. I guess I thought we would jack off, then play in the haymow or outside someplace. Big Al took us back in a shed on the side of the barn where the horse could get to the hay. Him and Jimmy and Ronal turned and faced me and Richard and Jerry back in the shed and worked around so our backs was to the wall.

"We want you to suck our cocks," Big Al said, unbuttoning his fly and taking his big old shiny-headed cock out.

"I ain't goin' to suck your dirty old cock," I said, looking for a way to get out of the trap we was in. I saw right off that there wasn't any. We was trapped just like Sam told me the Army was trapped at the Bulge by the snow and the Germans. Or just like one of them old cowboys in the western books did when they rode into the box canyon in one of them westerns that Big and Russ read and passed on to me before they took them down to Jap and Smokey's barbershop to exchange. There wasn't no way out, except to fight like hell. And as big as they was, that didn't look too promising. Big Al was more than four years older than me. Jimmy was three and Ronal was two. Jerry was ten, I was almost twelve and Richard was twelve. "I ain't no cocksucker."

"I'm not either," Richard said, stepping over to put his arm around Jerry when he started to cry. "An' neither is my brother. You don't touch him."

Jimmy and Ronal had their old peckers sticking through their jeans and overalls and walked closer to us. Jimmy was in front of me.

"I ain't goin' to suck your dirty ol' cock," I said, "you goddamn-sonuvabitch, you. You can kill me, an' I won't suck your goddamn cock."

Big Al moved Jimmy over in front of Jerry and held his cock up at an angle to me. "You can suck my cock, John Walter," Big Al said, grinning at me like a possum eating shit. "I think I'll like that pretty good."

"Over my dead body, you fuckin' bastard," I said, stressing the one word I knew would make him mad. He'd made up a big story about his father working up north and not coming home much because it was too far. I'd never seen him and had asked Russ about it one day.

"Well, he does work up north," Russ said, looked at me and smiled. "I don't think he comes back to see Verlie, though. He's the one she says got her knocked up. But I doubt if she even knows who Albert's daddy is. Mary Louise's either. Old Verlie was a rounder. She diddled first one, then the other."

Jack Berry later told me that she was "ready to fuck" just about anytime. And he told a story I thought was just awful about a bunch of boys around town going somewhere in the woods south of town to wait for her to come and meet one of them. The boy to meet her said he'd stamp his feet to let her know where he was just off the road. When she got there, first one of the boys stamped, then another. Jack said Verlie would run toward the sound each time, saying, "Don't move. Don't move. I'm acomin'." Finally everybody just ran off and left her in the woods.

"That's a bad way to treat her," I'd said to Jack.

"She didn't have no sense," Jack had said and laughed. "She should've knowed better."

Jack stretched stories a bit when he was talking to us boys, so I asked Coony Pfeiffer about it the next time I saw him up on the store porch. He was a bachelor and a painter who lived with his mother west of the store and pretty much came and went as he pleased. He had a Filipino girlfriend and had built a little one-room frame building so he could bring her home. People had a fit, but Coony didn't seem to care. He'd tell us how she could put both legs around her neck for him. He'd laugh and tell us what we asked and cuss just like he was talking to any bunch of men. Coony said what Jack had told us about Verlie was probably true. He'd heard the story, anyway, and a whole lot of others about her.

I didn't want to say any of that and really make Big Al mad. But I didn't plan on sucking his cock, either. He knew what I meant by calling him a bastard. So did the other boys. Jimmy was the only one who lived with or had both parents. My daddy got killed in the war, Richard and Jerry's folks was divorced and Ronal's mother was dead. We all knew about each other from the lies we told and from what we heard around town and what Russ told me.

"You're a bastard," I said, using the word again to make sure he knew what I was talking about and watching out of the corner of my eyes as Jimmy and Ronal started to stick their cocks in Richard and Jerry's mouths. "You ain't got no daddy."

"Come here, you little cocksucker," he said, grabbing me by the hair and pulling my head down to his big cock. "Get your mouth open an' suck my cock."

I was crying and hollering when I felt the head of his cock slip inside my mouth and just inside my teeth. Still crying and gurgling, I bit down as hard as I could. Big Al jerked my head up hardly before I opened my mouth and hit me with his fist at the side of the head, knocking me back into the manger with the hay for the horses.

"You dirty little sonuvabitch," he said. "You bit me. Little cocksucker bit me. My cock's bleedin'. I ought to kill you."

I wasn't quite sure how far along the other boys had got, but when I grabbed ahold of the hay manger and pulled myself up everybody was looking at me but Big Al. He was leaning over as far as he could and was blowing down on his cock. I could taste the blood and salt in my mouth and hocked like Big and Sam did when they'd swallowed coal dust for an hour while they scooped off a load of coal. Then I spit everything I hocked up between me and Big Al.

"I want to go home," I said. "An' I want Richard an' Jerry to go with me."

"Goin' to run home to Mommie an' tell, are you?" Big Al asked, sticking his old cock back in his pants. "I'll beat the shit out of you, if you do."

"Fuck you, bastard," I said. "I ain't tellin' nobody shit."

Jimmy and Ronal didn't say anything and just put their peckers away. Richard and Jerry and me edged along the hay manger and started running just as soon as we hit the door. We ran like hell about half way down the lane before I looked back and didn't see the other boys.

"They ain't comin'," I said, hollering and stopping to wait for Jerry.

For a minute, we just walked along and kept quiet. Then Jerry started crying. "Jimmy put his old pecker in my mouth," he said. "I'm goin' to tell my mommie when I get home."

"What for?" I asked, madder than I ever remembered being. "So everybody in the whole goddamn town will know that we sucked them sonsabitches' cocks? I sure as hell don't want Mother or Aunt Helen or Big or Sam or any-goddamn-body else to know that. Fuck them sonsabitches."

Richard had been quiet walking along with his arm around his brother's shoulder. Now he nodded and spoke. "That's right, Jer. Don't tell Mom. I don't want nobody to know that I sucked on Ronal's pecker, either. That'd just make things worse."

"But I don't want to do that anymore," Jerry said, still crying. "I don't want to suck anybody's pecker."

"I don't either," I said. "We just have to be careful about gettin' too far away from town with them or not let them get us off by ourselves."

When we got to the road, Richard and Jerry went off toward their house on the other side of the square, and I walked slowly down the road past Big Al's house toward home. Verlie came out on her little porch and hollered at me.

"Have you seen Albert?" she asked.

"He's back up the lane," I said, the dirty bastard, I added under my breath, jerked my thumb back over my shoulder and kept walking.

"Yooooouuuuuuhhhhhooooooooo, Alllbbbbeeerrrrtttt," she said sing-songy like. "Dinnnner is reaaddy."

I never thought about it being dinner time. Big or Sam stopped for dinner sometimes if they was close. And I sure didn't want to see them. Mother was at the store, so I didn't have to see her. I could see right away that nobody else was there. My eye was swelling a little where Big Al had hit me and it stung a little where it was near cut open. Everybody'd ask me about that.

Aunt Helen and the girls was sitting at the kitchen table having peanut butter-and-jelly sandwiches when I walked in. "You're just in time for dinner, such as it is," Aunt Helen said. "What in the world happened to your eye?"

"Oh, that?" I said. "Had a little accident. I was ridin' Jimmy's bike up the lane an' hit a big old rock. Throwed me off the bike, an' I landed on my head."

"Let me look at that," Aunt Helen said, then got a cold rag and washed my face. With a piece of cotton, she dabbed a little peroxide on the busted place. "That'll kill the germs. Hold this cold rag on it to keep the swelling down."

I held the rag on my eye while she made me a sandwich and got me a glass of milk. After a minute, I put the rag down and ate. The rag didn't seem to be doing any good, anyway, and I was hungry.

I was still hungry that night at supper and had just taken my second piece of bread and helping of gravy when Big looked over at me and asked what happened to my eye.

I told him the same story I'd told Aunt Helen when I got home and the same story I told Mother when she got home from the store. And it was the same story I planned to tell everybody. I'd been over it in my head quite a few times and knew the story inside and out. I could almost see myself riding that old Schwinn of Jimmy's down the lane under the trees lining the lane, hitting a rock the size of a grapefruit and getting pitched off the bike head over heels and landing on my head. It was easier to take than the real story that was just as clear in my mind as the one I'd made up. I don't know what Richard and Jerry said to their mother or anybody else. We never talked about that day again.

"Looks to me like somebody bopped you, Sedwick," Big said, forking a fourth of a piece of bread and gravy in his mouth while he looked at me. "You ain't fightin', are you?"

"Nope," I said, peppering the gravy pretty heavy just like Big. "I ain't been fightin' yet. But I 'magine I will have to one of these days. One way or the other."

Big started to say something, then went back to eating.

10

From then on, I looked around the corner and measured the distance between where I was and where I had to be to be safe. I felt a little like old Huck Finn did about being around his pappy when he was drunk and mean and wanted to stay away from him. Richard and Jerry and me still went to the graveyard and George Dewey's pond, the bluff on Borax out that way and all up and down that little crick, Madge's Old Mill and barn down on the Old Bed, the bridge on North Fork and all up and down it. We just made sure that we knew where the other boys was or that we was close enough to Bellair or a house on the outskirts when we played with them that we was safe. Sometimes I'd let my guard down and not be careful.

I hadn't been in Jimmy's barn lot since we'd been up the lane to his grandfather's old barn. We'd only played out in his big front yard once since then. Then one Saturday afternoon, we'd all started at the store and just ended up at the milk barn right behind the Barkers' house. It seemed safe enough. As we walked across the barn lot and past the windmill that was turning real slow in the slight midday breeze, I looked at the gate to Jimmy's backyard and the big gate that led to the lane, either back to the road or up the lane to the old barn. For a minute, I looked at the old windmill pretty close. It was disconnected from the pump and wasn't pumping any water. They didn't use it much to pump water anymore, but I was fascinated when it was connected and the windmill turned in the early morning breeze before it died down and kept the pump handle moving up and down like a piston in a car and filling the drinking trough with water without anybody but the wind or God doing a thing.

At the corner of the barn, Jimmy opened the door to where the cows were milked each morning and evening and stepped back for every-body to walk in ahead of him. In the middle of the day, it was empty. Nobody was around. Not even the cows.

"I ain't goin' in there," I said, looking back at the gates.

"We're just goin' to see where they milk the cows," Big Al said.

"Not me. I don't want to see where they milk the cows."

"Come on," Jimmy said. "We can play up in the haymow."

"Nope," I said and edged away from the other boys.

"Get in there, John Walter," Big Al said, holding out his arms and waving them at me like he was driving some hogs into the barn. I thought of what Barney Ford had said about us all "bein' a bunch of hogs, wallowing in our own shit." I didn't plan to wallow in no shit.

I had just a second before Big Al's arms would grab me and drag me into the barn, and I jumped toward the big gate. I knew he could catch me, if he tried. But I hoped he wouldn't try since I was running toward the house and town.

"Come back here, you little cocksucker," he hollered after me. "Ain't nobody goin' to hurt you."

Fuck you, sonofabitchin' bastard, I thought as I ran, they ain't going to hurt me, if I can help it. As I was passing the windmill, my legs pumping faster than I'd ever felt them moving, I looked at the gate and thought about climbing up the windmill ladder. But I'd be stuck up there, I knew, and kept pumping away for the gate that I thought I could climb over real quick and head for the road. Just then I felt something hit me square in the back, slide down a little and fall off.

"Bull's eye," Big Al said and the other boys laughed.

I slowed down and looked back. He was standing a little in front of everybody else with a big grin on his face. He'd taken a pile of cow shit that was dried and crusted over on the top but still plenty messy inside and on the bottom, flipped it over and threw it at me like the shotput that he threw for the track team. I could smell the cow dung and felt it running down my back and on down my jeans.

"Goddamnsonuvabitchincocksuckinbastard," I said when I got to the gate and knew I was safe except for all the shit running down my back. I still felt good but dreaded going home to change clothes. I was damned if I'd stayed at the barn, but I had cow poop all over me to deal with by not staying. I couldn't win for losing. It was sort of like

Andy Utley had told Russ and me about getting shot down on a bomb-ing raid a few months before the end of the war and being captured by the Germans, I figured.

"Hell, it was my first mission," he'd said, sitting out in the swing between two trees in Russ' backyard one early summer evening. "I was eighteen years old, for Christ's sake. Just out of high school. I was the belly gunner on a B-24 Liberator that was flyin' bombin' raids out of Italy to the Ploesti oil fields. Lash Griffin from up at Martinsville was the upper turret gunner. He was gettin' close to rota-tion. I think he had thirty-three missions. You had to have fifty to get rotated home an' out of the war at that time.

"Anyway, we was on a bombin' raid to Ploesti an' got hit over Albania about twenty minutes or so from our base at San Pancrazio on the way back. I felt three jolts in the plane an' knew we was in trouble. The tail gunner took a direct hit, an' the turret an' part of the plane blowed away. So I started tryin' to get out. My chute was bouncin' around all over the place. I chased it around the plane a little an' then had a helluva time gettin' the clips fastened after I got the chute on. But I got them fastened in time to roll out just before the plane started in a sharp dive to the left. That was close.

"Lash was still in the plane, standin' up with the navigator when I rolled out. Never saw him again or any of the other four who was still aboard. I reckon they went down with the plane. Four of us got to the ground in one piece. I landed in a tomato patch an' ran into some locals. I asked a woman to get rid of my chute so the Germans wouldn't find it. She did an' they put me up in an attic. I was shakin' real bad. They gave me some coffee. It was so strong, I couldn't drink it. I was up there for about half a day when some people came an' got me to go ID a body. It was Floyd Wilson, the tail gunner, or what was left of him. I couldn't recognize him at first. But he had red hair, an' he was the only redhead on the plane. He was all shot up an' looked just like a piece of raw meat wrapped in a flight suit. The whole left side of his chest was gone. Part of the plane was nearby. One of the locals had a shovel, an' I buried Wilson about four feet deep at the bend in a little stream. He had thirty-five missions when he died. I always wanted to go back an' get him, bring him home an' bury him. I think I could still find that place today," he said, looking off in the dark.

"Then I went back up in the attic. Next day they took me to the other crew members, an' we slept on the ground that night. Bill Samuels had a broken bone in his foot that hurt him so much he couldn't keep from hollerin' an' cryin' out. We all had first-aid kits, but the goddamn morphine packets was empty. Some asshole was takin' that shit back on the flight line. Wasn't even any aspirin or anything to help relieve the pain."

Andy looked kind of spooky to me then, sort of like I was feeling as I walked along towards home. He had a funny look in his eyes that I could still see in the fading evening light and a big frown on his face. He stopped to light a cigarette and the only noises I could hear was the blackbirds chirping in the maple trees around us and the rubbing of the chain swing on the metal pole as Russ moved the swing now and then. I could see Eunice washing the dishes through the kitchen window. I couldn't see anybody at our house over across Russ' garden. I could see the lights in the kitchen and the dim light of the front room shining through the hall and out the window and knew where everybody was and what they was doing just after supper. Andy's wife Naomi turned the kitchen light out as he blew his first drag off the cigarette out into the night. He smoked and talked quiet, and Russ and me listened. I wished I could have a cigarette like Russ and Andy, but I wanted to hear what Andy was saying more than I wanted a smoke.

"The next day, they came an' got us," he said, taking a long drag on his cigarette before he went on. "They didn't have any love for the Germans, but they had to look out for themselves, I guess. They put Samuels up on a horse an' headed us out of town, walkin' down the road with us. There was a bunch of them to start with. I looked around once an' saw a couple of them drop off an' go back. One by one, the people dropped off. Pretty soon there wasn't nobody except the four of us an' we ran into some German soldiers who'd been lookin' for us.

"'For you, the war is over,' a German soldier said when we stopped. They showed us Lash's an' Lt. McConnell's dog tags an' said some locals buried them where they hit the ground. The Germans didn't know about anybody else. The plane crashed on the next hill over from where we landed. The other three crewmen must have gone down with the plane. Captain Appleton's wife was due to have a baby anytime. He was the pilot."

That made me think about how my daddy got killed and I'd never seen him. I wanted to ask Andy about the baby and what happened to it, but he went on to say that the Germans split the crew up because Samuels had to go to the hospital and shipped them to different *stalags*. He never saw anybody again.

"The war still had a few months to go when I got shot down in August of '44. That winter was one of the coldest winters on record in Europe. We like to froze to death. The Germans was runnin' scared an' knew they couldn't last much longer. They took us on a march through that cold an' snow that killed half the men on the march. Somehow, I made it through to one place where we stayed 'til the weather broke. Then I got moved to another *stalag* in time to spend awhile there an' then see the gates opened an' the American Army come rollin' in to take us home. That was the happiest day of my life."

It sure as hell wasn't the happiest day of my life when I came walking down the street, and there wasn't any Army to take me home. I was headed there on my own, but I'd stopped in the lane on the other side of the shrubbery at Jimmy's house and taken my shirt off. After I'd unbuttoned it and leaned back to let it fall off of my shoulders, I took the shirt and tried to rub the cow shit off on the grass. Then I rolled the shirt in a ball and walked toward the street and home. I ran straight to the bathroom and slid the bolt home to lock the door hardly before it was shut. Not much cow shit had got on my jeans and only a little on my shorts. I could wash a little of that without doing the whole thing, I knew, but the shirt was going to have to be washed all over again. I threw it in the bathtub that just got put in less than a month before and turned on the water full blast, hot and cold both.

"What in the world are you doing?" Aunt Helen said over the splashing of the running water. "John Walter, answer me."

"What?" I'd heard her the first time, but was trying to get the cow shit down the drain before I answered.

"What are you doing? It's the middle of the afternoon."

"Oh, I fell down when we was playin' up to Jimmy's, an' I got pretty dirty. I'm just washin' up, Aunt Helen."

"You okay?"

"Yes, ma'am, I'm fine."

I started trying to go with Big and Sam more than I had been for a while and not playing with the boys when they all got together.

Richard and Jerry stayed on their side of the square, and I stayed on mine. But sometime later I saw Jimmy out in his front yard and went up to play with him. He said he had to feed the calves and asked me to come along. While he was getting a bucket of ground feed from the granary, he talked kind of quiet about what had happened with us boys. I didn't want to talk about it, but he keep talking in a quiet way that made me feel that he cared about us.

"You didn't tell anybody, did you?" he asked.

"Nope."

"Good. I've been wantin' to talk to you. It was bad the way Albert treated you. That wasn't right. I wouldn't treat you like that. An' he won't, either. If you'll suck me off, I'll make sure he won't bother you."

I couldn't believe what he was saying. One minute he was being real nice and the next minute he was doing the same thing him and the other two boys had done before. But as he was talking, he was taking his old cock out of this pants. It was hard and sticking up toward me at an angle, little black hairs sticking out of his jeans. He rubbed over his cock and moaned a little as he walked towards me.

"Just put your mouth down on it," he said. "I won't come in your mouth."

"No, get that thing away from me. You're crazier 'n a fuckin' bedbug. I don't want to suck your cock anymore 'n I do Big Al's. An' I sure's hell don't want to suck his."

"It's okay. Nothin' wrong with doin' it. Won't hurt a thing. I'll tell you when I'm comin', an' you don't have to worry about old Albert anymore. I'll take care of him."

"You can't whip Big Al," I said. "I can take care of that sonuvabitch my damnself."

"No, you can't," Jimmy said, walking closer to me with his cock still in his hand and looking bigger than before. "He'll catch you sometime. I won't let him do that. Just put your mouth down on it an' suck me off."

"No, get that fuckin' thing out of here."

"It's all right. I just want to see how it feels. I won't tell anybody, an' I will keep Big Al away from you."

I didn't believe that for a minute, but Jimmy kept on talking real soft and kind and said he wasn't going to hurt me or make me do it.

His cock didn't look big and red and ugly like Big Al's did. And I didn't feel as scared and upset as I did when Big Al was around and was going to force me to suck his old cock. I knew Jimmy wouldn't do that. He kept being nice and not being scary. But he kept following me real close, and I kept backing away.

"Just once," Jimmy said softly. "Nobody else will know."

"Just once?" I said, my back to the wall. "Why just once? Why not a hundred times? You're crazier 'n a goddamn loon. I don't even want to see that old thing. I want to go home right now. You said you wouldn't try to make me."

He smiled kind of crazy looking through glazed-eyes, mumbled something I couldn't make out and kept stroking his cock and jacking off. I looked around at the wall and backed into it, trying to buy time to figure out what to do. I couldn't believe I'd let myself get trapped again.

"I won't squirt in your mouth," Jimmy said real soft and took ahold of my shoulder and tried to bend me down to his cock.

I kept trying to back away, but he pulled me far enough down that my mouth was almost to touch the head of his cock. I shut my eyes, pulled my head back and gagged at the thought of what he was trying to get me to do.

"You dirty sonuvabitch," I said, screaming and jerking back. "You dirty, no-good sonuvabitch. Get away from me."

"It's okay, it's okay," Jimmy said and kept jacking off real slow and talking soft and low. "Just put your mouth down on it. That'll feel good to me. An' it won't take long."

Just then, he started jacking off faster and faster. I slid over to the corner of the shed and put out my right foot to kick him, if he came any closer. He jerked back and stood straight up as he started squirting and squirting out so far he almost hit me.

"You dirty sonuvabitch," I said, screaming again. "You dirty sonuvabitch. You aimed to put that old jazz in my mouth, you dirty sonuvabitch. I ought to kill you."

"No, I wouldn't have done that," he said. "I wouldn't have come in your mouth."

I turned away and headed for the door at the opposite corner of the granary while he buttoned up his pants. Tears wouldn't come, even though I wanted to cry. I was madder than hell, too. I'd come closer than I wanted to letting Jimmy get me to do something I'd have let Big Al kill me before I'd do. And there wasn't a goddamn thing I could do about it now. I should have kicked the sonuvabitch right in the balls and got the hell out of there when he took out his cock and started talking, I thought. But I hadn't. It was a close call that was over, one that I had just barely gotten through. I felt real bad about not kicking the shit out of Jimmy or dying while I tried. I wondered what Daddy and Sam and all the rest of the fellers I knew who'd gone off to war would think of me being so weak and cowardly like I was after I'd promised to make Daddy proud of me. And what would Big think? And Mother? And Aunt Helen? And the rest of my family? And the rest of the people in town? Not much, I thought. I didn't think much of my goddamnself, either.

Jimmy had other chores to do before dinner time. No way was I going to help him. I didn't even want to be around him and ran across the barnyard and out into the yard to my bike. I pushed it through the opening through the shrubs to the lane. Then I jumped on and had peddled the bike as fast as I could by the time I got to the road. Nothing was coming from either way, but I hadn't stopped to look. I bent low over the handle bars and kept peddling as fast as I could past Big Al's and Andy's and Russ' and our house and Miz Hancock's and Madge's and Horsey Matthews' and Miz Taylor's before I slowed down to turn the corner at Maggie Hamilton's and Joe Marshall's to the angling road out to the cemetery.

Lots of places around Bellair had something about them that let you be alone, if you wanted to. There was all kinds of toilets, even the girl's toilet at the school, the mulberry tree out back of Fannie Boone's old store, the tree house Richard and Jerry and me had cobbled up in the empty woods north of their house, a couple of old barns and an old brooder house behind Coony's little house that I wanted us to have club meetings at like Tom Sawyer did in Mark Twain's story about Tom that took place a hundred years before.

But none of those places could give me what I got at Charlie Kline's grave. I dropped my bike at the cemetery gate and ran down between the tombstones with family names of people who'd lived around Bellair since the early settlers came west. Miz Finley had told us that one day when she brought the whole school out to the cemetery on a field trip at dinner time and an hour afterwards. We'd eaten dinner out under the hickory nut tree in front of the cemetery, then walked among the tombstones while Miz Finley told us about the settlers coming west in covered wagons and by horseback. Some of them'd come from Kentucky and back East that way like they had in the McElligott family. But most of them had come from Ohio and on east from there. She talked about what kind of place Bellair was in her lifetime and before. That's where I learned that the Old Bed used to be a part of North Fork until they rechanneled the crick to take some of the water away from town when the bottoms got out and under water. After that, Jeff Williams' old mill was just a barn and the Old Bed was the town fishing hole in the summer and skating pond in the winter. Madge didn't like that, but that's the way it was.

"Did you know Jeff Williams, Miz Finley?" I asked when we walked through the corner of the graveyard where he was buried.

"Yes, I knew Jeff, John Walter."

"Was he a nigger, Miz Finley?" That was after I asked Madge if she used to be one and knew better than to use the word.

"He was a Negro, John Walter. And he was as fine a man as there was in this part of the country. That's what's important about a man. What kind of a man you are, what people think of you. That's what matters. Not your color."

I was thinking about that as I ran to Charlie's grave. I sure as hell wasn't a fine man or a fine boy or a fine anything. To tell the truth, I'd almost done what Jimmy wanted me to do because he talked so soft and nice and because it would have been easier than fighting. So I could've sucked a boy's cock for no goddamn reason and never fought like I should've. Ronal Crucell had told me not long before that it was just as much a sin in the Church of Christ to think something as it was to do it. That's what Horsey had said, too. I wondered if that had made me a cocksucker. All the names we called each other was mostly just bad words we used because we knew we wasn't supposed to say them. None of us wanted God to damn anybody, we didn't really mean that somebody's mother was a bitch or any of the other bad words we used. But I didn't want to be a goddamn cocksucker by any stretch of the imagination, whether it was real or just in my mind.

Usually when I went out to Charlie's grave I could talk and talk. That day I couldn't say a thing. I just sat there and thought about the whole thing and my goddamn life. After a while, I got up and walked back to my bike and rode home. I wished being in the granary had never happened. But it had, and I couldn't talk to anybody about it. Not even a dead soldier.

A couple of weeks later, I was up to the store where everybody else was that night. Big was playing forty-two and Aunt Helen was crocheting with a bunch of other women. It was almost dark, and Horsey had just turned the porch lights on. Some kids was playing Hide-And-Go-Seek on the east side of the store. Others was playing tag out in the street. Jimmy asked me if I wanted to go down to the Old Bed to see if there was any fish in the traps he had down there. At first I said no because I knew he'd try to talk me into sucking his cock. But I wanted to go and he promised me he didn't expect that. We walked down the road west past Coony Pfeiffer's house on one side and Ross Childers' on the other, past Maude Fell's and on past Alice Childers' house back up on the hill before he said anything else about it.

The lights from the store had slipped out of sight when we walked through the gate to Madge's place and the Old Bed. A bright full moon made it almost as bright as it was at the store. Jimmy started talking about cocksucking again.

"That wouldn't have been so bad the other day, would it?" Jimmy asked as we walked into the woods where the moonlight wasn't quite so bright. "My cock's clean."

"You want to try it?" I said. "Mine's clean, too. You can suck my cock. How'd that be?"

"No, I don't want to do that. But you can suck mine."

"No, I can't. I don't want to do that, either. An' I'm not goin' to. I'm goin' back."

"Don't go back. We got to check my traps. An' if there's any fish, we can build a fire over on the side of the hill by that old willow tree that sticks out over the water and roast the fish. Nothin' better than fresh fish, cooked over an open fire."

"Quit tryin' to get me to suck your cock."

"I'm not tryin' to get you to suck my cock."

"You sure as hell are."

"Well, it'd be okay. You don't have to do it very much, an' it'll be over. Just this time, an' I'll never ask you again."

By this time, we had walked to the west side of the Old Bed and stopped in the moonlight. It was hot and humid with the temperature still about ninety degrees. The moonlight filtering down through the trees gave the whole area an eerie look so you could see everything in light and dark almost at the same time. When I turned to see where Jimmy was, he had his cock out. I could see in the moonlight that it was hard. He was rubbing it and jacking off kind of slow.

"Just this time," he said. "I tell you when I'm comin', an' I won't never ask you to suck me off again. But please do it now. Ohhhh, please."

"No, goddamnit, Jimmy, I don't want to do that."

"Please. Just put your mouth down there an' suck it a little. Just a little. It'd feel so good, an' I'll never ask you again."

"You promise you'll never ask me again?"

"Promise."

"Then *don't* ask me again. I want to go back to the store."

"We will. Just do this first."

I was shaking from the cold and the dread and hating myself for even talking with Jimmy about sucking his cock instead of knocking the shit out of him. He was still bigger than me, and I looked around for a club to knock him silly but didn't find one. Then Jimmy squirted in the grass in front of me.

"I'll kill you if you ever ask me to do that again," I said, jumping back and away from him. "An' I mean that sure as hell."

He never said a word, and I turned and walked away. He soon caught up with me, but both of us was quiet on the way back to the store. I meant for him to never ask me to suck his cock again. I wasn't sure he understood that. But I meant it. And it'd be a cold day in hell before I'd do it, I was sure of that.

The first person I saw when we walked into the lights of the store was Jeremy Hamilton. He was out at the edge of the lights, looking up in the sky. When he saw Jimmy and me, Jeremy walked back toward us.

"Well, there's the tough little bastard," he said. "What've you been doin'? Off suckin' his cock? Or suckin' his cock off? Taste good, did it?"

He laughed.

I felt my face flush, lowered my head and ran straight at Jeremy's fat belly. I thought I could knock him down and beat the shit out of him. The picture of that had been in my mind over and over. But when I hit him, I just stopped. He was probably seventy-five pounds heavier than me and started hitting me with one hand while he held me by the back of my shirt with the other. His punches didn't hurt much, but I couldn't do much except cuss him.

"You goddamnsonuvabitchin'fat-ass cunt, Jeremy Hamilton. Let me go, let me go."

"I'll let you go when you say give," he said, dragging me to the front of the store and laying me back across the porch while the other kids gathered around to watch.

"Fuck you, fat ass," I said. "I ain't sayin' give to you."

He grabbed me by the hair and banged my head down on the concrete porch. I saw stars and started crying.

"Say 'give.'"

"Fuck you, you fat-ass. Kill me. But I'll never say 'give' to you ."

He banged my head down on the porch a couple more times, then slapped me across the face. I was crying and cussing and couldn't see what else was going on until I heard his mother's voice.

"Jeremy, whatever are you doing?" Fern Hamilton asked him. "Don't do that to John Walter. He's just a little boy."

"He's a smart-aleck little boy."

"You don't hit anybody like that. What's the matter with you?"

"Nothin' the matter with me, Mother. It's that crazy little boy there that's got somethin' the matter with him."

"You're a lyin' sonuvabitch," I said.

"That'll be enough of that kind of talk," Mother said from the door.

She and Aunt Helen took me off to the other edge of the porch and brushed the dirt off of me. Fern told me she was sorry and made Jeremy tell me he was, too. He said he was, but I knew he didn't mean it. That didn't matter to me either way. Jeremy Hamilton was a bully to little kids. He wasn't able to beat up on kids like Big Al or even Jimmy, but he could sure beat up on me. Mother asked Aunt Helen to take me home and get me cleaned up.

"Howard will be back in a few minutes," Mother said. "He's going to close up, so I'll be there pretty soon."

Riding home with Aunt Helen, I tried to sort things out in my head. Not long ago, things seemed so much simpler. Now, I wasn't sure what was going on or what to do. But I knew where I had to go and started getting things ready when we got home.

That night I went to bed long before I usually did and before any-one else. I couldn't go to sleep until after I'd heard everyone else turn in for the night. Then I'd sleep a little and wake up and think awhile about what had almost happened, about my daddy and about other things. I thought a lot about cigarettes and got up and went out to the pantry where Big kept his carton of Lucky Strikes. It was about half full, and I didn't think Big would miss a package. He'd grab two or three packages at a time and throw some in the glove compartment of the truck and maybe get another one or two the next morning. After I tucked the cigarettes in the pocket of my jeans, I slept until I heard Big start his truck and back out of the driveway.

I was dressed and ate a bowl of Wheaties and a banana before Mother went to work at eight o'clock. She always walked down to the corner on the narrow sidewalk, then turned and walked on the wider and newer sidewalk up past the Church of Christ, past Fannie Boone's old hotel and past Jake's old restaurant before she crossed the road and walked catty-cornered across the street to the store. I rode along with her all the way, feeling closer to her than I had for a while.

"What're you doing up and out so early, John Walter?" she asked as we passed Miz Taylor's house and I spied a hummingbird moving in a blurry line, darting from flower to flower and then going out of sight in the flash of an eye.

"Look at that hummingbird, Mother. How can they fly like that?"

"I don't know, " she said, watching the hummingbird with me. "Is that why you're up and out so early? To watch hummingbirds?"

"No."

"Where're you going?"

"Oh, just ridin' around the square an' down to the school like I always do," I said, almost falling off my bike as I slowed down and made slow circles in the street so I could stay with Mother. "Ain't nothin' else to do around here. Big's already gone this mornin', an' Sam ain't been here yet."

"Well, you just be careful what you're up to. It's like that time Freda Trout told me that you almost drowned over at the gravel pit. You wasn't even supposed to be over there."

"I didn't even about drown. She's crazy."

"You never did tell me what happened."

"We had our bottles of pop tied on a rope to keep 'em cold while we was swimmin' an' playin' around. When we got ready to eat what we brought for dinner, Ronal pulled the rope up an' my RC was gone. His was there an' so was Richard an' Jerry's. I didn't get mine tied so it'd stay. The rope was tied to that old cable that goes all the way across the gravel pit, so I just held onto the rope an' went down to see if I could find my RC. I wasn't under very long an' wasn't about to drown."

"But you can't even swim, John Walter."

"Can, too, But I wasn't swimmin'. I was holdin' onto the rope that was tied to the cable."

"Did you get your RC?"

"Nope. It was too deep. It went straight down from the little place by the bank where we was swimmin'. I just walked right off into the deep an' went down to the end of the rope an' hadn't touched bottom."

"John Walter!"

"I came right back up with the rope," I said, not telling her what it felt like to walk off the edge of the bottom where I was feeling along for my RC with my feet when all at once I just slipped off into the hole that went straight down. It was scary, but I held onto the rope and pulled myself back to where I could stand up and walk to the bank. It was exciting, too. As I'd walked toward the other boys and came up out of the water, I felt my cock starting to get hard. That'd never happened like that.

"Well, you stay away from there. Whether you about drowned or not, you stay away from there. I don't want to have to hear Freda Trout tell me where you've been or what you've done at someplace you're not even supposed to be."

There was a lot of places that I wasn't supposed to be, to hear Mother tell it. She was always telling me where not to go, what not to do and how to take care of myself. Mostly, I listened and then did whatever we decided to do. Maybe there was some places and things that was dangerous, but Bellair and the people and things all around was home. It wasn't the wild place like I'd heard it was, and still wished it was, during the oil boom days when Jake's place right down from the Church of Christ had gambling and drinking right when church was going on. Now a bunch of fellers sat on the store porch, smoking and chewing, telling stories about them times or something else for the hour Horsey closed the store on Sunday morning to go to church.

"Hey, Butchman, come here an' show these men how you can cuss," Ross Childers said one Sunday morning as he walked over from the house on the hill catty-cornered from the store and where Russ Taylor said old Doc Ferguson lived and practiced medicine after he came there from being a doctor in the Civil War. Ross wore a suit and tie, hat and overcoat like he did every day in the winter. When it wasn't cold he didn't wear the overcoat, but he always wore a suit coat. "Come on, Butch, show how you can say cocksucker."

"Goddamsonuvabitchincocksuckinlittlefucker," Butch said all at once. He'd been five or six then, a chubby little red-headed boy Ross had adopted when he married Vena who'd come up from Kentucky with Jack Moore where she'd met him when he was there in the Army. She got knocked up, Russ Taylor said to me one day when I was over at his house, and Jack got shipped off to the war where he got killed just like my daddy had and never came back to Bellair. I didn't know that Ross wasn't Butch's real daddy until Russ told me.

"Can't he cuss good?" Ross asked, smiling and then laughing a kind of cackle that went on down to his belly and made it shake. "Huh? Ever hear anything like that?"

Nobody said much. I looked at Big but couldn't tell anything by looking at him. I knew that if I ever used words like that in front of him, let alone in front of a bunch of fellers on the store porch on Sunday morning, I wouldn't be able to sit down for a week. "Boys that don't do like they're supposed to an' got hard heads will have sore asses all the time," Big had told me more than once.

Mother had told me what she'd been telling me a lot more than once. When she told me again to be careful and not to go anywhere but around the square, I nodded and said, "Yes, Mother." She walked up on the porch and on into the store as I turned north and rode up past Richard and Jerry's house and on up to the road to The Corners.

I figured she'd think I was just riding around the square, and Aunt Helen wouldn't see me heading east. There wasn't many houses on that part of the square. There was only Jake and Maggie Brummet on one side and John and Florence Hamilton, old Doc Ferguson's girl, on the other besides Lucy Childers' house where Richard and Jerry lived with their mother and grandmother. Then before you left town, there was only Sam and Josie Schaffner's place up on the other road, Coony's little house and the old Jones house that had been empty for years.

I sat back on the bike seat and let one hand hang down by my side as I peddled along like I did all the time riding around town. When I got out to Arthur and Fern Hamilton's place and started down the hill down to Borax, I started pedaling as fast as I could. I needed to go as fast as I could going down hill to get up the other hill without having to peddle too hard. And I had to be back in Bellair by noon.

The hard tracks in the gravel was easy to ride in. But riding got a little tricky when I had to cross a gravel ridge and get out of the way of a car coming from behind me. That only happened once before I got to The Corners. Going across the Willow Crick bottom, one of Big's trucks came down the hill behind me. The front wheel turned in the gravel ridge and slid out from under me. I caught myself with my right hand, skidded along the edge of the road and skinned the devil out of the palm of my hand. I looked up and saw that it was Sam. He stopped before I could get up.

"You all right, Sedwick?" he asked, a big grin on his face.

"Yep."

"Where you goin'?"

"Just ridin'."

"A bit far from home, ain't you?"

"Not on a bike."

"Watch out for them gravel ridges," he said and drove off down the road. He was empty so it didn't take him long to cross the bridge, get up the hill and out of sight.

I took my big red handkerchief out of my pocket and wrapped it around my scraped and bleeding hand. It stung and hurt as I got on my bike and started out again. At the top of the hill, Chris and Elsie Matthews lived in the place where my Granddad McElligott had built a house after him and Sam's grandma had got married.

She died is how come Sam and me didn't have the same grandma. I saw Elsie at the pump and left my bike at the edge of the yard and walked over to her.

"What happened to you?" she said, lifting the bucket of water off the pump.

"Had a wreck," I said, unwrapping the handkerchief.

"Let me look at that. My goodness, you've scraped that pretty bad. Come in the house and let me doctor that for you."

I didn't want her to make no fuss, but she took me inside. It was the only time I'd ever been inside the house except at the shivaree and everybody was crowded around. It wasn't a lot different than the house Granddad had built a little later across the branch from his mother where she'd lived in a little old house all of her life and raised four kids. Until he died, he lived there with Grandma and Marie, their girl who got some kind of a fever when she was young that gave her a bad heart. She'd stayed home with them ever since I could remember.

Both houses had a kitchen at the back with a porch leading in. One porch was on one side, the other was on the other side. The front rooms and bedrooms off the kitchen was pretty much the same. Just two rooms. Granddad had added another front room onto the new house but closed it off in the winter except on Sunday when his family came for dinner. Grandma Phoebe's house was just two rooms downstairs and one upstairs. We always went over and looked around when we was there on Sunday.

Elsie had me hold my hand under the pump at the kitchen sink while she pumped water. Then she dried it with a towel and poured some peroxide over the scrape on my hand and foam popped up everywhere.

"That'll kill the poison," she said. "I probably should put some salve on it and tie a rag around it to keep it clean."

While she was doing that I thought of the story about Granddad that Burns Larue was telling me up at the store one afternoon. That was the first time I even knew he lived in the house. "Oh, land sakes, yes," Burns had said. "He built the house an' lived there a good spell." When I asked Big about it all he said was that it was before his time. His time started years later up at the other place, he said.

By the time Granddad bought the place where he lived now there'd been eight kids born in the old place. And they'd buried four of them before they was eight or nine, Aunt Catherine Bryan told me when I asked her about it. She was one of the first kids and said she helped raise Daddy and Big and the rest of Grandma Mary Elizabeth's kids. Right after they moved to the new house, Aunt Catherine said her mother got sick and died. What Burns told me about Granddad when he lived there where Chris and Elsie Matthews did was something nobody seemed to know anything about.

"Your granddad raised hogs out there on the hill," Burns said. "He'd get a bunch fattened up an' drive them to market over to Palestine. When he got back, he'd ride into Bellair an' get in a poker game at Jake's. Back then, them poker games might go on for two or three days or until people went busted."

"Did Granddad go busted?"

"I 'xpect he did sometimes. Everybody did. But now he liked to play. He was a good poker player. Liked his whiskey when he wasn't playin' poker, too. He could shore put it away."

Burns was telling me the story just before Granddad died. And he was in bed most of the time by then and didn't say much more than hello when Big would take us in to see him. Then he'd just grunt. I don't think he always even knew who we was. One time he looked up at Big and said, "Who is it? Bill?"

"No. I'm Bob. This is Bill's boy."

"Thundernation. If that don't beat anything. Where'n Sam Hill is Bill?"

I looked up at Big. He just shook his head and looked back at Granddad. So with him not being able to talk much or know what he was talking about when he did, I never had a chance to learn anything from him about driving hogs to market and then playing poker and drinking whiskey for two or three days. I did tell Big what Burns had told me an' worked it in when I'd asked Big about who'd built the house Chris an' Elsie lived in.

"That's a bunch of shit," Big had said, putting his western book down in his lap and looking at me. "I never heard anything about Pop playin' poker an' bein' gone for two or three days. I reckon he did live there. You can't always believe what you hear."

Big went back to reading his western book, and I imagined Granddad driving hogs to market like the cowboys in the western books did cattle and then riding into town to play poker. That made me feel real good about him. That was him, I figured, before he was my old, sick granddad. The rest of the family, except Big and Daddy, didn't seem the cowboy kinds Burns made Granddad sound like. Big was kind of a cowboy, but he never played poker or drunk whiskey that I knew of, except times when he got sick that time. From what I'd heard about Daddy, he might have done a little of both. But nobody knew what he had done after he left for the Marines, except get killed. That was the end of that, and I never talked to him about nothing.

I thanked Elsie, got on my bike and headed east again. Garvey Charles waved from his barnyard as I rode past his place and out onto a stretch of pretty flat land. For a while I settled back to an easier ride and passed Claude Cottrell, Dave Crandall's, George Scott's and on past the wide gravel to the Willow Church and Smokey Cottrell's old home place. Just beyond there, I started down the hill into another little crick bottom. My legs was beginning to feel the strain of the effort to get up the hills. So I tried thinking of why I was taking this ride. Almost getting Jimmy's cock stuck in my mouth hadn't changed a thing about how I looked. I still looked pretty goofy, I thought. My hair was stringy and had a cowlick that would never lay anyplace that looked right. One of my eyes drooped more than I liked to see it droop when I looked in the mirror. I always squinted up so it didn't droop. One of Mother's cousins and his wife had come to visit at Christmas and looked me over like I'd seen Big look over a bunch of cattle he was fixing to buy. Mother and Aunt Helen both liked Victor Black, but they didn't like his wife Sharon a bit. I felt the same way pretty quick.

"He's got that droopy eye like the Garners, Lorene," Sharon said, turning to her and laughing. "Isn't that cute?"

Wasn't nothing cute or funny about it that I could see. I tried to keep my eye squinted up but didn't always remember. And I still looked the same, anyway. No matter what Sharon Black said.

At the top of the hill, the land flattened out so you could almost see The Corners down the fence-row lined road. Closer to town some of the fence rows had been taken out and you could see farther around the countryside. Right at the edge of The Corners, the school marked the beginning of town and led up past old Doc Bates' house and office and on to the center of town and a four-way stop. Aunt Helen said one time that the old doctor had delivered every baby all around in every direction for miles and saw all the old folks die off there, too. I reckon he was still at it.

I turned north at the stop sign and went out of town past Charlie Franklin's Garage where Big always got his trucks worked on and out the tree-lined street with houses clear to the edge of town. I'd been afraid I'd run into Big along the road but felt pretty safe as I rode out of town. I figured I had about three miles still to go on what was pretty close to a ten-mile trip. The road north had a grade built up over the little crick, so there wasn't any hills to climb. I peddled fast and easy around a big sweeping S-curve and back north to the next crossroads. I was almost there before I could see the little church on the south side of the road and the cemetery on the other side. I'd only been there for Daddy's and Granddad's funerals and on Decoration Day every year since, when we'd decorate their graves. The American Legion boys put out little flags for them that'd been in the service and had a ceremony that ended with a rifle salute. I always felt real proud then.

I dropped my bike in the ditch outside the gate to the cemetery and went in to the McElligott part. There was a bunch of them that I didn't know much about. Nobody talked much about the family too far back. I thought maybe there must have been a thief or a murderer or something back early. But I just imagined that. According to what was written on the tombstones, some of the fellers had been in the Revolutionary War, the War of 1812 or the Blackhawk War. One of them even said War of the Flags. I didn't know anything about that one, I reckoned. I saw my great-granddad's grave. His tombstone said, William G. McElligott, June 6, 1838 - April 23, 1866, War Between the States, Union Army.

Grandma and her sister, Aunt Tilda, looked darker and had different-looking faces than other folks, high cheek bones and broad noses. Daddy and Big and Aunt Harriet favored them some, too. I asked Grandma one day if she was part Negro like Madge. She just shook her head and said, "No." That was good enough for me. I knew Grandma wouldn't lie. She looked different. Acted different. Didn't matter, though. She was Grandma. She once pointed to the fried chicken plate she'd just sat down and say to me, "There's the pulley bone, son." I looked up at her, wondered how she knew I liked the wishbone and felt real special. She had a soft look in her eyes.

Years later, I learned that her grandmother was an Indian. She never talked about it, and nobody knew anything about her.

Daddy's tombstone was off behind his granddad's grave. Daddy's said: William S. McElligott, Illinois, Sgt. USMC, 1st Bn. 7th Reg. 1st Marine Div., World War II, March 7, 1917 - Oct. 25, 1942. I sat down in the grass in front of the tombstone and took out the package of Lucky Strikes I'd taken out of Big's carton. For a while I just sat there smoking cigarette after cigarette. Nothing would come out of my mouth except smoke. I couldn't talk about what had happened or what to do about it. Then it just started pouring out.

"I'm sorry, Daddy," I said, holding back a sob to keep from crying but feeling my eyes water up. "That goddamnsonuvabitchin' Big Al Matthews grabbed me an' stuck his cock in my mouth that day. An' it's been one fuckin' thing after another since then. Now I almost let that goddamnsonuvabitchin' Jimmy Barker stick his goddamn cock in my mouth an' didn't knock the shit out of him for even tryin' to do it. He acted like he's goin' to keep Big Al from botherin' me or that he wants me to do somethin' with him. All Jimmy wants is to stick his cock in my mouth, too. He's no different than Big Al. I want to be strong an' tough like you was, Daddy. How can I do that an' let myself get in such tight spots? How can I be tough like you?"

I went on for a little longer and got so I was tired and couldn't talk. Then I just stared at the tombstone as a soft breeze blew across my face and made my face feel cold. What would my daddy think of his little boy having somebody trying to stick a cock in his mouth, I wondered. Or having a little cocksucker for a boy? I let loose with a holler that almost took my breath. What was the matter with me? My daddy and none of the fellers I knew would ever have somebody trying to get them to suck their cock. And they'd kick the shit out of them, if they did, I knew.

I don't know what I expected, but nothing much had happened besides me talking my feelings out. I still felt like it was me against everybody else, that I was still alone in the world. More alone than I'd ever been. But I was plumb worn out, and it felt good to feel that way. A few minutes later, I picked up the pile of cigarette butts I'd smoked to throw them in the ditch and walked back to my bike. The sun was getting pretty high in the sky. I had to hurry to get back to Bellair by dinner time.

11

That morning in the cemetery at Daddy's grave helped some with handling things. I was able to go on and watch close enough to stay away from Big Al and Jimmy unless other fellers was around like they was when I started working out with one or both of them hiring out to the same farmer. And baling hay was a job they was on when I was getting big enough to be able to help out on by the summer after I turned eleven. I was almost as big as some of the older boys, but I wasn't as strong. At least I could drag a bale over to the edge of the truck. I couldn't throw one up in the truck yet. I could get one up on the back of a wagon by sticking my knee in the bale and shoving it up to the edge and then shoving it on up. Both arms and both knees got all scratched up, but I liked to work with everyone else and not just stand around and watch.

Back at the barn, I'd always get up in the haymow and catch bales coming off of the corn hiker and drag them away. Two fellers would unload the wagon and two or three of us would stack the hay in the mow. One day over at Leland McCallister's, I was dragging bales off the hiker and dragging them to the back of the mow where Big Al and Ronal was stacking. Ronal was up on the stack, Big Al would throw them up after I drug them back to him. I stood at the door to the mow and watched Leland and Bennie Miller laughing and talking as they looked at a bale Bennie kicked off and on the hiker. The bales had been coming up almost faster than I could drag them back to Big Al. But the one Bennie had kicked off was the only one coming up. I was glad to stick my head out the haymow door and get what breeze there was. I waited until the bale was almost at the door before I drew my head back and stood up to catch the bale and saw what they'd been talking about down on the wagon, a snake caught up with the hay. I jerked my hands back and let the bale flip off the end of the hiker and fall on the floor away from me.

"Goddamnsonuvabitchinfuckin' snake," I said, screaming and looking down at Leland and Bennie who stood laughing hard. Leland doubled over and nearly busted a gut. "What'd you goddamnsonuva-bitches send a goddamn snake up for?"

"You afraid of snakes, John Walter?" Leland asked, still laughing. "Hell, that old snake won't hurt you. It's dead."

"I don't give a dang if it's dead or alive. I don't want to see no goddamn snakes."

Big Al and Ronal had come over to see the snake. The baler had picked it up in the field and baled it up right along with the hay. The old snake was smashed in with the rest of the hay the length of the bale with the head sticking out under one of the baler twines. I'd almost put my hand right on the head.

"Here, John Walter, look at this sonuvabitch," Big Al said, picking the bale up and turning toward me. "It's deader 'n hell."

"I don't care if it's dead or alive. You get that fuckin' snake away from me right now or I'll kill you."

Everybody laughed and I knew that the kidding wouldn't go much farther right then. Leland hollered up to me to take the bale over by the manger and throw it down. "I'll take the snake over for the hogs after while an' leave the hay," he said. "Or do you want to take the snake over to the hogs now, John Walter?"

"Not hardly," I said. I didn't know why I was afraid of snakes, but I didn't like them one bit. I was all right if I saw them first, like when Madge or Aunt Helen or Russ chopped one's head off and left it laying in the road or in the garden, still moving until night. "Them sonsabitches won't die all the way 'til the sun goes down," Russ said one day, leaning on a hoe and watching the snake he'd just killed wiggle and slide around. But if I didn't see the snake first, I was scared about as much as a feller can be scared. I never been more scared, anyway. Maybe as scared.

One day just after we moved to Bellair, I was taking the shortcut to the store through Madge's backyard, across Miz Taylor's yard that I mowed years later and on through her old barnyard where there was a path through and on across the Church of Christ yard and past Fannie Boone's old hotel where she still lived with her son George — or him with her. The paint had peeled off the old two-story house that had been a hotel during the days of the county oil boom forty years earlier. The out-buildings wasn't painted, either. The grass was hardly ever mowed and looked more like a field than a yard. Everything taken together gave the place a kind of eerie, half-lived-in look that made it hard for me to imagine it being a lively hotel and stable back in the old days. But I always tried to see it that way when I passed the place after we'd moved in from the farm.

Just before I got to the churchyard and Fannie's place, about half way into the path and weeds almost as tall as me, I stepped on a snake laying across the path. I saw the snake about the same time I put my foot down on it. I let out a yell and jumped straight up in the air. When I hit the ground again, I was running full speed out of them weeds. My heart was beating so fast and I was breathing so hard by the time I got to the road that I had to sit down at the edge of the yard and rest. Looking back toward the path, I could see me jumping high in the air and legs pumping through the air before hitting the ground running. It was awhile before I took the shortcut to the store again.

But not long after that, George Boone was finally getting around to raking the yard and cleaning up a little like he did once in a while. He'd run across a snake and cut its head off and left it laying at the edge of the road. Big Al, Jimmy, Ronal, Richard and Jerry and me was walking along the road towards the store when Jimmy saw the snake. Richard and Jerry took off running. Jimmy picked the snake up by the tail, looking at the rest of us standing around in kind of a circle at the edge of the road. He faked throwing it at us a little bit and then threw it straight at me. That's what I'd been afraid he'd do while we stood as I turned right into the snake flying through the air. It hit me in the neck and wrapped all the way around. I let out another yell and clawed at the snake clinging to my neck. By the time I'd flung it away, I was a ways out into the churchyard. The boys laughed and went off to the store. I went off toward home. I was ashamed and mad as hell.

I'd asked Sam one day if he was afraid of snakes. For some rea-son, I figured he'd not like them, either. I could hardly believe what he told me.

"I used to have a pet snake when I was a kid," he said. "I'd let it slide around on my neck an' coil around my arm."

"You're kiddin' me. I'd have a heart attack."

"No, I've always liked snakes. Mice an' rats are somethin' else. I hate them little devils. My mother made me carry one she'd caught in a trap to throw out to the cats when I was four or five. I screamed an' hollered all the time. Ain't liked 'em since."

Later I rode with him one time when we got over to the hog alley in the stockyards in Indianapolis about midnight to unload a double-deck load of hogs. We was driving them down the aisle to a pen a ways off. Just as we turned a corner in the aisle, a big old rat that was bigger than any rat I'd ever seen come scurrying across in front of us. I kind of froze and watched it go under a pen on the other side. Sam jumped up on the opposite side of a pen hardly before I'd seen the rat. The old stockyard feller who'd been standing to turn the hogs and get the ticket laughed and said, "Afraid of them rats, huh? I'd ought to go get you a couple to take home with you. They's plenty of 'em around here that I could give you."

"Be the last goddamn time you'd ever do anything like that," Sam said and handed the feller the ticket to sign. "I'll guarandamntee you that right now."

The feller took the ticket and we left.

"You should've seen old John Walter's face," Leland said when we was washing up at dinner time, still laughing about the snake. "His eyes got as big around as silver dollars, an' he jumped back like he was shot."

I knew he was kidding me and that other fellers were scared of snakes, too. Now, though, everybody knew that I was scared of them and had seen me show just how much. That was bad enough. But then there'd be other fellers hearing about it from stories that are told all your life. Some of them are good, some funny and some bad. Whichever, Dad Garner was always telling me that they get around and that a feller's name was the only thing he could take to the grave with him, so he'd better watch out how he lived his life. I thought that was a little silly, but I was beginning to see what he meant. Maybe being afraid of snakes wasn't a bad thing, but I didn't want to have to hear it all my life.

I'd never heard any bad stories about my daddy, and stories was about all I had of him. I'd ask Mother and Big about him now and then. Big'd always tell me stories about when they was kids.

"He thought he was big enough to come out an' help in the field long before he could do much," Big said on the way to the gravel pit one afternoon. "We was cuttin' fence row down there west of Wiley's barn one afternoon. Your dad wanted the ax. I told him he'd cut his leg off an' to just stay out of the way or drag brush over to the pile. Your Uncle George an' Uncle Vern was way up ahead but come back to burn the piles. I was cuttin' an' stackin' brush as we come. It was a pretty cold day, but I got hot an' took my waist off an' hung it on the brush pile an' we went on stackin'. George come along an' lit that pile after while. He didn't see my waist. But in just a little bit, your dad seen the dang thing burnin' an' pulled it off. Instead of puttin' the fire out, though, he held the waist up an' hollered at me to look. It was burnin' pretty good by the time I grabbed it an' stomped the fire out. Had a hole in the back big enough you could put your head through.

"How old was Daddy?" I asked, laughing and picturing him holding the waist, an old blue coat of overalls material like Grandma wore outside now. I imagined hers had belonged to Daddy.

"Oh, I 'xpect he was nine or ten. I don't know. Somewhere around your age, I reckon. Maybe younger. But old enough to know better than to stand there laughin' an' let my dang waist burn. He still laughed about it when we talked about it later. Told me I ought to look out for my own things. Him an' Harriet kept us entertained."

Mother'd tell me stories about the little time they had together. She lived on up toward Martinsville and never got down to the Moonshine Store where Daddy's family went. One night Josh Ruffner who lived across the field from them came by and got Daddy and Big to go to the Needmore Store to hear somebody play guitar and sing. Turns out it was Uncle Homer Workman and some fellers. Aunt Millie was married to him and Mother and Aunt Helen was along with them. They was standing over by the sacks of beans to the side of the store. Mother said her and Aunt Helen had spied Daddy and Big when they come in the store and talked about how handsome they was next to Josh and anybody else in the store. He was a big old feller now who walked bent over a little to one side and limped along.

He still lived across the field from Granddad and Grandma. I asked Sam about Josh one day when we loaded a load of hogs there.

"He jumped in with the 101st at the Invasion," Sam said. "Hurt his leg when he landed but went clear on through to the Rhine. By that time his knee was swelled up twice as big as the other one. Couldn't walk anymore. Thought for a while that he'd lose it. He's had a couple of operations on it, but they can't do nothin' with it. Sort of looks like he's drunk when he walks now, don't he?"

"I reckon he does," I said as I remembered how Josh stumbled along all the time.

But Mother and Aunt Helen wasn't interested in him. They was interested in Daddy and Big who seemed to be paying more attention to the music than to girls until two of them started throwing beans. Mother says it was Aunt Helen's idea. She says it was Mother's idea. When they talk about it, Big always says, "Biggest mistake I ever made was going up there with Josh Ruffner." Whichever one started throwing beans, they had got soup beans out of the sack and tossed them at Daddy and Big. Nobody would tell me much else, except that they started talking to each other. I could see where things ended up.

After everybody was washed up for dinner and Leland had kidded me a little more about the snake in the bale of hay, the talk turned to other things. I didn't know where this snake business was going to end up, but I didn't like the idea of it being a part of stories fellers would tell about me. The rest of them was more interested in what there was to eat than anything else. I was glad for that. I was hungry, too. Maude McCallister set a good table, and she put out plenty. The fried chicken on the first plate sort of disappeared. The second one didn't go away so fast. But I managed to eat three pieces of chicken, a couple of helpings of mashed potatoes and corn and three pieces of bread and gravy before I started slowing down much.

"Old John Walter's puttin' her away like we was puttin' the hay away this mornin'," Leland said. "You don't watch out, you won't have any room for pie."

"Looks like you put a little away yourself," I said. "I don't eat pie, anyway."

"Not even with a scoop of ice cream on it?"

"Nope, I don't eat no sweets," I said. And except for pop and candy, I usually didn't. That was because Sam didn't put sugar in his tea and said he'd got used to things without sugar when he was in the war and didn't like sweet things. So I said I didn't, either. It was kind of hard to not eat Aunt Catherine's pecan pie or Aunt Rosemary's Spanish cream pie, but nothing else bothered me much. I did drink a bottle of pop or eat a candy bar every chance I got, but I didn't put teaspoons of sugar on my cereal like everybody else in the family did. I was tempted to ask for a scoop of ice cream without the pie, but I knew that'd only bring on more teasing like I'd got about the snake. So I sat and watched the rest of them eat the pie and ice cream.

After dinner, we always laid around under a shade tree for a few minutes. I wanted to take a nap but didn't dare. I knew that was another thing I'd never hear the last about if I did. To help stay awake, I asked Leland where he was in the war.

"What war?" he asked, cupping his hand around a match to light a Camel. "Was there a war?"

"World War II," I said, thinking about Daddy getting killed in it. "You know what I'm talkin' about."

"Yes, I know which war you was talkin' about," Leland said, a crooked little smile pulling at the corner of his mouth and a playful twinkle flickering in his eyes. "I was in Europe."

"Was you in the Army?"

He laughed. "Not on your life. Not the regular Army, anyway. I was a flyboy in the Air Corps. Flew on B-17s over there an' was always scared to death that that airplane was goin' to fall out of the sky every time we went up. Never did. But we caught flak an' got hit on about every mission I ever flew on, all twenty-five of them. An' I thought there'd be more of them. When I first got to England, you had to have twenty-five missions to rotate home. They kept talkin' about raisin' it to thirty because the rookies was losing' more planes than the squadrons that had more experience, more missions. I figured they'd raise the numbers, an' it'd go up to thirty-five, forty, forty-five or even fifty, like it got to be or was down in the Mediterranean, by the time I got to twenty-five. Then I figured if I made fifty, they'd raised it to sixty. That's the kind of outfit the Air Corps was, any military outfit. They got you by the balls, no matter what it is."

He talked on for a few minutes before he said, "Let's go to work, boys. There's daylight goin' to waste an' hay waitin' to be baled. Got to give you somethin' to work off that big dinner."

We headed back to the field and hauled four more wagon loads to the barn before the baler broke down. These were the kind of breaks I liked. There wasn't anything else to do but wait when the wagons was empty, if it was something that could be fixed pretty quick so Leland didn't have to pay us too long for sitting around. He didn't seem worried about that and sat around with us telling stories while the baler was being fixed. It wouldn't be long before we was back in the field. Until we was, I asked Leland more about the war. He didn't mind talking and always had a little smile or a crooked grin on his face when he did. His eyes would sparkle the closest thing to a diamond in a goat's ass I reckon I ever saw anywhere.

"We was gettin' ready to go overseas," he said, standing off aways from us and in the sun, "an' was just killin' time, goin' out on liberty, drinkin', screwin' an' havin' as much fun as we could. Some of the boys got a little penny-ante game goin' a day or two before we was movin' out. I had this little blonde on my lap. She wasn't wearin' any panties that day. She didn't wear any most days."

He stopped and looked back at us. His eyes was dancing, and he had a devilish little smile on his face. He laughed and his eyes sparkled even more. His smooth and handsome face didn't have lines. He put me in the mind of the movie star Jeff Chandler. Both had tanned, leathery faces and hair gone gray young. Leland was always kidding and playing around. Sometimes I didn't know if he was telling the truth or kidding. But after seeing that snake him and Bennie sent up the hiker, I listened and watched him like it didn't make any difference.

"I kept my hand up under her dress most of the time, playin' with that old snatch," he said, kneeling on the ground in front of us, "an' playin' cards with the other one. She'd light a cigarette for me an' hold it for me between drags. 'Are we goin' to get married, Le-land?' she'd ask me an' wiggle her little ass on my lap. 'Hell, yes, Bet-ty, we're goin' to get married,' I'd say an' we'd laugh. Neither one of us cared much. I was goin' overseas, an' she was goin' to find another GI on his way to the war. But we had a helluva time for a few days. She was a some kind of woman is about the best I can tell you.

She had one of them snappers like you hear about but never find. I'm tellin' you now, she could make that thing talk. We had us some fun."

He sat back on the ground, put his hands behind his head and told us more about Betty than I'd ever heard about a woman. We laughed and listened. I felt a little funny hearing a grown up talk to us about women. But Leland was just entertaining us while the baler was down. He was a good storyteller.

"You always tell funny stories or stories where you're havin' a good time," I said. "It must have been a lot of fun bein' in the Air Corps."

"Oh, it was a blast," Leland said, chuckling a little and smiling. "I had more fun 'n a barrel of monkeys."

"Well, you talk like you did."

"I reckon I do. You remember the good times an' forget the bad ones. Don't do you no good to remember the bad ones. They're over an' done with. You can't do nothin' about 'em, except go on. The good times are worth rememberin'. I met some good people like that old Betty an' a lot of good men, saw places I'd never have seen an' done things I'd never have done. But there ain't enough money to pay me to do it again. I'd hate to be one of them poor bastards in Korea that got called back."

"How'd they do that?"

"Oh, they tried to get you to stay in the reserves when they let you out at the end of the war. Some of 'em did. Then them that come in at the end of the war got a choice of comin' home early an stayin' in the reserves or servin' their time out before coming home. Lot of guys chose to come home early. An' they went back to Korea a few years later. Royal Walker from over at Stoy was one of them that wasn't so lucky. He got killed right after he got called back."

Miz Finley had talked to us about the war in Korea in current events from time to time. When President Truman fired General MacArthur for what I reckon was not having the proper respect and wanting to disobey orders about flying across the Yalu River after the Chinese planes that would attack across the river and then fly back into a safety zone, Richard, Wayne Atkins, Joe Douglas, Marvin Miller and a bunch of us in fifth and sixth grades stood up in front of the room at recess and talked about what the general could do.

All of us thought he'd been treated much too bad for what he'd done and why he'd done it.

"Maybe he could join the Army as a private an' work his way back up to general again," Wayne said. "That'd show old Harry Truman."

We all nodded. That'd show old Harry Truman for sure. Dad Garner said that wasn't the way it worked since Harry Truman was running things. He was in charge, Dad said, whether anybody liked it or not. And I took it that he didn't like it from the way he sounded. He said the problem was that MacArthur was trying to run things, too. MacArthur didn't agree with Truman and wasn't going to keep his mouth shut about how to run the war and just follow orders. That's the reason he was fired, Dad said.

"But wasn't General MacArthur right?" I asked.

"I don't know about that, but right has nothin' to do with it," Dad said, looking through thick glasses at his twirling thumbs and his hands folded on his belly. "Accordin' to how you look at it, I reckon. But Truman's president. He told MacArthur not to cross the Yalu River. MacArthur said you can't fight a war where an army attacks you, then runs back across the river an' you can't cross that line. Truman doesn't want a war with China. An' MacArthur didn't want to fight a war where there are rules like that. Both of them have good points an' strong personalities. I 'xpect they both thought they was doin' the right thing."

"Maybe the war'll go on long enough," I said, "so I can go fight there an' help out."

"You won't have to worry about that. If there's not one there, there'll be one someplace else. People don't know how to get along. Probably never will. But we'll find someplace else to stick our nose where we have no business."

Dad and me listened to General MacArthur's speech to a joint session of Congress after he'd been fired and sent home in April 1951. Dad just sat there listening, not saying anything, after he told me a joint session of Congress meant both the Senate and the House of Representatives met together.

"Be still now," Dad said when General MacArthur started speaking. "I want to hear this."

The old general sure could talk. After a while, I wasn't even able to say a word. He had me nearly crying when he finished with the part about old soldiers never dying but just fading away. I wasn't sure how that could be, but it sure sounded good. I figured he'd get his job back after his speech. But that never happened. He did seem to fade away.

A long time later, I saw General MacArthur's farewell speech to the cadets at West Point when he'd been accepting some kind of an award that somebody had printed out poster size. It was hanging up above the store in Bellair with the rest of the pictures and the board with the Gold Star boys on it. The poster was pasted to a piece of cardboard with some string through the top so it could hang from a nail on an old door set back against the wall where anybody who still went up there now and then like I did could see what the general had said. His general's hat was at the top of the page, all proud and tall up there hovering over the words he said. I stopped to read them every now and then and saw others stop once in a while. It wasn't that old "Fourscore and seven years ago ..." of Lincoln's Gettysburg Address, maybe. But it wasn't far off. That old general said some things that I thought a feller could do well to remember and live by.

When he'd talk about "duty, honor, country," I'd think of my daddy, Charlie Kline, Sam and all the rest of the fellers around the country that had been away to the war. They'd done their part for duty, honor and country, just like the general said they could and should. By the time MacArthur made that speech at West Point, I was taking my turn.

Next chance I had to ride with Sam was one night when he had a straight load of cattle to take to Indianapolis and was going to stay at the stockyards and get a load of coal on the way home. He picked me up when he gassed up before we went out to Red Wilson's place to get a few head of his feeder cattle. I'd just come from the store to tell Mother goodbye. She told me to be careful and gave me a quarter. I took it because I knew it'd make her feel better and could give it back later. I knew I wouldn't have to spend it because Sam would buy us supper at the truck stop where he filled out his tickets for the stockyards and commission houses. We loaded up and got headed east in no time. And it wasn't long before we was sitting there in the truck stop.

"Where these steers goin' tonight, Sam?" I asked after we'd ordered supper. The meat loaf, mashed potatoes and gravy and green beans I'd seen go by looked almost like what we had at home. And for a minute, I was back home sitting with everybody instead of in the truck stop. Then another waitress stopped in front of us and put our supper on the counter in front of us, and Sam never answered.

"Here you go, sweetie pie," she said to Sam. "Is this Bob's brother's boy?"

"Yeah, this is John Walter."

"Pleased to meet you, John Walter," she said, holding out her hand. "I'm Maggie. Now you be careful with that meat loaf. It's hotter 'n the dickens."

"You can call me Sedwick like 'bout everybody else does," I said and went to shoveling the food in. By the time I finished the mashed potatoes and gravy and the green beans, the meat loaf was only lukewarm. I looked at the pie in the case but knew Sam and me never got pie and forgot it. He was eating slower than me. Maggie had stopped in front of him and stood with her arms leaning on the counter, looking into his eyes.

"You've not been in for a week or two," Maggie said. "Got another girlfriend someplace else?"

"Have I got one here?" Sam said, grinned and took the last bite of meat loaf and doubled the last piece of bread to stick in his mouth.

"You might have," she said and grinned back, "if you wanted one."

I twirled around on my stool and looked at the back wall. When I twirled back around Maggie was walking back to the kitchen for someone else's order. Sam picked up the check and his tickets and walked around to the cash register. Maggie came back to take the money. I saw that our supper was not quite two and a half bucks and Sam gave her three bucks.

"Keep the change," he said and took a toothpick. "I'll see you here Saturday night."

"Sure will."

Sam flipped the toothpick away and lit a Lucky Strike.

"Let's get them cattle to Indianapolis," he said. "I want to get a little sleep tonight."

He had the truck started and in gear hardly before I was in the truck.

I watched Brazil come into view as we rounded the curve on Route 40 and headed across the railroad tracks and down the main street of town. Since we left the truck stop and was heading out for the stretch on into Indianapolis and the stockyards that was always the best place to talk or be quiet or whatever you felt like doing, I'd been trying to decide whether to ask Sam about Maggie or the war. I'd waited to ask about the war after we'd got loaded up because the stock and us had to get settled down after being on the road for a while. Then we stopped at the truck stop and Maggie was there.

"I reckon you got a girlfriend now, Sam," I said just out of Brazil when we was picking up speed on the open road. "Looks like she likes you pretty much."

It was getting on towards night, but I could still see Sam's face turn beet red. I'd seen him mad and glad and a lot of other things when his face would get red with the feeling. But I'd never seen him embarrassed. His face was a different kind of red. The look on his face was one I'd never seen before.

"You little dickens you," he said and went back to driving up and down the big hills that led into Putnamville and on through Stilesville, Belleville and Plainfield before getting on into Indianapolis and the turnoff to the stockyards. He was always shifting up or down with the gears as we drove through the hills and the towns. I watched him every time he shifted, whether it was just putting the stick up or down for the two-speed axle or going up or down with the five gears. He always double-clutched when he shifted and got a rhythm going that he never stripped the gears like Big'd raise the devil with fellers, if he ever heard it. Sam was so smooth when he shifted. He told me to listen to the motor to tell when it was time to shift. I did and got so I could tell just a second before he'd shift. That made me feel like a million dollars.

I'd feel good every time I saw another town sign at the city limits show up in the headlights, too. They all seemed like a foreign country to me. It was kind of like the places they'd gone through after the Invasion and on through to the end of the war that Sam ticked off when I could get him to talking about it. I could check off another one of the Indiana towns as we rolled towards Indianapolis with the load of cattle.

"Why didn't you go to Korea, Sam?" I asked when we reached the top of a hill outside Putnamville. "Leland McCallister said something about it the other day, but I didn't really understand what he was talkin' about. Reserves an' things like that."

"Oh, they had this point thing durin' the war," Sam said. "You got so many points for how long you'd been in, how long you'd been overseas an' one thing an' another. After the war was over, they was processin' men out accordin' to point totals. Lot of 'em that came in right at the end of the war hadn't been in long enough to have many points. So they offered them a year early out if they'd sign up for the reserves. Quite a few of them fellers did. Then when we got tangled up in that mess over in Korea, them fellers got called up."

Sam allowed he didn't want to have nothing to do with that mess over there. He said he was danged lucky that other time and had no desire to go back to the Army for another hitch.

"No, sir," he said. "I got my fill of it a long time ago. It's like I've said before, I wouldn't take a million dollars for what I've seen. But I wouldn't go through it again for a million dollars. I'll bet a lot of them old boys who signed up for the reserves an' are over there in Korea freezin' their asses off wish they'd done another year before gettin' out that other time."

"But they're doin' their duty," I said, thinking about how it'd be to go through something you wouldn't take a million dollars for and doing your duty. "Ain't a feller supposed to do his duty for his country? That's the good thing about bein' able to fight in a war, I reckon."

"Ain't a damn thing good about fightin' in a war," Sam said, shaking his head all the time I was talking. "If they'd let them sonsabitches fight them that start them, there wouldn't be as many wars. It ain't always about duty, honor an' country an' all that horseshit. When it comes right down to it, it's about your outfit. For them that's doin' the fightin', anyway. You try to look out for each other. An' you can't always do that. The rest of that bullshit is for the politicians an' the recruitin' posters."

"Our family must've believed all that stuff."

"How'd you reckon that?" Sam asked, settling back a little and looking over at me.

"Well, I'm doin' this family tree thing at school," I said. "An' goin' way back there's McElligotts in 'bout all the wars goin' back to the Revolutionary. One of 'em was at Valley Forge. One or two of 'em was in the War of the Flags, whatever that was, the War of 1812, maybe, because they was some of 'em in that one. Another one was in the Blackhawk War. Three or four of 'em was in the Civil War, one of 'em even fightin' for the South."

"How'd you find all that out?"

"I talked to Grandma an' Aunt Christine, mainly. An' I looked in the graveyard over at Wesley Chapel where Daddy is buried. I wish I'd thought to talk to Granddad, but I wasn't much interested when he was still able. An' I read in Marie's scrapbook that's got all kinds of things in it, stuff about Daddy an' you, an' talked to her an' Aunt Annie. Russ tells me a lot about people around Bellair, the ones that went off to war an' them that stayed. That tells me a lot about our own people an' the fellers around home.

"I learn about my ancestors an' the way they lived back then an' what they done. Big says it don't matter none who your people was or where they came from, but I want to know what kind of people I come from an' what they've done in their lives. Maybe it don't matter, but it's interestin' an' helps me see how a feller ought to live his life."

Sam nodded and laughed. Then he turned to me and said, "Don't go gettin' them ideas in your head too much, Sedwick. I love this country. But this bein' in a war ain't what you seem to think it's all cracked up to be. I wish I'd never had to go through one. An' you'd have a daddy to grow up with, if he hadn't been in the war."

After that he didn't say anything for a while, and I just sat there thinking about what he'd said. I figured he was probably right, but it was one of them things that I'd have to find out for myself one day. I'd already decided that.

Thinking about things like I was, time went by real quick. Sam turned off on Kentucky Avenue for the stockyards in no time. With a straight load of cattle, all we had to do was back up at the cattle pens and let them all out at the same place. It didn't take long at all before we was unloaded and pulling over to the side where Sam stopped to scoop the sawdust out of the bed we'd gotten from the sawmill for taking the load of cattle. It was a little before midnight Indiana time, same as ours 'cause we was on fast time in the summer. We was going to stay at the Stockyards Hotel and go back to Brazil to get a load of coal

in the morning. Sam said he slept in tanks and on the ground enough
to do him for a lifetime and he was going to sleep in a bed like a feller
had ought to whenever he could.

I'd never stayed at the Stockyards Hotel or in a hotel anywhere
for that matter. The last time Big had stayed over there was when he'd
brought bedbugs back. Aunt Helen just had a fit then. They took all
the bed clothes outside and hung them on the clothesline before she
washed them. And they opened the doors and windows and gave the
house a good cleaning. The bedbugs was everywhere, biting everybody. I reckon that's where that old saying came from that Mother and
everybody had always said to me when I went to bed. "Sleep tight and
don't let the bedbugs bite," they'd said ever since I could remember.

"They still got them old bedbugs here, Sam?" I asked as we walked
down the halfway. I liked the old stockyard building. Four hallways
led to a big center opening that looked like the four-way stop at The
Corners where each road led out to Bellair one way, the Busy Bee
Farm another, Porterville another and out towards Martinsville the
other way. At the stockyard office, we came in from the outside and
took the tickets to the commission houses and walked to the center
and on around to the restaurant and hotel. There was sale bills and all
kinds of notices tacked on the walls or boards.

"I imagine they have somewhere around here," Sam said, smiling
down at me. "They fumigated after that time Big an' Gus Trout brought
that bunch home. But they ain't far away."

At the restaurant, we sat at one of the horseshoe-shaped counters
while Sam got us a room. He got a glass of water. I was thirsty but
didn't get any. I was always so afraid I would wet the bed when I was
little that I got in the habit of not drinking anything after supper. Back
then, there wasn't a thing in the world worse than to wake up in the
middle of the night while or just after I'd wet the bed. I was always
too ashamed to get up and tell Mother. So I just laid there in it and
went back to sleep. At first, it'd be warm and wet. When I'd wake up,
it'd be smelly and cold. I hated to see Mother take the feather bed out
to the clothesline to hang it out to dry and air out so everybody could
see and never took any chance that it'd happen again.

Sam got the key, and we went up some stairs to the rooms. I felt
like I was staying in one of them hotels in the cowboy movies.

There wasn't nothing fancy about the rooms. Ours had two beds and a dresser was all I could see.

"I'll take this one," Sam said, then pointed over to the far wall. "You take that one."

"Do we take our clothes off?" I asked.

"I'm just going to pull my shoes off an' lay down. We ain't goin' to be here long enough to get comfortable, Sedwick. I'd like to get back down for breakfast by four so we can get back to Brazil by the time the mines open."

He turned off the light. I pulled off my shoes and laid down on the bed like I figured Sam was doing. Tired as I was, I went out just about as quick as that light. It didn't seem like no time until I heard Sam say, "Time to get up, Sedwick. I can smell the bacon cookin'."

I couldn't smell bacon cooking, and I didn't feel much like getting up. But I rolled over and slipped my shoes on and had them tied before I could keep my eyes open. It was dark, anyway, so I didn't figure it made any difference.

We stopped at the toilet down the hall. I washed the sleepy dirt out of my eyes while Sam used the stool. I could just see in the mirror and smiled a little at the sleepy-eyed little boy looking back at me. Ain't this living? I thought. I went in and peed and peed after Sam was done. He'd lit a cigarette while he was doing his business. The smell of that mixed with the smoke and the match and the old pee smell. It put me in the mind of what I smelled in the old outside toilets.

At breakfast, a few other truckers was scattered around the two counters that was open. Sam ordered sausage and eggs with a side order of biscuits and gravy and coffee. I nodded and said, "Give me the same."

"Coffee, too?" the waitress asked, looking at Sam.

I nodded, hoping that I could have a cup of coffee. I knew I couldn't smoke in front of Sam or other grownups, but I sometimes had coffee. It tasted read good early in the morning like when Uncle Billie and Aunt Annie came up and we had fried catfish with bread and butter, which she'd churned, and black coffee.

"One cup," Sam said and nodded. "Over easy on the eggs."

I nodded.

He'd hardly finished his second cigarette and ground it out in the ashtray on the counter when our breakfast was put down before us.

I felt my eyes get big. There was two thick cakes of sausage, the eggs, two pieces of toast and a bowl of biscuits and gravy. It was almost falling over the edge of the bowl. I was hungry, but I didn't know if I could eat all that sat before me. But I salted and peppered the eggs and the gravy pretty lively and dug in.

Sam forked a big bite of biscuits and gravy in, looked over at me and grinned while he was chewing and swallowing. "You pepper things like Big does," he said. "You'll burn your stomach up someday with all that pepper."

"Nah," I said. "Big says pepper's good for you."

Sam just laughed. We didn't talk much after that; we just ate. I was getting full, but I was coming more and more awake. The coffee didn't taste as good as what Aunt Annie made with the fish that time, but this old coffee perked me up as I drank it. I began to feel like it was almost noon. I finished up eating just after Sam pushed his plate back and lit another cigarette. He smoked it and drank another cup of coffee before we left.

It was still pitch dark outside. As we headed out of the stockyards, I could see trucks still coming in and hear the sounds of livestock and truckers hollering as they unloaded their trucks. Things looked pretty much the same as they did when Sam backed the big Dodge ten-wheeler up to the cattle pens. Not until we got out on Route 40 did I look in the mirror and see the sky lighting up behind us. The sky was still pitch black ahead of us.

"I like mornings," Sam said, looking out over the road and letting go of the tight grip on the steering wheel he'd kept since we'd got on the road. "Wakin' up an' lookin' at everythin' comin' alive. Here, we're already up an' at 'em again this mornin'. Had our breakfast an' gettin' back to work. We've got another day."

I nodded to agree with him. Getting up in the morning was always good when I had something to do. Sometimes at home, I slept until eight o'clock or after because I didn't have anything to do or because I'd just lay there thinking about things and didn't get up until after almost everybody else had left. But there wasn't a thing like trucking with Sam early in the morning. Things seemed to be just like they ought to be. I reckon the way I was feeling was about how I wanted to feel all the time; I was doing what I wanted to be doing;

and I was the kind of feller I wanted to be. It was almost perfect. The night went away kind of gradual, but then all of a sudden it got light when the sun popped up behind us. I could see folks all over everywhere then, things taking on a look of something besides headlights.

It didn't seem to take us no time before we was in Brazil and turning off to go to the coal mine. Five other trucks was already there. Not much of a line, Sam allowed. Sometimes trucks was lined up all back down the road. I went to Indianapolis with Big one time when we came back to get a load of coal and there was at least fifty trucks in line for coal. Big rolled up a coat and went to sleep on the truck seat. I slipped some Lucky Strikes out of his package and smoked to stay awake. That's how Big said he started smoking when he was keeping his trucks busy all the time.

"There was time when I didn't pull my shoes off from Monday morning 'til Thursday or Friday," Big had said one time when Mother had caught me smoking. "That was back durin' the war when I'd take a load of stock at night an' haul gravel or somethin' else all day. I'd pick up soldiers whenever I saw them to help keep me awake. Most of 'em went to sleep right after they got in the truck an' wasn't no help atall. Only one time over on the state line I was just about to run through a barricade when this soldier reached over an' shook me before I hit it. I'd run through one in the same place a night or two before but got stopped before I hit anything else. So I started buyin' cigarettes to smoke at night to keep awake an' got started smokin' a long time after I was old enough to know better. You don't want to get started at somethin' like this."

I was already started, I thought. Since I quit picking up butts and gotten older, I'd think a lot more about how to get money for cigarettes or how to get a pack out of Big's carton. Anytime I saw a chance, I'd puff away on an old cigarette. The taste was really awful, to be honest. But it still made me feel so grown up to have a cigarette in my hand. After Big talked to me about smoking and told me about picking up hitchhikers to keep him awake, I still kept on smoking every chance I got but tried to stay awake to watch more than I did before. On the way back home with a load of coal one afternoon when we'd been to Indianapolis and came back to the mine like Sam and me was doing, I stayed awake and noticed Big going to sleep and drifting off

to the side of the road ever little bit. I was almost afraid to say anything as long as he was on the road. And every time I'd get ready to
say something, he raised his head a little and pull the truck back straight
on the road. One day coming into The Corners, I hollered just as I
thought we was going off the road.

He raised his head like he always did when I'd hollered before,
pulled the truck back on the road and said, "I'm awake."

I was still wide awake when Sam stopped behind the last truck.

"We're goin' to have to get this rack down in a hurry, Sedwick,"
he said. "They'll be loadin' coal in a few minutes."

Sam had the clamps out of the corners of the stock rack and started
letting the sides down for me to start clamping down. He'd have to
tighten them, but I could get everything ready for him. He sat the
stock rack gate across the back and let the front part lay on the sides
until we got under the coal hopper.

"How much we gettin' today, Sam?" I asked when we was done
with the rack and moving up in line.

"Around twelve ton, I reckon," Sam said. "Whatever we can get
on this old tandem outfit, twelve to fourteen ton. You goin' to help me
scoop it off?"

"Reckon I can. I can help, anyway."

Sam grinned and moved the truck up again. He stood outside the
truck and held the front part of the stock rack up while they loaded us. He
told me to stay in the truck. The truck bed bounced and rolled when the
coal began falling. I looked out through the little back window and then
in the mirror. I couldn't see much except coal dust and could only hear
the thumping of the coal as it hit the truck bed. Sam pulled the truck
up a couple of feet when the front of the bed was loaded and the front
part of the rack could lay on the coal. Then I saw him stand out on the
running board again and wave and tell somebody to shut 'er off.

We went back to the scales where we weighed empty on the way
in and stopped to weigh loaded. He went in to get the ticket and take
care of the paper work. From being around Big and Sam all the time,
I knew that trucking was more than just driving around the country,
seeing and doing things that was fun and interesting like I used to
pretend when I rode my bicycle up and down the streets in Bellair,

and Nancy, Mary Beth and Cheryl played like they was the waitresses at the truck stops. But I liked the trucking life.

"Reckon we'll have to stop at the truck stop," I said when we headed out of the coal mine.

Sam jerked his head over and looked at me. "I thought we might stop an' let me get a cup of coffee. Don't want to be too long. It looks like there's a storm coming up down in the southwest. See how dark it is off in the distance? It's comin' this way, I 'magine."

It did look dark off where he'd pointed when I could see through the trees. But it was a warm morning outside. The sun was shining real bright. And it was still shining like that when we pulled into the parking lot of the little truck stop just west of Brazil. Maggie was sitting in a booth drinking a cup of coffee and working a crossword puzzle out of the paper. She looked up and smiled. She got Sam a cup of coffee without asking. I didn't want anything because I had to use the toilet so bad. When I got back, Sam had finished his coffee and was ready to go.

"There you are, Sedwick," he said. "We've got some coal to scoop. I'll see you 'bout six Saturday, Maggie."

"I'll be right here," she said.

I wasn't right sure, but I think her face got red. She giggled some. Sam grinned real big at her. I sort of felt like I was not supposed to be there. The whole truck stop with the other waitress and help and some customers was somehow like players on a stage like the one where the high school kids did when they came to the grade school and acted a play for us. The people in the truck stop was real but didn't seem real as they walked around and talked with each other. I walked to the door ahead of Sam and went on out to the truck. The sky was getting darker over towards Terre Haute. Sam looked off to the west as he walked out.

"We're going to get our ass wet, scoopin' this danged coal off," he said. "Not much we can do about that."

"We could wait until tomorrow to unload it," I said. "It might not be rainin' then."

Sam laughed. "We've got to get a double-deck load of hogs out to Wes Davis' an' take them to Indianapolis tomorrow," he said. "Coal's got to be gone."

"You ever have another girlfriend, Sam?" I asked as both of us stared out at the sky. That was something I'd been wanting to ask him about for some time. I'd liked Betty Newlin for a long time. But so did everybody else. She liked us all at one time or another. I walked around on air when she liked me and felt like crawling in a hole and pulling the hole in after me when she liked somebody else. Richard and Jerry didn't fawn over her like the rest of us did. Betty was their cousin, and they looked at the other girls. I couldn't decide if they was lucky they didn't have to worry about whether she liked them or whether they was unlucky because they didn't have somebody as pretty as Betty to like. "I mean one that you liked like you an' Maggie like each other."

"You think we like each other, huh?" he said and grinned at me as I sat there nodding my head. "I reckon we do. Last time I really felt like that was before we went overseas durin' the war. My outfit was out east trainin' to go when I met somebody I thought I'd come home an' marry after the war. She was from 'Napolis, too. 'Napolis, Maryland."

Sam talked quiet like while he drove into the darkening sky. He said how good looking she was, blonde hair, copper skin and an eye tooth that was crooked in a pretty kind of way, not a real beauty queen, but nice enough to him because she liked him and was such a good lady. He only knew her a few months before he shipped out for overseas.

"What happened?" I asked when he stopped talking.

"Absence don't make the heart grow fonder, I guess," he said, shrugging his shoulders a little. "We was in England gettin' ready for the Invasion, an' she was back in the States. Guys had been going overseas an' not comin' back. It was kind of a live-for-today-because-tomorrow-might-not-come time for everybody. Out of sight, out of mind, I guess. Don't make it any easier. I found another girlfriend in England; she found another guy in Maryland. That's just the way it was for a lot of us. Things changed real quick for just about everybody in them days."

That pretty well put the clamps on us talking anymore for a while. Sam kept watching the sky. It wasn't noon yet, and it was getting real dark out. The sun had disappeared behind the clouds not long after we had left Terre Haute. He pushed the big Dodge ten-wheeler as fast as he could through the little towns, up and down the hills and around the curves. At The Corners, Sam rolled through the four-way stop and went on west to the wide gravel that went to Oblong. At the first road back east, he turned and right away we started going down the hill to cross a one-lane bridge across the little crick.

"Hang on, Sedwick," Sam said. "I'm goin' to save a little time."

When the bottom leveled out, Sam gunned the motor and started moving faster towards the bridge. I held on to the door and put my hand up on the dash. He didn't say why I should hang on, and I didn't ask. I felt the truck sag before the front of the truck had reached the other side of the crick. Then the load of coal dropped the back end of the truck down real quick on the tandems as it fell through the little bridge and into the middle of the crick. When the back of the truck dropped, I scooted back on the seat and was looking at the tops of the trees on the hill in front of us. My heart was pounding so hard I thought it would jump out of my chest.

"Son-of-a-bitch," Sam said. "Son-of-a-fuckin'-bitch. We're up shit crick without a paddle now."

For a minute, we just sat there, him cussing and me scared to move. Then he ran out of cuss words or breath one. I wasn't sure, but he quit cussing and said, "Well, let's get out of here. It's goin' to be rainin' cats an' dogs before long. An' I got to get ahold of Big. Open your door an' climb out onto the hood an' down to the road."

That was easier said than done. Sam somehow got up to the hood so quick I didn't see how he'd done it. I couldn't hold the door open and crawl out at the same time. Finally, I just climbed up the front of the truck bed and got on top of the cab to make it to the hood. He helped me down off the bumper and started walking towards the house at the top of the hill. I hurried to catch up.

"What're we goin' to do, Sam?" I asked.

"We're goin' up here to Johnny Goodman's place an' call Helen. She'll have an idea where Big is. He'll want to get this coal off there today an' get that truck out as soon as we can. He's goin' to be madder 'n hell, too. He told me to go around an' come in past Virgil Schafer's, that the bridge wouldn't hold the tandem outfit with this much coal."

I guess it didn't, I thought, but didn't say anything. I wondered why Sam had come this way if Big told him the bridge wouldn't hold the load.

"I thought I could get across this once an' save a little time before the rain came," Sam said as if hearing my thoughts. "See how things you do in your life change the way it turns out. We could have been backin' up to Johnny's coal shed an' gettin' ready to unload, if I'd gone the other way. The shit's goin' to hit the fan sometimes when you can't do much about it. But there's a lot of times when, if you'd just watch what you're doin', you can keep yourself out of trouble. Like the time them Germans walked up on us there in France, an' I made a beeline for the hatch after gettin' one of 'em. I grabbed his rifle an' scrambled in like hell an' that old hatch came down on my head an' stuffed me in the tank. Knocked me out. When I came to, I felt like my head had been jammed down into my chest. Hurt like hell. Still feel it today."

"Did you go to the hospital?" I asked.

"Oh, yeah, I'd taken a little shrapnel, too. I went to the field hospital for a few days, then went right back to my outfit. But what I'm sayin' is I should have been watchin' that hatch door. I'd been banged before, an' I'd been in an' out of a tank a thousand times. I knew how heavy it was, how it bangs shut an' how to avoid gettin' hit. An' I knew Big was probably right about that damned bridge."

"What's he goin' to say?"

"He's goin' to raise hell, then he's goin' to come over here an' work like the dickens to get that coal off an' that truck out of there."

We saw Johnny in the barnyard when we walked into the front yard. He met us at the gate and walked with us to the house when Sam told him what had happened and that he needed to use the telephone. I sat out on the back porch and played with Lady, a Collie that had come to the Goodmans a couple of years ago. She'd sit on the porch and nuzzle my hand with her nose until I'd start petting her head. I threw a stick out towards the well. She bounded off the porch, got the stick and brought it back to me, wagging her tail and smiling at me in her eyes. When I took the stick and told her, "Good girl," she jumped back on the porch and stuck her wet nose under my hand again.

"Thanks, Johnny," I heard Sam say as he walked through the door and out onto the porch. "I'm goin' to need it."

He didn't say much on the way back to the truck. I was dying to know what Big said but didn't want to ask. At the truck, Sam started talking again and opened the tool box opposite the gas tank on the saddle-tank setup Big had had made to be able to carry more gas and tools. Sam got the flares to set up for the night. He showed me how to set them up and gave me one set.

"You take that one back up yonder about half way to where the hill starts up an' set it up," he said. "We can light them later. Maybe Big will have some flashers."

"You talk to him?"

"Yeah, he was just gettin' ready to leave Charlie's garage. Had a blowout on an inside dual an' had to get a new tire. He was already fit to be tied."

"What'd he say about this?" I asked, pointing to the truck with its nose up in the air.

"What do you think he said?" Sam asked, grinning for the first time since we broke through the bridge. "He raised hell. First thing he said when I told him was, 'Oh, well, bullshit, Sam. I told you not to try an' cross that danged bridge.' He went on for a little bit, then said he'd be over here to help get this truck unloaded. He'll be here anytime."

And by the time we got the flares out, Big was backing his truck down the hill and bearing down on us before I climbed across the crick on the truck. He stopped and was out of his truck to look at the job ahead of him when I got to the other side.

"Sonuvabitch," he said, spitting a stream of tobacco juice on the road where the bridge had torn away. "This is goin' to be a bitch to get that coal unloaded. I'll back my truck up as close as I can get. We're goin' to have to throw some off the front so we can get the scoop under this coal. Then that fuckin' rain is goin' catch us before we get done."

Big backed the truck up and took out the end gates while Sam started clearing out room to get the scoop in to start unloading. I stood out on the road for a while just watching. Neither one of them said a word while they scooped coal from one truck to the other. Then it started raining, just a few drops at first, then it started pouring. I ran for the cab of Big's truck.

"Sonuvabitch," I heard Big say again as I shut the door. I figured they'd be right after me. But I kept looking in the mirrors on both sides and never saw them. After a while I took the big winter coat Big kept in his truck in the summer to use as a pillow and draped it over my head to go see what they was doing.

What they was doing was scooping coal. Even though I'd been in the truck ten minutes or so, I was still surprised. I thought they'd probably got over in Sam's truck or even under the back of Big's truck right in front of them. But they was scooping coal, side by side, in the pouring rain. They'd pulled it away from the front of the truck and had it piled more to the back. First one would get a scoop full and throw it up and into Big's truck, then the other one would do the same. They wasn't working as fast as they would if they'd been scooping corn or something else out on the flat land. But they was working steady, their caps pulled down lower than usual and their shirt sleeves buttoned down. Neither one of them paid any attention to me. I didn't see any sense of me getting wet, so I went back up to Big's truck and waited. It keep on raining hard for a bit longer, then it slacked off and just kept slowing down until it wasn't raining anymore. I got out and went back to see how the coal scooping was going.

It was going pretty good. About five minutes later, they quit and threw their scoops out on the road. They had about as much of the big load off and on the littler truck that they could, I reckoned. Standing there on the road peeling off their shirts, I thought of old-time fighters like John L. Sullivan and Jack Jefferies. Sam was taller, leaner than Big. He was thicker through the neck and shoulders, and inch or two shorter but heavier. Both of them was stripped to the waist and was wringing the sweat and rainwater from the shirts. Their muscles rippled in and out as they worked. Sam had a tee shirt, Big an undershirt. They put both shirts back on and tucked them inside their trousers.

"Let's get that over to Johnny's an' get it unloaded," Big said. "We might be able to get back over here an' get the rest of this this evening. Charlie can get the winch truck over here an' pull you out. See if you tore anything up. Then Bud Boudreau can get this bridge fixed. He was over at Rapier's when I started over here. I stopped an' told him. He said it needed replacin', anyway, so the township will take care of it. But, dang it, Sam, I want you to watch what you're adoin'. You could've tore the devil out of that truck. Maybe you did. You ought to know better that to try an' cross a little fuckin' bridge with that kind of a load on, even if I hadn't told you to go around."

Sam stood there, puffing on a Lucky Strike, looking down just a little and nodding every once in a while. I felt bad for him, but it was better him than me, I thought. I'd had Big talk to me pretty rough a couple of times like when I pinched Cheryl Matthews or swiped a package of his Luckies and got caught smoking them. I didn't even like to be around when somebody messed up or he got mad. Same with Sam. Both Mother and Aunt Helen had told me that their old family doctor had asked them if they was "going with some of them fightin' McElligotts down there by Moonshine" after daddy and Big started coming to Martinsville. I never figured that out. I'd heard about a fight or two some of them had had, but it didn't seem like much to be calling the whole family fighting.

In the cab, I was stuck between two big wet men. They smelled a combination of coal, sweat, rainwater and cigarettes. With the windows rolled down, the smoke from their cigarettes drifted outside. Things was starting to dry out. Off to the south, I saw a rainbow in the sky.

"Oh," I said, crying out when it popped into sight as we drove up the hill, "look at the rainbow. Maybe that means you'll have some good luck now. Ain't that what that's supposed to mean?"

"Luck don't have nothin' to do with it when you try to take a tandem outfit with twelve or fourteen tons of coal on it over a little bridge like that," Big said, flipping his cigarette out the window as he finished and staring straight ahead. "That ain't usin' common sense."

"That's right, Big," Sam said, flipping his cigarette out his window and saying something for the first time I'd heard him say anything since Big backed up. "It won't happen again. Now let's get this dang coal unloaded an' do whatever else we have to do."

I sure wasn't going to say anything else. Neither of them did, either. They unloaded the coal at Johnny Goodman's and went back and finished unloading the coal from the other truck before either of them said a word. The sun was still up, but it was pretty low in the sky when we drove up the hill to the wide gravel again.

"I'll take you up to your mom's now an' come get you in the mornin'," Big said. "We can get down here an' unload this little jag at Johnny's first thing, then I'll take you to 'Napolis so you can come with Charlie when he comes to winch you out."

By the time we'd taken Sam home and got back to Bellair, it was nearly dark. I was starved. Me and Sam had eaten at the stockyards early and hadn't had any dinner. And now it was past normal time for supper.

The kitchen light was on when we turned into Bellair. That was a good sign, I thought. But there wasn't no supper waiting on the table. Mother and Aunt Helen made us a couple of toasted cheese sandwiches apiece and gave us a big slice of apple pie. That and a glass of milk was it. I was hungry enough that I never gave a thought to not eating the pie. Big sat hunched over his plate with both elbows on the table.

"You goin' with me tomorrow, Sedwick?" he asked, looking over at me.

"I think I'll stay here."

"That's just what I figured," he said, smiling a little.

I figured I had about enough trucking for a while. When I finally crawled into bed a little later, I don't know whether my head really hit the pillow before I was asleep. Light was streaming in the front door, and I could hear Nancy and Mary Beth playing in the front room before I ever opened my eyes again. I stretched and yawned. It felt good to still be in bed and the sun up so high in the morning.

12

After we fell through the bridge with that load of coal, I started hanging around home or the store more for whatever jobs I could get and worked quite a bit all through the summer. So I didn't spend as much time out in the trucks with Big and Sam. I'd usually ride to Oblong with one of them on Saturday afternoons to get the truck greased or whatever they had to do. But that was about it. I liked to go with Big. Sam took care of his business and was ready to go home. Big would play pool or go down to Joe's Tavern for a pork sandwich and a beer. When Joe Marshall went with him, he'd stay in the tavern and drink mugs of Sterling beer and Big would play pool.

On the way home, Joe would smoke a King Edward cigar and offer Big a beer and cigar as soon as we got out of town. Big didn't always take a cigar, but he would take a beer and drink it in three or four long drinks. Joe'd drink his slower. I always looked at him and the can of Greisedieck Brothers beer until he'd smile a bit, his bloodshot eyes watering. "You, you, uh, you want a drink, John Walter?" he'd say. When I'd nod, he'd look over to Big and say, "That all, uh, right with you, Rob — er, uh — bert?" He'd always say, "I reckon. But just one an' don't you tell the women." That one drink always tasted so different from any other drink I'd ever had. I can't say that I really liked it, but it gave me a memory of the real taste of beer that stayed in my head from then on. And afterwards, I always looked for that taste in beer that reminded me of growing up and being in the truck with Big and Joe. I didn't often find it.

Joe wore bib overalls, a shirt and work shoes during the week. On these Saturdays, he'd dress up in a khaki set of shirt and trousers and a pair of ankle-high dress shoes. A khaki cap always sat cockeyed over to the right side of his head. I was pretty shocked one day when he took his cap off to wipe the sweat from his head to see that he was bald. Tiny beads of sweat stood out all over his milk-white bald head. He sure looked different without a cap. He never smoked or drank through the week, but on these Saturdays he did both. Sometimes he'd fish a half pint or a pint of Four Roses whiskey out of one of his beer sacks of Greisedieck Brothers six packs and take a drink. At the edge of Bellair, Big'd stop the truck to let Joe out. He'd always look over and say, "Much obliged, Robert." He'd nod and would get out and walk or wobble a little, carrying his beer and a few groceries to the house.

Big never drank much and seemed a bit uneasy that Joe did.

"Is Joe drunk, Big?" I asked as we pulled away one time.

"If he ain't, he will be. He'll sit there an' drink 'til it's all gone. I don't know what he sees in that stuff."

"Maybe he likes it," I said. "It tastes pretty good."

"That stuff's poison, if you drink it like Joe an' some of 'em does," Big said. "You're only twelve years old. You don't want to get started foolin' with that stuff too much. Probably be better off, if you'd just leave it alone all together."

It was nearly dark when Big turned in the driveway. We'd been gone a big part of the day. Saturdays like these were the ones I liked best. When Joe went with us, I knew I'd have more time to roam around. I could nearly always get a haircut if I needed one, go over to the drugstore and get an ice cream cone or a toasted ham-salad sandwich, stop by the pool hall and work my way back to Smokey Cottrell's barber shop. Some Saturday afternoons, the barbering business would slow down, Jap'd be gone and I'd find Smokey sitting up in the chair, reading something and smoking cigarettes. He said he still read four or five books a week, mostly novels.

"Hello, there, John Walter," he'd always say with a smile on his face. He'd stop whatever he was doing right away. Sometimes he'd ask if I wanted another haircut, and sometimes he'd ask if I wanted another boot camp haircut. But he'd always talk to me until he had a customer walk in. And I'd always try to steer the conversation around to the Marine Corps and the war. Over the years, he'd answered my questions and gave me an idea of what the Marine Corps was like and where he and my daddy had fought in the war. He didn't know much more about what had happened to Daddy than Mother and the rest of the family did.

"I wasn't on Guadalcanal," he said one day. "But I can imagine what it was like. You don't want to know. I know what I saw in just a few days is more 'n I ever want to see again."

"Do you ever think about bein' on Iwo Jima?" I asked, sitting in the chairs against the wall, knowing that I did want to know what it was like.

"Every day," he said. "Every day. Maybe less the more time that passes. But every day. When the time in February that we went in rolls around, I think a lot more about it. I think how lucky I was that I'm here when a lot of them ain't. Just like your daddy. I've had a lot of bonus years since that Iwo deal. By the time I got hit on the forth day, there wasn't many men left in my outfit that hadn't been hit or killed. Only twelve or thirteen was left in my platoon."

"Did the Japs shoot you?" I asked, seeing one in my mind's eye pointing a rifle at him and pulling the trigger. "Did you get any of them?"

He chuckled a little.

"That wasn't quite the way it was. I got a round through my pack from some Jap old boy in the first ten minutes on the beach when I was horizontal to the ground. That was the closest I come to gettin' shot that I know. 'Course there was rounds of all kinds flyin' around everywhere from the time we went in. They was closer than I wanted 'em to be."

"Was you on the first wave?" I asked.

"Nope," Smokey said. "We landed on Green One with the third wave at 0830. We circled around a little an' saw what was goin' on there on the beach. It wasn't a pretty sight to go in behind. One old boy from down deep in Southern Illinois who was one of my favorite people looked a bit grim. I said, 'Scared, John?' He grinned a thin little grin an' said, 'Hell, yes, I'm scared, Smoke. But I've been scared most of my damn life, anyway.'

"We landed at the narrowest point in the island an' was to cut through to the other side an' then turn left to Old Baldy, Mt. Suribachi. I was in one shell hole, or whatever was there that'd give a little cover, after another across that narrow stretch. I got rid of that pack on the beach after I raised up to look around an' that round went through the pack, an' I didn't have a bite to eat from mornin' chow the day we went in until after I got hit."

"That mornin' chow was steak an' eggs, wasn't it?" I asked.

"Not where I was," he said, chuckling and smiling again with his eyes just dancing the way he always did when something amused him. "We had a regular Navy fare for mornin' chow. I guess we was supposed to get steak an' eggs. Even the book that came out later said we did. Somehow we must've been the only ship that didn't get the word. Somethin' happened to our steaks. We got a hunk of bread, two boiled eggs an' a canteen cup of coffee. Probably got some shit-on-the-shingle, too. I don't remember. I didn't have much of an appetite. We was snafued before we ever got started."

"Snafued?" I said. "What's that?"

"Situation normal, all fucked up," Smokey said and laughed, "That's the way things was. I hadn't slept much. Nobody did. People sat around talkin', writin' letters, cleanin' gear, whatever. A bunch of us played penny-ante, quarter-limit poker most of the night. When somebody went broke an' wanted to keep playin', he'd just reach in the pot or in somebody's pile an' take some money. Nobody cared. We didn't figure we was goin' to be needin' any money where we was goin'. Then reveille came at three o'clock."

"Do you reckon my daddy got steak an' eggs before he went in on the 'Canal? Or done like you say you fellers did at Iwo Jima?"

Smokey sort of chuckled again.

"He was in the Marine Corps, wasn't he? I can see now that they just didn't have the facilities to prepare steak an' eggs for us on one of the oldest LSTs in the Pacific an' hundreds of men over its usual complement. We usually got the short end of the stick. Your daddy might have got steak an' eggs, but I doubt it. That's the way the cookie crumbles sometimes. Your daddy probably ate about like we did an' wasn't very hungry before goin' in.

"But I was hungry as an old bear by the time I got back down to the beach after gettin' hit. The corpsmen left me on a litter with lots of other wounded Marines. The ones of us who didn't have real serious wounds wanted some chow. It didn't take long for me to figure out that we probably wasn't goin' to get any, though.

I knew we'd get some chow on the hospital ship the next day, an' they'd move the chow in to the troops still fightin'. Nobody paid much attention to us after we was dropped off that night.

"Bullets was still zippin' about when they put me in a pup tent with an unconscious Marine down on the beach. A few minutes after that, Father Bradley, our battalion Catholic chaplain, squatted down in front of our shelter. I'd never spoken to him before, or he to me, but he called me by name, asked how I was, how the rest was, an' talked as calmly as if we was in a pew back in the States. 'How would you like a canteen full of hot coffee?' he asked me. I didn't see any PX about, but I said, "That'd be mighty fine.' He took my canteen an' trotted down the beach about two hundred yards or farther to a beached LST. In a few minutes, he came hotfootin' up the beach, handed me the coffee, wished me well an' trotted off for the lines.

"Just after dark, we was put aboard an LST on the empty tank deck. It was full of wounded. They was to be transferred the next day to hospital or secondary hospital ships. The officers an' crew threw open the ship's store an' mess an' carried us food an' drink far into the night. No one could have treated us with more compassion. They wasn't medics, they was just good people."

I was almost speechless, sitting there listening to Smokey talk. He'd never told me quite so much before and never about getting wounded. I asked him how that'd happened.

"My outfit was turned toward Suribachi when I got hit," he said. "We'd cut the island in half an' was movin' up the side of Old Baldy. It'd taken us three days to do that. Them damn Japs was dug in everywhere. The Navy was still shellin' with their big guns, our artillery was layin' down fire ahead of us an' the Japs an' us was crankin' out a helluva lot of rounds. Looked like a damn war zone."

Smokey chuckled and stopped to light another cigarette. After he'd taken a couple of drags, he said, "But I think I got my ticket out of Iwo courtesy of the United States Navy."

"You mean the American Navy shot you?"

"Not on purpose, I reckon. But they'd been shellin' that rock for days an' kept right on after we landed. Didn't do a hell of a lot of good. The Japs was dug in an' hard to get at. We was just startin' around Suribachi on the west beach in the evening an' movin' up the hill when the shells started comin' in, some of them ahead of us but a couple behind us. I think I caught some shrapnel from one of them rounds.

"Funny thing," Smokey said and laughed all of a sudden. "I got hit in the thigh an' the calf. A corpsman came over to take a look at me an' called for a stretcher. 'I can walk,' I said. 'Save the stretcher for somebody else.' 'You can't walk,' he said. 'Sure I can,' I said. I got up an' tried, an' he was right. I couldn't walk. I'd hunted rabbits all of my life, an' I always wondered why they didn't run when they just got hit with a little shot that knocked them down but wasn't going to kill them. I knew when I tried to walk: the muscles in my calf an' thigh was stiff an' paralyzed an' my leg wouldn't work.

"Like I said, there was only twelve or thirteen left in my platoon then. Stretcher bearers was about wiped out, too. So four of the men put me on a poncho an' took off for the ambulance jeep. Just before that, Skaggs whipped off his combat jacket in a pouring rain an' wrapped my leg with it. I protested that I'd be aboard ship an' it was cold, but he said, 'I'm fat enough to keep out the cold, so who needs it?' I saw him later in a hospital in Honolulu. He said he liked to froze his butt off.

"Anyway, the poncho split an' my tail bounced off a rock, which hurt more than the original wound. So they got me on a stretcher an' I got a ride back to the beach on a jeep. I gave the boys my cigarettes, chewin' tobacco an' stuff that I could get aboard ship after I got in the jeep."

I was seeing my daddy and how he died much clearer.

"Was a lot of 'em gettin' killed?"

"All the time, John Walter," Smokey said quietly. "All the time. Dead Marines an' dead Japs all over the place."

"Did you see anybody get killed?"

"Too many, John Walter. People gettin' killed all around me. Kids, eighteen, nineteen, twenty years old. They called me Pops, an' I was only twenty-six. The kids got killed before they'd hardly lived, just like your daddy did. He wouldn't even be forty years old today. That's the way it was. Old Tony Stein was about twenty-two when he went in with us on Iwo. Handsome as the devil. Cocky little guy from Ohio who'd worked in a machine shop. He took a .50 caliber out of a crashed airplane and rigged that .50 up so he could carry it an' fire from the hip.

Called it his *Stinger*. He was up an' down the beach a dozen times that first day, coverin' for somebody or just attackin' a position with that .50 poundin' rounds into it. He opened up a lot of ground for us. Been a lot more dead a lot quicker if it hadn't been for old Tony. A few days after I got hit, he was headed for a strongpoint when they caught him in a crossfire an' dropped him right in front of everybody. I can see him on the beach that day just like it was yesterday. He got the Big One for what he did. An' if anybody ever deserved one, it was him.

"The Big One?"

"Yeah, the Medal of Honor. 'Course he was dead before they could give it to him. So was a lot of others. When I got down to the beach that night after gettin' hit, they had bodies laid out off to one side an' litters with the wounded laid out everywhere. Wasn't much of an atmosphere to eat, but like I said, I was starved. Nothing to eat, though. Later on, after Father Bradley brought me the coffee an' before we was taken aboard the LST, I saw a couple seabees off toward the water a few yards cookin' somethin' in a five-gallon bucket. I thought maybe they was cookin' stew to feed some of us who was able to eat. Then one of them fished in an' dug somethin' out with a bayonet. Later somebody told me they'd had two Japanese heads they was boilin' the meat from so they could take the skulls as souvenirs."

"God!" I said. "That's awful."

"People do awful things like that in war, John Walter. On both sides. Always have, I 'xpect; always will."

Years later, I read a book about the Iwo Jima campaign. In the front of the book, it said something like, "If the United States Marines will return just one grotesque souvenir taken during the invasion of Iwo Jima, the terrible deeds of them all will be forgiven. The Japanese Iwo Jima Survivors' Association." I remembered the day in the barber shop and the story about the two seabees. The next time I was in the area and went in for a haircut, I reminded Smokey of that story, then told him about the book. He hadn't read it. I told him about the part in the front of the book and what it said.

"Fuck them sonsabitches," he said with the nastiest look I'd ever seen on his face. He said it so quick and so hard-sounding that I flinched. He'd always seemed so gentle and easygoing. He'd talked soft, laughed quick and always had a warm look in his eyes.

"What do you mean?" I finally managed to ask. "You told me about the two seabees boilin' the Japanese soldiers heads when you was there on the beach after you was wounded. That was for souvenirs. An' I've been readin' other things like some Marines carried pliers to pull the gold teeth from dead Jap soldiers when they found them."

"That may be," Smokey said, pausing to light a cigarette. "There's assholes everywhere. There's always that ten percent that don't get the word, like they say in the Marine Corps. You know what I'm talkin' about. I heard about a couple of guys pullin' some teeth. Never saw anybody do it. But did them Jap bastards say anything about what they did to Marines they got ahold of there? I'll bet they didn't say shit about anything like. Did they say anything about how they'd cut a Marine's cock off an' stick it in his mouth, then laugh like a fuckin' hyena an' tell us about it all night? I'll bet they didn't say a fuckin' word about that shit. Or anything like it.

"Tough old boy from Texas, Sgt. Harrell, almost got overrun on an outpost one night. I was gone by then, but some of the others in my platoon told me when I rejoined them in Hawaii to get ready for what we all feared was the invasion of Japan — thank God we didn't have to do that. The boys said the Japs throwed grenades in the hole two different times an' took both of Harrell's hands an' cut his legs up pretty lively with sabers. But he kept them bastards from breaking through all night. They got another feller alive out there somewhere an' dragged him off a ways. Before he died he screamed out a couple of times, then hollered out to Harrell to surrender to save both their lives. After a while he didn't scream out or holler anymore. When our outfit got out in front of the listenin' post the next morning, the man was dead. He'd been beaten, an' his cock had been cut off an' shoved in his mouth. Them Japs was mean, cruel little bastards. They've got a helluva lot of nerve tellin' anybody they'll forgive them for anything after all the things they've done. They apologize for Pearl Harbor? Or anything else before or after Pearl Harbor?"

I shook my head. Smokey just looked at me a minute before he continued. Then he said, "Harrell was still alive the next mornin'. He'd kept the Japs away all night, hearin' them torture one of our men an' being wounded pretty bad himself. He lived but wound up losin' both hands. When the platoon got there the next mornin',

Jap soldiers was strung out all over the place, a couple of them right at the edge of his foxhole an' another one in the foxhole. Sgt. Harrell shot them with his .45 while he still had a hand."

I was quiet when Smokey stopped talking that time and both of us smoked a cigarette before he spoke. He was telling me the kind of things I wanted to hear, just like he always had. It made me feel closer to my daddy in understanding how he'd died when I was just a little boy. And it gave me a different point of view than I had ever got in school where World War II came at the end of the year when everybody was already thinking about summer vacation.

"Maybe Sgt. Harrell should take his Medal of Honor an' send it back to this outfit an' apologize for killin' all them Japs at his listenin' post in front of the CP that night an' leavin' his hands out there," Smokey said. "That sounds like what them sonuvabitches want. You think that'd be the thing to do?"

I shook my head.

"I don't either," Smokey said, relaxing and smiling now. He soon looked more like his old self and went on talking about other things like we always did. His mind seemed to be able to set things aside and go on with whatever was at hand.

My mind stayed on what Smokey'd been saying every time he talked about the war. Like Sam had told me, the movies I'd seen showed war in a different light and never showed anything about how bad things was in the way Smokey told me. 'Course that was the movies, and I knew Sam had told me a long time ago that war movies was "phony as a three-dollar bill." But even most of the books I'd read never even come close to the way things Smokey and Sam and other people said it was. And I'd read every book I could on the war and talked to anybody who'd talk to me to see what I could find out about what it was like and how Daddy got killed. All of the talks and books gave me a better idea of that. Just a better idea, though. Not the real thing. The books seemed so far away. They was just stories like any other book. I wanted to know what it was really like to be in a war. And I wanted to know how Daddy had got killed.

It was only a few days after I'd talked with Smokey that Saturday and he first told me about being on Iwo Jima that I was in the store talking with Mother when Ross Childers and a tall, dark-haired man I'd never seen before came in with him. Ross was dressed in one of his double-breasted suits, tie and tie clasp neat and showing, shoes shined and a dress Stetson hat on his head. The diamond ring on his left hand sparkled in the bright light of the morning sun as he walked through the door. He came to the counter and flashed a smile at Mother and me.

"Hello, there, Lorene," he said. "This is one of Lela's cousins from North Carolina that I'd like you to meet. Lorene, this is Claude Pleasant. Claude, Lorene. An' this is her son, John Walter. Claude thinks he knew Bill when he was in the Marines."

I saw Mother gasp and put her hands to her throat.

"Where?" she asked real quick.

"In the States," Claude said softly, "an' on the Island."

Ross waved his hand, the diamond flashing again, and said, "I'll see you later, Claude."

"Right pleased to meet you, ma'am, an' you too, son," he said and held out his hand to me. I looked him over as I took it. He wore a Stetson, too, but more country than Ross' dress hat, and a sports coat, dark shirt open at the collar and cowboy boots. He was quite handsome and reminded me of pictures of Daddy in that they was both tall with dark hair and dark skin. "I see you're your daddy's boy. The eyes."

I grinned. That's what everybody said that knew us.

"Thank you, sir," I said. "That's what everybody tells me."

"Please have a seat, Mr. Pleasant," Mother said. "Could I get you anything?"

"No, ma'am. An' Claude is fine, Mrs. McElli — "

"Lorene, please."

"Yes, ma'am. Ross was just tellin' me about the store an' things around town. When he mentioned you an' your name, I just knew you had to be Sgt. McElligott's people. I just wanted to tell you how much respect I had for him as a man an' as a Marine. I thought he was one of them people who'd never get killed. He was like old Gunny Basilone, who was on the Island with us. Got the Medal of Honor there in the Lunga area where your husband got killed. You just thought Gunny'd never die, either. He'd bellow out right in the thick of things to get us goin', 'Let's go, people. Nobody's gonna live forever.'

An' he'd be right there with you. Nothin' touched him. Then at Iwo in '45, his luck ran out. He was doin' the same thing there, even almost got another Big One — just the Navy Cross this time. But then he got cut in pieces by a Jap machine gun."

Mother made some kind of little gasp that stopped Claude short. Her face was white and looked pinched together. She had a hurt look in her eyes that put me in the mind of the look in Richard's and Jerry's dog Skipper's eyes when they made him stay inside and left him behind when we all went some place.

"I'm sorry, Lorene," Claude said, removing his hat and revealing a much lighter forehead. "I'm talkin' too plain, ma'am. Thinkin' about Sgt. McElligott an' all took me back to them days 'fore I realized it. I'll keep still."

"No, no. You keep talking, Claude. I want to know."

"You sure, ma'am?"

Mother just nodded and wiped her eyes.

"Well, ma'am," Claude said, "if you want to know. Sgt. McElligott wasn't just like the gunny, but both of them always seemed to know just what to do in any situation. Your husband knew his men an' knew how to treat 'em. We'd have followed him to hell an' back. An' did. We took casualties, but he saved us from gettin' wiped out a couple of times, too."

"What happened, Claude, when Bill got killed?" Mother asked, sitting on the edge of the bench with my hand in hers, looking across at the big man on the opposite bench. "Was you there?"

Claude sighed and nodded.

"I was. We was cleanin' out a Jap strongpoint one afternoon after two days of havin' it pretty rough. Had the position about secured. We'd lost a couple of men. Sgt. McElligott was walkin' around checkin' things out when a Jap popped up out of nowhere, out of a little cave we'd missed, an' shot your husband in the back. He never knew what hit him an' never suffered a bit. Rounds from three different weapons hit that skinny Jap at the same time. That's about all I can tell you, ma'am. The graves registration people buried him in a cemetery back towards the beach. I stopped by your husband's grave on the way off the Island to tell him goodbye. There was rows an' rows of crosses with name, rank an' serial number on each one. I guess you had him shipped home, Lorene?"

"Yes, he came home in '48. He's buried over with the McElligotts at the church north of Annapolis."

"There's McElligotts buried there that was in the service back through the Civil War, the War of 1812 an' the Revolutionary War," I said, adding to the family history and being kind of proud to be able to tell somebody about my people. "My great-granddad, Daddy's granddad was in the Civil War. Aunt Catherine said he never recovered from whatever happened to him at Chickamauga an' all through Kentucky an' Tennessee before that. He died before he was thirty."

"I come from them kind of people, too, son," Claude said and smiled down at me. "They're good people. A lot of 'em don't live long lives. Guess that's just the way it is. I'm just thankful I knew your daddy. He was a good man."

He looked back at Mother and said, "I'm not stayin' here long, Lorene, but I'd like to visit Sgt. McElligott's grave before I leave an' pay my respects. Would you care to go with me?"

"I don't think so, Claude. I've got to mind the store. And when I do go, I prefer to go alone."

"I can understand that."

"But John Walter can go with you. He knows how to get there, where the grave is an' can go about anytime today, can't you, John Walter?"

"Yes, ma'am," I said. I was pleased that Mother had offered to let me show Claude Daddy's grave. That was a place I went anytime I had the chance, which wasn't often. This time, I'd get to talk to somebody who was right there with my daddy when he died. And I wasn't sure Claude had told us exactly how Daddy had died. It seemed after Claude had noticed Mother was upset with his story that he tried to make sure he didn't let that happen again.

"I'd like to go right now, Lorene," Claude said. "I've thought of Sgt. McElligott a great many times over the years. An' if I can, I'd like to see where he's restin' today. I'm headin' for St. Louis on some business this afternoon. Only time I'll have to go is now."

"I don't know why not. John Walter, please show Claude to your daddy's grave and take him up past your grandmother's on the way. She was going to the doctor with Annie this morning, or you might've wanted to stop there so Claude could meet Bill's mother."

"That's fine, Lorene. That would have been nice, but I've got to get on down the road. I'm just pleased to see the country where he grew up an' where he's restin'. It's been very nice meetin' you an' John Walter. I hope to see you both again sometime, Lorene."

"It's been nice meeting you, too, Claude. I hope to see you again, too. This has been a pleas — well, it's been a surprise. I've always wanted to talk to somebody who was with or knew Bill. Thank you so much for stopping by."

Claude put his hat back on and touched the brim of his hat before he turned to me. "Let's go, John Walter," he said. "I appreciate you accommodatin' me here this morning at the drop of a hat. Anything I can do for you this mornin'?"

"Tell me about my daddy," I said, feeling a chill run up and down my spine. "Mother, Grandma, Big an' all of 'em have told me about him growin' up an' all. But nobody ever told me anything about him when he was in the Marines or the war. An' you can call me Sedwick. Everybody does. That's my nickname."

Claude nodded as he walked out the door and said, "I'll tell you what I know about your daddy, Sedwick. I met Sgt. McElligott at New River before we shipped out. He was the platoon sergeant when I reported in to Charlie Company."

"You didn't go to boot camp with Daddy?"

"Lord no," Claude said and smiled. "I was only fifteen when I joined the Marine Corps, an' your daddy had already been in quite a while then. He'd already been overseas before the Japs bombed Pearl Harbor an' was on his way back to the States. He came to Tent City there at New River in North Carolina an' joined our outfit. I was fresh out of boot camp. My daddy had nine kids back there in hard times. My mother died when I was fourteen. Daddy was havin' a hard time takin' care of us all, so I joined up just before Pearl Harbor an' ended up on the Island when I was sixteen years old. Your daddy knew how old I was an' sort of kept an eye on me when he could."

That made me smile. I pictured that in my mind. It was kind of like Big and Sam and some of the others trying to look out for me the way they did sometimes, even when I hadn't done quite the right thing like one night over in Indianapolis with Big. We was unloading a double-deck load of hogs for Joe Wertz at the hog alley.

After Big run them out of the truck, a feller came to the gate to get the hogs.

"Where they goin'?" he asked.

"Producers," Big said. "We'll go with you."

"Okay, follow me."

He took the ticket out of the post and opened the gate for the load of hogs to go to a pen where they'd be kept until they was sold the next morning. I had a hotshot in my hand and walked along with Big to drive the hogs to the pen. I felt pretty grown up to be driving hogs along the alley at the Indianapolis stockyards at a time of the night when Richard and Jerry would be going to bed or already there. Even Big Al and Jimmy and Ronal would likely be in bed, too.

"Sssssuuuuiiiieeeee," I said a couple of times and put the hotshot to a slow hog that was lagging behind a step or two. Both times the hog squealed and ran into the rest of them. They would all squeal and run forward, bunching up so they could hardly move.

The second time, the feller with the stockyards said, "Tell that damn kid to put that hotshot up."

"I don't see no 'damn kid,' Mister," Big said, not even looking around. "This here's my brother's boy. He's the only kid I see around here. You ain't talkin' about him, are you?"

"Tell your brother's boy not to use the hotshot on the hogs," the feller said, not answering Big's question. "Makes 'em run an' bunch up."

"I'll tell 'im," Big said and turned to go back to the truck. "An' you can take these fuckin' hogs on back to the pens by yourself."

On the way to the truck, Big said, "You oughten to use the hotshot like that, John Walter. Gets the hogs all riled up."

While I was thinking about how Big looked out for me, Claude was pretty quiet. As he drove along, I gave him directions and told him who lived in each place along the road. At Chris Matthews', I told him that my granddad had built that house and lived there at one time. When we passed Garvey Charles' place, I waved at him and told Claude we butchered hogs there. He just smiled and nodded as I talked and didn't say much unless I asked him a question.

"How did Daddy try to look out for you, Claude?" I finally got around to asking.

"Oh, in different ways," he said. "He was more patient with me when I fouled up in trainin' than he was with other people. He didn't cut me any slack. But he'd be more patient with me because I was so young. He didn't make it obvious. Out in Jacksonville one night right before we shipped out, though, a bunch of us was in a bar. The bartender took one look at me before anybody ordered and said, "I don't sell milk in here."

"'I didn't hear anybody order any milk, sonny,' Sgt. McElligott said. 'You hear anybody order milk, men?'

"The whole bunch of us hollered, 'Hell no.'

"'I'm talkin' about that kid there that's not old enough to be in here,' the bartender said and pointed at me. 'He's not even dry behind the ears.'

"'Where he's goin' you don't have to be dry behind the ears,' Sgt. McElligott said. 'That's not a requirement.'

"'All you gotta do is be alive an' be able to shoot straight,' an old boy from Oklahoma named Carter said. He was a corporal an' one of your daddy's old buddies an' squad leaders. 'An' Pleasant can do that 'bout as good as anybody I've ever seen. But maybe we can take the barkeep an' stick him in my squad instead of Pleasant.'

"'Barkeep don't pack the gear to replace Pleasant,' Sgt. McElligott said and looked straight at the bartender. 'He's with us, son. Give him what he wants. An' that milk sounds good for me. I think I'll have a glass.'

"'I don't have milk to — ' the bartender started to say.

"'I'll have a glass of milk,' your daddy said.

"An' he got one, an' I got a beer."

"Daddy didn't drink?" I asked.

"Oh, he'd drink a beer now an' then, but that was about it. He never bothered nobody else about it as long as the feller could do his job. It was another story, if he couldn't. Then your daddy could flat tear a man a new asshole. He told me one day that he never dreamed that some people drank the way they did. 'It's like sloppin' hogs, Pleasant,'" he said.

"That's what Big says," I said and laughed. "Big's my uncle, Daddy's brother. Did my daddy smoke?"

"Yeah, a little. But I guess he didn't start until he'd been in the Marine Corps for a while. Said it was a stupid habit, suckin' hot smoke into your lungs an' then blowin' it back out again. Out in the field, he had a chaw in his mouth a lot."

It sort of surprised me what Daddy said about smoking. I'd always figured that he liked to smoke, I guess. Everybody else seemed to. Maybe I could chew tobacco when I got a bit older, I thought. But right then, it made me sicker than anything. I didn't see what anybody could get out of chewing tobacco.

Claude slowed to a crawl as we drove past Grandma's place. He took it in and nodded all the while. His lips moved a little, and he said something aloud once, but I couldn't understand what he'd said. Something about the look in his eyes and on his face told me it was private and I shouldn't ask what he'd said or what he was thinking. His jaw muscles was working back and forth.

"Nice place where your daddy growed up," Claude said after a while. "Nice place."

I nodded and told him where to turn again.

"Did my daddy really get killed the way you told my mother he did, Claude?" I asked when we'd made the last turn and we were headed straight for the graveyard.

"Pretty much. He'd been hit in the shoulder while we was puttin' that pillbox out of commission. I don't know how that happened. He just kept us movin' straight ahead. With rounds flyin' everywhere, I didn't see that he was hit until it was over. He was regroupin' us an' checkin' casualties. His left arm was hangin' limp at his side, an' he had a glazed-over look in his eyes. But he was okay. Then that little bastard popped up out of nowhere an' zapped him. That was the end. It was all over for your daddy. He was dead when he hit the ground."

We was both quiet after that. Claude turned his big Chrysler in the driveway to the graveyard and stopped. For a minute, he just sit there looking out over the rows of tombstones. I wondered again what thoughts was running through his head but didn't ask. After a minute, he turned to me, and I guided him out through the graveyard.

"Here's the McElligotts," I said, stopping by my granddad's grave. "This here's my Granddad McElligott. He died in '48 or '49, right after they shipped Daddy's body home. That's Granddad's first wife there, Sam's an' some of my other cousins' grandma. Some of the kids that didn't live long are buried back there with Daddy an' some of the others."

"How many children did your granddaddy have?"

"Fifteen, I think it was. There's six buried back there, countin' Daddy, an' there's nine livin'."

"Your granddaddy kept himself pretty busy, I'd say."

"I reckon so."

"My daddy had nine of us to feed an' take care of after Momma died," Claude said, going over what he'd already told me about himself. "That's the reason I joined the Marine Corps, so he'd have one less to look after. It was still hard times where we lived in North Carolina."

I had asked Mother, Aunt Helen and Big about how they lived in the Depression. There had just been three of the Garner girls and ten of the McElligott boys and girls. The four older ones had been gone before the hard times hit, Big'd said. The two girls got married, and two boys went off to France and the war over there. When they got back, they worked out awhile and then started farming. Both of them went busted, Big said, because of low prices and bad weather. Sam's folks' marriage went busted, too, at the same time. But other than that, Big said the family didn't feel the Depression that much.

"It was hard times," he said. "We didn't have much money, but we always had something to eat. Mom would keep a batch of buckwheat pancakes goin' in the kitchen all winter. She canned danged near everythin' from the garden an' orchard. We had chickens for eggs an' fried chicken on Sunday. We'd butcher two or three hogs every fall for meat. We hunted rabbits an' quail. We had a couple milk cows for milk an' butter. Our eatin' was a whole lot better than it is now."

When the boys turned twenty-one, Big said Granddad McElligott gave them three hundred dollars. He gave the girls one hundred dollars. They was out on their own from then on. They could always go back home or even stay there, as long as they got up and had breakfast together. Daddy was the only one who was ever able to sleep in after he left home. He'd stay out late on Saturday night and sleep past breakfast on Sunday morning. Big said Granddad would growl some but let Daddy sleep. Nobody else could get by with it, though.

The Garner house wasn't much different during the Depression, Mother said. They always had plenty to eat, enough money to send all three girls to high school in Martinsville and pay board for them to stay in town through the week. And both families had always looked after grandmas who lived close by. At times, both families had other parts of the family in the house for long periods of time. Mother said one of her mother's cousin's husband got killed in a logging accident. The cousin and the little girl came and lived with them for five years before moving to Oklahoma with her new husband. That was sort of like Mother and me living with Big, Aunt Helen and the girls, I thought.

"It was normal to have family around all the time," Mother said one time when I got everybody talking in the living room after supper one evening. "Old people, young people. A houseful all the time."

Big nodded his head and said, "Some of Aunt Tilda's family, or Uncle Otis' would come an' stay for a month in the summertime. Mom'd just cook a little more."

I didn't know much about the names they mentioned. I knew they was family, but I didn't know much about them. Aunt Tilda was the dark-skinned, black-haired woman with the piercing eyes. She was my grandma's sister. I asked Grandma one time if Aunt Tilda was part Negro like Madge and some of the rest of the people around Bellair. "No, son," was the only answer I got.

That's all I heard about it until Aunt Christine, one of my aunts who was not much younger than Grandma, was down to our house one day. She started out telling me a story about the McElligott side of the family. She said two of the McElligott girls got captured by the Indians in the east somewhere when they were eleven and thirteen, got raped and was kept by the Indians for a couple of years before coming back with babies. She said the Indians was worried that the white man was going to wipe them out and wanted to have some off-spring. That sounded a bit farfetched to me, but it made a good story. Aunt Christine also told me another story about her great-great-grandfather being in the Revolutionary War and owning slaves later. After his first wife died he'd married a real young woman and the rest of the family had a fit. But the couple'd had her great-grandfather and several more kids. There was even rumors, she said, that he'd had some children with a slave woman he owned down in Kentucky.

"Now I don't know if that's true," Aunt Christine said, "but that's what they said.

After I'd ask Grandma Mary Elizabeth about Aunt Tilda being part Negro because she was so dark skinned, I started looking closer at everyone else in the family. Daddy and Big was sort of dark skinned and had high cheek bones. Maybe they was part Indian, I began to think after I'd heard hints of Grandma Mary Elizabeth's grandfather having an Indian squaw for a wife. I didn't know for sure what was really truth or if anybody even knew for sure. Or if they'd tell me if they knew. So I asked Aunt Christine about that.

She looked at me with a tight smile on her face. "Now, John Walter," she said, the smile still tight and a trace of twinkle or gleam in her eyes. "I'll tell you what little I know about that, but you mustn't tell Grandma Mary Elizabeth that I told you or that you even know a thing about it. She don't ever talk about it. Promise, cross your heart, hope to die, stick a needle in your eye."

"Promise," I said.

"This is only what Pop told me one night when I was sittin' up with him not long before he died," Aunt Christine said. "He only talked about it with Grandma Mary Elizabeth one time a long time ago. She just wouldn't talk about it atall. But on her mother's side of the family, she thought hers an' Aunt Tilda's granddad had taken a squaw for a wife when he settled in Ohio an' had some children that was half Indian. That's all I know, John Walter. And that's about all you'll ever know. There's no way to find out anymore, I reckon."

"This must be Sgt. McElligott's granddaddy — the one you told me about," Claude said as he walked slowly through the gravestones, stopping to read names and dates. "'William G. McElligott, 123rd Reg., Ill. Inf., June 6, 1838 - April 23, 1866, War Between the States, Union Army.' He wasn't very old."

"No, sir. Aunt Catherine said her grandma — that's her layin' there," I said, pointing at her grave, "told her that he never got over the war, never got much better an' died right on their weddin' anniversary. Granddad was only a year or so old. He had two older sisters an' a younger brother that was born later. They lived in that little house across the branch from Grandma's where I showed you when we came by there. Granddad built his house on the other side of the branch from where she lived, drawing her veteran widow's pension until Vincent an' Vernon come back from the First World War. She died not long after they got back to the farm."

"Yeah," Claude said, "I see she died in 1923. She lived alone for more 'n fifty-five years. That's a long time."

"She wasn't exactly alone, though. She had four kids. I don't know how many the others had, but like I told you, Granddad had fifteen kids altogether. Ten of them lived. My daddy was only seven when she died. So there was somebody always around. Aunt Catherine said somebody, either one of them or some of the rest of the family, I can't remember because I didn't know any of them, was always there with her. Visitin' or just stayin' at night an' then helpin' take care of her when she took sick."

I counted seventeen tombstones with a McElligott on them while Claude wandered around. I knew there was a bunch, but I'd never counted them. A few of them were babies and little kids. And some of them was the David McElligott side of the family, a feller who lived around the corner from Grandma's place. Their farms joined up. Aunt Helen had told me one time that Granddad McElligott had told Mother and her that his dad and Dave's dad was first cousins. Aunt Helen had that figured out back through all the cousins so many times removed. I couldn't keep track of that. They was McElligotts was all I knew. They must have come from the same place somewhere way back down the line, I figured. Granddad had told Aunt Helen and Mother after they married into the family that some of the McElligott families had come together, out from Maryland and Virginia to Kentucky and then up through Indiana to Illinois. That was in the early 1800s. Other parts of the family had stayed in Kentucky; other parts went off later to Missouri and Texas.

Uncle Billie Peterson's mother was from the Illinois part of the family, too. When I stayed down at Uncle Billie and Aunt Annie's, they told me a little about the family history that had been handed down to them. The one I'd heard more than once was about the move up through Indiana to Illinois was one I liked. A couple of the men had ridden ahead of the wagons to find a place to camp for the night when they came upon the hot springs over in Indiana. It was cold and the steam rose over the springs, giving it a pretty scary look in the dreary winter day. The men turned their horses and hightailed it back to the wagons as fast as they could get there.

"'Let's get out of here an' head them wagons off to the west,'" Uncle Billie said the man had said. "'We're not more 'n a mile from hell right now.'"

I could picture that in my mind's eye. The image got even clearer years later when I read a Thomas Hardy novel where the characters would somehow find themselves out in the heath where it was dark and eerie and scary. I thought of that as I walked along behind Claude and looked at the names and imagined the men and women who went with them. I'd seen some old photographs with names written on the back. They didn't mean much to me, if I couldn't put something of their lives to the face. I stopped at my great-great-granddad's grave and read, "John McElligott, born Kentucky, July 10, 1791, died August 20, 1873. War of 1812." I figured he was a tall old feller like his son who would have been the one Aunt Christine used to tell me about.

"Only one of them that ain't here is old Sam," I said when Claude got back close. "That'd be Samuel McElligott. He was my great-great-great grandfather an' was the oldest feller in the bunch that any of the family knows about. He was born somewhere in Maryland or Delaware on October 2, 1745, and died in Kentucky August 5, 1822. He was the one Aunt Christine had told me about when I was doin' the genealogy project at school who'd been in the Revolutionary War an' all. They think his daddy was Robert, the one my Uncle Big is named after, who was Scotch-Irish an' came to this country from Ireland just before old Sam was born."

Claude smiled at me.

"You sure know your people's history, son," he said. "I can't take my people back past my granddaddy. Wish I could."

"Big says it don't make any difference," I said, proud of what I'd been telling Claude, proud that I knew. "But I figure that a feller ought to know that kind of stuff. That's one of the reasons I wanted to know so bad about how Daddy got killed. A feller's got to be proud of his people an' know as much about his line an' what they done as he can, I reckon."

"I reckon you're right," Claude said as we walked among the McElligott family graves. "Helps a feller keep life in focus, if you know where your line of people's comin' from. We all probably ain't much different than them that come before us."

I walked a bit straighter as we looked at other McElligott men's stones that had some war on their tombstones like Daddy had WWII on his marker. The women just had date of birth and date of death. Sometimes there'd be a little biblical verse or something. One a couple of plots away from Daddy's said, "That mortal coil unfoldeth." That was on the tombstone of U.S. Grant McElligott. At the bottom of the stone, it said, "Spanish-American War." While I was standing there looking at that, I saw Claude out of the corner of my eye. He squatted down, hat in hand, in front of Daddy's marker. While he was squatted there, I never saw him move a bit. He stared at the grave marker for a long time before he got up. I stood behind and waited, a tear rolling down my cheeks now and again. I kept them wiped off.

"Thanks, son," Claude said, putting his hat back on. "Let's get you home. I've taken enough of your time today."

"You're welcome, sir," I said. "But you ain't took none of my time. I've been wantin' to talk to you for as long as I can remember. And that's the god's truth."

Claude smiled again.

Meeting him was one of the biggest moments I ever remembered in my whole life. He was someone who had been right there when Daddy got killed. I'd wondered for so long how it'd happened. To have somebody who was actually there and saw what happened was almost like a miracle to me. Big didn't think so when I told him.

"Your daddy's still dead, ain't he?" he said. "It don't make no difference how it happened; he's still dead."

"Didn't you want to know, though, Big? Didn't you just wonder how he died? What happened to him? Why it was him an' not the next feller? What it'd be like to have him here now?"

"I think about him all the time, John Walter," Big said, tears welling up in his eyes for the first time I'd ever seen them. "I wonder why it was him that lost that coin flip an' not me. I wonder why it wasn't me who went off an' got killed an' not him. I wonder a lot of things, but it ain't goin' to change anything an' knowin' how he got killed don't give me much peace. All's I know is that he's dead."

Big turned and walked away. I figure he was crying some and didn't want me to see was the reason he left. I didn't know. But he walked off, and we never talked about the war or my daddy getting killed in it again for a long time. With Big the facts was still there, but he went on and never talked about them like he didn't a lot of things in his life. I reckon he thought it'd go away, if he didn't talk about it. Or at least he wouldn't have to bother nobody else with it. With me the facts was there, and I thought about them and talked about them all the time. It was the only way I could live. I wanted to know whatever I could about Daddy and the war. Almost everything in my life somehow related to him and where he got killed. That changed things in my life — pretty considerable. And I knew that what had happened to him and what kind of a man he was was going to help me get through the bad things I'd have coming up in my life. I figured bad things had happened or would happen to most everybody at one time or another, things that you just had to live with and go on, like Big said. It was the going on that was rough sometimes. Sam was right about that. Meeting Claude and hearing about how Daddy got killed helped me some in going on.

Mother seemed a little more at peace after Claude's visit, too, and brought up his name from time to time. For a long time afterwards, I'd look for Claude's big Chrysler at the store or over at Ross' every time I was on that side of the square.

13

A couple of big storms covered the Illinois and Midwestern countryside with several inches of snow before Christmas. The first one hit
when Big and Sam and Dad Garner and me was bringing two truck
loads of cattle from the sale barn in Paris out to the Red Wilson farm
Big had rented to feed cattle. He was feeding about a hundred and
fifty head and would take a load out or another one in from time to
time. Right after we got to the sale barn, it started snowing pretty
heavy and the wind picked up so much you could see things blowing
across the parking lot. Big walked through the cattle pens looking for
what he wanted to buy while the rest of us went to get sandwiches. I
was thinking about getting back home and going sledding with Richard and Jerry and anyone else who wanted to go. We'd have a fire at
the bottom of the hill down by Jim Miller's old place or down at the
Old Bed and spend all day sliding down hill and even staying into the
night. But I knew we'd have to hurry home with the cattle to do any
sledding before dark.

Sam ordered Big a hamburger and a Pepsi that was waiting for
him when he got back from the cattle pens. He salted and peppered
the hamburger and splashed some ketchup on it before taking a third
of it in one bite. I started taking bigger bites and chewing faster, because I knew when Big finished his sandwich, he'd be off to the sale
ring without the rest of us. Sam was done before Big, and I shoveled
mine down but was still eating when he washed his last big bite down
with the last of the Pepsi. Dad still had half a sandwich left when Big
and Sam stood to leave.

"Better stay here with me an' take your time," Dad said. "You
didn't half chew that sandwich."

"I'm goin' with them," I said, finishing off the Pepsi.

"We better get them dang cattle bought an' get out of here," Big said as we headed to the sale ring. "Ought to get 'em bought right today. This looks like a devil of a storm."

That made me smile. I hoped he was right. We didn't have many snowstorms like that at home. And I was afraid that we wouldn't get that much down there. Paris was farther north and always got more snow. I always liked to go to the sale barn there, anyway. The auctioneer sat in a little booth at the edge and just above the ring. Two or three fellers walked around the ring looking for bids and worked the bidders when things wasn't moving fast enough. These fellers in the ring knew the bidders in the crowd and went back and forth from one to the other. They didn't even look at Sam, Dad or me. They went right to Big and on to another feller that was a bidder. Big said you had to watch who you was bidding against because he thought sometimes they'd have somebody running the bid up. When he thought they was doing that, he'd stop bidding and just sit there. The first bunch that Big bid on had a feller bidding against him he thought was doing that. I didn't see what was going on at first because I'd been up at the top of the seats looking down at everything from the highest spot. The way I could see things changed with each step I took back down to the top of the sale pen. I counted eighty-nine fellers sitting around on all sides, watching the cattle being sold. Most of these fellers never came to buy anything or even made a bid on anything. They just watched what was going on.

When I got back, two of the fellers in the ring was trying to get Big to bid. All he'd said was "Nope" once and then just sat there ignoring them. They finally turned to the auctioneer and shook their heads.

"Sold for $28.50 a hundred, ten head of prime western steers an' heifers," he said over the loud speaker and slammed the gavel to the table top, then pointing to a feller on the other side of the ring.

"Didn't take 'em long to start, did it, Big?" Sam asked, resting his chin in his hands. He had a smile on his face that was mostly covered by his hands, but I could see his eyes smiling.

"They come right at you," Big said. "You got to watch these cockwallopers. I'll bet you anything them feeders was Frazen's cattle. He'll split 'em up an' run 'em through again Tuesday. Maybe even today."

A little later Big bought ten head of western feeders. They had a brand on their hips that looked like a J with a circle around it. I'd never seen any cattle with a brand on their hip. And I never even knew that Big bought them. I'd seen him nod once, but that was all I'd noticed.

"Sold right over there," Frazen said, pointing to Big with his gavel and then banging it down on the table, "ten head of prime western feeders for $26.50. You can't buy cattle any lower than that, gentlemen."

The auctioneer went on to the next bunch of feeders. I liked to hear him talk as he told about each bunch and started the bidding with the same line each time.

"Now who's goin' to give me twenty-five dollars," he'd say or call out the amount wherever he started the bid, "for this good-lookin' bunch of feeders that. ..."

Sam and Dad and me heard Frazen over the loud speaker as we went to load the feeders while Big stayed to buy another truckload. We'd only been in the sale ring for less than an hour, but in that time it had snowed quite a bit. Everything was covered. The scenery had changed from dreary gray to a bright white that was dulled a little by the falling snow so you couldn't see more than a few hundred feet in front of you. The other fellers didn't look happy about the snow. Sam had his mouth shut, and I could see his jaw muscles move back and forth as he backed the truck up to the loading chute.

We had the feeders loaded and the truck pulled out in the parking lot when Big came out to get his truck with the sale bills in his hand. I ran over to him and walked onto the truck with him.

"Did you get some more with brands?" I asked.

"Nope," he said. "Just some plain old feeders."

He backed his truck across the lot while I walked along beside him. At the chute, he stopped an inch or so away and then eased back to the platform. We climbed over the chute to the pens. Sam and Dad was there waiting.

"Ain't this the shits?" Big said.

"It's more 'n the shits," Sam said. "Let's get these cattle loaded an' headed south while we can."

"There's only nine in this bunch," Big said and nodded. "Right here. Got 'em bought right."

I held the gate open while Big and Dad drove the feeders out. They was Herefords like the western cattle, but they didn't look as good. They looked more like what Big called common. He said they was mixed with something else.

Sam went back towards the loading chute. The feeders ran out of the pen and straight to it. We was loaded and heading south in ten minutes. It was snowing so hard I was a little scared. I didn't know how we could see to drive if it got worse. All I could see was the heavy snow coming straight down for a bit, then getting caught by the wind and blowing straight into the windshield or the other way across the hood. The wind seemed to change directions and back again in no time. Cars and trucks coming from the other way was right there hardly before you had any warning. The lights would just pop out of the darkness of the afternoon and the whiteness of the snow right in front of us on the other side of the road. It wasn't two o'clock yet, but we was about an hour from home when it wasn't snowing.

I looked over at the speedometer. We was going thirty miles an hour. It'd take us a lot longer than an hour, I thought, if we even made it home. I'd read stories in Big's and Russ' western books about blizzards out West where cowboys or settlers got lost and either froze to death or by some miracle or another made it to a little line shack. I didn't want to freeze to death or even get stranded out along the road in the truck. The thought of it scared me more than I wanted to admit.

"Thought you liked this snow, Sedwick," Big said.

"Not like this," I said. "Can we make it home, Big?"

"I reckon we can, unless it starts driftin'."

That I trusted Big and Sam as much as anybody could be trusted was the only comforting part of what I thought and saw as I stared out through the windshield of first Big's truck and later Sam's the rest of the way to Red Wilson's place. The snow let up some the farther we drove, but there was still a lot of it. I thought of all the stories Dad had told me about the storms they had when he was a boy growing up on a farm back in the old days in the 1800s. He said they just holed up in the house and waited the storm out. They only went outside together and only to feed the livestock or milk the cow. In bad snowstorms, he said they had some twine stretched out from the barn to the house to make sure they didn't wander off into the storm. The storms in his days seemed much worse than any I'd ever been in before.

But Big and Sam remembered the same kinds of things about winters when they was growing up. Maybe it was just them living out in the country a half a mile or so from the nearest neighbor that made the storms seem worse. In Bellair, I could always look out the windows and see Madge's house on one side and Russ and Eunice's on the other. I could always see Miz Hancock's out the front door. And I could usually see the back of Richard and Jerry's across the garden on the other side of the square. Looking through the windshield of Big's truck into the snowstorm, I couldn't tell what anything was.

We pulled off the road at the little restaurant in West Union to see how Sam and Dad and the cattle was getting along. I wonder what Sam thought about the storm and asked him if I could ride the rest of the way with him. He nodded over to Dad and said, "Ask him."

Dad was closer to Big's truck, so he just turned that way.

Only the part of the windshield where the wipers waved back and forth was clear of snow. Sam hunched over the steering wheel and gripped it with both hands. I tried talking about the cattle, but he'd just grunt or say something I couldn't understand. He smoked a cigarette ever little bit and kept the window open so much that it was cold even with the heater running full blast. I shivered and thought about going sledding down on the hill.

I started telling him about sledding and how I wished I'd been living back in the olden days when they had real snowstorms so I could have lots of days to sled and play out in the snow. That's when I found out that he hated snow about as much or more than he hated mice and rats.

"I've had enough snow to last me for the rest of my life," he said, the muscles in his jaw twitching as he clamped his teeth together. "Livin' through a winter durin' the war gave me a bellyful of that stuff. I hope I never see another flake. Cold weather either. They say that that winter over there in '44 an' '45 was one of the coldest on record in Europe. It was colder 'n any damn thing I've ever seen, an' I know there was more snow than I'd ever seen before or since. An' we was out in it with Germans everywhere. Particularly at the Bulge."

When I started to ask him to tell me more about everything, he stopped talking, held onto the steering wheel like he was afraid it would get away and kept on driving through the storm like we'd hadn't even been talking about war and storms or anything else. I figured he just didn't like what we was driving in coming from Paris and quit talking myself. But as we drove through the storm, I let my mind drift away and started thinking about what Sam had said. It was easy for me to imagine us as an Army convoy back in the war. Looking out as far as I could see, it was plain that we could be ambushed almost any place along the way. Mother didn't even want me to play out in the snow when there was far less that it was snowing. It was hard to think somebody could live outside all winter and on top of that, be in the middle of a war like Sam and the other soldiers had been.

It was war enough for me to help get the cattle unloaded and fed and on home. The snow was still coming down and the wind was still raging when we pulled in to unload the cattle more than three hours after we'd left the sale barn in Paris. My imagining being a convoy in the war had stopped long before. I felt lucky to only be helping Big sit up the loading chute to get the feeders unloaded in the middle of the snowstorm rather than off fighting in a war in a foreign country.

After we dropped the chutes and let the two loads of steers and heifers out, we carried hay and feed for them and the other cattle that had gathered to eat and see the new feeders. By the time we got the unloading and feeding done, the snow had tapered off to nothing, but the blowing snow had covered the tracks in the lane out to the road. You could hardly see where the lane was because there was already nearly a foot of snow on the ground. Standing at the back of the two trucks, we watched Big lay the two-by-four in the iron slots in front of the door to the feed shed made from an old stock rack, make sure the door was shut tight and walk back to us.

"I think we'd better go around by Red's an' in past Mulberry School," Big said, lighting the first Lucky Strike I'd seen him smoke for more than an hour. "It was driftin' bad over there by Charlie Russell's when we was comin' in. Them north-an'-south roads are goin' to be a bitch, whichever way we go."

Sam nodded and said, "'Xpect that's right."

"Be fewer north-an'-south roads goin' back out the way we came in," Dad said. "More hills the other way."

"But we're empty now," Big said. "I don't think we can get through them drifts over there north of Charlie's house. More protection the other way. I think we better try it that way."

I got back in Big's truck, and we headed out first. He had to cut a good track to the road. I jumped out and opened the barbed-wire gate and drug it across in front of the truck and stood waiting until Sam had gone through. Dad walked up just as I drug the gate back across to shut it.

"I can do this," I said, aggravated that my granddad hadn't stayed in the truck and let me shut the gate on my own. "You didn't have to get out in the snow."

Dad was almost eighty years old. He never complained about anything, didn't talk much when we was working but done his part and then some most of the time. Dad and Big was quite a bit different to work with. Big told you to do something — or maybe ordered you to do something would be a better way to put it — and left you to get the job done. Dad asked you to do something and stayed around to help you do it.

"Two's better 'n one out in a storm like this," Dad said, stepping through the gate to the road side of the fence. "Let me help. If you'd pull it tight, I'll slip the wire over at the top."

I didn't argue with him. Just as soon as the gate was in place, we ran for the trucks. The stretch going south from there was pretty well protected by the trees on both sides of the road and the hills. We moved right along. On around past Red's house and through the Willow Crick bottoms was no problem, either. The snow was a foot deep, but the trucks cut through. It was just slow going. Big run in second or third gear all the time.

Even the road north up to the Mulberry School wasn't too bad. The fence row on the west side of the road kept the drifts in the fields. When there was a drift, it would only be a few feet where there was a break in the fence row. Big run it in third gear with the stick down in low axle and barreled through.

At Mulberry, we headed back west. It was past supper time, and the snow wasn't blowing now. The whole countryside was covered with snow like I'd never seen. Only the trees cast a dark shadow in the otherwise bright whiteness of early evening. It looked so peaceful out with the moon starting to break through the dark clouds that I started to say what I was thinking when we turned the corner towards Louis Edwards' place.

"Son-of-a-bitch," Big said, saying each word by itself instead of the whole thing as one word as he usually did. "Look at that dang snow."

I couldn't even tell where the road was supposed to be. The snow had drifted across the road like it was open prairie on most of the half of a quarter of a mile or so where Bus Scott had bulldozed the fence rows on both sides of the road to make more farm ground. Big shifted down to second as we turned the corner and gunned the motor. By the time we hit the highest part of the drift, he was in third gear. We plowed through until the drifts got higher than the truck bumper. He shifted back down to second, then to dual low before we stopped completely and couldn't go any farther.

"Sonovabitch," Big said. "We're goin' to have to walk in."

Sam and Dad had stopped right behind us and was getting out of their truck when I stepped out into the snow that was more than knee deep on me. I started to go back to them, but Dad waved me the other way. We all met in front of the truck. I wondered what Sam was thinking. He looked tired and his face was drawn. With that look, I knew he wouldn't want to talk. And Big still had the mad look on his face. I knew I didn't want to talk to him.

"Fuckin' weatherman don't know what he's talkin' about," Big said. "Nobody knew anything like this was comin'. We're goin' to have to walk in. You okay, Selva?"

"I'm fine," Dad said. He was wearing gloves for the first time I'd seen him wearing them. He'd always told me that you couldn't tell what you was doing with gloves on and never wore any. "What would we do, if I wasn't?"

"Holler if you need to stop," Big said, not answering the question. "Sam, you lead out an' break a path. You an' Sedwick follow. I'll be right behind you. It's goin' to be slow goin'."

Sam nodded and turned away to start toward Bellair and home. And it was slow going. Sometimes the drifts was almost waist deep, and Sam would have to go off towards the east ditch to find a way through. I didn't know how he knew where he was going. It wasn't that you couldn't see.

You just couldn't tell where you was or where you was going to end up. Or I couldn't.

"How can you tell where you're goin'?" I asked.

"Can't tell," Sam said, laughing a little for the first time I'd heard all day, "unless you find a reference point out in front of you to keep your bearings. Just use my tracks an' I'll get us up to Louis Edwards' place. The drifts'll not be so bad from there on into town."

I looked out in front of Sam and could see Louis' house and barn less than a quarter of a mile away. Then I looked back to the tracks I was supposed to be stepping in to follow Sam. It was all I could do to keep up and not flounder around in the snow. I couldn't watch where I was going and off in the distance, too. I wondered how Dad was getting along. Both Big and Sam was six feet tall or better. Dad was three or four inches shorter and had shorter legs. I was about as tall as Dad, but I had longer legs and was having trouble following in Sam's tracks. When I looked back at Dad, I couldn't tell how he was doing. He was putting one foot in front of the other and not saying anything or showing how he felt one way or the other, taking things the way he always did. I wondered why he was out working with us at all when he didn't have to. He rented his farm out, had enough money to get by and lived with us. He didn't have to be out taking care of cattle in a snowstorm, even though he owned some of the cattle with Big and helped take care of them until they sold them.

That was another thing I couldn't figure out. All along while they was feeding the cattle, Big had said he was going to sell them at election time. That was in November 1952. But the prices didn't get to what he wanted for the cattle, and he kept feeding them. Then he went and bought two more loads in a snowstorm right before Christmas and was going to feed them, too. I thought that if I'd been doing things, I'd have sold the cattle before winter set in and spent my time down at the Old Bed, skating on the ice or just sitting around the fire and roasting a potato rather than wading through the snow to feed cattle. Then I wouldn't have to worry about how much money I was going to make or lose, and I wouldn't have to work out in the bad weather. At the Old Bed, I could play with Richard and Jerry and imagine I was one of the early settlers camped out just below the settlement or a soldier off in a war like Sam had been back when he was young.

Big and Dad would never say much about why they kept feeding the cattle in the winter when prices was so low. When I'd asked Sam, he'd looked over at me and smiled.

"It's like old Kentuck used to say," Sam said. "Cut your losses. Throw your cards in if you ain't got a chance to win the hand. Don't bet on the come. There'll be other hands. Don't throw good money after bad. That's what it looks like to me they're doin'. But it's their call."

Their call didn't look real good to me as we walked along through the knee-deep snow. Dad was more than twice as old as Big and Sam, and they wasn't moving real fast. I asked Dad how he was doing once.

"Just keep goin'," he said.

And I did. I figured that if Dad could keep going at his age, I could keep going at mine. Wasn't much choice, anyway.

We made it to Louis' house and turned on the angling road to Bellair. The snow wasn't drifted as bad there, and Sam walked along the right edge where there was little snow much of the time. The wind had swept the higher edge bare in places and made for easier walking. That didn't last long, but we never had to pass through any more big drifts as we followed the road around slow curves and up and down little hills.

At the graveyard, the little lane that ran back on the east side of the small, cleared hilltop was drifted fence-top high. The gate to the cemetery was just sticking out over the top of the snow. Parts of the fence was all covered up. I could see the tops of the tombstones, but it sure looked funny to me to see only the tops sticking out. Charlie Kline's flat marker on out away from the drifts was covered in nearly two feet of snow, I could tell in the moonlight that now made the countryside bright. It was probably cold like this when he died, I thought. He'd been killed on February 23, 1945, when Sam said "the end was in sight." That's the way he put it when I'd been with him at the restaurant in Oblong when a feller named Hal Holden, who'd lost an arm in the war, was eating dinner with us. Hal started driving an oil tanker after the war and was with Charlie when he was killed. Hal and Sam got to talking about the war in Korea, and Charlie's name came up and him getting killed.

"Didn't know what hit him," Hal said. "We was runnin' across an open field one mornin' when Charlie got caught in a crossfire from a German strongpoint we was clearin' out. He was dead when

I dropped down beside him a couple of seconds later. Took a round right through the chest. Damn shame! He was only twenty-two years old an' a helluva feller. An' you know how handsome he was. First Sergeant an' some of the boys always called him Clark Gable. Strong as a bull, too. He told me one time about wrasslin' with Big. Said he could throw him sometimes, but he was the toughest man he ever got tangled up with."

Feller'd have to be a whole bunch tougher to fight a war in cold weather, I thought, as Big and Sam and Dad and me started down the hill to Borax and the last stretch on into Bellair. I couldn't imagine soldiers fighting in cold and snowy weather. I didn't even know how they could hold a rifle. My fingers was tingling and burning. I was cold and wet all over. Sam seemed to know that I was about all in by the look on his face when he looked over at me. He hadn't said anything since he struck out through the snow back where the trucks stalled.

"How you doin', Sedwick?" he asked while we leaned into the hill and walked up to where we could see Bellair.

"Okay," I said, lying and picturing Charlie running across that field in Germany and falling dead in the snow. "I'm cold."

"We're almost there. Just keep puttin' one foot in front of the other one for five more minutes."

"You makin' her okay, Selva?" Big asked.

"Yep," Dad said. "For five more minutes, anyway."

"That's all of us, Selva," Sam said.

"They'll have the maintainer out early in the mornin'," Big said. "We'll have to get out there an' dig the trucks so Golf can get on through."

I don't know when I'd ever been more happy to see Bellair. Lots of times I thought I wanted to get out of there so bad I didn't know what to do. I wanted to go out West and see where the cowboys and the Indians lived. I wanted to go to Mark Twain's hometown on the Mississippi and see where Tom Sawyer and Huckleberry Finn lived — I thought Huckleberry was about the best name I'd ever heard and wanted to do things like he'd done. And I wanted to go out to California where Dad Garner's brother Harry lived. He'd told me about taking a train to San Francisco in the winter of 1895. "They had a stove in each car," he said. "But out in Utah, we ran out of wood.

It was cold, down around zero. We got so cold that we started bustin' up the seats an' burnin' them to keep warm." He laughed. I wanted to have experiences like that. I even thought about seein' what it was like to be in a war, but Korea didn't look like it was going to last until I got old enough to fight. If it didn't, I didn't know what I'd do to get in a war. I was so cold that I knew I'd have to worry about that later.

When I saw the outline of the town, the faint lights in the windows and chimneys with smoke drifting straight up now that the wind had died down, I didn't want to be anyplace except at home in Bellair. I wondered if Daddy or Charlie or any of the rest of them that went away to fight in the war ever felt like that. It felt real good to me that I was getting home. Inside, Dad and me stood around the stove in the dining room and thawed out. Mother stood with us. Big and Sam stood around the stove in the front room. Aunt Helen and Nancy and Mary Beth stood with them.

I was shivering so much I could hardly get my coat unzipped and out of my wet outer clothes. Russ had said something about being so cold out on a drilling rig one night that he "started shiverin' like a dog shittin' peach seeds." I laughed and laughed at him when he said that. I couldn't quite imagine that picture. Now I could. I laughed and laughed at the picture.

"What's the matter with you?" Mother asked.

"Nothin'," I said. "Nothin'. I'm just glad to be inside."

Slow but sure I got warm. I stood right next to the stove until I nearly burned myself. The steam rolled off both Dad and me as our wet clothes turned hot wet instead of cold wet. Mother put my pajamas close to the stove to warm. When I warmed up enough, I went to the bathroom and stripped out of my clothes. Away from the stove and nearly naked, I started shivering and thought of the dog passing peach seeds again. I laughed and laughed again.

"Whatever is the matter with you?" Mother called from the hallway.

"Nothin'. Not a thing."

"Bring those wet clothes out here. Don't put 'em in the hamper."

I finished dressing and grabbed the rest of my clothes as I went out the door. Mother looked at me a little funny, I thought, but she didn't say anything else about me laughing so much. Dad had gone off to his bedroom to go to bed, leaving the dining room empty so

I could crawl in the daybed where I always slept. I started to go to bed, then thought of Sam. I wondered where he was going to sleep.

He was still standing around the stove with Big when I went to the front room to see. Aunt Helen was making a bed on the couch. Mother was moving a little table and chair over to the wall by the flower window.

"You goin' to sleep on the couch, Sam?" I asked.

"I've slept on worse things," he said. "I told Helen I could sleep on the floor."

"You can have the daybed," I said. "I can sleep on the couch."

"I'll be fine, Sedwick. Thanks, though. You go on to bed. It's been a long day. I know I'm ready for some shut-eye."

I didn't need any coaxing. I was almost asleep on my feet. My head had hardly touched the pillow before I was asleep. I must have slept like a rock, as they say, because I was still in the same position when I woke up the next morning. The light had been on in the hall when I passed out. Sunlight was streaming in the front door when I opened my eyes. It was real quiet in the house. I knew from the sun that it had to be after eight o'clock. Mother had already gone to work at the store. But where was everybody else, I wondered and ran to the front room window to look out. Dad wasn't sitting back in the corner in his chair. And the car was gone. The sidewalks and driveway had been shoveled. I couldn't believe I'd slept through everybody getting up and around.

Golf Blakeman roared by from the south about that time, and I knew where everybody was. Aunt Helen had taken them out to get the trucks out after Golf had plowed the roads open out past Louis Edwards' place. Getting left behind made me kind of mad. I'd ought to be out there helping them get the trucks shoveled out instead of laying in bed all morning, I thought. But I felt good, too, rested like you do after a night of sound sleep. I was kind of glad that I got to sleep until I woke up.

Aunt Helen, Nancy and Mary Beth drove up about that time. Big and Sam and Dad got back with the trucks about an hour later. They decided not to do anything for the rest of the day.

"We'll feed the cattle tonight," Big said to Sam, "an' you can take that pickup load to Indianapolis tomorrow night. Let's stay in the rest of the day."

That made me feel pretty good that they was going to stay in, too. I still felt a bit guilty about being in bed while everybody else was outside.

But nobody working for the rest of the day sort of let me off the hook. I went sledding with Richard and Jerry.

We hadn't been down on Jim Miller's hill anymore than to have time to get a fire going when Big Al, Jimmy and Ronal came up over the hill. They'd been rabbit hunting and saw the smoke from the fire from the field across the road. I looked around when I first saw them. We didn't have much of a way out and back to town, but I didn't think they'd stick their cocks out in the cold. They hadn't even tried anything like that in the last year or so. But it wasn't something I forgot about. What'd happened was always there between us when we was around each other, even though nobody ever said a word about it. Most of the time they just tried to run over us or push us around. I could hardly wait until they couldn't do that anymore, and I told Big Al one time that would happen.

"The time's comin', Big Al, when I'm goin' to be just as big as you, an' I'm goin' to kick your fuckin' ass all over town."

"That ain't goin' to be right away," Big Al said. "Probably never. But you ever try it, I'll turn you ever' which-way but loose. I'll get on you like stink on shit, you little cocksucker. I ought to cornhole your little ass right now."

"You an' what army, you big bastard?" I said, firing right back at him that day. "It ain't goin' to be long 'til I kick your ass all over the place."

Big Al grinned as he walked up to the fire.

"It goin' to be now, Jackie?" Big Al asked. "The day you're goin' to kick my ass all over the place?"

"Fuck that Jackie shit," I said. "That ain't my name."

"That right?"

"That's right. We're just sleddin', Big Al. We ain't lookin' for no trouble."

"We're sleddin', too," Jimmy said. "We're not lookin' for trouble, either. Looks like the snow's good for slidin' downhill. Let's get to sleddin'."

The three of them unloaded their shotguns and lay them on Big Al's coat at the top of the hill. Then they walked over to the sleds and started to take them.

"I didn't say you could use my sled," I said.

"Neither did I," Jerry said.

"I don't think nobody asked you," Ronal said, letting off his neighing laugh. "We just want t' slide downhill a little."

"Not on my sled," I said. "You can't use it."

Jimmy was closest to mine. He laughed and picked it up. Big Al and Ronal picked up the other two sleds. They all turned toward the track downhill. I didn't figure there was any use of saying anything else and lowered my head and ran at Jimmy. I hit him just as he started to lay down headfirst on the sled and knocked him over on the other side. We landed on the downhill side of the hill and started rolling down. Jimmy never quite recovered from the first hit I landed on him. As we rolled down the hill, I threw a couple of haymakers at his head that glanced off his shoulders and hit me in the face. When we finally rolled to a stop about halfway down the hill, I jumped on top of him with my knees on his arms. Holding his hands down and leaning close to his face, I said, "You goin' to leave me an' my fuckin' sled alone, asshole?"

"Yes, I'll leave it alone. Just get off of me."

"Promise?"

"Yes, I promise."

"Cross your heart, hope to die, stick a needle in your eye?"

"Yes, yes. Let me up."

"Say it."

"Cross my heart, hope to die, stick a needle in my eye."

"What?"

"What?"

"That you'll leave me an' my sled alone."

"That I'll leave you an' your sled alone."

"Okay," I said and let him up. I walked up to the sled, flipped it over and started back to the top of the hill. Jimmy followed after he'd brushed the snow from his clothes. Big Al and Ronal was hooting and laughing when I got to the top.

"You goin' to let this little cocksucker get the best of you, Jim?" Big Al said. "He ain't — "

I ran at him just as I'd done at Jimmy. Only Big Al didn't go down as easy. He sort of fell over in the snow, grabbed me with one hand and halfway tossed me up in the air and down the hill. I just missed Jimmy walking back up as I rolled past him. He kicked out at me as I rolled past, hitting me in the ribs with his toe. I grunted and came to a stop about where Jimmy and I had a few minutes earlier. I looked up to see Big Al throw my sled high in the air towards me.

"Fuck you, your sled an' the horse you rode in on," Big Al said. "You ain't got a lick of sense, John Walter."

"Look who's talkin'. You're dumber 'n owl shit to boot."

Richard and Jerry stood off to the side of the others and waited for me to get back up the hill. By the time I got to them, the others had picked up their shotguns and headed for town.

"You've got 'em all pissed off at you now, John," Richard said. "One of 'em's goin' to beat the shit out of you now. Or out of Jerry an' me.

"Big Al's the only one that can beat anything out of me now. Them other two can't whip me anymore. They never could fight their way out of a paper bag, anyway. They was just older than me. An' Big Al can't whip all three of us right now. We've got to stick together an' not let them assholes hurt us anymore."

"Me an' Bub'll just stay away from 'em," Jerry said.

"You do that," I said as they turned the corner for their house. "Ain't no fuckin' reason I have to stay away from 'em. It's a free country."

14

I reckon living in a free country and having the freedom that goes with it is a risky deal. Because of all the choices a feller has when he's free, it's hard to decide which way to turn sometimes. Big knew he was losing money right along and didn't buy any more cattle. But he kept on feeding them through the winter, hoping the prices would go up. I could tell he was real worried. Him and Dad talked about things getting back to where they was in the Depression. With prices down around twenty cents a pound, Big said he couldn't even break even and pay for the feed. Yet to keep on feeding the cattle like he was seemed to be what Sam said the poker player meant about "throwin' good money after bad." That's sure what it looked like Big was doing instead of cutting his losses and selling the cattle.

And with the losses piling up and Big all worried about what was going to happen, it was more quiet around the house than usual the rest of the winter, even with Nancy, Mary Beth and me all there together for the evening. Mother and Aunt Helen would talk quietly and crochet nearly every night. Sometimes Dad listened to the news on the radio. But he mostly just sat in his chair, holding his hands together in front of him and twiddled his thumbs together, first one direction, then the other. Big just sat in his chair in front of the big window smoking cigarette after cigarette, reading western book after western book. Some Sundays, he'd read three whole books and never say a word all day. I'd get outside as soon as I could then, but there was nothing to do at night except stay in and read.

I'd reread sections of *Huck Finn* or *Tom Sawyer* every now and then and think about doing some of the things they did in Mark Twain's books. And I was still reading the western books Big or Russ had around and would get off in a corner most every night and read until bedtime. Almost every western book had a character that I could always side with who reminded me of Big or who I thought Daddy had been like. The cowboy or rancher would be a loner or a feller trying to start a little spread where he'd run his own outfit. He always had a hard way to go. There'd always be rustlers, a range war, some old grudge from long ago, the weather or something to stand in the way of getting along easy. That stuff still interested me, although I'd been reading anything I could about World War II to learn what I could about what Daddy had gone through. What Claude Pleasant had told me made me want to know more, and the history classes didn't teach me the kinds of things I wanted to know.

I read everything I could get my hands on about the Marines. These war books was kind of like the old western books with the good fellers and bad fellers always getting into it and the good fellers coming out on top. Some of the good ones got killed but died so everybody else could go on. With the books and what Sam and other fellers had told me or that I'd heard, I thought I had a good picture of what was going on back then and what Daddy went through. The books helped complete the picture. One book I really liked was *The Magnificent Bastards*, a story by some woman about a bunch of Marine Raiders between battles in the South Pacific close to where Daddy had been. They sure seemed to have a good time when they wasn't fighting. Another book I liked was *Guadalcanal Diary*. The picture I got from it was more outside looking in than what I wanted, but it was another part of the picture. It was by a reporter who was with the Marines on Guadalcanal. They didn't seem to have such a good time there, other than what Claude Pleasant had told me, but they did the job they had to do. That's what I figured Daddy had done and saw him somewhere in about every book I read. I was pretty proud of him. Reading about the Marines made me even prouder. Probably the best book about them was *Battle Cry* by a feller named Leon Uris who'd been a Marine infantryman in the war.

"Here's one that hits the nail on the head," Smokey said one day just before Christmas, handing me the book when I got up in the chair. He pulled back any books about the Marine Corps that went in the trading box at the barbershop and saved them for me. That kept me in reading material without the western books. "This old boy knows what he's talkin' about. Thought you might want to take a look at it."

The old boy who wrote the book had been in the landing on Tarawa and a couple of other islands out in the South Pacific. He'd been what Smokey called a grunt, an infantryman, just like him and Daddy. The book was supposed to be fiction, but I wasn't so sure how that worked. In the western books I read, the stories seemed real even through the fellers who wrote about the Old West hadn't lived back then. And I didn't know any real cowboys. In the war novels I'd read, the stories seemed pretty real about what had happened, too. I could see Daddy running up a hill with his men to clean out a Jap machine-gun nest so the rest of his outfit could move up and get some kind of picture of what war was like. So I figured the fiction was mostly real.

That's the kind I liked best. But the soldiers and Marines I read about in the books I was reading didn't talk like the ones I knew around home. If the fellers in the books didn't talk like the ones I knew, I wondered if everything else was cleaned up to be what everybody thought was fit to print. And that made me wonder if I ever got the real picture of war from reading the books. I'd heard for a long time about an old boy from Robinson named Jim Jones who wrote a book called *From Here To Eternity* about his time in the Army that was supposed to show things like they was. But I couldn't get ahold of the book. Some places like the drugstore and the newsstand in Oblong wouldn't carry the book because of the "bad language," and I wasn't anyplace else where I could buy the book, even if I would've had the money. Most of the fellers I was around all the time who'd been in the war had read the book after it came out in paperback, and I wanted to read it, too. Big read it after his brother Vincent, Sam's dad, had read it and passed it on. "It ain't fit for a woman to read, now Bob," Vincent told Big one Sunday when he gave him the book up at Grandma's house when we all got together for some of her fresh-killed fried chicken, mashed potatoes and gravy for dinner. "It's not really fit for anybody to read. It's filthy. I'll let you have it, but don't let Helen or Lorene read it. It ain't fit now, I tell you."

That probably made me want to read it more than anything else. I'd never heard anything filthy from Sam or any of the others and tried to imagine what Uncle Vincent meant. Filthy was something dirty, vulgar as far as I knew. So it was hard for me to figure out how a book was filthy that showed what it was like when the Japs bombed Pearl Harbor and throwed the country into war. I wanted to know what happened and what it was like to go off and fight in a war like Daddy and the others had done. They was off fighting "to save our asses from Hitler an' Tojo" was the way old Wes Davis put it. I didn't see anything filthy about that. I didn't get into all the details about why I was wondering with Miz Finley, but I asked her what filthy meant first chance I got.

"Well, John Walter," she said, the little twinkle in her eyes when she was tickled about something or was teaching somebody, "I'm sure it means different things to different people. If you play out in the mud, you'll get filthy. Dirty. If you use vulgar language in your talk or think crude thoughts, you could be said to have a dirty mouth or a filthy mind."

I figured that must be it, then. Everybody said there was all kinds of cussing and fighting and drinking and whoring and gambling going on in Jones' book. "Sounds like the Army I was in," Sam said when I'd talked to him about it. "It's a little raw, just like the book says. I reckon it's all right for us to go off an' fight an' die in the war, but it ain't all right for anybody back here to read about the way it was when we was off fightin' an' dyin'."

That sounded about right, I figured, but wanted to know more.

Early one morning when Smokey was sitting in the barber chair reading the newspaper, I walked in and asked him about the book and why people thought it was filthy and what I could believe about what I read in anything. He laughed as he folded the paper and looked up at me.

"That all you want to know this mornin'?" he asked, chuckling now as he talked and fished a cigarette from his shirt pocket. "You don't want to know much, do you?"

"Not much, I reckon," I said quite seriously. "Just them things I don't know an' asked about."

"Well, I'd say as a general rule not to believe anything you read or anything you hear an' only half of what you see yourself. That's a good place to start."

"I'm serious, Smokey."

"So am I. Every one of them old boys I landed on Iwo with had a story to tell, none of 'em exactly the same. An' then after-wards, none of 'em remembers most of it exactly the way the others do. By the time it gets filtered through everybody's eyes an' ears, editors, censors an' time, an' the different experiences, you've got a mirrored reflection of what happened. An' it's a blurry reflection at that. The best of what makes it to the books an' becomes a part of tradition or legend captures the essence of the situation, I reckon. So what can you believe? Who can you believe?

"Here's an example: I saw the first flag being raised on the top of Old Baldy there on Iwo after I got hit. I was being hoisted up the side of a hospital ship that mornin' an' turned on my side an' looked back towards The Rock. An' there on the top of Suribachi, a bleak sky in the background with the sun's rays shinin' on it just a little, was one of the most beautiful sights I'll ever see. The flag stood out in Technicolor against the drab background. I got all teary eyed. Still do. An' that flag gave Marines all over the island an emotional charge. They was goin' to take that island in spite of the odds. The boys told me later that they didn't even take notice of the second flag raisin'. But that photograph you always see from then looked like the Marines was fightin' like hell in takin' Old Baldy an' became symbolic for victory to the American people everywhere. But was it the truth? Not in the real sense. We'd already cut the island in half, taken Suribachi an' put the flag up. That second flag was larger an' was raised later to replace the first one an' didn't mean nothin' to the men there. Helluva picture, though."

"You was there?" I asked, hardly able to imagine somebody I knew seeing something like that. "That's something."

"It was something all right, a real tear-jerker," Smokey said, tears in his eyes. "An' like I said, I'll never see anything like it again."

I reckoned I'd never see anything like it at all. Smokey turned, took his glasses off and wiped his eyes. When he turned back to me he had a little smile on his face and looked happy.

"What about *From Here To Eternity*?" I asked, going back to my original question. "What's the truth about it? What's wrong with it? Why is it filthy an' not fit to read?"

"You're wound up like an eight-day clock, ain't you?" Smokey said and laughed. "I don't know what's wrong with the book. It's thick, pretty well written, but hard to read sometimes, tells a story about the Army the way things was, usin' the language soldiers use. It wouldn't do for some of the people who complain about the language in the book to be around a bunch of Marines. Or sailors or soldiers, either, for that matter.

It's a different world in there. A whole different world. Old Jones came in for a haircut a year or so ago, an' we was talkin' about that."

"Don't he say fuck a lot?" I asked, using the word to a grown-up person for the first time in my life.

"That's the way it is," Smokey said, smiling slightly. "You hear the word all the time. It's the way people talk. You get so used to sayin' it, that you don't even know you're sayin' it. Jones said every time he used 'the word' in the book, including all the ones that he wasn't able to keep in, the word wasn't used with a sexual meanin' that has always kept the word out of books in this country. It was just how we talked. It was fuck this or fuck that, this fuckin' thing or that fuckin' thing. It was the ultimate negative verb and modified everything that took on any negative or bad meanin'. How can somebody writin' a novel about the Army or the Marine Corps not use the word? That'd be like a bunch of jarheads goin' on liberty without drinkin' beer."

"You sound like a teacher, Smokey," I said, watching him chuckle and looking at him in a way I never had before. "Or a writer."

"I thought about teachin' at one time. I'd liked to have been able to work with young people. I used to help boys learn to swim or shoot a rifle an' just about anything we did growin' up out in the country. It's a mighty good feelin' to see somebody learn somethin' good that's goin' to stay with them for the rest of their lives an' know you was a part of it. Good teachers are worth their weight in gold, an' we pay 'em like day laborers.

"An' I wanted to write at one time, too. One of my high school teachers told me I 'had a flair for writin'.' I could 'turn a phrase,' she said. I tried my hand at it a little after the war, an' I'd planned to go to college on the GI Bill. But then I got married an' had to make a livin'. I'd always cut hair around home an' for the boys in the Marine Corps, so I went up to Decatur to barber school on the GI Bill after I got home. Been here ever since I finished school. Probably be here until they carry me out. I reckon that's a lot better than if I'd never got off The Rock. There was a lot of good men that never made it off like I did, never had the chance to do anything with their lives but grow up, fight an' die young. An' die hard."

"I reckon so," I said quietly, thinking about Daddy as I watched Smokey turn his head away and stare out the window to the street. "But I wish you'd been a teacher. You'd been a good one."

Smokey turned back to where I was standing in front of him and laughed softly. He looked so kind and gentle. It was hard to imagine a feller like that off fighting in the war.

"An' you'd have been a good writer, I'll bet. Maybe you'd have wrote a book like Jim Jones did. You could have really wrote how it was to be out there fightin' in the war."

"I don't think anybody can do that," Smokey said. "About the best you could do is try to show what it's like. It's like when you look there in the mirror. You see us here talkin', the chairs an' everything here in the shop. But what you see in the mirror is only a reflection of us. It's not the real thing. Can't be. To really know this barber shop an' us in this moment, you've got to be right here with us, not just see the mirrored image."

"I reckon that makes sense. But how do they write about the war the way they do an' call it fiction? My teachers say fiction ain't true."

"Oh, I'd say most of the stuff happened that you read about in these war novels, even a lot of the real gung-ho stuff. But it didn't necessarily happen in the way it does in the book or to the characters there. An' nobody can tell you or show you how godawful bad war really is. Men who was there take their experiences an' fashion stories out of them that uses anything that fits the situation from anything they've ever done, saw, heard about or thought. They just paint a picture of what it was like. That's about the best anybody can do. Jones does a good job at it. 'Bout as good as a feller could, I reckon."

"That's what I've heard fellers say. I ain't read the book yet, but I aim to soon. What kind of a feller is Jones?"

"Kind of like most of the rest of the men around here an' across the country who saw any combat," Smokey said. "He's not much different than the rest of us. Only he's a writer an' wrote about it."

Smokey said Jones probably did what he had to do, got lucky and pulled through and got back home when he wasn't always sure he would. Like everybody else, Smokey said Jones came home to a different world, no longer a boy, and spoke for them that fought the war. Smokey figured a lot of people around our part of the country didn't like Jones because of that book and the way he acted, the drinkin', the fightin', the cussin' an' so on, just like the soldiers did in the service.

"It was okay when we was off fightin' an' dyin' over there," Smokey said. "But now that the war's over an' times are good again, people don't want to hear any of that kind of stuff an' don't understand why some of us act crazy like Jones an' what happened to us that made us that way. They particularly don't want to have somebody writin' about it, livin' among 'em an' still actin' like a soldier on leave.

"Most of us fell in back home just like we did in the war an' done what we had to do. We lived with what we'd seen an' done but never really put it in the past. Jones couldn't put it in the past, either, and wrote about it because I imagine he had to write about it. Probably gone crazy, if he hadn't. At the time, I thought I could write, too, considerin' where I was. But I wasn't there long, didn't take it all in when I had the chance, didn't work at writin' like Jones did an' just came back an' went to work as a barber. I had to make a livin'. An' makin' a livin' as a writer is hard to do at the start, I'd judge. You don't become a writer overnight. It takes time I didn't have.

"Jones, from a writer's point of view, was lucky to be there when Pearl Harbor was attacked. Bein' there let him give you a bird's-eye view of where he was at the time, life in the peacetime Army and the beginning of the war for us. I wouldn't be here cuttin' hair right now if I could do something that good. I'd be doin' just what Jones is doin'.

"But to answer your question, he's a hard-nosed feller that tells it like it was in the military an' in the war, as best as a writer can, I reckon. Not many of 'em do that. Or can. Lots of people who complain about the book wasn't in the service an' probably haven't even read it. That's the kind of thing that really frosts my balls. People need to know what wars are like before they go to sendin' young men off to fight an' die in 'em. Might not do a damn bit of good, but people still need to know."

Smokey didn't have a copy of Jones' book that I could borrow then, and I couldn't find a copy from anyone else. So I saved up a buck and a quarter to buy my own. But I was never anyplace to buy one. Smokey finally loaned me his copy a year or so later. By then the movie was out, and I didn't get to read the book until after I'd seen the movie. The movie was okay, but I liked the book so much because the fellers in it was pretty much like the fellers I was around every day. I could see them in my mind's eye as they was sitting there in the mess hall eating morning chow when the Japs started bombing Pearl Harbor and what happened later. Frank Sinatra and Burt Lancaster and Montgomery Clift and Ernest Borgnine and the rest of the Hollywood actors I'd seen in other movies looked the part in the movie but never came close to what I thought was the real thing or the fellers I knew who fit the parts and had lived the life.

Fellers like Sam and Wes Davis. I was helping them load a double-deck load of hogs one day when they'd talked about *From Here To Eternity*. All Sam had really said about it when I'd talked to him earlier was that it sounded like the Army he was in and that the book "was pretty raw." When we was getting the loading chute set up that day, him and Wes talked some about when they was in the Army and how true-to-life the book was.

"Now, by god, Mac," Wes said, stopping to spit a stream of tobacco juice, "I wasn't where he was, an' he wasn't where we was. But I could goddamn sure tell he'd been somewhere. Some of these books I read, I wonder if the feller writin' it was in the same goddamn Army or the same goddamn war I was in. A feller didn't know a helluva lot about what was goin' on except right around where he was. But by god, I know what went on when we was fightin' them fuckin' Germans. They was fightin' sonsabitches. I know what that chickenshit, fuckin' Army was like, too. An' that goddamn Jim Jones puts you right there in them little places where you can tell he's been there an' knows what he's talkin' about."

After listening to Sam and Wes and other fellers who'd been there talk, I started thinking about books a bit different and about how much of what I read was real. I thought about how real the story in Jones' book sounded and what it would have been like, if I'd really've been there, knowing how different that'd be from any story or book. And I wanted to know what was real.

Being around Bellair after my daddy was killed in the war and me and Mother living with Big and Aunt Helen was the only *real* real I knew then. None of us had much. And times wasn't good for Big, so Christmas wasn't much that year. I had my heart set on getting a pool table. Mother had told me that there wasn't any room for a pool table. I didn't expect a big one like they had in town. But the Sears and Roebuck catalog that I leafed through almost as much as books had a little pool table that I figured I could set up about anywhere. On Christmas morning, I ran into the front room where the tree was and stopped short when I didn't see any package big enough to be the pool table. The one I got was a couple of feet long and a foot or so wide and sat on top of a table. The balls was marbles, and the cues was so short I couldn't even hold my fingers and stroke the cue the way I watched Big do at the pool hall. Tears welled up in my eyes when I opened the package and set the table on the floor.

I'd also wanted a cowboy shirt with arrows on the pocket corners like one I'd seen in the catalog. Aunt Helen made me one. Her and Mother still made clothes for themselves and the girls out of feed sacks and material they'd buy like they'd done at home during the Depression. I'd watched Mother cut out the patterns and sew the different parts together on the old Singer sewing machine over in the corner of the dining room. And I could hardly tell the dresses wasn't store-bought. But she had never made clothes for cowboys. Neither had Aunt Helen. The shirt itself was okay. I couldn't tell much that it was homemade except the arrows on the pockets. The arrows wasn't really arrows. They looked more like thread wrapped around the end of a stick. I thanked everybody and ran to the bathroom. I didn't want to hurt anybody's feelings. I knew there wasn't much money, and they was doing the best they could. That didn't keep me from feeling bad about not getting what I wanted. I was just feeling bad all over and wanted to be alone. That was my Christmas, and it was real.

The best thing about the Christmas was that there was no school. I got to sleep until I woke up on my own and then play with Richard and Jerry all day. The big snow was gone by Christmas, and it didn't look like any more was coming soon. We kept hoping for another snow so we could go sliding down hills and have some snowball fights. Instead the weather stayed wet and miserable. It was gray and overcast most of the time with the sun hiding behind the clouds.

"You just watch," Richard said one day between Christmas and New Year's when we stood around the stove in the store, "it'll snow the day we get back to school. If it does, we ought to lock Miz Finley out an' go slidin' downhill."

With Miz Finley, I couldn't imagine that. She was a tall, big old woman with short gray hair. Looking out through her rimless bifocals, her eyes kept the classroom with eight grades in it running as smooth as the big engines inside the power houses in the oil fields off in the countryside. Her eyes could cut through you like a bolt of lightning when you'd done wrong, or dance with laughter and make you feel like a million dollars when you'd done right. It was always clear which was which, too.

She had her way of doing things. School started on time. Everything had a place. And you stayed on the job she told you to do, or she made sure you did. As far as I could tell, she never brought out a paddle to use on anyone in the years I'd gone to school to her. In her first year at the school and when I was in the third grade, Big Al, Jimmy and Ronal and some of the other older boys led a mini-rebellion against her strict rules and high expectations. Like most of the other younger kids, I joined the boys on the fox hunt as we ran off south through the snow toward the North Fork and circled back around to get back at the school fifteen or twenty minutes after afternoon recess ended.

Miz Finley never got the paddle out even then. She just talked to the bunch of us a little when we got back, then talked with us alone. I don't remember all she said or what the other boys said she said to them. Maybe she said the same thing to us all. But she wagged her finger at me and said, "I hope you don't always plan to follow the pack, mister."

That always stuck with me. So when Richard talked about us locking her out of school by getting there early and wiring and screwing the doors shut from the inside, I just laughed. I'd sneaked in with Big Al, Jimmy and Ronal a year before Miz Finley came to lock the teacher out. Miz Ryan was gone, and it was Mr. Riggs then. But the boys waited until his wife's day to teach to lock him out. Big Al'd opened the door then, even before school was to start, for Miz Riggs after she asked him several times. I knew Miz Finley would have the door open the minute she told us to open it.

That's the way it was with everything with her. She had a no-chewing gum rule and could smell gum in the air from the front of the room and walk right to the boy — and it was always a boy — with her nose up in the air, sniffing like one of Woodrow Cash's bird dogs pointing quail, and tell whoever it was to "go fertilize the wheat field" or whatever was planted in the field to the south of the school. She always caught us, and we always went. So I knew we'd be going to school and wouldn't lock her out.

"You better think of something else, Richard," I said. "That one ain't goin' to work. We ain't lockin' Miz Finley out. We're just goin' to have to stay in here around the stove or go outside an' do something else. We ain't goin' to melt."

The days of the Christmas vacation drug by and stayed the same dreary way. I went to feed the cattle with Big and Dad every day. The lot was muddy and dirty. We'd wade from the old stock rack feed house to the feeders, sinking into the mud ankle deep. The cattle waded and waddled to the feeders through the mud, making it sloppier each day until it finally got to the point where the mud and everything else was mixed smooth and looked a bit like mashed potatoes and gravy did when I stirred them up until I couldn't tell one from the other. We'd get back in the middle of the morning, giving me time to have a full day of doing whatever I wanted to do.

When I wasn't outside playing with Richard and Jerry or up at the store watching the old men play forty-two or listening to other fellers tell stories, I just stayed home and read. That was all that kept the cabin fever from making me go crazy, I thought. In the evening, I'd listen to fifteen minutes of Hank Williams from WGN Radio in Chicago. I'd only get to hear four or five songs, but when he sang "I'm so lonesome I could cry," I'd almost cry myself. His mournful voice and the words spoke right to my heart. It really made me feel downhearted and alone.

I was fixing to get more downhearted. On the last day of the year, it turned off cold and started freezing things up. The sun still wasn't shining much, but the ground wasn't soft and muddy like it had been since the weather turned warmer and all the snow melted and soaked down into the ground as far as it could, then stood in puddles where it couldn't run off to a ditch. New Year's Day was Aunt Helen's birthday. Mother wouldn't let her cook or do any work. We had bacon and eggs for breakfast and sang "Happy Birthday" to her.

"How old are you, Mommie?" Mary Beth asked.

"Old enough again as half," she said, "count it up and it'll make you laugh."

We just looked at her. I had no idea what she was saying.

"What does that mean?" Nancy asked.

"Means I'm old enough to know better, too young to care."

I left them talking about how old Aunt Helen was and told them I was going over to Richard and Jerry's to see what we could do outside.

"You be careful, John Walter," Mother said. "You don't want to take a cold right before you have to go back to school."

Richard and Jerry didn't have a cold, but they was feeling sick like I was about going back to school without the usual days of freedom to roam the countryside over the Christmas vacation. They had just eaten their breakfast and was ready to get out of the house. Ruby said the same thing to us about being careful when we left that Mother had said to me. We walked toward the store, closed for the day while Horsey and Arletta did inventory, Mother called it, and walked on east past Fannie Boone's old store, the bank building, Jake's Restaurant, the Bellair Post Office, now the Ladies Aid Society, the old hotel and the Church of Christ, all closed and rarely used except the church and the hotel where the Boones lived, and headed out of town on the angling road to the cemetery. We hadn't been out that way for a long time. We thought Borax might be froze enough to skate on. And I wanted to go to the cemetery. I wished I could see Daddy's grave, but Charlie Kline's had to do. I always thought about Daddy more than usual on the first day of the year and how another year was starting that I wouldn't have a daddy. I tried to do something to mark the turning of another year. A couple of years before I took some ten-penny nails and made 1951 on the side of the maple tree just outside the garage. I saw that about every day.

At the top of the hill, I looked off to the south and tried to imagine the log schoolhouse there Russ had told me about. It had been there before they built the two-story schoolhouse Joe Marshall used as his barn. I could just see Joe's field and the trees starting and crowding the field all around. It was harder to imagine the log school being moved on skids and pulled by horses to where it became the EUB Church. I could see the big, spreading oak tree at the foot of the cemetery and the tombstones scattered across the top of the hill. It was a good picture. I always wondered why there was no church by the cemetery as there was for others. That would have been a picture right out of a painting, I thought. But Russ had told me the cemetery was Bellair's "buryin' place," not a church cemetery. Seeing the names on the tombstones I'd heard any number of the old men and women talk about always gave me a bit clearer idea of the stories they was telling about earlier days in Bellair. Somehow that gave me a good feeling.

Leaning over the concrete bridge abutment when we got to Borax, we could see that the shallow water was frozen in places. "I think we can skate in a couple of places," I said. "It looks thick enough."

"I ain't goin' to skate on that ice," Richard said. "I don't want to get my ass wet."

"Let's go on up to the graveyard first," I said. "That'll give the ice more time to freeze.'

"That ain't goin' to make any difference," Richard said.

"Sure as hell is," I said.

"Bub knows what he's talkin' about," Jerry said. "He knows more 'n you."

"Bub don't know shit 'bout nothin'," I said as we cut through the old weeds at the bottom of the hill and walked to the big, old oak tree to climb the fence to the older part of the cemetery.

"Does, too," Jerry said.

I laughed and never said anything else. Him and Richard walked around among the tombstones while I went to Charlie's grave. Some of their relatives, including their granddad, was buried there. When we came to the cemetery, they always went to that part and left me alone. I sat down on the ground in front of the flat government marker for Charlie's grave. I couldn't imagine what was buried down there in the ground that nobody had seen when he was shipped home any more than they'd seen what was in the casket that was supposed to be Daddy's remains. I fished a Lucky Strike butt I'd picked up that Big had hardly smoked and lit it. It was so long, I didn't think it counted as picking up a butt. While I smoked, I talked to Charlie and Daddy in my mind about how it was not to have them alive and around all the time. It didn't make me feel as good as it sometimes did. I was feeling kind of empty, like there wasn't nothing there to hear me talking, that I was just talking in the wind and the words floated away.

I sat there a couple of minutes, trying to get the old feeling I thought I used to get. It didn't come, so I got up and left. Richard and Jerry angled over to meet up with me as we walked to the gate and out to the road on the way back towards Bellair. We didn't say much until we got to the bottom of the hill, and I started veering off to climb down the bank to Borax.

"I told you I ain't goin' down there," Richard said. "Jerry's not coming, either."

"You don't tell me what to do, Bub," Jerry said. "I'll go if I want to."

He followed me off to go down the bank.

"I'm tellin' Mom," Richard said.

"Tattletale," Jerry said.

I tuned them out and concentrated on getting down the bank. It was much colder than it had been for days. We'd all dressed warm and had gloves. I even had a pair of Big's overshoes on over my shoes. Richard was still hollering back at Jerry when I reached the ice.

"It's hard here," I said, inching my way along on the ice.

Jerry stopped about halfway down and watched me.

"Come on down," I said.

"No, I think I'll go home with Bub."

He disappeared up the bank, and I walked under the bridge. I could see water running at the other edge of the bridge, but thought I could stay out away from it and on thicker ice. It got thin quicker than I expected, and I fell through in the deepest place in that part of Borax. That was only about waist deep. But the water was so cold that I let out a yell of shock and surprise that echoed under the bridge. I grabbed an old gate wired to the fence that went across Borax when Joe Marshall or Arthur Hamilton had cows in their pastures and started walking to the bank. My teeth was already chattering like a squirrel on a hot summer morning.

Jerry was standing at the end of the bridge when I waded out and up on the bank. He started down the bank towards me when I started shaking so much I could hardly stay standing. By the time he got to me, I'd stopped shaking quite so much. With his hands on my arm and shoulder, he helped me get to the top of the bank and out on the road.

"Let's get out of here," I said.

"Leave me go get your Uncle Bob. He'll come an' get you."

"I don't want to stay out here that long. I need to get to the fire an' out of these wet clothes."

We started moving as fast as I could. I'd walked fast and try to run for a little bit, then I'd slow down as I got started shaking real bad.

"You okay?" Jerry asked at the top of the hill when I was shaking pretty hard.

"I'm so fuckin' cold I don't know what to do. I'm shakin' like a dog shittin' peach seeds. It's so cold it'd freeze the balls off a brass monkey. Let's get out of here."

"You're turnin' blue," Jerry said. "You goin' to be okay?"

"Maybe that means I'm goin' to die."

"Leave me go get Bob."

"An' let me die here alone," I said, teeth chattering and laughing at the same time. "If I'm goin' to die, Jerryeee, I want to dieeee by the fire. Take me home to dieeee, Jerryeee. Oh, take me home to dieeee, Jerryeee. Tell 'em I love 'em, if I don't make it, tell 'em I love 'em."

"You're crazy," he said. "You're not goin' to die."

"Pro-oooo-bb-lly not," I said, stuttering and almost unable to talk. I thought of Sam and what he'd told me about being out that winter in the war and how cold the soldiers on both sides must have been. I'd been not quite five that year and remember Uncle Billie Peterson parking the car down the road from Granddad and Grandma McElligott's house on Christmas Day and walking down the road dressed like Santa Claus with a bag of gifts for us kids slung over his shoulder. We waited inside, warm and happy, and watched him come down the road. Now, I wanted to be inside near the stove at Big's.

At the corner of the square, I told Jerry to go on to his house and turned toward home without waiting for him to answer. With each step, I wondered if I'd make it to the house before my legs froze solid, and I couldn't walk any longer. I looked toward the corner as I walked into the yard and saw that Jerry stood watching me. I waved and ran up on the porch.

Mother opened the door when I reached the top step.

"Why, you're all wet, John Walter," she said. "Get in here and get those wet clothes off. You'll catch your death of pneumonia."

"Oh, I'm dyin', Mother, I'm dyin'."

"Stop it," she said. "Somebody did die, though. It just came on the radio that Hank Williams died."

I stopped.

"Hank died?" I asked when I could get the words to come out. I couldn't believe that Hank Williams was dead. I'd been listening to him on WGN Radio every evening when they played his songs for quite a while now. It hadn't taken any time at all for me to get to feeling that there wasn't anybody anywhere I could feel closer to than old Hank. The songs he wrote and sung had things in them that I felt or knew I would feel sometime. And the way he sung the songs you knew that he was talking about things he knew about. The words was still there but the feeling wasn't when somebody else sung Hank's songs. They didn't have the same feeling then. "Hank died?"

"That's what the radio said."

"What happened?"

"I don't know. They just said he had died; they didn't have the details. I just heard it when I saw you walking down the road."

I felt like a ton of bricks had just been dropped on me. The few songs I could hear in the fifteen-minute part of a program on the radio every evening was something that helped me through times when I was real lonely and there wasn't nobody to talk to about some things. Mother and I didn't talk much about Daddy. But every fall about the day Daddy had got killed on, she'd get in a quiet mood and stay that way for a long time. Daddy had got killed ten years ago last October, so long ago to me that I couldn't even remember it. Mother said it seemed like just yesterday. On that last anniversary of the day Daddy got killed, I saw her sitting on the edge of her bed with the faded yellow telegram in her hands. I walked in and put my arms around her. Neither of us said anything until she finally folded the telegram and said, "I've got to help your Aunt Helen with supper."

We hadn't said anything about Daddy since then. So it usually helped me to go out to the cemetery now and then and talk about Daddy to Charlie Kline. It hadn't helped much earlier when I'd felt like I was just talking to the wind. But there was always a whole bunch of other things I wanted to talk with somebody about, too. Since there wasn't anybody else, listening to old Hank Williams was something that always made me feel better. Some of the things he was singing about wasn't the things that I was thinking about, but the feelings he put into his writing and singing was so strong and so close to what I felt that I sometimes thought he was right there in the room with me when he was singing.

He was as real to me as anything ever was. And now he was dead, gone like Daddy and Charlie.

Mother took me by the arm that day and led me to the front room stove. I was still shaking like the leaves in a tree during a windstorm. The stove felt better than anything I could imagine right then. And I got as close as I could to it without hugging it. Mother went to get a towel while I started peeling off wet clothes. The water was sloshing around in my overshoes, and I was wet up to my chest. When I'd first fallen through the ice, I had reached out for the gate and splashed around like a hog in a mud hole. After I got stripped down to my underwear, I took the towel and dried off. Mother was holding a blanket up to the stove and put it around me after I'd dried off. The heat of the blanket warmed me up so fast I could hardly believe it. Except for the wet underwear, I was beginning to feel almost hot.

I remembered thinking I wouldn't break through the ice just a second before I heard the ice start cracking and felt myself sinking into the cold water. It didn't seem like something that could happen. That's what I was feeling about Hank Williams dying. How could he die? He was young, he was rich and he was a star. Words from a song I'd been hearing on the radio kept working their way into my mind, and I kept saying them over and over on the way to the bathroom to change underwear and get dressed.

"I want to live hard, love fast, die young an' leave a beautiful memory," I said, singing the words aloud and off key in the bathroom. The words said what I thought Hank had done. That kind of life, dying young and leaving a beautiful memory, would sure beat getting old and not being able to take care of yourself like I saw Granddad J.W. get and then stay bedridden for a long time before he died. I didn't exactly think I wanted to die, but there was something kind of magical about the idea in the song. Daddy and Charlie Kline had both died for their country, I thought, and died young. They wouldn't ever get any older and was stuck in everybody's mind as young heroes who helped win the war against Hitler and Tojo. That wasn't a bad way to go, I decided. But it was hard on the ones left behind. I never had my daddy take me fishing or hunting or lots of other things I thought fathers did with sons. And I didn't care much about doing those things. I'd gone hunting on my own a couple of times. Once I'd knocked down a quail and couldn't find it after looking for nearly an hour. Even if I'd have found the quail, I didn't want to clean it. I'd helped clean rabbits and butcher hogs. The sight of all the blood and guts put me too much in the mind of Daddy getting killed. Even after Claude Pleasant told me how Daddy got killed, I still could see his guts falling out all over the ground and blood oozing out of his mouth and nose as he lay dying in the jungles of Guadalcanal. I had to force myself to look at someone gutting any kind of animal. Maybe if Daddy would have been around, I would have been different about things like that. But I wasn't sure.

I often wondered what Mother and Liz Miller, who I'd heard was Charlie Kline's girlfriend when I thought Mother might be, thought about how things turned out for them. They never had the chance to live their lives and raise their families like Aunt Helen and others who had men who either didn't go to the war or came home to somebody. Liz and Charlie wasn't married and had broken up a couple of times before he went overseas, but everybody said they'd get married when he got home. By the time what was left of his body was sent home, Liz had picked up her life and got married to an ex-GI who did make it home. Mother had me to raise and didn't seem to want to go on with her life beyond that. It was comfortable living with Aunt Helen and Big. Their doors was always open to family. And with a big house, there was always somebody coming or going. Mother never had any boyfriends that I could tell. I knew Claude Pleasant wrote letters to her ever once in a while. I didn't know if she wrote him, but I knew she liked him. Whatever, she never seemed to be able to go on with someone else like Liz had done. I thought that was because of me.

More about Hank's dying was on the radio Dad Garner was listening to when I came back into the front room. The details was "sketchy," the radio announcer said, but Hank had been on the way to a show in Ohio when they thought he might've had a heart attack. His driver tried to rouse him from sleeping in the back seat. When he couldn't, the driver took him to the hospital. He was pronounced dead on arrival. That was it. Dead on arrival. This was one time the details didn't really matter much to me. Hank Williams was dead. It wasn't a good way to start out a new year with an old friend dying. I couldn't remember feeling quite so shocked and hurt with anyone else's death.

When Mom Garner and Granddad J.W. had died, I wasn't even able to feel real sad and cry like everyone else. They'd both been sick and in bed for so long that it seemed more like a blessing when they died. I didn't want that, and I doubted that they did, either.

I'd tried to cry at Mom's funeral when I saw Mother and Aunt Helen and Aunt Millie and everyone crying. Uncle Homer's sister, Audrey Ralston, was crying and wailing and carrying on more than I'd ever heard anyone. I was surprised. I hadn't known Audrey even knew Mom. Mother later told me that Mom was a Ralston and related to Audrey's husband Hiram. No matter how she was related, I didn't think there was any reason to carry on like she was. I was listening to her and trying to cry myself, but the tears wouldn't come for me. I didn't understand how they could for her.

I'd felt the same way when Granddad J.W. died right after they shipped Daddy's remains home. When Grandma called Big and told him that night, I felt something like relief go through me. Granddad was through suffering, I thought. I was standing on the fence at the Oblong Fair the next day, listening to Ray Price sing on the stage in front of the grandstand, when Uncle Billie Peterson walked up beside me. I looked up at him and back to the stage.

"I reckon you heard your granddad passed away last night," he said. "'Bout midnight."

"I heard," I said, looking up at Uncle Billie.

"Too bad. It'll be hard on Grandma Mary."

"Yeah, I reckon," I said, not knowing what else to say.

"How many times have you heard someone say," Ray Price was singing on the stage, "if I had his money, I'd have things my way? But it's little they know that there's not one rich man in ten with a satisfied mind. ..."

That was one of my favorite songs, and I wondered then if Granddad or anybody else who never had much money could have a satisfied mind. I'd told Big about the song before and how not one rich man in ten had a satisfied mind. He'd laughed and said, "I'd like to try it as a rich man. They's a lot of fellers out here who ain't rich that don't have a satisfied mind, either."

At Granddad's funeral, nobody seemed to have a satisfied mind. Big sat over at the end of the pew by Grandma with his head in his hand while the preacher talked. He was saying something about "cryin' at birth and rejoicin' at death." I didn't understand all he was saying, but in Granddad's case, I thought I understood the rejoicing part. Grandma and Aunt Marie had taken care of him for a long time. The rest of the family helped and began sitting up with him every night. In the last weeks before he died, I heard Big say they had to feed him everything he ate and even had to turn him in bed. Grandma had to wipe his behind, Big said. I figured even Granddad J.W.'d rejoice at getting out of being in that kind of shape.

I didn't feel that way about Hank's death. I figured he must've had that satisfied mind old Ray Price had been singing about all the time. I thought Hank had about everything a feller could want. And now it was over. That evening the station played Hank's songs for a solid hour in tribute to him. I felt some better after hearing all his old songs that I didn't hear often. And I felt better knowing that I could still hear fifteen minutes of his songs each evening like I always did. Him dying wouldn't stop that. But I felt him being gone worse than anything I'd ever lost since I got old enough to know.

I fell asleep, still sad. Afterwards, there was an emptiness in me that didn't seem like would ever fill up.

The rest of the winter was pretty much the same dreary weather, cold, damp and wet. I didn't always go out to feed the cattle during the school week, but I didn't miss many days. The feed lot was a pool of mud where one hundred fifty head of cattle waded through for feed and hay at feeding time. I stumbled and fell one day while I was walking with Big. Part of the bucket of feed I was carrying went flying ahead of me, spilling half of it out in front of me. I had mud from head to foot and felt like crawling in that hole Aunt Helen talked about and pulling my hole in after me. Messing up or not doing right in front of Big always made things worse than ever.

"Son-of-a-bitch," Big said as he jerked me to my feet and helped me stand. "Watch what you're doin', Sedwick."

Watching what I was doing didn't have anything to do with it. I stepped in a hole and stumbled. Watching things didn't always mean you didn't catch one right on the chin. I was watching Ronal as close as I could the day we had a fight over his arithmetic in a forty-two game that he put him and Jerry out by cheating with the figures. Mother was standing up behind the cash register, so we couldn't say much inside. I said we should go outside where we argued about his addition. At the time, I thought I was a boxer. I was a couple of years younger than Ronal, but I was as tall and thought I could whip him if we boxed and I just stayed away from him. I danced around with my hands up like Joe Louis, watched Ronal and jabbed at him with a left when I saw an opening to land a punch on his nose. I felt the jab land, then saw stars flashing through my head and across in front of my eyes. Ronal had come in with a right hook and caught me on the jaw. That was the second time he'd knocked me down. Like the first time, the punch took me completely by surprise.

I looked up at Ronal from the ground through watery eyes. He was standing over me with his fists cocked ready to punch again. I shook my head to clear my eyes and got up. This time I watched closer and didn't get knocked down again. But I didn't whip him like I thought I could, either. We finally started wrassling. He was a lot stronger than me and finally got on top of me and wouldn't let me move. I wouldn't give, and he finally let me up. All that had changed as I'd grown older. The last time we'd wrassled, I threw Ronal and pinned him to the ground so he couldn't move. He didn't give, either, and I finally let him up.

By the first of March, Big had watched the markets long enough to figure they weren't going to change much and might even go on down. He was ready to say give. It was time to take the cattle to Indianapolis, he said, and "stop pourin' money into feed. It's like pourin' sand into a rat hole."

On the morning Big had set to sell the cattle, the sun was shining like it hadn't been for a long time. Dad Garner drove his old Hudson. Joe Marshall was going to help and rode with Big and me out to start hauling cattle. The ride was quiet. Big smoked a Lucky Strike. Joe had a chew of Beechnut in his mouth. Tobacco juice seeped out from the corner of his mouth, leaving a little stream moving down his chin. I sat between the two wanting a cigarette and wondering how I could get one after we started loading cattle.

They was standing around the feeders waiting to be fed. Big filled a basket about half full and started walking south toward the loading pens. The cattle started following him when they saw he wasn't filling the feeders. The rest of us walked behind to bring up stragglers and make sure none dropped out. Dad and me brought up one side, while Sam and Joe brought up the other. If we'd just had horses to herd the cattle with rather than doing it on foot, I'd have felt just like the old cowboy I wanted to be.

Everybody else seemed gloomy. I knew Big and Dad was losing money on the cattle, but I just thought better luck next time and told Dad as we walked along.

"There won't be a 'next time,'" he said. "Mr. Quinn from up at Oakland bought the place an' will be movin' in soon."

That was a shock. I knew Big had talked to Red Wilson about buying the place and the section of ground for pasture and cattle feeding but didn't think he could pay the sixty thousand dollar price for it and make enough to pay for it. Since Big figured that, I thought nobody else would buy it at that price, and we'd go ahead renting the pasture and feeding cattle there. I'd already been thinking about getting a horse and keeping him on the place since I still had no place to keep him in Bellair. Big could use my horse to ride around the pasture when he was looking for missing cattle instead of walking. Without the place, I knew that idea was down the drain. Maybe we could even move there, I thought.

"Why didn't you buy the place from Red Wilson, Dad?" I asked.

"Couldn't pay for it at that price," he said, walking along with a large broken tree limb that looked like a shepherd's staff from a Bible picture hanging on the wall at the UB Church. "No use workin' for nothin' an' losin' money like we are with these cattle. Money don't grow on trees."

"We could sell the house in Bellair an' move out here."

"'We' could do a lot of things, I 'xpect."

I walked away and didn't say anything for a while. Dad never liked any of my ideas. I thought this one was one of my best. The pasture and rolling hills wasn't a ranch out West, but we didn't live out West. Maybe sometime. I was only twelve years old and wanted to grow up on the closest thing to a ranch I could see around Bellair. The Red Wilson place was it. Not only could I have a horse, but we'd have all kinds of other animals on the place. We could even have a brand on the cattle like the western feeders Big had bought at the Paris sale barn. I liked the Bar None for the brand, a bar with a slash through it for the branding iron and for the name of the spread. I still wanted to join the Marines like my daddy had done, but I figured after that I'd come back, get married, have kids and raise cattle on the Bar None after Big and Dad got through with it.

The place was perfect for that and would be a good place to live and grow up. I really liked the house. It was a rambling two-story house with probably five or six bedrooms, one all to myself, a big downstairs with the kitchen leading out to a breezeway connecting the main house to a summer kitchen where Mother and Aunt Helen could can and cook in the summer. The only drawback was the big yard. I knew mowing it would fall to me. All we had was a push mower that would take all day to mow the big yard with, no matter who you was. I'd have to have a power mower like Harl O'Connell's that I used to mow his yard. Later on, I figured the hired hands could do the mowing when they wasn't taking care of cattle.

Looking out across the pasture and seeing the cattle strung out behind Big made me think how it could be when we owned the place. I could see us on horses the next time we was taking the cattle to market. It'd be so much fun. Not that it wasn't fun now. I was just thinking as the cattle was moving along without any problems. It sure looked pretty with them strung out behind Big for nearly a quarter of a mile and us bringing up the rear. It'd be a dream come true to own Red Wilson's place and run a ranch just like the ranchers did out West. I angled back over towards Dad.

"I'm goin' to own this place someday, Dad," I said. "That old Quinn ain't goin' to have this place long. He'll be done with it by the time I come home from the Marines."

"I 'xpect," Dad said, ambling along. "You better stay out of the Marines. But right now we've got to get these cattle loaded an' hauled off to market before they put us in the poorhouse."

I'd heard him and other people say poorhouse and always thought of Jim Miller's old house south of Bellair that was falling down since he died. It was a poorhouse. I reckoned that that wasn't the kind of poorhouse Dad was talking about, though.

"We ain't goin' to no poorhouse, Dad," I said. "We're not even poor. We're just in debt an' don't have much money, Big says."

"That's for sure. That's not the way I like to do business."

Big was opening the gate to the barn lot as we came over the rise. He had a wagon with a little jag of feed to help keep the cattle settled. After we'd all gotten in the barn lot, we put feed out for them and filled the stock tank so they could drink all they wanted before loading.

"Selva'll take us up to get the trucks, Sam," Big said. "You load out first. By that time, Matt an' Ralph will be here with their trucks and drivers. Jim Richards is comin' with one truck. So we should be able to get seven loads hauled to Indianapolis today. An' we'll get seven loads tomorrow. That'll leave another load that I'll get Wednesday."

Joe and I sat on the fence while they went after the trucks. Just before they got back the other truckers started rolling in and lining up to load. Sam pulled around them, circled in and backed up to the loading chute. Big pulled in behind the other trucks and stopped. He hadn't seemed to be in a good mood earlier. I didn't expect him to be when he got out of the truck.

"'Bout time you fellers 're agittin' here," he said as he walked up to Jim Richards, Matt McIntyre, Ralph Barber, and Pete and Gene Shaw, who drove for Matt and Ralph. After the two brothers had worked for Big after they came home from the war, they had gone on to drive for other fellers. With more small truckers and farmers getting trucks, Big started cutting down on the number of trucks he run awhile after the war was over. He sold a truck and then didn't put a new motor in his truck to haul lime when it threw a rod through the block. The truck had stayed parked too much of the time, he said. So he didn't need as many drivers. Gene had been with Ralph when he started taking two trucks out West to follow the wheat harvest. Pete had been with Matt almost as long.

"Good mornin', Big Mac," Pete said, squinting from the cigarette smoke that had curled into his left eye. "Where are them cattle? We ain't got all day to sit around here, bullshittin' an' lollygaggin'."

"I'll bullshit an' lollygag you, you little prick. Don't you have any drivers down there, Matt? This boy don't look like he can see over the steerin' wheel."

"He can't," Matt said. "He looks under the top of the steerin' wheel. But he does a fair job of puttin' a truck down the road."

"I met the little fucker the other day," Jim said, "down there north of Oblong on the wide gravel, an' I thought the danged truck was drivin' itself. Didn't look like there was a soul in the cab."

Pete cackled and the rest of the fellers laughed a little. I liked this bunch about as well as any fellers I knew. They treated me like one of them, I thought, and they all laughed a lot when I was ever around them. I remembered seeing a picture of Matt in a sailor's uniform down at Uncle Billie and Aunt Annie's and talking to him before about being in the Navy during the war.

"I saw a picture of you in a sailor's uniform here while back," I said to Matt when Sam was finishing his tickets on the load. "How'd you like bein' in the Navy?"

Matt laughed. He'd told me before that he didn't like it.

"Better 'n bein' a dogface or a jarhead, I reckon," he said, still laughing. "I didn't want to be in nothin'. But they was takin' warm bodies for about anything when I got called an' went to Chicago to take my physical. I remembered what old Smokey Cottrell said about them takin' ever' other one for the Marines when he was called. So I listened for that when I got to the head of the line, but they was just askin' everybody what branch of service they wanted to go in. Couple of guys right in front of me told 'em they wanted to go in the Navy. 'Army,' the old boy hollered, stamped a paper and handed it to the first guy. 'Next.' Same thing with the next guy. The old boy didn't even look up at me when I stepped in front of him. 'What about you, sonny?' he said. 'Where'd you like to go?' 'I'd like to go home,' I said. 'But since I can't, anything but the damn Navy. I can't stand the water.' 'The Navy it is,' he said, stamped my papers and handed them to me. 'Next.' I guess they didn't want anybody to be happy."

Everybody laughed. The fellers all sounded happy while they was talking and laughing and waiting to load. And it wasn't long before Big was ready for Sam to load the first bunch of cattle, and everybody started walking to the scale house and loading pen, still talking and laughing. They'd all been places and done things I wanted to do. I couldn't wait to grow up and go to all those places and do all those things they'd done.

"One of you run the scales, boys," Big said. "I want to see how they weigh here before we load 'em. I've got 151 head. Some of these cattle are awful big. I think we can get nine or ten head on each truck with no trouble. I'll take the last load Wednesday."

The scene over the next two days really made me feel like a cowboy on a cattle drive. I got out in the barnyard and helped drive the cattle in the pen outside the scales. We'd drive ten head at a time into the scale shed and closed the gate on the cattle. Matt weighed them when they stood still enough, hollered, "Yeah," and waved them on through the other gate to the loading chute. One time Big saw a smaller heifer and told us to run it in with the ten we had on the scale so he'd be sure to be able to take the last of them with the last load. Everything went smooth, and we had all seven trucks loaded by three o'clock. That'd put us in Indianapolis by around eight or nine that night and back home by an hour or so past midnight. I knew I'd sleep in the truck some, but I'd also get to sleep late the next morning.

I'd never seen seven trucks out on the road together in a convoy like we was in when we headed out with Sam in the lead and Big bringing up the rear. Dad surprised everybody by deciding to go along and rode with Big. I was in the lead with Sam and could see the other trucks in the side mirror after we'd turned a corner as they followed us. This was a real live cattle drive like they had in the Old West, I thought, only we was hauling the stock to Indianapolis in a few hours rather than driving them to Dodge City in a few weeks or months. Big and Dad was the cattle owners. Big was the trail boss. Sam was the foreman. The other fellers was top cowboys that hired on for the drive. I was the kid that stood to inherit the spread when my uncle and granddad died or turned it over to me. It sounded like a good story for a western book I could write someday. I folded Sam's coveralls and sat on them so I could look out the windshield and see just what Sam did and what he was doing. That'd be important for me to know no matter what I did. And I knew it wouldn't be long before I'd be driving one of the trucks and hauling cattle and whatever else there was to haul.

The trip to the stockyards was no different than most others I'd taken. It was just more fun that there was seven trucks of us, and it was our cattle we was hauling. Sam didn't seem like he wanted to talk much, though, so it was a pretty long ride. He said his neck was hurting, and I saw him put an aspirin in his mouth every once in a while and chew it. He said it was to kill the pain. On the way home, I slept from east of Indianapolis to The Corners where I got in the truck with Big and Dad and went on home with them.

Next day, we did the same thing, except Dad didn't go back to Indianapolis. I rode with Big that evening. He didn't have much to say, either. I tried to talk to him about us buying Red Wilson's place, living out there and feeding cattle. He smiled a little when I brought it up and seemed to listen to me. It wasn't until we was unloaded and started back home that Big said anything about what I'd said. I'd started talking again, wide awake with the excitement of the trip and my ideas.

"I 'magine we'll buy it," he said. "Your daddy an' me used to talk about gettin' us a place to feed an' farm. We had all kinds of big idees, too. Look where we got with them. He went off to the Marines an' never come back. An' I'm about to go belly up. I'll end up losin' more on them cattle that I'll ever be able to pay back an' live an' keep these dang trucks arunnin'. I 'xpect I'll lose ten thousand dollars an' Selva'll lose three or four. I should've knowed better than pourin' feed into them all winter when there was more cattle on the market than they needed. I've hauled stock over there to Indianapolis for fifteen years an' seen fellers bringin' their feeders in an' losin' their shirts an' everything they had doin' the same thing I done with this bunch. I knowed better. I could've sold them all at election time in November an' got about the same price I got now. All that feed that went into them from then until now was just more money to lose. I knowed better. Or should have. I ought to have my ass kicked up between my shoulders so I'd have to take off my hat to shit."

I didn't know what to say and didn't say nothing. That pretty well took care of the conversation the rest of the way home. The next morning, we got up and had ham and eggs at about ten o'clock. Big didn't seem to be in a hurry to get the last load and sat there drinking another cup of coffee and smoking one cigarette after another. Sam didn't have any hauling to do and came by at noon to help load the cattle. Later that afternoon, he dropped Dad and me off at home and went home himself.

We was out of the cattle business.

Big didn't make it home that night nor the next day. I could tell that Aunt Helen was worried but didn't say anything until he'd been gone the second night. The next morning she called Sam at his mother's and asked him to come to Bellair. He got there at noon, ate dinner with us and tried to talk Aunt Helen out of going out to look for Big.

"He's okay, Helen," Sam said. "An' he's goin' to be pissed off, if we're out huntin' him."

That didn't matter to Aunt Helen. We waited a bit after noon to see if Big got home before she told Sam she was going whether he did or not. He said he'd rather go and drive the truck than let her go alone. I said I wanted to go, too. Nancy and Mary Beth stayed with Dad while we got in the truck and headed east.

"Why are we takin' the truck?" I asked before we got out of Bellair. "We could go faster in the car."

"He could be over there along the road someplace," Sam said. "An' if he is, we could pull him in somewhere."

"And he may be over there someplace shacked up with some woman," Aunt Helen said. "Where else would he be and not call and let us know where he is?"

"Now Bob ain't got a woman anyplace, Helen," Sam said. "He don't hit the bottle or anything like that. He might be playin' pool or checkers. But he's okay. He's probably over at the truck stop playin' checkers with Marion. They sit there for hours studyin' each move an' not sayin' a word. Then they go off an' drink coffee an' talk about the markets or where to drill an oil well. This cattle business has been pretty hard on Big. He probably just wanted to get away for a little bit. That's how he's dealin' with everything."

"He didn't have to worry me to death over it."

I tried to imagine where Big was and what he was doing. I remembered Burns Larue and what he'd said about what Granddad McElligott did after he sold a batch of hogs.

"Maybe he took the money from the cattle an' is off playin' poker someplace," I said. "That's what the cattlemen did in the western books."

Aunt Helen gave me a dirty look. Sam laughed.

"He ain't playing poker, either," he said. "That's not the kind of gamblin' Big does."

"Maybe he took the money from the cattle an' ran off to South America," I said. "That's what Butch Cassidy an' The Sundance Kid did in the western stories when they had to leave the country."

Both of them laughed at that.

We all looked at the traffic coming from the other way to see if we could spot Big headed home. A few times before we got to Terre Haute, we saw stock trucks. But Sam said he could tell from quite a distance that they wasn't Big's red Dodge. As we started across the Wabash River into Terre Haute, we saw his truck in the other lane. The sun was in his eyes, and he didn't seem to see us, although Sam blinked his lights and honked. He drove on into the edge of the downtown area before he could turn around and start back west.

"He didn't act like he saw us," Aunt Helen said.

"He saw us," Sam said. "I'll try to catch him."

He drove as fast as he could through West Terre Haute, Toad Hop and up and down the hills on U.S. Route 40 and into Illinois without any sign of Big. Finally on the south side of Marshall, we saw the back of his truck. Sam flashed his lights when we got closer. Big pulled to the side of the road and stopped. We piled out of the truck and met Big between the two trucks.

"What 'n the devil're you fellers doin'?" he said, growling.

"Lookin' for you," Aunt Helen said. "Where in the world have you been? I've been worried sick that you're over here along the road somewhere or somewhere else you hadn't ought to be."

"Why'd you bring her over here, Sam?"

"I didn't want to, but she was goin' to come by herself."

"You fellers don't need to worry a dang thing about me. I can take care of myself without being wet nursed by any of you."

"I'm not so sure of that," Aunt Helen said. "I'll ride home with you, an' we'll see about that."

Sam and me pulled out ahead of them and went on home.

"I'm glad I'm not in that truck," Sam said.

"Me, too."

15

Sam and Maggie got engaged right after Big sold the cattle. It still seemed like the dead of winter. The weather was cold, and another snowstorm hit in the middle of March. Both trucks stayed parked most of the time. Sam took off for a week and worked on the house he had bought at the east edge of The Corners. I never saw much of him after that. Most of the time when he wasn't driving, he went there to get the house ready for him and Maggie to move into when they got married the first week in June rather than come on over to Bellair. His neck had begun to hurt him more. Driving a truck didn't help it, he said. The neck brace he'd started wearing didn't help much, either. He'd been looking for another job because of his neck and because he said he needed something that paid more and had better hours now that he was getting married.

After he finally got a job working in the coalyard at the light plant early in the summer, he didn't tell Big until almost the last day. That aggravated him pretty lively because it was during a busy hauling time. But he paid Sam straight time and was beginning to have a week or two now and then when he paid Sam more than his truck made or for doing nothing at all some days. Big's kind of trucking business was dying out, and it wouldn't have been long before he had to let Sam go or go broke, I reckon. So Big was glad Sam had found a good job in the long run. Big even said that's what he should do instead of trucking. I wasn't too happy about that. But farmers was buying their own trucks and doing most of their own hauling. Big had bought a new truck just before Sam quit and traded one of the others in on a tractor.

When I came home from school and saw that tractor setting in the yard, I threw my books on the porch and jumped up on the tractor like I was going for a ride. For a little bit, I was satisfied to just act like the tractor was running and I was driving it. I'd shift gears from the little yellow sticker on the gas tank and plow and disk and think about getting to drive the tractor. Then I had to start it up. It scared me that it fired up so quick. I pushed the choke in and the motor started purring like a sewing machine. I looked through the steering wheel and followed the sticker to shift into first gear and let out on the clutch and slipped back in the seat. The tractor jumped forward and died. And it was probably a good thing it did or I'd have run into the house.

I looked around to see if anybody had seen me. I didn't see anybody and started the tractor again and backed it back in the spot it had been in earlier. This time I made sure the clutch eased out rather than popped out. I was about to get off when I heard Russ holler.

"Better get off that damn tractor before you run it into the house," he said. "You'll kill yourself."

"Won't either," I said, jumping off the drawbar to the ground. "I'm goin' to drive this old tractor in the field."

"Which field would that be? My garden?"

"We'll be farmin' ground somewhere."

I didn't know then that Big was going to start farming Grandma Mary Elizabeth's land. Getting out on a tractor and farming was in my blood, I reckon. For a long time, I'd wanted us to have a tractor to do some farming about as bad as I wanted a horse to do some riding. The horse almost came true a few weeks later, probably about as close as it ever would, I figured. Dad Garner had gone up to stay with Aunt Millie for a while. He said it was because the house was too full in Bellair. He was right, but I still didn't get to sleep in his bedroom while he was gone.

I came home from school one afternoon and saw the pinto horse he'd bought after he moved up there, tied to the clothesline pole at the edge of the garden. I was more excited than when I saw Big's H Farmall sitting there in the front yard. The horse was saddled, standing there patiently on three legs with one back foot resting while the other three bore his weight. My heart was beating double-time as I walked up to him as though I was going to mount him and ride away.

He looked around at me, curious like. I rubbed his nose gently and caressed the worn saddle on his back. If I could have a horse like this,

I thought, I'd be happier than anything. The horse tossed his head and jumped sideways as I turned quickly and dashed to the house, completely missing the two steps on the back porch when I jumped and landed right at the door. I banged the screen door shut and ran wildly to the front room where I saw Dad sitting in the big stuffed chair in the far corner, quietly talking to Nancy and Mary Beth, one on his knee and the other on the arm of the chair. Mother, Aunt Helen and Madge sat on the couch and a nearby chair.

"Hi, Dad," I said. "Is that your horse? He's a purty one. Where'd you get him? What're you goin' t' do with him?"

"Whoa, there," he said, chuckling a little, his eyes bright with laughter. "You talk too fast. Slow down. Yes, the horse is mine. Homer bought him from Vern Samuels here while back an' then decided he couldn't keep him. I bought the horse the other day. An' just rode him down here this afternoon."

"You rode him all the way down here from Aunt Millie's?" I asked. That was at least ten miles, I was sure. And I thought Dad was much too old for that kind of a ride.

"Thought I'd bring him down here for you," he said quietly.

"For me?" I hollered, looking quickly at Mother and Aunt Helen. I knew Mother didn't like for me even to be around horses, let alone have one of my own. When Jimmy Barker and Ronal Crucell brought their horses around and let us younger boys ride them, she always told me not to ride, telling me I'd get hurt. But I always rode anyway. And I could sure take care of a horse. "Yippee!"

"I brought him for you," he said, "but your mother an' your aunt won't let you have him."

"You'll get hurt," Mother said. "You don't know a thing about taking care of a horse or even how to saddle one."

"I've known how to saddle a horse an' take care of one since I was just a kid."

"You're still just a kid," Aunt Helen said. "You're not even dry behind the ears. And you don't have any place to keep him. Where you goin' to keep a horse around here? In the coal house?"

"Rocky won't hurt me," I said, giving him the name I'd always planned on giving my first horse. "An' I'll take good care of him. Honest I will. Can I have him? Please, can I have him?"

"Now you know you don't have any place to keep a horse, John Walter," Mother said, emphasizing the Walter because that was one of Dad's names, too.

"That's right," Aunt Helen said. "I don't know what he even brought it down here for, anyway."

"For me, for me. That's what. I'm goin' to move out in the coal house. An' we could keep him over at Russ' place so I could walk right out of the coal house an' over to take care of him."

Madge snorted and said, "Keep a horse in Russ Taylor's chicken yard? I wouldn't hold my breath for that. He ain't goin' to let you keep a horse in his chicken lot, I can tell you that. An' I ain't talked to him fer thirty years 'r better."

I hoped she was wrong. I dashed out of the house and ran over to ask him. He looked at me with the stern look he sometimes put on his face when he thought I was doing something that didn't make any sense. His eyes sparked a little, but he shook his head no and went back to reading his western book.

"Madge said you wouldn't let me," I said and started out the door to find someplace else to keep the horse.

"Oh, she did, did she?" he asked, his eyes turning stern like his face was earlier. "Why don't you keep that damn horse down there on her place? Jeff Williams used to have horses down there. So did Hank Lewis. I've never kept no damn horses here."

"I'll ask her," I said and ran back home.

I did ask and she said no, too. I tried to reason with her and Mother and Aunt Helen, too, then cried a little. That worked sometimes. But I knew it wasn't going to this time and finally just shut up like everybody did about me asking Madge if she used to be a nigger. My heart felt like it was breaking in two as my grandfather patted my shoulder, said, "I'm sorry, John Walter," and swung up into the saddle. "I never thought about them not lettin' you have a horse."

Neither had I.

I watched him ride off and ran to the corner where he turned east and watched him until I could no longer see his lone figure in the fading evening light. Then I walked slowly down the road, kicking a rock and watching the dust puff up between my toes. Shoot, I thought, I won't ever get a horse.

After that, I wanted to move clear out of the house, and the coal house Aunt Helen had mentioned for the horse sounded good to me. Since Big had gone to burning coal oil to heat the house, the coal house was empty. It was a little lean-to attached to the back of the garage. It had a door leading into it from the sidewalk to the house. The room itself was about a twelve-foot square. The place had coal dust everywhere, but I figured I could get that cleaned out with a little sweeping. Then I could bring the sweeper out and finish cleaning it.

"Not with my sweeper, you're not," Aunt Helen said when I asked her about it, not telling her what I'd planned to do with the coal house. "You'd ruin a perfectly good sweeper out there in that mess."

When Big had me clean out the garage like he did in the spring, I cleaned out the coal house, too. Nancy and Mary Beth came outside to play after they'd washed the breakfast dishes that morning. I had most of the stuff moved out of the garage so I could sweep it out and move things back in so you could get around in there. I'd planned to do the same thing with the coal house. When the girls came out, I got them to sweep out the garage and start straightening up there while I cleaned out the coal house.

"I don't want to sweep that old garage out," Nancy said. "We're going over to Madge's. She's got some oatmeal cookies. She said we could have one. Then we're going over to Cheryl's."

I dropped the old rotary tiller I had in my hand and walked towards Madge's back door with them. Her oatmeal cookies was as good or better than Grandma's. It also gave me a minute to make a deal with Nancy.

"If you'll help me finish cleanin' out the garage," I said, "I'll do the dishes, wash an' dry, tonight."

"Tomorrow night, too," Nancy said at Madge's back door. "And let me see your hands. No crossed fingers."

"But two nights — "

"It's either that or nothing."

"Okay, it's a deal," I said, admiring Nancy's will. She had me over a barrel, and she knew it. "You an' Mary Beth help me finish up the garage an' the coal house, an' I'll do dishes for two nights."

"Wash and dry. Tonight and tomorrow night. Cross your heart?"

"Both, tonight an' tomorrow night. Cross my heart, hope to die, stick a needle in my eye."

That was good enough for her. We went on in on Madge's back porch and into the kitchen. She was standing at the stove stirring something like she almost always was when I was there. At first I'd thought that was real funny, her being by herself since Hank died and cooking so much. But then I saw her carrying some cookies or a pie over to some neighbor's house when they'd been sick or had something else going on. Sometimes she just slipped in our back door unannounced as she always did and left something on the kitchen table. I was real sorry for what I'd asked her, but nobody ever mentioned it.

"You fixin' something to take over to Russ?" I asked, knowing that I might not get a cookie. But I liked to pester her about things, particularly the way she and Russ didn't get along. We lived right between them, and I liked them both. Truth be known, I often imagined them to be married and living in one house or the other. Probably in Russ' since he had so many things around that you could tell the place was his. Madge's house and everything was neat and clean so you could hardly tell it was hers, if you didn't know her. I figured since they used to like each other, they could've ended up married, but I never got around to telling either of them what I'd imagined. Both of them would've cussed me out from one end to the other, if I said anything like that to them. Madge could cuss with any man I'd ever heard cussing.

"I'd put rat poison in there, if I was," Madge said. "Piss on Russ Taylor. Who invited you here, anyway?"

"Nancy said you invited us over for one of your mouth-waterin' oatmeal cookies."

"Us? You got a mouse in your pocket? I asked Nancy and Mary Beth to come over for cookies. You an' the mouse wasn't invited."

"I guess I just thought you'd include me. Ain't I just like a grandson to you, Madge?"

"Not hardly," she said, laughed and shook her head. "You're like a pain in the you-know-where."

I liked to see her when she laughed. Much of the time she didn't even smile much. But come to think of it, I didn't see many of the women around town, a lot of them widows, smile too much,

except when they got together every Thursday at the Ladies Aid and
worked together piecing quilts and talking. They laughed and talked
all day then.

"Your cookies are always so good. They'll sure hit the spot right
now. I've been cleanin' out the garage all mornin'. The girls are goin'
to help me after we get some cookies."

She brought out three small glasses and poured milk in them. Then
she set the cookies she'd just taken out of the oven on the table. I
could feel the warmth still there when she put one in front of us and
started around with another one before I'd taken a bite.

"Now that's it," she said. "Don't try grabbin' another one, or it'll
be your last time you ever grab anything. I'll chop them dick skinners
off slicker 'n a whistle."

"You'll shit, too, if you eat regular, Madge. Ain't that what you
told me?"

"I never told you no such thing," she said, the fire shooting from
her eyes like bolts of lightning. "But you try takin' another cookie an'
see what happens."

"What's 'dick skinners'?" Mary Beth asked.

"Ask Madge, she'll tell — " I said, then looked at Madge's eyes
again. "No, don't. Hands. Bye, Madge. Thanks for the cookie."

"You rascal, you," Madge said. "Get out of here."

Back outside, the girls and me went to work. By noon, we had
the garage pretty much straightened up and cleaned out and was
started on the coal house. I had seven gunny sacks of junk for Big
to haul away. Most of it came from the coal house where I carried
the tin cans and glass from the house to haul away a couple of
times a year. The rest was odds and ends of broken or worn out things
from the garage. I was pretty proud of the work we'd done and how
things looked.

"Now let's get the coal house cleaned out an' things put back in
there," I said. "You kids can come out an' visit me anytime after I get
moved out here."

"You're crazy," Nancy said. "Why'd you want to live in the
coal house?"

"I'd never live out here," Mary Beth said. "What if the snakes
crawl in an' get on you?"

I'd thought about snakes and mice. Russ even said there were probably a few rats out there, too. When I first thought of living in the coal house with rats and mice and snakes, I almost forgot the whole idea. I'd just filled the coal buckets for the evening and filled the kindling box when I sat down and told Russ what I wanted to do. He smiled a little as he shook a Chesterfield halfway out of the package, offered me a cigarette for doing his chores like he did a time or two after he'd got hurt helping a farmer get his corn in. Then he told me what he figured would happen in the coal house.

"Them snakes will come in for the rats and mice," he said, lighting his Zippo and holding it for me to light the cigarette. "An' they operate at night. They'll run you out of there."

I sucked in hard and got more smoke than usual and coughed it right back out. My throat burned and my eyes watered. Russ was sitting back in his rocking chair, holding his arm on the arm of the chair with a Chesterfield between his little finger and the index finger of his right hand. He'd lost the middle finger and ring finger when he got his hand caught in a corn picker the fall before. I saw him through watery eyes and saw that he was still smiling a little, but his eyes was laughing hard and his stomach was moving up and down like an old car on a bumpy gravel road.

"You son-of-a-bitch," I said through clenched teeth when I had stopped coughing long enough to talk. "You aimed for me to choke on that drag. I ought to kick your ass up between your shoulders so you'd have to take you hat off to shit."

"My, my, my," he said, laughing harder. "You're learnin' every old sayin' in the world, ain't you?"

"I'm tryin' to. I listen to you an' Madge all the time. I might even write a story where you an' her was married an' talked to each other usin' them sayin's."

"You can leave me out of anything that's got her in it."

"Well, I got me a list started of them old sayin's," I said. "I'm goin' to have a whole book of 'em. That's what I'm goin' to do in the coal house. An' I'm goin' to write a western book like you an' Big read, too."

"How you goin' to do that?" Ross asked, shaking his ash off, taking another drag and flipping the cigarette in the coal bucket. "You hardly been out of Bellair, let alone on a cattle drive or in a saloon fight."

"I've read enough westerns to know a little about them things. An' I've seen old Jim Richards kick the shit out of Fred Campbell over there at the Porterville Tavern years ago. Other 'n that, I'll have to depend on what I've read until I can go out West for myself. I want to work on a ranch, stay in a line shack by myself an' ride herd in a storm. But until I do, I'll just have to use my imagination an' get by with it."

"You've got quite an imagination."

"I reckon I do. An' some writers just use their imagination. You said yourself that that Crane feller who wrote *The Red Badge of Courage* hadn't even been born until after the Civil War. I ain't read all of it yet, but it's purty good. An' you said it was a good book."

"I said that?"

"Yeah, you said that. Don't you remember we was talkin' about the Civil War an' you told the story about old Doc Ferguson, who you said had been a doctor in the war, hittin' that old pregnant gypsy in the gut when she was trying' to rob him?"

"Yes, I remember that — an' I talked to Leland an' Ronald after that," he said, mentioning his boys who'd been in the war. "They hadn't read the book. But I told them how the boy wanted to see how he'd react in war an' run the first time he was in battle, showin' his fear an' how afraid he'd been. Then goin' back an' stayin' to fight. They said it was the other way around for them. They didn't find out how horrible things really was 'til they was there. That's when they wanted to run. So Crane may have told a good story, but maybe that ain't exactly how it is when somebody's really shootin' at you. Anybody ever shoot at you? Tried to kill you?"

"Not yet. I probably won't find out until the next war. Dad says Ike's goin' to finish this one before I get old enough to go so I can write a book about a war an' show what it's like. I've never fought in a war an' don't know what it's really like. But I'll find out. An' I ain't never slept in the coal house with snakes an' rats an' mice yet, either. But I will. After it's cleaned out, I'm goin' to put some shelves around the walls, kinda high up, for books. I'm goin' to make a little desk out of an old piece of plywood or an old door, sleep on the daybed an' take one of the chairs of Dad's that Aunt Helen was goin' to have you recover. I'll just have to deal with the snakes an' rats an' mice when I get there. How'll that be?"

"Oh, that'll be just peachy," he said, laughing and shaking his head. "I can hardly wait 'til you move out there. I'll probably hear you screamin' all the way over here some night when you wake up with a goddamn snake in bed with you, an' you haul ass through the door without even openin' it. An' if you ever have to go to war, you'll probably find out you won't like that any better than you'll like livin' in the coal house."

"Maybe," I said, but Russ had pretty well made me decide I'd try to live out there. I'd been thinking a lot about what to do. I wasn't about to give him the chance to kid me about being afraid of anything.

And I told Nancy and Mary Beth how I'd deal with the snakes and rats and mice while we finished cleaning the place. "First off, I'd set traps an' put out rat poison. The rats an' mice would either get caught in the traps or eat the poison. Then the snakes would eat the ones that eat the poison. That would poison the snakes, too. I'll plug up all the holes, an' that'll be the end of rats an' mice an' snakes."

"Eewww!" Nancy said. "All the dead things in here would stink to high heaven. I hate the smell of dead snakes worse 'n I hate gravy. You remember that one Fannie Boone left over in her barn to keep you and Richard and Jerry out of there?"

"She didn't do no such thing," I said. "It just crawled up in there an' died. That's all."

"Well, I hate the smell of them more 'n anything, anyway."

"Eewww!" Mary Beth said. "I do, too. I don't want to be in the coal house anymore. I'm not coming to visit you here, Bubby."

"Don't come an' visit me, then. An' don't call me Bubby."

Nobody came to visit me because I never moved out there. Aunt Helen was the main thing in the way of the move. She said I was crazy to want to live in an old lean-to on the back of the garage.

"Why, the garage's not fit to live in," she said, "let alone that filthy coal house. Who's going to wash your clothes? You'd have coal dust on you, your clothes and everything else. I know you wouldn't expect me or your mother to wash 'em."

Mother agreed with Aunt Helen but wasn't as plain about it. After the girls helped me clean out the place, I sat some orange crates and an old chair I'd found down at the junk pile south of town and tried to make the coal house livable. But it wasn't long before things started piling up in there again. Big always stacked the tin cans and glass jars in there before he hauled them off to the junk pile. Dad had moved back in the spring and took over the garden. He put hoses, tillers, plows and everything else in there. He'd even brought his big black kettle for butchering down from his place to store in the coal house.

With Dad back in the house and the coal house filling up, I didn't see anyplace else to sleep except on the daybed in the dining room. The only way I'd ever get the back bedroom was when Dad died. He was old, more than eighty, but I didn't want him to die just so I could have a room to myself. Even if he didn't get to give me his horse, it was good to have him around. As old as he was, he could still work all day. That helped me and Big both. Already since Dad'd been back to help us get started farming, he had shown me he could work me into the ground. The first time Dad and me worked together, I was driving the new H Big had taught me to drive by putting me in Joe Marshall's little patch south of town with a seven-foot disk and telling me to "cut it once" and leaving me to figure out how to do it. By the time I'd finished disking the patch and turned the front wheels too far a couple of times and they scooted straight ahead instead of making the turn until I learned to use the brakes and steering wheel together, I was driving good enough to do the disking and started doing it pretty regular whenever I was needed. That got me out of the house.

Dad was driving an old Farmall M that day, pulling an eleven-foot disk back and forth across forty acres twice, first catty-cornered to get it to dry and then straight up and down. After I'd finished the old pastures south of Grandma's house, I waited in the truck for him to finish and was fast asleep when he crawled in the truck to take us home after dark. I was bone tired and knew he had to be, too. But he didn't say a word. He just jumped the truck along, never shifting gears until the engine was about to die. I figured he thought he was still driving a team of horses that he only had to pull back on the reins and say, "Whoa," or loosen them and say, "Giddup." But the way he drove didn't bother me much as I drifted between sleep and not quite asleep. I went straight to bed when we got home. He washed up first. I was asleep the minute I shut my eyes and never heard him go to bed.

He was sitting at the breakfast table the next morning, looking bright-eyed and bushy-tailed. I didn't much care how I looked. I just wanted to sleep.

With school out, I was working more and more in the field or helping with the trucking rather than just riding. I still had a couple of yards to mow, but I was working with someone most every day. Sam came by on his last day driving for Big and picked me up early in the morning to help him haul hay for Tops Calvert before I could find another job. It was right before the Fourth of July when we always went to Casey for the celebration. Before the fireworks started at dark, a carnival with rides and corn dogs and gypsies and all kinds of things brought people out early. I needed some money to have a good time on the Fourth. Working for Big wouldn't make me any money, except what he'd give me when we got to Casey. And that wasn't much.

I could have a good time without much money, but it was always a little bit better if I could have a corn dog or two, some lemonade and a bag of saltwater taffy that I could see being made before my eyes. A ride or two was always good, too. But just seeing the people and what they was doing was as good as it would have been going to the show for a double feature and sitting with Beth McMahon, a real pretty girl I liked who'd just moved to Bellair from someplace in Indiana. One year at the Fourth of July celebration, I'd been walking behind my cousin Bernie Bartlow, who was in the Air Force and on his way to Korea, a bunch of my other older cousins and a couple of their friends. This gypsy lady bumped into my cousin Bobbie Gene, one of Vernon's boys who'd just come back from Korea and was home on leave from the Army, as he passed a tent where you could get your fortune told. He stepped away from her and hit her with a backhand slap that knocked her to the ground. I stopped in my tracks, shocked that Bobbie Gene had knocked a woman down. Then he stepped over to her, reached down and took a billfold from under a fold in her dress garb.

"I ought to slap you sillier 'n you already are, bitch," he said and looked in the billfold. "They better run your sorry ass out of town before you get hurt."

A Casey police officer worked his way through the crowd of people looking on and took the gypsy by the arm to help her up.

She stood up and came face to face with Bobbie Gene before shrinking back, bringing her hands to her mouth and moaning.

"What's goin' on here?" the officer asked.

"This phony gypsy tried to pick my pocket," Bobbie Gene said. "I felt her hands on me after we'd bumped into each other. I backhanded her an' got my billfold back."

The officer looked at Bobbie Gene's ID he'd taken out of the billfold and asked, "You in the service?"

"Sure am. An' this billfold she lifted sure is mine, too."

The officer turned to the gypsy.

"Officer, officer, that is not true. In the crowd of people that is here, I stumble and fall into this man. His wallet, it falls from his pocket to the ground. I try to pick it up to give it back to him, and he hits me very hard and knocks me to the ground for trying to get his billfold to him."

"That's bullshit," Bobbie Gene said. "The billfold didn't fall out. You took it out with your grubby little hands. An' if you ever try it again, I'll hit you so hard it'll knock you into next week."

"Take it easy, soldier," the officer said. "I'll take care of this gypsy."

He took her back to the tent and told her and the rest of the gypsies to pack up and get out of town or he'd arrest the woman for pickpocketing. They started packing while the officer stood watching. I edged over by Bernie to watch with the others. He grinned down at me and tousled my hair. Seeing what had happened was more exciting than anything I'd ever got to see up close. And it didn't cost me a penny.

So I could still have some fun whether I made any money to spend before the next day's celebration. I knew I could depend on Mother for a dollar or two, but I hated to ask her for money. Sam said he'd need Dad and Joe Marshall to help get all of Tops' hay in before the Fourth. He didn't want to have to work any then, or any time after his last day, and wanted to have the hay all out of the field and in the barn by evening. I knew I'd get a couple of dollars for helping.

It was about ten o'clock when we got to Tops' field. It was just getting dry enough to start baling, and Tops was climbing up on the tractor to start. He was a barrel-chested feller wearing Levis and a cowboy shirt, boots and a Stetson. Sam had told me Tops'd lost one of his legs as a Marine infantryman on Tarawa during the war that one time when we'd stopped to load a couple of steers to take to Indianapolis. Tops and his hired hand had been roofing the barn.

"How's he get up there an' get around if he's only got one leg?" I'd asked as I'd watched Tops shimmy up and down the roof just like the hired hand. I couldn't tell he had only one leg. "He don't look like he's got only one leg."

"He'll hold his own just about anywhere. He says he's well off compared to a lot of other men. He's right about that."

I watched Tops climb up on the tractor as we drove into the hay field. Now that I knew he'd lost his right leg, I could tell he favored it and always tried to keep his weight on his left foot. He'd put his weight on his right to get up on the tractor high enough so he could swing his right leg up over the seat like he did when he was mounting a horse. I was amazed at the man and always looked hard at his right leg. It was stuffed down in his boot just like the other one. I imagined a piece of wood tied to a string on his leg and stuck down in the boot. I wanted to see the wooden leg. Sam laughed when I told him what I imagined.

"I don't think it's quite like that," he said. "It's a piece of cork or somethin' that the stump sets in an' fastens on. Tops an' me stopped in a tavern over at Toad Hop, just west of Terre Haute, a few years ago. Pretty rough place. A bunch of hoods kept lookin' our way an' sayin' things about us loud enough that we could hear. When our sandwiches come, Tops takes out a big old pocket knife, opens up a long blade an' cut the first sandwich in two. Then he wiped the blade on his thigh an' jams the knife into his calf. After he took a bite of the sandwich, he reached down an' took the knife again an' cut the other one in two pieces. This time, he just wiped the blade off an' stuck the knife back in his pocket. It got real quiet over in the corner. We ate an' got out of there before them fellers figured out how he was able to do that. They was dumber 'n a box of rocks but would've finally figured out that Tops had a wooden leg. We'd probably had to fight our way out of there then."

In the field, Sam jumped up in the back of the truck so he could load the hay the way he wanted it. Dad and Joe would walk along behind, picking up bales while I drove the truck. I didn't want to, but Joe didn't drive anything but a tractor and Dad had never driven a truck much and wasn't a good driver. So it was left up to me. I'd got so

I could drive without popping the clutch out and jumping along. I stopped every so often and got out and carried a bale or two before jumping back into the truck and moving up again. We only got one load picked up from the field and put away in the haymow in Tops' barn before it was time to get dinner.

Most of the time I ever helped anybody haul hay, everybody ate dinner wherever we was working. Probably we would have eaten at Tops' house, too, but Sam wanted us to eat at his house a couple of miles away. When he had sent the last bale up the hiker and shut it off, he hollered up at us, "Get 'er stowed away, boys, an' let's go. Maggie'll have dinner waitin'."

I bellied under the haymow door on the hiker, then stood up and walked down to the ground on the hiker chains. A little breeze blew in my face as I walked down the hiker that was at a forty-five degree angle to the ground, cooling my sweating body. Dad and Joe climbed down the haymow ladder and came out the barn door as I jumped to the ground.

"That ladder in there is for gettin' out of the haymow," Dad said. "What if you fell out of the hiker?"

"But I didn't," I said. "I was hot up there doin' all the work for you old fellers. I must've packed two bales to your fellers' one, don't you think, Joe?"

Joe smiled and shook his head. "I ain't in this," he said.

"The air cooled me off, Dad. I'll ride in the back so I can get real cooled off before dinner. I'm starved."

"You better have an appetite," Sam said, grinning from ear to ear. "You're fixin' to get some real eatin'."

"I'm ready," I said and jumped in the back of the truck.

"Here, Sedwick," Joe said, coming around to the back of the truck, "give me a hand. I'll ride back here with you an' give Selva room up front."

Joe climbed up in the hiker and held his hand out to me. When I grabbed his hand, he put his foot up on the back of the bed. I pulled him up and in. Sam pulled away before we got situated and had a good hold on the stock rack.

"He sure is in a hurry," Joe said when we got our feet planted in the bed.

"He wants to see Maggie," I said. The wind felt good in my face as I turned to watch the woods and fields flash by. I was cooled off and ready to eat by the time we turned east and headed into The Corners. Joe looked cooler, too. He had taken his cap off. At first, beads of sweat had stood out on his milk-white bald head and dripped down on his forehead. He wore a long-sleeve khaki shirt and a pair of overalls. The shirt was soaked down to his wrists. Dad and Sam didn't have overalls on, but they both had their sleeves rolled down. I wanted to get a tan on my arms and only wore a tee shirt. I'd taken it off at first, but I was getting scratched on the belly by the hay and put the tee shirt back on.

Sam wheeled the old Dodge in his driveway and stopped right behind his Dodge coupe. I jumped to the ground before he'd hardly stopped. Joe shook his head at me when I looked back at him. He sat down on the bed and pushed out and down to the ground. Sam had started peeling off his shirt before we got to the pump. He had an ugly pink hole just above his right shoulder blade and some other smaller scars on his back. My eyes locked on the ugly scar on his shoulder. I knew he'd been wounded in the war, but I'd never seen any of the scars. Dad and Joe didn't seem to notice and just rolled their sleeves up to wash. I peeled my tee shirt off and stood in line at the wash pan sitting on a wash table near the pump. Sam held the bucketful of water he'd pumped while we washed. When one of us finished, we'd throw the water out towards his barn and he'd fill the wash pan again.

I'd never been inside the house before. On the outside it looked pretty much like Grandma's old two-story farmhouse and the one Sam grew up in across the field a mile from there. Inside, it looked kind of like Grandma's, too. But all the furniture and things was much newer. And Sam had a new refrigerator and stove. Grandma still cooked on her wood-burning cook stove in the kitchen. She finally got a refrigerator after her kids talked her into getting the house wired for electricity a year or so before. The next spring they dug a line from the well to the house so she could have running water in the house. But there was no hot water and no bathroom. "No place for one," she'd said. "Don't need it, anyway."

Maggie had the table set for five people and steaming hot dishes of food already on the table when we walked in the dining room. Her face was flushed, the smile she gave us as we walked in stayed on her face all during dinner.

"Have a seat," she said. "Mr. Garner, you can set there. And Joe, you and John Walter can sit over on that side."

"Sit down an' dig in," Sam said. "The tea's not sweetened, but there's a sugar bowl, if you need some. See what you think about Maggie's cookin'. This is the first time she's cooked for any hay hands, an' I told her to make plenty."

And there was. I'd never seen Sam so happy. He laughed and talked about Maggie, the food and everything. He kept a smile on his face, too. He kept a steady stream of talk going as he passed me the mashed potatoes, then a huge dish of chicken and noodles. I saw the strings of white meat in the noodles.

"That's the way Big likes chicken in the chicken an' noodles," I said, piling a big scoop on top of the mashed potatoes before passing it to Joe. Then there was corn and green beans and sliced tomatoes. I was running out of room on my plate.

"He can have some anytime," Maggie said, smiling.

"Here now, Sedwick," Sam said. "I raised them 'maters. You can eat more than one little slice."

I took two more and salted and peppered everything pretty lively before I dug in, using my fork backhanded almost like a shovel. Maggie was a good cook, I thought, as I shoveled in a bite.

"I can go get a scoop shovel out in the truck," Dad said. "That fork's to take bites with."

"Let him eat," Maggie said. "I like to know that you like my cookin'. Looks like he does."

"Looks like a pig the way he's shovelin' it in," Dad said. "He didn't learn that from me."

Me and Sam filled our plates about as full again but ate a little slower the second time around. Dad and Joe pushed their plates back and nodded at Maggie when she asked them if they'd like a piece of cherry pie. Because Sam had started eating some sweets, I'd been eating some and a little pie now and then. But I didn't really like cherry pie all that much. She had a big scoop of vanilla ice cream right on top, though, melting and running down the side and puddling all around the bottom of the crust. I knew I'd have to eat the pie to get the ice cream and started going after the seconds a little faster.

"You won't be worth a dime this afternoon," Dad said when I finished my second helping and dug into the pie.

"All I got to do is drive the truck," I said, "part of the time, anyway. This pie is great, Maggie. An' the ice cream tastes homemade."

"Thank you, John Walter. The ice cream is homemade. Sam made it last night after he got home."

He smiled and backhanded a big bite. Being married was a good thing for him, I decided. He'd always been good to me, friendly and helpful. But he always had a distant side to him and didn't smile and laugh quite like he had been since he got married. When we got up from the table, Sam waited for us all to go. He was bending to kiss her when I looked back, and he grabbed her behind with one hand. She opened her eyes and looked right into mine.

"Sam," she said, shrieking and turning beet red.

I followed Dad and Joe out on the porch. The thermometer on the wall of the house and in the shade said it was ninety-eight degrees. That meant it was going to be up more than a hundred out there in the hay field and 115 or 120 in the haymow. I was beginning to really see what Big had told me over at Garvey Charles' a year or two before about finding something else to do besides trucking. He'd just wrassled a couple of veal calves into the truck on a real hot summer day. His shirt and the top of his trousers was wet like he'd been swimming upside down. Sweat was running down his face and to the end of his nose and dripping off on the bill of lading he was writing on the calves. Delia, Garvey's wife, handed Big a cold Pepsi cola that looked awful good to me. He turned the bottle up and swigged it down faster than I'd ever seen anybody drink a Pepsi. A little foam was all that was left when he handed the bottle back to her and grunted, "Much obliged."

The heat had made me sleepy. And the sleepier I got, the more I thought about what Big had said about finding something else to do to make a living. Even sitting on the floor of the truck bed, jostling around as Sam headed back to Tops' hay field, I was sleepy and didn't want to go back to work. Sam drove pretty slow, and I did nod off a couple of times. When he slowed and pulled into the field, I was ready to nod off and sleep the rest of the afternoon. Instead, I went back to driving up, getting out to load a bale or two and driving up again. Sam drove into the barn and let me ride on the running board on his side. Joe rode on the running board on the other side. The wind in my face dried the sweat and cooled me off before we had to climb up in the haymow where it was like an oven.

I went through the motions in the heat, wanting to be somewhere else but knowing that it was Sam's last day and hating to see it end. When it finally did, we drove off towards Bellair and home. Sam waved at Tops, who was on a dapple quarter horse riding back toward a herd of cattle in the next field. He waved back and galloped along with us on the other side of the fence for a few yards. Him on that horse was sure a pretty picture.

It was too noisy to talk in the back of the truck. You had to holler real loud to be heard. So Joe and me just held on and stared out through the slats of the stock rack. Sam pulled in the driveway and stopped long enough for Joe and me to hop down. Dad was walking to the house when I walked around to the front of the truck. Joe waved at Sam and walked off toward his house down by the schoolhouse.

"Ain't you comin' in, Sam?" I asked from the front yard.

"Nah, I got to get home. Maggie'll have supper ready. Big's not here, an' I can settle up with him later."

"Here?"

"Here or over at 'Napolis. One place or the other."

"I ain't goin' to hardly see you now."

"Sure you are. It ain't like I'm movin' to Chicago. I live five miles from here."

"You'll come back an' visit."

"Sure, an' you'll come over an' visit," Sam said, grinning great big like he did sometimes. "Anytime you want. Tell Big I'll leave the truck there in my driveway until I can bring it back. An' take care, Sedwick."

"I will," I said. "You, too."

"Don't take any wooden nickels, either," he said and eased the truck out on the road and headed for his house at The Corners.

I watched until the truck was around the corner and out of sight, then listened to Sam shift from third to fourth to fifth and finally hesitate a minute while he pulled up the stick and was in high gear and axle speed.

16

Not having Sam stopping by the house for gas or to pick me up to help him somehow, even if it was just cleaning out the bed and putting in decking, seemed strange. He'd been stopping by for a long time and was just like one of the family. He'd never stayed with us overnight unless he had to because we didn't have enough beds. But he'd just as likely be there for breakfast or any other meal as Big when both of them was running trucks and burning the candle at both ends, as Aunt Helen said about them. With both Big and Sam there, the table talk got pretty loud sometimes. Dad and Mother would be the only ones not talking. I'd sit next to Sam and talk his ear off, if he'd listen.

Big would sit across from us with Aunt Helen and Nancy on one corner and Mary Beth on the other. He'd usually tell Sam a dozen things that had to be done that had been forgotten at other times. When one'd come to mind, Big would just start talking to Sam no matter who else was talking. It was like nobody else was around. Since Big'd lost the money on the cattle, he seemed to be far away in his mind most of the time.

Mother would sit at the end of the table on my right. She'd seem lost in her thoughts quite a bit, too. I always figured she was thinking about Daddy getting killed. It didn't seem like she was able to get past that and go on with her life, even though he'd been gone a long time. It seemed so long ago that he'd gotten killed to me because I didn't even remember it. But Mother said it seemed just like yesterday to her, that that part of her life stopped forever that day and she couldn't get it out of her mind. So I reckoned she must have been thinking about Daddy and what it was like for us to be left behind to get along the best we could. Nothing else seemed like it could bother her so much and keep her mind occupied like that.

Whatever she was thinking, she never talked about it much. I knew she was worried about me some. She never talked about that, either. I had a few years left before I finished my schooling, but I think she thought ahead to when I was out of high school. I'd told her I was going to the Marines like Daddy had just as soon as I graduated. She didn't say anything; she just had a painful look on her face and in her eyes. I reckoned it was because she missed Daddy and worried about me.

"You do and you'll come back like he did, too," Aunt Helen said. "You stay here and get a job. Let somebody else go."

After that I never said anything, but I still aimed to join up as soon as I could. Kenny Palmer had joined right at the end of the war in Korea. He kidded me about going with him at the time. He was seventeen and his mother signed for him. I wasn't near seventeen and knew my mother wouldn't sign for me, even if I was. Kenny said I was big enough that I could get by with it with the right papers. That made me feel good, but I wasn't ready to go then. Mother probably couldn't have stood it. Not only not wanting me to join up, she had a hard time thinking about her life after I was gone. She still wrote to Claude Pleasant some, I thought, and he wrote back. I got to thinking they'd get together sometime, and she'd marry him and move away after I was gone. Or maybe before. I didn't know what to think. That meant moving away, and I didn't think I wanted to leave Big's like that. But Claude lived a long way off and hardly ever come anywhere near Bellair. After a while, I didn't see any more letters. And she didn't seem to be interested in other fellers. Sometimes some feller'd try to talk to her, kid her about something like the gray in her hair at the temples that she kept out in the open by pulling her hair back over her ears, and she'd just smile and not say anything.

I'd noticed, too, that Mother and Sam always seemed uncomfortable around each other from the time he'd come home. I didn't know what to make of that and thought it was strange since they was related. They avoided looking directly at each other at the table and only spoke to each other if they had to, I'd noticed. And Sam never went to the store like everybody else. I asked him about that one day awhile after he quit driving for Big.

"Don't have any business there, I guess," Sam said.

"But you don't even go there for a bottle of pop. Why not?"

He didn't say anything for a long minute and just stared out at the road while we rode along. Finally he said, "I never did go there much before the war when Uncle Billie an' Aunt Annie ran it. An' your mother's there now."

"What's that have to do with anything?" I asked. "Don't you like her?"

"I like her fine. She's one of the nicest ladies I've ever known."

"So what's the problem then?"

"I came back from the war, an' your — "

"Daddy didn't. That don't have nothin' to do with you."

"Why him an' not me, though?" he asked. "It'd be so much better if it'd been me. You'd have had a daddy, Lorene would have had a husband an' maybe you'd even have a brother or sister like you want."

"But that ain't the way it is, Sam," I said, talking louder than I usually did with him. "You told me all that stuff. That them that make it was just lucky. You was; he wasn't. I wish he was here, too, but he ain't. An' that's nobody's fault. Mother doesn't think that way, Sam."

"I'll bet she has. An' I'm not blamin' her for it. Why wouldn't she?"

"She'd never wish you was dead, Sam."

"I know she wouldn't, but she can't help but to wonder what if or why not. We don't feel comfortable around each other. But now don't you say nothin' to her about what I told you. She's one of the ones who's had to suffer the loss for all these years an' will have to for the rest of her life. Your daddy, the war an' all that went with it'll probably be the last thought on her mind before she dies. I know it will be on mine. Maybe your daddy was one of the lucky ones. His sufferin' is over."

"I never looked at it that way," I said.

"I did," he said. "An' have. All the goddamn time."

Later in the summer, we heard Jim Taggert was bringing his family back to visit his mother, Clara, who lived south of the store. His father, Jim, had died right after the war. The younger Jim had only stopped through Bellair for a few days after he got out of the Army Air Corps. Sometimes his name came up in talk around the store, but I didn't remember seeing him, except in his picture in uniform around an airplane upstairs with all the other boys from around Bellair who was in the service. Like a lot of the others, he looked like a movie star to me, standing with his hand on the wing of an airplane dressed in a leather flight jacket with a white scarf around his neck and tucked in at the front. His hat was cocked to the left, and he had a crooked grin on his face.

Bart Finley, who had lived east of town before the war, stopped by one day when I was sitting on the porch. He'd heard Jim was coming by and wanted to know if he had made it yet. I didn't know. Neither did Richard and Jerry. And there wasn't nobody else there.

"You boys want a bottle of pop?" Bart asked. "I'm buyin'."

He didn't have to ask again. We followed him inside to the pop case. I lifted the lid on the end of the bright red case with Coca-Cola written across it in big white letters and looked down at the RC Colas and flavors. That part also had a small section of little Cokes. Horsey had arranged the different pop in the case in a way I always knew exactly where the bottle of pop I wanted would be. He still started with the little Cokes, then went to flavors, which was a slimmer bottle than the big Pepsis or RCs, and on to a few RCs before getting to nearly half of the case filled with Pepsis, all sitting neck deep in ice cold water. It'd been like that at least since Charlie Kline had bought me a bottle of grape just before he went overseas during the war.

"I believe I'll have a Pepsi," Bart said and lifted the other lid. And then walking back to the middle of the store he said to Mother, "Hello, Lorene. I'm buyin' these boys a bottle of pop. Would you like one, too?"

"No, thank you."

While they was talking, we all took RCs. I had a nickel in my pocket so I grabbed a package of Planter's Peanuts and took the nickel to Mother. On the way out, I took a couple of big swigs from the pop. Outside, I cupped my hand around the neck of the bottle and dumped the peanuts down through the funnel my hand made. Bart came out a few minutes later and reached for my bottle after I'd taken another swig and four or five peanuts with it.

"What'd you do?" he asked. "Dump them peanuts in there?"

"Yep," I said. "Makes everything taste better, mixin' the salty peanuts an' the RC. Takes away a little of that mediciney taste of the pop."

"Whatever floats your boat," he said.

"Was you a sailor?" I asked.

"Not quite. I was on a little island out in the Pacific that made me feel a bit like I was in the Navy, though."

"What was you in?" Richard asked. "My Uncle Ed was in the Navy."

"Yeah, I know. I was in the Air Corps."

"What was the island you was on?" I asked.

"New Guinea."

"What did you do?" Jerry asked.

"Everybody I could, an' the easy ones twice," Bart said and laughed. "I was on ground crew that kept the planes flyin'."

I laughed, too, and remembered after Bart had stopped by the store one time before, Johnnie Larson and some of the older men had been talking about when Bart came home from the war. "He'd run around all night," Johnnie said, pausing for a swig of his Pepsi, then going on, "an' sleep all day. Edward told me he'd hang a sign outside his door when he came in that said, 'Do not disturb.'"

I'd hear one story after another about the boys around Bellair who went off to the war when the fathers and neighbors got started talking. Johnnie didn't say much because his boy, Morris, had stayed in the Army. Edward was Bart's daddy. Him and Lela came to town all the time, but they wouldn't say much about Bart. I asked Edward about the sign one day, and he just shifted the cigar holder in his mouth and smiled.

"We didn't bother him," he finally said. "He'd been gone a long time an' saw quite a bit, I 'xpect, that played on his mind. He finally got it out of his system. Then he went to work, got married an' started a family."

Bart had a glint in his eyes and a smile on his face as we talked on the store porch. It was sort of a devil-may-care look that seemed to say he was having fun.

"Did you put a 'Do not disturb' sign on your door at your folks' house when you came home?" I asked.

"You betcha," he said, smiling even bigger and laughing. "I'd been gone for almost four years an' wasn't sure I'd ever be back. I had some catchin' up to do. Edward an' Lela didn't know what to think. But they was good about it."

"Was you on New Guinea when the war was over?"

"Yeah, that's where I was. An' it was one of the most dangerous times of the war. When the word came down that the Japs had surrendered an' the war was over, everybody started firin' off rounds of whatever they happened to have — .45s, rifles, machine guns, 105s — you name it, an' somebody was crankin' off a round somewhere.

The ships anchored out in the harbor started crankin' off rounds everywhere. The sky was lit up like a Christmas tree. It looked like the Fourth of July fireworks for half the night. I don't know how many guys was killed an' wounded that night, but I'd bet there was a bunch."

Bart talked and we listened until he finished his Pepsi.

"Nice talkin' to you boys," he said.

"You, too," we said together.

"Tell Jim Taggert that Bart Finley'd like to see him when he comes home. Tell him I'm workin' midnights."

"Was he in the Air Corps, too, Bart?" I asked.

"Was he ever!"

"What do you mean?" I asked.

"He flew 'The Hump,' that's what I mean."

"What kind a airplane is that?" Richard asked.

"It's not an airplane," Bart said, laughing again with his eyes dancing wildly. "That's what they called a route over the Himalayan Mountains that got our planes goin' an' comin'. They was carryin' ammunition an' supplies to the Chinese who was fightin' on our side against the Japs an' to our boys who was stationed in China. Flyin' over the Himalayas was the only way to get the supplies to where they needed them across the mountains. The planes used a lot of their fuel to get over The Hump with a full load. Then if they did make it over an' delivered their cargo, they had to hightail it back to base or they'd run out of fuel an' crash in the mountains. Which a lot of them did."

Richard asked what kind of a plane Jim flew over The Hump.

"A C-46 transport," Bart said. "That's what they used a lot. They could carry a helluva load an' had the power to pull it over the highest mountains in the world an' deliver it on the other side. Took some great planes an' terrific pilots an' crews to get the job done. An' old Jimmy flew The Hump a ton."

I looked at Jim a little closer when he did come to town. Him and his three kids, two boys and a girl, got to Bellair a couple of days after Bart was there. Jim still looked like a movie star, I thought. He was taller than average and had dark wavy hair and a handsome face that was beginning to show crow's-feet at the corners of his sad-looking eyes. He smiled when I told him Bart Finley wanted to see him while he was home and other lines in his face appeared.

"I'll try to see old Bart Finley," he said. "He's a good old boy. I always liked him."

"I reckon he likes you, too. He said he'd sure like to see you but said to tell you that he's 'workin' midnights.'"

"Okay," Jim said and smiled a little. He introduced me to the kids. The oldest, Jimmy was a year younger than me, Johnny was a year younger than Nancy and the youngest, Kathy, was Mary Beth's age.

The kids and me went off to play around the store. Jim talked to Mother and other people who were there to do their trading. I could tell right off that the Taggart kids was city kids. They laughed and made fun of the way I talked and about everything else they saw.

"You'ns come see us, now hear," Jimmy said when his dad waved at them to come from the store porch. "I reckon we'll be aseein' you'ns around somewheres."

"I reckon you will, iffen I don't see you first," I said, laughing at him trying to sound like a hick.

"Ha, ha," he said. "You're funny. Bye."

He herded his brother and sister before him like me and Big and Sam or anybody herded hogs or cattle. Jim waved at me from the porch. Both boys looked like him, but they sure didn't act like him, I thought. But while they was in Bellair for the next few days, I played with them about every day. Richard and Jerry played with them once and stayed away from us the rest of the time. When I'd ask them to come out and play with us, they always said no. Richard told me later that he'd played "with enough brats" when they lived in LaPorte and "didn't need to play with more." They didn't live in Indiana, I told Richard. They lived in Illinois. He said that didn't matter, that "they was city slickers from up North."

I never quite felt that way. But I didn't always like the way they acted like they graced us with their presence or the way they made fun of everything I thought was pretty normal around Bellair. Next day after they showed up, I walked around Bellair with the boys — Kathy stayed at our house to play around town with Nancy and Mary Beth — and we got to know each other. On the way out to the cemetery to see their granddad's grave, Jimmy kept calling me Jackie. I asked him a couple of times not to do that, that my name was John or John Walter.

I didn't even tell him my nickname was Sedwick. I didn't feel right with him calling me the name I really liked.

"Why do you hillbillies always go by two names?" Jimmy asked, laughing at his own smartness, I thought. "Isn't one good enough?"

"I reckon it's just our way of doin' things."

"I reckon," he said, mocking me.

I felt my face getting hot and my heartbeat starting to race. I hated this feeling when you knew what was going to happen and there wasn't a thing you could do about it. Once that feeling got there, though, everything was better.

"I wish you wouldn't mock me," I said quiet as I could, trying to keep the shakiness out of my voice. "An' I wish you wouldn't call me Jackie. Name's John Walter."

"'Name's John Walter,'" Jimmy said, mocking me again and standing stiffly, saluting. "Come on, Johnny, stand and salute John Walter of Bellair upon North Fork."

I took a deep breath, knowing I didn't have any other choice, and ran straight at Jimmy, ramming my shoulder into his gut with his hand still up saluting. He grunted and fell backward.

"You're an asshole, Jimmy Taggert," I said, jumping on his arms with my knees and holding his hands still with my hands. "I ought t' kick your ass halfway to Georgia. But I like your daddy. You quit actin' like an asshole an' give an' I'll let you up."

About that time I felt Johnny jump on my back. I straightened up and grabbed one of his arms. He was pretty little and light as a feather, so I was able to flip him off to the ground and still hold Jimmy down.

"My dad doesn't have anything to do with this," Jimmy said.

"Sure he does," I said, cocking my right arm back with my hand balled into a fist. "He's from here. I don't want to beat the shit out of you, but if you keep actin' like an asshole makin' fun of me, I'll do it whether you're Jim Taggert's boy or just any old boy that happened to blow through Bellair, lettin' everybody know that you think you're hot shit an' better 'n everybody else. Well, there ain't nothin' to that. Now you goin' to give an' behave or do I have to knock some sense into you?"

For good measure, I jumped off the ground a little and came back down with both knees into Jimmy's arms. Then I pushed forward and put all the weight I could on his arms.

"Okay, okay," he said, "I'll give. You don't have to be a bully."

"You'll behave yourself? Cross your heart an' hope to die, stick a needle in your eye."

"I can't cross my heart with you holding me down."

"Do it in your head an' say it: I'll be good, cross my heart, hope to die, stick a needle in my eye."

"That's silly."

"Say it or I'll kick the shit out of you."

"I'll be good, cross my heart, hope to die, stick a needle in my eye."

Johnny stood right close, looking at us and crying a little. Nancy, Mary Beth and Kathy had just walked by the corner and stood off a ways when they saw us fighting. I wondered if Nancy and Mary Beth would have helped me if the boys would have been able to take me down. When Billy Snider had picked on Nancy after school one day, I chased him across the road from the store and had him on the ground just like I had Jimmy Taggert, only then I kept hitting Billy Snider and hitting him until Nancy got me to stop. So I knew she'd help somehow. Mary Beth was still pretty little but would do what Nancy did or what she told her to do. The girls looked on for a minute, then went on towards the store.

"Okay," I said, easing my knees off of Jimmy's arms and getting up. "Let's get on to the cemetery, if you still want to go."

He nodded and said, "I thought it'd be called Boot Hill down here."

"That's out West in the old days," I said, seeing that he was still going to carry on. "You through with your bullshit yet, or do we have to keep it up?"

"I'm through, I reckon," he said and grinned, friendly like.

"I reckon you better be," I said, friendly like right back.

Jimmy was quiet afterwards as we walked together down the hill and across the Borax bridge at the foot of the cemetery. He stopped and looked over the side of the bridge down into the narrow crick with shallow running water, laced with oil everywhere and marking the high spot of early rains with deposits of oil on the bank and high up on the grass.

"Why do they call this Borax?" Jimmy asked.

"Because of the stuff they put in there with all this oil that gets dumped in here? It's a mess. You can't even go wadin' or swimming in any of the cricks around here for the oil. Willow Crick ain't too bad. Not much oil over that way."

"They dump oil an' stuff in here? That's dumb."

"What they goin' to do with it?"

"I don't know, but look what it does to the water an' to the whole area touched by the water. It's disgusting."

Maybe it was disgusting. I didn't like the oil and stuff all over everyplace, either. But I just figured it was the way things was done, and there wasn't anything I could do about it. Johnny walked a little ways ahead of us and was turning into the cemetery at the top of the hill when Jimmy and me turned and started up the hill.

The burying part sat back away from the road and sloped down toward Borax and off to the woods the other way. Like always, I tried to imagine a church somewhere close like there was at other country cemeteries. At the Bellair Cemetery, the front part was kept mowed and looked sort of like a park with a hickory-nut tree off to the side after you turned in and a big old oak tree shading some of the place off to the back. Maybe they was going to build a church there in time, I thought. As it was, it made a nice place for parking or playing for us kids. The two churches in Bellair had no cemetery and, like Russ told me back when I'd asked him, people used the town's burying place east of town for their dead. South of town was the junk yard, west was the North Fork of the Embarras River and what was left of the Old Mill, north and some east was the oil fields that gave the only jobs available besides them connected with farming.

The Taggert boys had been to the cemetery with their daddy but had to hunt for their granddad's grave. I went off with Jimmy as he wandered through the old gravestones. He rattled off names as we walked and asked me if I knew the people when they lived. I told him I knew Charlie Kline and about him getting killed in the war. And I told him I knew just about everybody else he asked about; but except for Charlie, they'd been dead before I could remember. Madge's folks was there, of course. And so was some of the Taylors, the Hamiltons, the Larues, the Brandywines, the Pfeiffers and others in town.

At Jimmy's granddad's grave, we stopped and looked at the headstone that had Clara, his grandmother's name, cut into the stone, too. "That'd be weird," Jimmy said, "to see your name on a grave marker."

"You're right," I said. "I never thought about that."

"What's even weirder is to know that none of these people here, including my granddad, will ever get to heaven," Jimmy said, folding his arms across his chest and shaking his head.

"How do you know that?"

"They're not Catholic."

"What the hell does that have to do with it?"

"If you're not baptized Catholic and don't die in a state of grace, you'll go to hell."

"Who told you that bullshit? That's the biggest bunch of bullshit I've ever heard."

"The nuns told us in catechism classes."

"Them nuns don't know shit, then."

We argued religion quite awhile. I wondered about it all the time, but we didn't always go to church down at the EUB Church. Big didn't go to church anymore and got his annual visit from the preacher about coming to church. Dad never had been a church-goer. Mother and Aunt Helen tried to take us, but it was never possible for us to go all the time. When we'd miss a couple of weeks, it just got easier not to go. Going to hell was a scary thought, but somehow I just couldn't think that the people in my family who didn't go to church at the Church of Christ like other families in town did or wasn't Catholic like nobody in town was would end up in hell. If that was so, that meant that my daddy would go to hell, too.

My eyes watered up, and I ran at Jimmy again, crying and hollering at him. "Fuck them old Catholics," I said through clenched teeth, "if that's the way they think. My daddy already served his time in hell, Sam says, an' there ain't no way in the fuckin' world he's goin' to hell after that."

"He might as well have killed himself as not be a Catholic," Jimmy said smugly. "He'd have just as much chance of getting to heaven as he does now."

I grabbed Jimmy by the shirt and pulled him toward my raised fist. Nothing else I could think of except kicking the shit out of him would make him understand how wrong he was, I felt. He looked at me with fear in his eyes, but he made no effort to defend himself. That made me stop. I couldn't hit him like that.

"You're not worth it, you dumb sonuvabitch," I said, letting go of his shirt and dropping my cocked fist. "You don't know nothin'. You're dumber 'n owl shit. An' that's dumb."

I turned and walked out of the cemetery and back to Bellair. Jimmy followed me a few steps behind me and never tried to catch up with me. Johnny brought up the rear, and we run into Nancy, Mary Beth and Kathy at the corner again. I didn't feel like talking to anyone for the rest of the evening. After supper, I listened to Hank Williams sing three songs and headed outside to sit on the porch and stare off into the dark. "I'm so lonesome I could cry," the last song I'd heard, kept running through my mind for a long time.

The next morning, Jimmy knocked on the door when I was just finishing breakfast. Nancy answered the door and came back to the kitchen to tell me that he wanted me to come outside. I picked up my bowl and emptied the last of the Wheaties and milk into my mouth, wiped the milk mustache from my lips and went to the door.

Jimmy was standing quietly, blocking most of the sun from my eyes so I could see him good. His face was white and looked a bit drawn, like something was hurting him. I felt that way sometimes when I had a pair of shoes on that was too small or I was outgrowing my jeans and they was so tight they made my stomach hurt.

"Could I talk to you, John Walter?"

"I reckon."

"Could we go down to the school?"

"Don't see why not."

We headed off the porch and down the road to the school. Neither one of us said anything as we walked along. He had his head down most of the time like he was thinking of what he wanted to say.

"Let's sit on the porch," he said.

I nodded and went to the end of the porch and sat so I could lean my back up against the schoolhouse. Jimmy sat opposite me, leaning against the corner pole. They was larger poles than the ones on the store porch and harder to lean into, hold onto and stiffen your legs and body so they was parallel to the ground than it was on the skinny ones.

"I'm sorry for the things I said and the way I acted yesterday," Jimmy said. "I knew some of those things hurt you when I said them. That's why I said them. My mom and dad are getting a divorce, and I've been mad at the world lately. We're here for a few days to visit my grandmother and be with Dad. Then we're going to go live with Mom. For a while yesterday, I was picking on you and didn't think about all that. But I didn't know your father had been killed in the war. I thought you lived with your mom and dad.

"I got to talking with Dad last night. He's not been drinking down here, and we can talk a little to each other. I asked what you meant about somebody saying your father 'already served his time in hell.' And he told me about your father being in the Marines and getting killed at some place called Guadalcanal. I'm sorry for what I said, John Walter — I do think it's funny that people down here use two names a lot, but it's just different. My mother's Catholic and that's the way I've been raised. I go to Catholic school, mass on Sunday and Holy Days and catechism on Saturday. I believe in the teachings of the church. My dad's not Catholic, though, and I can't believe he's going to hell because he's not. He does a lot of other things like drink and run around that may get him there. But that's beside the point and has nothing to do with the bigger question about faith."

"Your daddy went through some bad times in the war, I heard," I said. I'd been listening to Jimmy pour his heart out to me. It felt awkward in a way. But I felt different about Jimmy almost at once. Between feeling sorry for him for what he was going through and thinking about my own life, I felt the tears welling up in my eyes and fought to hold them back.

"We know that," Jimmy said. "And we love Dad. When he's not drinking, he's a great dad most of the time. Even then he has nightmares about airplanes crashing where he'll start screaming and wake up the whole house. Not long after one of the bad ones, he'll start drinking and not come home for days at a time. When he does come home, he's drunk and smelly. Mom just couldn't take it any longer."

"I'm sorry to hear that, Jimmy. My daddy's gone, too. But I'm pretty lucky to have Big an' Sam an' all the other men around here to talk to. I don't know what I'd do without them. Don't worry none about yesterday. It's over an' done with. Let's play together an' have a good time while you're here."

"I'll shake on that," he said, reaching across the steps with an outstretched hand. "Thank you, John Walter."

And we did have fun for the next few days. The best time I think was during a summer rainstorm that drove us inside the store where Richard came in and him and me taught Jimmy and Johnny how to play dominoes and forty-two that afternoon. We all sat around the card table under the florescent light with the rest of the kids standing around looking on.

It was pretty easy to teach them to play dominoes by laying down the first one and talking them through the plays and telling them how the game was scored. By the time we'd played a few hands and they knew how to play, Richard went out at a hundred even. The rest of us weren't far behind.

Teaching them to play forty-two took a little longer, but with Richard and Johnny partners and Jimmy and me partners, it didn't take long for them to figure the game out. We never threw our hands back in because nobody bid. Somebody would always bid thirty to open. And they would bid wildly until somebody else finally said, "Forty-two." It took Jimmy and Johnny awhile to figure out how much they could bid based on what they had in their hands and how their partners might help them. Several times both of them went set by large numbers and laughed like a baboon when they did. Then they settled down and we raced out of the hole and towards a hundred again. Jimmy and me just barely went out with Richard and Johnny at ninety. When we finished the game, Mother said, "Pop's on me. You kids have been wonderful."

We dashed for the front of the store and the pop case with Mother laughing as we went. That sounded good to hear her laugh like that. Jim had just walked in the store and laughed, too, "Candy's on me then," he said.

I snagged a Royal Crown and a package of peanuts and went back to the domino table. I went about the process of draining a little of the RC with a couple of big gulps and was pouring my peanuts in when Jimmy got back.

"Whatever are you doing?" he asked.

"What?"

"Dumping a bag of peanuts into your soda. I've never heard of such a thing."

"There's a boat load of things you've never heard of, Jimmy

Taggert. You ought to try it."

I was surprised when he took his Baby Ruth back and got a package of peanuts. He dumped the peanuts into his Pepsi and looked over at me when he'd finished.

"Satisfied?" he asked.

"Satisfied?" I said, echoing him. "It don't satisfy me. You don't have to do nothin' to satisfy me. I just wanted you to know what you're talkin' about before you go judgin' everything. You jump on anything you see that you don't like or don't know anything about with both feet."

He laughed and tilted the bottle up and took a drink of the pop with a few of the peanuts. I took a swig of my pop and took some peanuts, too. We stood at the edge of the stove, eyeing each other and chewing.

"Taste good?" I asked.

"Not bad," he said. "I still think it's rather strange. It's not something I'd do again."

"But it's okay if I do?"

"Sure. Why not?"

"I was just checkin'."

That was the last time I talked with Jimmy before they left. We all said goodbye when they left the store that day. Although they said they'd be back to visit the next summer, I never saw the Taggert kids again. Jim came back just after Labor Day and school had started. Mother told me he'd been in for a package of cigarettes earlier one Saturday morning when I went to the store. Right off, I decided to go talk to him. He was walking around his mother's yard, smoking and looking at the two cows grazing in the pasture off to the east. They looked past him to me as I walked across the yard. Jim turned and followed their gaze.

"Hello, John Walter," he said, a faint smile on his face. "What're you up to?"

"I come to see you."

He laughed, bringing the glint to his eyes that I remembered from other times I'd talked to him. He still had that movie-star look about him, but his face was a little puffier than I remembered it. I was sorry to hear that he didn't get to see his kids much now that he was divorced and not living close to them.

"I'm lookin' for work right now," he said, taking a drag on his cigarette and flipping it away. "I'm goin' to look around here for a few days, then go to St. Louis an' see what I can find there. If your dad needs any help this fall, tell him I'm lookin' for work. I'll scoop corn or whatever he needs. Be good for me to get back outdoors an' do some hard work."

"I'll tell him, but he's sold one truck since Sam quit."

"Sam quit? What's he doin'?"

"He's workin' over at the light plant in Hutsonville."

"Are they hirin' there?"

"Sam had his application in for a long time. He got the job last summer. The truckin' business has been fallin' off for a long time, an' Big sold the other truck after Sam quit."

"That's too bad. He still might need some help this fall. Tell him about me, if you would."

"Okay."

"Thanks for spendin' time with my kids last summer, John Walter. Jimmy talks about you an' bein' down here all the time."

"Well, I think about him all the time, too. It was good to have all of you here this summer. Hope you stay around an' find a job, Jim."

Jim did stay for a few days, but he never found a job an' was gone by the next Saturday morning. And I was gone by the time Clara died and Jim came back for the funeral. After that, I never heard much about him but thought about him from time to time and wondered how his life had gone after that last time I'd seen him. I hoped things worked out for him. Somehow, I figured he deserved that.

17

Before I had finished sixth grade and we'd just started feeding cattle, somebody had decided the seventh and eighth grades should go to Oblong. The old Bellair school was in the process of closing like other one-room country schools and was consolidating with the Oblong Grade School a few miles down the road. I was twelve years old and excited to go but soon wished I was back in Bellair. At first, the kids treated me like I was retarded or wasn't right bright, I guess because I was taller than everybody except Grant Harrison. And he was three or four years older than the rest of us and a bit "teched in the head" was the way Dad Garner put it. When everybody saw that I wasn't retarded, it was more like I was the country hick instead of a town kid. After a while, I decided that wasn't so bad and didn't let it bother me.

By the time Sam left the summer after my first year at Oblong Grade School, I was beginning to feel more at home at the school and with the people there. I even missed them during the summer and couldn't wait to get back for eighth grade.

I'd learned pretty quick that the kids in Oblong who called me a country hick wasn't any smarter than me. In fact, most of them wasn't as smart, I didn't think. The teachers there wasn't any better teachers than Miz Finley, but there was several of them that was good like she was. Miz Stone made history and current events even more interesting to me than they had been by following the news all the time and relating things that happened to things that had happened in the past. Miz Patrick made English fun and assigned good stories to read. Grammar lessons made me want to gag, though. And Mr. Lincoln made me like arithmetic and math, which I thought was impossible. We all called him Abe behind his back because of his last name and the way he looked like a young Abraham Lincoln.

But he really made me feel good about myself the first time I got a hundred on a test, the only one in the class, and a "Congratulations!" in his stylish handwriting on the paper under the score.

It was in his class one day that I got caught in a game trying to be one of the town kids that ended up embarrassing me more than I could ever remember being embarrassed. Like the feller said, it got my goat so much I didn't know whether to shit or go blind. Usually when the other boys started something in Abe's class, I tried to stay out of it. I liked him for one thing. But the biggest reason I paid attention to him and didn't join the other boys when they acted up was that he'd been a sergeant in the Army and he'd fought in the war over in Europe. I liked all that and just liked the feller who was the first man teacher I'd had who was more like other fellers I knew than anybody I ever figured I'd have teaching me in school. He was big and lanky, not quite as tall as the old president from the Civil War days. But tall. Abe treated me like he liked me, too. He was kind of awkward and homely looking, like I felt. He could have grown a beard, put on a top hat and passed for Honest Abe in some of the centennial celebrations going on in towns across our part of the country.

All that respect and good intentions went out the window the day Lonnie Dailey, Pete Hillary, Gale O'Neal, Mike Stevens, Ed Wooten and another boy or two, all on the basketball team that I wanted so much to be a part of, started sneaking their hands up under their armpits and bringing their arms down on the cupped hand to make it sound like a fart. I listened to one after the other make the sound while Abe would raise or turn his head at each noise, never catching the guilty kid. But I figured he knew where the sounds was coming from and who was making them. I waited patiently for the right place to get in on the fun and really become one of the boys. Abe was reading the directions for a bunch of problems he was assigning. With his head down, I slipped my left hand inside my shirt, cupped my hand under my shirt and came down hard with my arm. The noise was so loud and sounded so real it scared me, even before I saw Abe's head snap up and heard everybody laughing and snickering. To make things worse, I let a little fart that everybody around me heard. And smelled. That made everybody laugh even harder.

Old Abe came up out of the seat like he was shot and headed back to the corner where we all sat. The others was still laughing like anything when Abe made his way to us in three or four giant steps. I thought he was coming straight for me, but he stopped by Ed and ask him what was so funny.

"I was laughin' at him," Ed said, pointing at me.

"How about you, Donnie?" Abe asked another basketball player and the only one of us who hadn't been making sounds.

"I was laughin' at John Walter, too."

I kept my head down when Abe stopped beside my desk.

"Well, what did you do that these boys think is so darned funny?"

I couldn't say a word. Abe was dark skinned, but I could see the red in his face and knew he was mad as hell. My own face felt hotter than a firecracker about to explode.

"What's so funny, John Walter?" Abe asked, towering over me. "What did you do? Or say?"

His voice was loud and angry-sounding. I had my head down, almost on my desk. I felt like Aunt Helen always said about "wanting to crawl in a hole and pull my hole in after me" when something had happened to embarrass her. With Abe standing over me and with nowhere else for me to go, I understood exactly what Aunt Helen had meant.

"Get your head up, John Walter. Look at me when I talk to you. Look me in the eye. What did you do?"

"I-I-I couldn't help it," I said in a squeaky, shrill voice that sounded like a girl to my flaming hot ears. I couldn't think of another thing to say and couldn't have if my life would've depended on it. I couldn't even have told him what it was that I couldn't help. "I-I-I'm sorry."

That made the boys laugh more.

"That's enough out of you," he said, barking at them and starting back to his desk. "I'll deal with the lot of you in practice tonight. You've all been actin' up today. That won't do."

And he did deal with us. I don't suppose the practice was much longer than usual. But when he walked on the gym floor that evening and blew his whistle, he was all business. There wasn't any taking a break so he could teach a play or a move, show how to get position for a rebound or tell a little story about something in life that he found that went along with what he was trying to teach us.

We gathered around him when he motioned us to circle around.

"We've got some boys on this team who like to fool around in class," he said, looking right at me. "I've told you all many times how I feel about your behavior in general. You represent Oblong Grade School when you're on this basketball team an' you're a reflection of my teachin' an' my coachin' to the people of this community when you're on this basketball team. It's a privilege to have the freedom to be able to be on this team an' represent this school an' this community. You will behave accordingly, or you won't be on this team any longer. Is that clear?"

We nodded.

"I'm not goin' to go into the details. I know you all know what I'm talkin' about. Some of your behavior has been less than exemplary. So this evenin', we're goin' to play a full game with no time between halves. We're goin' to run some of this nonsense out of you. Doc is goin' to coach one team; I've got the other. McElligott, Hillary, Dailey, Stevens an' O'Neal are the Shirts, an' Donnie an' Ned Ennis, Wooten, Manson, Manley an' Edwards are the Skins. Doc, you can have the rest of the boys to substitute with. We won't need any subs."

Doc Winston was the assistant coach. I thought we had the best team and wouldn't have any problem beating Donnie Ennis and his bunch that didn't play much. They was little kids, except Donnie, who usually played with us, and Lawrence Edwards, who was a big, rugged seventh grader with arms and shoulders like a grown man. And for the first quarter, we was beating them like an old drum. I got two baskets in close, one on a rebound from a set shot Dailey missed and one on a pass over Manley from Mike Stevens. Everybody else had a basket, and we led 12-3. It was a different ball game after that.

"It looks like this isn't quite fair, Doc," Abe said, standing at the center line for the jump ball beginning the second quarter. "We're goin' to have to do somethin' about this."

"I think so," Doc said, taking his glasses off and wiping his forehead and face with a towel. He'd been a Navy corpsman aboard some ship out in the Pacific back during the war. He was an easy-going and quiet-spoken feller who was the speech teacher. I'd never heard him raise his voice or get mad about anything. He'd just smile and go on. "How 'bout lettin' me have another man? You've got the first five, except Ennis."

"Good idea. I should have Wooten over here, but I don't have room for him. So that'll work. Okay, let's go, boys, an' let's pick it up."

"Let me have a minute with my team, Coach."

"Okay. You've got it, Doc."

He gathered his team around him at the side of the court. We stood and watched. At the end of Doc's talk, everybody laughed, then all yelled together as they broke out of the huddle.

Doc put Wayne Manley in as the sixth man. He was a tall, skinny kid who maybe wasn't as fast as he looked when he raced around the floor, always moving, never standing around. But he was faster than most of us and raced toward their basket as Abe threw the jump ball up between Donnie Ennis and me. He jumped as Abe brought the ball up and swatted it to Wayne who got the ball several steps ahead of everybody else, dribbled a couple of times and made an easy lay-up. I turned toward our basket and started for it when I heard Abe holler, "Press. Press. Pay attention to what you're doin', John Walter. Keep your eyes open an' your mind on your business. Get in position. Don't just meander around like you're lost."

By the time I'd turned around, I saw Wayne shoot another easy lay-up. Our lead was cut in half in less than ten seconds. This time I was facing the other end when O'Neal threw the ball in to Dailey, who was immediately covered with two players from the Skins. He jumped in the air and threw a pass toward half court where I was standing. Big Lawrence Edwards came over and grabbed the ball and bounced a pass to Manley for an easy lay-up.

"Good job, boys," Abe and Doc both said in unison.

Our lead was now only three points. Dailey pushed Hillary to the center line to get into position. The rest of us was more or less in position for the press. We'd never practiced against six men and didn't quite know how to handle that. But O'Neal threw the ball to Dailey. He dribbled once and flipped it to Hillary who threw it to me. I pivoted to face our basket and passed to Stevens as he was cutting to the basket. The pass was almost behind him, and he barely caught the ball and was able to throw it out front to Dailey. He'd gotten down the floor to get the ball back and start our revolving offense that had worked real good against the Skins in the first quarter.

"Well, girls, it's about time," Abe said to our team as we got the offense running. "It only took you about twenty seconds to figure out what was goin' on an' how to handle the press. In combat, you'd all be as dead as a door nail; in a basketball game, you'd just get the tar beat out of you. You let these guys score six points about as quick as I've ever seen anybody score six points. Imagine if that were the last twenty seconds of a close game. You just lost. Got your butts beat because you didn't react quickly enough to the situation an' do what had to be done."

"Yeah, but they've got six players," I said, turning for the rebound as Dailey shot a set shot from the top of the circle. The ball swished through the net. "That wouldn't happen in a real game, I don't think."

"You won't have to play against six men, but you will find yourself in situations where you have to act much more quickly than your team has. You don't have all day to react. You'll lose a lot more than you'll win, if you do."

And we lost the practice game by ten points. We'd hold our own for a while, then the Skins would go on a run where they'd steal the ball two or three times in a row. If they didn't, they'd manage to score or get fouled when they had the ball. We could hardly touch the Skins without getting called for fouls while we got shoved around, elbowed and held without ever hearing the whistle. Doc had three or four other players to substitute with, where our team had none. The players he'd put in as the sixth man wasn't as good or as quick as Wayne, but they'd run around and double team somebody all the time. And by the fourth quarter, our butts was dragging. My legs felt like they was filled with lead. We still shot twenty-five free throws each before practice was over.

Afterwards, our part of the locker room was quiet as a congregation of church mice. The Skins was whooping and hollering while we showered. They didn't really brag about beating us, but they walked around and talked a lot more cocky than they ever had before. Abe hadn't said a word to anybody after the game was over. He'd made his point and then some.

"Tired?" Big asked when we got in the truck to go home.

"Yep. We played a full game straight through. I can hardly move, I'm so tired."

"That's when you've got to be able to do whatever you have to to get the job done. There'll probably be a lot of times in your life that you'll be tired like that. But there ain't goin' to be nobody there to take you by the hand an' lead you along the way. That'll be all up to you. There was times back durin' the war when drivers was scarce an' there was a lot of haulin' to do that I never pulled my shoes off from Monday mornin' 'til Thursday or Friday. I'd get so tired that. ..."

I'd heard that before and heard Big talking, but I lay my head against the window and drifted off to sleep thinking about Daddy as the truck rumbled along on the washboard of the gravel road. Big shook me by the shoulder when we got to Bellair. That night, I went to bed right after supper and dreamed that Daddy was driving the truck along the gravel road with me on the other side. He was dressed in the green Marine uniform with his hat sitting directly on his head as it was in the picture Mother kept put away in a photo album on her dresser. I was kind of surprised that he was driving the truck in uniform. While I was looking over at him, wondering about that, he looked over at me and smiled. I smiled back and reached out to touch him. He'd float in and out of the driver's seat as I held my arm straight out in front of me feeling through the air. I woke up crying, sorry that I had only been dreaming.

A couple of weeks later at lunch, somebody who got to the tables in the cafeteria where we always ate unscrewed the tops of both the salt and pepper shakers before anybody else saw them. I sat down with Mike Stevens and Pete Hillary and reached for the salt and pepper. They got to them first. Mike dumped the salt all over his barbecue, and Pete dumped the pepper in his mashed potatoes.

They hollered and cussed while the rest of us laughed. It was funny as long as it was somebody else. But over the next two weeks, just about everybody got caught except Donnie Ennis. He moved to another table. That was about the only way you could keep from getting a plateful of either salt or pepper, unless you quit using them. I tried to remember to check each time to make sure the caps was screwed on. But I was in a hurry one day and forgot. I had a mountain of pepper to scrape out of my mashed potatoes. That's about all you could do. The cafeteria ladies had quit giving new plates when it happened.

Embarrassed again, my face flushed, I kept my head down and my eyes on my tray. I was ashamed of myself for being dumb enough to dump all that pepper on my food.

Right then I began figuring how to get even the next day. I knew I'd have to get to the cafeteria early enough to get the tops unscrewed on the salt and pepper shakers. Maybe I wouldn't get the feller that got me, but I might get two fellers who'd not be thinking to check before they shook a shaker over their food.

I got there the next day with Pete and Mike again. They was arguing over who was going to win the World Series, the Dodgers or the Yankees. I hated both teams and didn't care. But I had time to salt and pepper my goulash and unscrew the lids before I put them back down. Other kids got in on the argument with Pete and Mike.

"The Yankees are goin' to win," Dailey said. "They always do, don't they?"

"The Dodgers in five," Ronnie Manley, a skinny seventh grader who wore thick glasses that made his right eye that looked off to the side bigger and more noticeable and who was the only Brooklyn Dodger fan I knew in the whole country.

"You don't know nothin'" O'Neal said. "Them Yankees are Dodger killers. They'll eat 'em alive."

I was listening but watched the shakers. Grant Harrison sat down almost directly across from me and reached for the salt shaker right away. I couldn't move. He looked up at the boys at the other end of the table and grinned that goofy grin he always gave everybody when he saw them as he started salting his food. Before he could look back around, nearly all the salt in his shaker made a huge mountain of salt right in the middle of the goulash. The salt started sinking and soaking up the red tomato sauce, leaving only a dry ring of white at the top like a real mountain and me feeling sick to my stomach.

"Oh, uook, uook at dat," Grant said, his face turning red and looking confused. "Who did dat?"

That stopped the World Series argument. Everybody looked at Grant and laughed. His face turned redder. So did mine. I felt real bad that Grant had dumped the salt. I hadn't thought about him sitting at our table. I was sure somebody would see how red my face was and point me out as the one who had unscrewed the top. On top of already feeling bad, having anybody know I was the one who let somebody who wasn't quite right dump the salt on his goulash was about more than I could take. I could hear Hank Williams singing, "... I've had lots of luck, but it's all been bad an' no matter how I struggle or strive, I'll never get out of this world alive. ..." I wasn't sure I would get through the noon hour alive. But nobody said a word. They was too busy laughing.

The head lady in the cafeteria came walking real fast towards our table. Not trusting myself to talk, I shoveled a big bite of goulash in my mouth, then tore off a big piece of bread and shoved it in my mouth.

Grant looked up at the woman, tried to talk but just managed to point at his plate. Her face was flushed.

"Who did that?"

"Grant did," Pete said and giggled a little.

"Stop that giggling like a little girl, Pete Hillary. I mean who un-screwed the salt shaker top and you know what I meant."

"It was unscrewed when we all got here," Lonnie Dailey said. "Grant was just the first one to use it."

"I don't believe that for a minute. Whoever would pull a dirty trick like that on Grant ought to feel ashamed of himself. Come on, Grant, I'll get you another plate."

Then she turned to us, pointed a finger at us and said, "Make this the last time that happens. Shame on whoever did this to poor Grant; shame on all of you for laughing at him."

I was quite ashamed of myself as the woman led Grant to the kitchen. Nothing seemed to work out for me. I knew other boys had unscrewed the tops of salt and pepper shakers and never had Grant dump the salt on his tray. After a while, I think just about everybody had taken the tops off to get even through somebody else's bad luck. But nobody could figure out who had started unscrewing the caps. I figured from the look on his face when somebody got caught that it was Bobbie Manson. He'd grin like a possum eating shit, and we started calling him Possum.

"Now you guys don't need to try pinnin' that on me," he said, still grinning. "I take the blame for all kinds of shit around here that I don't do."

He was right about that. But he did a lot of the things he was accused of doing. When I first came to school at the beginning of seventh grade,

Bobbie had borrowed fifty cents of my lunch money from me twice and not paid me back. I did without lunch for two days, and I quit loaning him anything. He'd put a thumb tack in my seat one day right after I wouldn't loan him another fifty cents, and I came into my seat and plopped down like I always did. I let out a yelp and jumped out of my seat. When I felt the tack and pulled it out, Bobbie was laughing like an hyena. I knew he had put the tack in my seat, too, and wanted to get even with him. The next morning, I went to homeroom early. Miz Stone wasn't in the room, so I put the tack in Bobbie's seat right in front of her desk and hurried back outside. I laughed to myself until the bell rang for school to take up and kept laughing all the way up the stairs and down the hall to Miz Stone's room.

I felt like dropping dead when I walked through the door. A light-haired girl with a hook nose was standing in front of the desk by Bobbie's desk. I'd never seen her before. She looked like she was about to cry. Miz Stone's face was red, and her eyes had that narrow look about them that I'd seen her use a time or two when some kid got out of line. Even then she'd never looked that fierce, though.

"Get to your seats immediately," Miz Stone said, her face still red and her voice mean-sounding. "Somebody put a thumb tack in Bobbie's seat this morning. Only this morning, we have a new student, Mary Kay Masters. This is her first day here. So I assigned her to Bobbie's seat. And what do you know? When she sat down right before most of you got here, she sat down on a thumb tack that was apparently meant for Bobbie. Who would do something like that?"

"He probably put it there himself," Mike Stevens said.

Bobbie had been standing beside Miz Stone's desk, laughing and grinning all the time. Now he hooted and hollered. She pointed her finger to the door and pulled him along by the ear as she walked out with him. Nobody dared laugh while she was still in the room. Just as soon as the door closed, everybody but Mary Kay laughed. She stood there with a tear rolling down the cheek I could see. Her eyes had a sad look in them.

My face was flushed beet red and even my ears was hot. I couldn't look at the girl but was glad Miz Stone was out of the room. By the time she brought Bobbie back in and sat him two rows away from me, I had time to collect myself and act like I didn't know anything.

"I don't know who did that mean trick," Miz Stone said, "but I hope you've all learned a good lesson today. Don't do something to somebody else that you wouldn't want done to yourself. In this case, an innocent bystander comes in and sits on the tack."

I squirmed again and thought about sitting on a tack myself and how I had felt. Watching the new girl and knowing who it was intended for, I felt awful about what happened but wasn't about to admit that I'd put the tack there. Bobbie asked me if I'd done it sometime later when Mother had let me stay with him for a basketball game one night when nobody could come and get me.

"Wasn't me," I said, walking toward his grandmother's house. "I thought we was goin' to stay at your house."

"We are," he said, "but the hero had to take my mother an' Little Rickie to the Legion for a feed before the ball game."

"The hero? Your dad."

"Hell no, he ain't my goddamn old man," Bobbie said like he was mad. "I ain't got no fuckin' old man."

"Everybody's got a daddy."

"I ain't. Whatever he was, he knocked my mother up an' ran away an' joined the fuckin' Army. Got his arm blowed off at some fuckin' place overseas. Good enough for him. Too bad he didn't get his fuckin' ass or his fuckin' head blowed off. I wouldn't have to see the cocksucker all the time an' hear my old lady tell me how much I look like him. The old lady married the other goddamn hero after he got back from the war. Got his sorry ass shot down in a big-ass plane an' spent the rest of the war as a prisoner. Fuckin' Krautheads probably kept him around to send home when the war was over to give us a pain in the ass. All he does now is piss an' moan about how the younger generation don't amount to shit."

I asked Bobbie if he'd started unscrewing the salt and pepper shakers or was the one who got me. He grinned at that and said, "It's like I tell you fuckers all the time. You always try to blame me for every goddamn thing that goes on around there. I don't do half the shit I get blamed for. Everybody tries to put somethin' off on me or get even with me, like I'm the only one that ever does shit."

I hadn't had him in mind when I unscrewed the salt shaker. All I was doing was trying to do to somebody else what had been done to me.

But the somebody turned out to be Grant Harrison, a feller who didn't deserve it and wasn't smart enough to watch out for the tricks we was pulling. It seemed like everything I tried to do was wrong. And I figured the salt-shaker trick was even more wrong because it was Grant who got caught in our stupid games. That made me think my luck was bad all the time and would probably run out just like my daddy's luck had run out.

"Here's the old lady's house," Bobbie said.

His grandma was a white-haired old lady who shuffled around in house slippers all the time we was in her house up in the north end of town. He asked her for money before he said anything else.

"Give me a dollar, old lady," he said to her through the screen door. "I'm flat-ass broke."

"I ain't got no dollar fer you," she said.

"You got more goddamn money than Carter's got little liver pills. Now gimme a dollar before I kick the shit out of you."

I stood there listening to the two talk in a way I would never have even dreamed of talking to my own grandparents. The closest I ever came to it was a time or two when Dad Garner would get me so mad I didn't know what to do. Then I'd cuss at him a little, but nothing like I heard Bobbie do with his grandma. Mother and Big and probably even Aunt Helen would have whipped me something awful for that kind of talk to Dad. But there was no way I'd ever even thought of talking to Grandma Mary Elizabeth that way. Nobody did.

"This heah peckerhead is Jaahhhnn Walltttter McEllligutt, Grannie," Bobbie said and laughed. "He's one of them goddamn hicks from up to Bellair. He's goin' to stay all night with me."

"Pauline know that?"

"Pauline don't know shit."

That kind of talking went on the whole time we was there. I wanted to get out of the house and away from it and did right after Bobbie finally talked his grandma out of fifty cents.

"Now that's the last I'm givin' you this week," she said as she snapped her coin purse shut. "Don't be comin' 'round askin' fer more."

He laughed as we walked down the street toward the drugstore and the center of town. "That makes two dollars this week," he said. "She's loaded, but gettin' anything out of her is like pullin' teeth. She's tighter 'n the bark on a fuckin' tree."

We went to the drugstore and had a ham-salad sandwich and a milk shake. Then we went across the street to the pool hall. I'd never played much pool, but I'd watched Big and lots of other good players and thought I could learn to be a good player.

"Want to bet fifty cents on the game?" Bobbie asked with a half-sneer on his face as he stood there chalking his cue. "Or are you goin' to play chickenshit an' not bet."

"I reckon I'm goin' to play chickenshit," I said. "I ain't played much pool."

"Neither have I. But I'll even play left-handed against you."

"You are left-handed."

He talked constantly while we played a game of eight-ball. I still had five striped balls on the table when he sank the eight ball by banking it in the corner pocket, the length of the table.

"Want some more, McEllie?" he asked. "I'll play right-handed."

I shook my head and threw a dime and a nickel on the table to pay for the game. What I wanted to do was watch somebody else play for a while. Older kids were playing eight-ball on the other two slop tables. But Duke Leonard, Perry Milner and Cap Massey was playing snooker on the front table. They'd been in the Army in the same outfit during World War I and had fought together in France, I'd heard somebody say. Besides putting on quite a show when they played pool, they played better than most anybody else around.

Duke stood watching the game and holding his cue out in front of him. He was usually the quietest of the three. Perry leaned over the table, shoved his Stetson back on his forehead and shifted the smoking pipe to the corner of his mouth. He cradled the cue in his hand and let the tip glide real smooth over the bridge he made with his thumb and index finger. His right leg stuck straight out from the table as he leaned over and stroked the cue that was lined up for an easy shot.

"Talk about shootin' cripples," Duke said. "I thought you was a pool player, you red-headed prick. What kind of shape you goin' to have, if you shoot that cripple? You're goin' to leave a table run for me."

"I'm goin' to shit, too, if I eat regular," Perry said, smiling as the smoke continued curling up over the brim of his hat. He hit the last red ball. It rolled in the end pocket and disappeared. He stood and studied the table before he finally bent over again and stood on his toes and held the cue almost straight up and down. When he hit the cue ball, it shot out and barely kissed the seven ball in between the four and the five balls and did a reverse and headed back to the end rail and stopped behind the three ball. "Now let's see you run the fuckin' table, Duke."

"You chickenshit sonuvabitch."

"That's why they call the game snooker, Duke," Cap said, cackling and taking his pipe from between his clenched teeth.

Perry smiled and puffed on his pipe.

They played a good game of pool, and I could see things they was doing that I wasn't that would help me become a better player. But the talk that went on between them was more interesting. I couldn't concentrate on watching them shoot when they was talking, so I mainly listened. They was old men dressed in overalls or gabardine or khakis who seemed to really like each other and liked playing pool. They acted like it really mattered who won the game, but I had an idea that they didn't care one way or the other. If they'd only admit it.

From the pool hall, we went directly to the grade school for the basketball game. Bobbie was about as awkward as a cow on crutches, even more than I was, and never played much. Abe had asked him one day if he wanted to be the manager for the team.

"Are you serious?" Bobbie had asked. "I ain't goin' around pickin' up nobody's dirty old jock strap an' handin' out towels."

Paul Thornton took that job and kept it all through high school. Bobbie never played much the night I stayed with him or any other night. On the way to his house after the game, Bobbie cussed a blue streak again. I cussed some, too. But I tried not to cuss in front of big people. Bobbie didn't care, except at school where he was usually careful not to cuss in front of teachers.

"Old Abe don't like me," Bobbie said when his mother, Pauline, and his stepfather, Whitey, asked him about the game. "Ugly sonuvabitch let everybody else play before I did. Goddamn chickenshit asshole don't know any more 'n a pissant about coachin' basketball. All he knows is what he got from that goddamn bulldog Butzholtz. Old Butthole. An' that cocksucker didn't know as much as he thought he knew. About anything or anybody."

"Bob, Bob," Whitey said in a normal voice, so low I could hardly hear him. "There's no reason to talk like that."

"Hell no, there ain't no reason," Bobbie said. "But there ain't no goddamn reason not to, neither."

I shuttered to think what would have happened to me if I'd talked like that at Big's. He'd have given me a whipping I wouldn't have soon forgotten. Like the time when he was gassing up on his way to Indianapolis with a load of livestock, and I was down the street playing with Nancy, Mary Beth and Cheryl Matthews. Cheryl was always doing something to make me mad. This time she told me I couldn't play with them because I was a boy. I pinched her by taking a piece of fat on her arm between my first and second fingers and then twisting the way Big had told me Granddad would do to any of them when they didn't show proper respect, even walking through a doorway instead of stopping and letting him through first. I gave the fat part of Cheryl's arm an extra twist and let go. She began wailing and crying like she was going to die. I'd never heard anything like it in my life.

Big looked down the street and bellowed out, "What'n the Sam Hill is goin' on?"

Cheryl ran crying to her mother who came out on the porch to meet her just as I walked toward Big with Nancy and Mary Beth following me. Arletta gave me a dirty look as I passed and looked at her only out of the corner of my eye.

"What did you do to Cheryl?" Big asked.

"She said — "

"I don't care what she said. What did you do?"

"I pinched her like this," I said, holding out my hand to show him, "like you showed me Granddad did to you."

Big reached out and grabbed my arm and drug me to the other side of the truck where he untied the rope from the end of the stock rack and put me down on his bent-out knee. I cried out the first time the rope came down on my legs. Then I gritted my teeth and closed my eyes. Big brought the rope down on my legs seven or eight times in short, quick swings with the rope clutched in his hand. Tears was streaming down my face when he let go of my arm. He was breathing hard as he put the rope back on the stock rack. The hogs in the upper deck was moving around and squealing. I was trying hard not to sob as the places where the rope hit on the backs of my legs started stinging and burning more after the first pain of the whipping faded away.

"You keep your dang hands off o' them girls," he said. "An' quit that blubberin'."

Standing there in the kitchen with Bobbie, his mother and Whitey and watching and listening to the conversation, I felt like I was intruding someplace where I had no business being. All the talk made me feel very uncomfortable and uneasy. Later, when we was getting ready for bed, I told him what would happen to me if I used language like that at home.

"Whitey ain't got the balls to give me a whippin' or hit me," Bobbie said, throwing the covers back and getting in bed. "That little cocksucker would have to kill me if he ever started in on me. An' you keep your goddamn hands off my pecker tonight or I'll knock the shit out of you, too."

My face flushed hot just as I started to get in bed. With the lights out Bobbie couldn't see me. I sat down on the edge of the bed, trembling and shaking a little. Pictures from the past that I'd tried to forget flashed across my mind, almost making me gag.

"You don't have to worry about that," I said, laying down and pulling the covers up over my shoulders. I laid there a long time, not saying a word but not listening to Bobbie talking, either.

When I finally drifted off to sleep, Bobbie was still talking. Sometime later, I was dreaming about Big Al and Jimmy walking toward me with their hard-ons in their hands and smiles on their faces. Both of them was beckoning me to come to them. I was getting up to run when Bobbie's arm came down hard on my back. Already part way up, I flung his arm back and jumped to the floor.

"Jesus H. Christ," Bobbie said. "What the hell's the matter with you? You're crazier 'n a fuckin' bedbug."

"I was havin' a bad dream, an' — "

"Have them someplace else," Bobbie said and rolled over to go back to sleep. "You scared the shit out of me."

" — you hit me across the back with your goddamn arm."

"You're crazier 'n hell."

I stood there until I heard Bobbie's breathing even out, looking at his shape in the faint light coming in the window. When I got back in bed, I scooted out to the edge and laid there, stiff and wide awake, for a long time. I hated dreams like that. And I hated sleeping with Bobbie.

18

With Sam not being around anymore and Big having more to do to keep up with the hauling by himself, I went with him to help when I could. But I also started spending more time with Richard and Jerry. We'd meet at the store or out on the street on a bicycle and roam around the countryside. I felt at home just about anywhere close enough to ride a bicycle in a little bit. Most people didn't seem to mind us being on their ground. Madge had told us a couple of times to stay away from the Old Bed and the Old Mill because she was afraid we'd get hurt, though. We just started going around the back way when we wanted to go fishing or ice skating or play tag in the Old Mill that was filled with old loose hay and you could climb around on the beams and rafters and jump a long ways down into the loose hay.

At the store one Saturday morning when Mother had to work because Horsey had to go back to Terre Haute for something, we played forty-two with Ronal Crucell while it drizzled outside. We'd had a rain or two but nothing like we had during other springs I could remember. When it cleared off and the sun came out a bit, Ronal went home and we headed out to get our bicycles.

"Now you boys be careful," Mother said. "And don't go near the gravel pit. You know you almost drowned over there last summer."

"No, I don't know that, Mother," I said. "Freda Trout don't know nothing. I told you what happened with that."

I was tired of hearing that story. Richard and me was both just about out of the eighth grade, yet Mother and Ruby Owens both tried to mother us boys like we was little babies. Just the week before when we'd been hanging around and couldn't find much to do, Richard and me decided we'd go camping out at the cabin on Willow Crick.

It was at a place called Broadwater because it was a lot wider than the rest of the crick. When they wouldn't let us go, we got some coffee and bacon and stuff and took off walking out there with our sacks slung over our shoulders like a couple of hoboes. That tickled us.

About a half an hour after we'd left Bellair and walked out the angling road towards the cabin, I saw Big's old Plymouth coming up the hill and out of the trees across the field by the cemetery.

"They're comin'," I said, pointing at the car. "Let's get in the ditch."

The ditch was deep enough and had enough of last year's weeds standing tall that we both got down so we couldn't be seen from the road. Richard's dog Skipper went down with us at first. But he didn't seem to like to stay down at the bottom. Richard'd whistle and coax him to come to us with no luck. When Aunt Helen stopped the car where Skipper was walking, he went over to the car and put his paws up on the window. I could see her from the ditch as she pushed Skipper away and looked along the road.

"I don't see them," she said.

"I wonder where they are," we heard Mother or Ruby say. I couldn't tell for sure which one.

The girls hollered out the window at us. We could hardly keep from laughing as we looked up at the car and everybody was only a few feet away. They finally drove on down the road. We got up and slung the gunny sacks over our shoulders and headed east again. Skipper ran along beside us, in front of us and behind us. When we got to the north edge of the Red Wilson place where Big used to feed cattle, we cut across the field.

"Nobody'll be able to see us now," Richard said.

"No," I said, feeling closer to him than normal as we walked back through the pasture and followed the fence over to Willow Crick. It always kind of surprised me to hear him talk much. Sometimes he could be real quiet and not much company. "But what about gettin' across the crick to the cabin?"

"There'll be a tree across the crick or somethin' that we can get across on."

"I can't wait to get over there an' make some coffee an' fry some bacon for supper."

"I can't either."

I'd been wanting to come out there to camp ever since I'd seen the one-room lean-to cabin when some of Big's feeders got out and headed up the crick. It was just north of where we fed the cattle. When Dad and me had walked up the side of the crick bank looking for strays that day and came upon the cabin, I thought I'd stumbled on a line shack from some western book I'd read awhile back. The front was open and looked out on the crick and across to the other side. I'd thought about camping up there since we had run across it. In my daydreams, I had a buckskin quarter horse tied to the hitching rack to the side of the cabin or hobbled a few yards away in a thicket of grass. Pictures like that ran through my head as we got closer to the crick. Richard grabbed my arm and pointed ahead of us. I saw the cabin, then I saw Jerry and their uncle, Ted Childers, standing in front of the cabin. We crouched behind a tree and looked across the crick.

"Bub," Jerry hollered out through cupped hands. "Bub, come on. Uncle Ted an' me are goin' to take you home."

"Don't answer," I said.

"I ain't goin' to."

We could see them plainly through the trees. I had Skipper by the collar this time so he wouldn't give us away like I thought he would back in the ditch. But he seemed to know what was going on and kept quiet. Jerry kept hollering ever once in a while. Ted paced back and forth, smoking and drinking a Schlitz beer. I couldn't see the can, but I knew that was the only kind he ever drank that I knew about. And we'd been seeing him drink beer since he came home from the war. Ted was never too friendly to me or anyone else I knew. He gave Richard and Jerry some pieces from his Army uniform but never told them much about what he did, where he was or anything about the war. I asked him where he'd been one time when he had his head under the hood of his car. The leg that stuck straight out over the fender jerked. "I was there," he said and went back to work. Him and Alice stayed pretty much to themselves and went off to Casey to the taverns on Saturday and brought beer home for the week. He tossed the can off the bank and hollered out, "Bub, now you get on in here. If you don't come now, I'm goin' to tan your hide good when I do find you."

Richard started to get up, but I touched his arm.

"They're about to leave," I said. "He ain't goin' to kick your ass.

Even if he does, it'll be tomorrow after we've stayed out here all night, fished an' done what we want to instead of what our mothers want us to do. Be worth an ass whippin' then."

Richard liked the idea of camping and fishing, but he didn't see it as an adventure like Huck Finn and Tom Sawyer did in Mark Twain's books or like I did. I liked the idea of being modern-day Hucks and Toms, doing like we was doing, exploring the whole country around us and even taking a raft down the Mississippi and eating fish every day like Nigger Jim and Huck Finn did on their trip. Wouldn't be no mothers or teachers always telling you what to do and when to do it like it was now. Richard just wanted to be off away from everybody.

A few minutes later, Ted and Jerry turned and started walking away from their cabin and toward the car. We waited until we heard it start up and begin going off to the east. I took out a package of Lucky Strikes and shook one out for both of us.

"I think we made it," Richard said, taking a drag on the cigarette after we'd got them lit. "I didn't know there for a while."

"I didn't either. I just don't understand what's the big deal. Ain't no reason in the world we can't stay out here all night an' not have our mothers an' Aunt Helen throw a conniption fit 'bout it."

"They're women."

"I reckon that's what it is. But Big wouldn't let me go, either, because Mother an' Aunt Helen would nag him to death, if he did. I hear that tale Freda Trout told about me almost drowning over at the gravel pit so much that it makes me puke to even think 'bout it. Let's get across this crick before dark."

A little ways up stream we found a big cottonwood tree had nearly uprooted from erosion along the bank and had partly fallen across the crick. We decided for Richard to shimmy up the tree first and jump over to the other bank and let me throw the gunny sacks to him, then jump myself with Big's .22 rifle. It looked like a pretty long jump to me, but Richard made it with inches to spare.

Skipper looked up and then across at Richard and ran back and forth along the bank. I laid down on the tree as far out as I could get and swung the first sack towards Richard. It was a little short, but he stepped out in the crick and caught the sack before it hit the water.

"Throw the next one a little harder," he said. "I've got my damn feet wet already."

I laughed and let the sack with the coffee and bacon swing back and forth a couple of times before I gave it a pitch toward the bank on the last swing. The sack hit Richard right in the chest and he stumbled backwards and sat down on the bank.

"You didn't have to throw it so goddamn hard."

"Get out of the way," I said, standing and getting to a limb where I could jump off and land on the bank. I jumped and pitched forward when I landed and fell right on top of Richard, the rifle between us.

"Get off of me, you asshole," he said.

Again, I laughed but rolled off and laid on my back, looking up through the budding trees at the darkening sky. This is what life is supposed to be like, I thought. We ain't hurting nobody, and we're having fun.

"Okay, Owens," I said, getting to my feet and watching Skipper finally decide to jump in and swim over to us. "Let's get down to the cabin an' get set up for the night. I don't think we'll have to worry about anybody comin' back tonight. We're safe from an attack 'til mornin', don't you think? Skipper'll hear anybody or anything that comes in the night an' let us know. Big won't get back from Indianapolis until two or three o'clock, an' he ain't comin' out here after us until after the sun comes up. An' we'll be up an' fishing up there on Broadwaters an' out of here by then."

"I hope. I'd hate to see Uncle Ted an' your Uncle Bob come walkin' down that path behind the cabin, though."

At the cabin, we unloaded the gunny sacks and put our blankets on the smooth, hard dirt floor and gathered wood for a fire. After we got it going, Richard threw half of the bacon in the skillet and put it on top of the metal grating we'd rigged up to cook on. In no time, the bacon was sizzling and the smell filled the cool evening air. I was starved. While Richard poured half the coffee we brought into the pot and filled it with water from the gallon jug of drinking water, I put two pieces of homemade bread Mother had just baked before she went to work on the old dish rags we brought for plates and to wipe our hands.

"I don't reckon I've ever had bacon that tasted any better than this," I said after I'd taken a bite of the sandwich with four slices of crisp bacon on it. "You cooked it just right."

"It is good, ain't it? Wait'll you taste this coffee. Uncle Ted showed me how to make it."

"It's cowboy coffee," I said. "I reckon that's the way cowboys made coffee back in the old days when they was out on the trail. Some coffee, a slab of bacon an' some beans is about all a feller'd need to get by."

"Tobacco," Richard said. "Have to have somethin' to smoke. An' I ain't goin' to smoke no fuckin' coffee grounds or corn silk or anything else you want us to smoke when you can't steal cigarettes from your uncle or I can't get some from Mom."

That was quite a few words for him to say at one time. I nodded and said, "Bull Durham. We could take a sack of Bull Durham. That's what the cowboys smoked."

"I hate that shit. I can't roll a cigarette for anything."

"You'll get better," I said. "Old One-Armed John, that feller that hangs around the pool hall in Oblong, the one lost his arm fightin' overseas in World War I, he rolls cigarettes with one hand. Spills a little tobacco, but he rolls a pretty good smoke."

"Bullshit. Can't nobody roll a cigarette with one hand. I can't even roll one with two hands."

"Go to the pool room with me sometime an' see for yourself."

"I'd have to see it to believe it."

"You'd see it," I said.

Richard dug out an opener and the can of dog food he'd brought for Skipper. He opened it before I made my second sandwich. Skipper took the food in a couple of quick bites and stood before Richard with his tail wagging, his eyes begging and his tongue hanging out.

"Get down," Richard said.

Skipper turned to me.

"You might as well go away," I said. "You ain't gettin' any of this. I didn't get none of yours."

Circling the spot three times, Skipper plopped down and looked up at Richard but stayed quiet. The two of us ate in silence for a while and just looked out over the crick at the brush on the other side. The chirping of the birds had died down, and the sounds of crickets calling through the evening was all you could hear. After the coffee boiled, Richard sat it off to the side of the fire and poured a little cold water in it.

"That's to make the grounds settle," he said, stopping to light one of his mother's Old Gold filter cigarettes, then pouring us both a cup of the coffee. "Nothin' better 'n a cup of coffee an' a cigarette after a good meal."

"You're right about that," I said, lighting a Lucky Strike and sitting back to enjoy the evening. "This is livin'."

By nine o'clock, it was completely dark, the fire had died down to glowing embers and we crawled under our blankets for the night. We laid there and talked a little before I finally tried to go to sleep. It was almost good to be going to sleep, though, and I felt my heart racing under my shirt as I thought about how good it was to be camping. Richard was quiet, so I didn't say anything. I wondered what he thought about the thing with Big Al, Jimmy and Ronal up at Chester Bayne's old barn. I didn't say anything about that, either. Neither him nor Jerry had ever said a word about it, but I thought about it every time I saw them, just as something always brought it to mind every day. I was still thinking about what had happened as I began drifting off to sleep.

"What the hell is that?" Richard said, bringing me awake. He was already sitting up when I opened my eyes.

"It's a fuckin' tractor comin' back here," I said. "They've got somebody comin' for us. Ain't that a bitch?"

We decided there wasn't nothing to do but wait. I picked up Big's old single shot .22 rifle. But I knew there wasn't anybody coming back here in on a tractor in the middle of the night that was going to hurt us. So we just waited. The tractor stopped, and it was quiet again.

"It's Old Hallie, boys," a voice I recognized called out through the night. "It's Warren Halliburton. I'm acomin' in."

"You hear me," he said after a while. "I'm acomin' in."

"What you comin' back here for?" I finally asked.

"Comin' fer you boys. Your mothers are worried sick about you."

"Ain't no need for 'em to be," I said. I couldn't believe it. Sending Dizzyfuckin'Halliburton after us. I was madder 'n an old wet hen. What a fucking insult, I thought. Richard and me was all settled in for the night, safe and sound as if we'd been home in our own beds. Then they send Dizzyfuckin'Halliburton in after us. Wouldn't no other man even think about coming to get us. But old Dizzy came walking in with a strong light showing him the way. Two blue tick coon hounds ran a little ways in front of him.

"Keep them coon dogs back," I said, holding Skipper by the collar. "I'm holdin' Richard's dog."

Dizzy hollered at the dogs and they ran nervously back and forth in front of him. When he got up to the cabin, he stopped and smiled at us. "You boys got your mothers worried to death," he said and stopped to take a drag on one of the fat cigarettes he'd rolled himself and always seemed to have hanging from the corner of his mouth. "I told Helen that you boys would be all right back here 'til mornin', but it wouldn't do her but what I come on back to get you. So gather your things up. They're awaitin' fer you out in the car at the road."

"Let 'em wait," Richard said.

"Now come on, boys," Dizzy said. "Ain't no use fussin'."

I started to argue but knew it would do no good and banged the skillet to the ground. We started poking things in the gunny sack, poured the rest of the coffee and the water on the fire and followed Dizzy to the tractor. Richard had to carry Skipper to keep the coon dogs away from him. I just couldn't believe that they'd send Dizzy Halliburton after us. I'd never been around him much. But I knew he was sort of a neighborhood black sheep, even though he was always around somewhere. He wasn't known as an honest man a feller could trust, Big told me one day after we'd picked up a veal calf to take to Indianapolis. Big said the feller didn't always act like he was playing with a full deck most of the time, either.

"Ray Fountain found an old sow missin' one morning," Big said when I asked him how he knew Dizzy wasn't somebody a feller could trust. "There was a light snow on, an' Ray tracked Hallie an' the sow right to his barn. Fellers say they've caught him stealin' corn, too. You just can't trust him out of your sight. I'd rather be poor all my life than to have fellers think about me the way they think about him."

That was the feller Mother, Aunt Helen and Ruby sent after us. But when he came back to get us, he talked like he had some sense. Men just see things different than women, I decided.

We was quiet on the ride. At the road, Dizzy stopped the tractor and shut it off. He walked with us over to the car and told Aunt Helen we'd turned in for the night and would've been safe until morning.

"They'd had supper," Dizzy said, chuckling and opening and closing his lips to breathe and to let the smoke go. "Had a good fire goin' that had burned down to the coals an' they had things set up s' good I durn near stayed with 'em myself."

Nobody in the car laughed or said a word.

"Much obliged for gettin' them, Hallie," Aunt Helen said. "I don't know what we'd done without you."

"You'd have worried your pretty little heads off," Dizzy said and chuckled louder and laughed down in his belly. "That's what you'd a done. An' them boys would've had the time of their lives."

By that time, Richard and me had climbed in the back seat with Ruby and Jerry. Nancy and Mary Beth was squeezed in the front seat with Mother and Aunt Helen. She rolled the window up and started to drive away.

"Couldn't you get anybody else from Bellair to come?" I asked. "An' gettin' Dizzy Halliburton to come after us. That beats about anything I ever heard."

"Watch your mouth, John Walter," Mother said. "Don't make it any harder on yourself."

"Why'd you wait until Bob left to pull a stunt like this?" Aunt Helen asked. "You didn't have the nerve to do it when he's home, did you?"

"I didn't even know he was going to Indianapolis tonight until we was leavin'. Ain't that right, Richard?"

"That's right," he said, the first word he'd said since we'd heard the tractor coming. "We didn't know that."

Which wasn't exactly true. I knew at noon that he was going to Indianapolis because I'd helped him put in the decking boards and fresh bedding. But we'd already planned to go by then and was going to ask him first. When we found out that he was going, we decided to wait and ask our mothers. With Big gone, it just made it a bit easier to go after they told us we couldn't.

"Whatever made you decide to pull a stunt like this?" Ruby asked Richard. "You don't usually do things like this."

"Oh, shut up, Mom," Richard said. "You've got us. Now let's go home an' go to bed so I can get back to sleep."

That was a mouthful for him, too. And it quieted everybody down. I jumped out of the car and hurried into bed when we got home. I heard Aunt Helen tell Big when he got home a few hours later. He didn't seem too mad, but I made sure I was up and gone by the time he got up.

It was just before noon when I came in for dinner and talked to him. And then all he said was, "I don't know what you fellers meant, scarin' them women an' makin' 'em worry about you. I ought to kick your ass."

But he didn't.

Richard had to stay home that next day as part of his punishment for going out to the cabin, but Jerry and me was loafing up at the store and met up with Strawberry Cottrell. He had a day off from the shoe factory and was sitting on the east end of the porch away from the old men when Jerry and me got there. Strawberry was a little older than the rest of the boys around Bellair. The bushy reddish hair that covered his head and grew long down the back of his neck was the color of a big old ripe strawberry. He'd dropped out of school as soon as he could and went to work at the shoe factory at Casey. So he always had some money. He never talked much and blushed and laughed a laugh from down in his belly when fellers talked to him.

"What the hell you doin', Strawberry?" I asked.

"I'm loafin'," he said, laughing and his face turning redder than it already was.

"We loaf all the time," Jerry said.

"You do?" Strawberry said, laughing again. "Ain't no money in that, is they?"

"Nope. But the loafin' ain't too bad."

"Let's go get some beer, Strawberry," I said. "That wouldn't be too bad, either. You could drive up to Casey to get some an' bring it back here for us to drink. I've got a buck an' a quarter for a six pack."

"Aw, I couldn't buy you boys no beer. I'd get in trouble."

"Won't be no trouble," I said. "But we can't go with you to Casey. Here's a buck an' a quarter. Get me a six pack of Greisedieck, an' we'll meet you at the school in half an hour."

Strawberry took the money, giggling as he did. I figured if he took the money, he'd get the beer and I turned to go. Mother was working at the store, and Aunt Helen and the girls was over across the bottoms helping Flossie Pierce wallpaper her living room. That was on the way to Casey, so we couldn't go with Strawberry. Couldn't go, anyway, even if she wasn't there. I knew it wouldn't do for us to ride to town with him. But we had the whole afternoon to drink the beer when he got back with it.

"You say you got a greazy dick?" Strawberry asked, giggling more and turning redder. "I — "

"I didn't say nothin' about me have a greazy dick," I said, cutting him off and looking over at Jerry. "I said to get a six pack of Greisedieck Brothers beer. That's what Joe Marshall drinks sometimes. I like that beer. It's got a kick an' tastes good. See you at the schoolhouse in half an hour."

Jerry and me jumped on our bikes and rode away. I thought about what Strawberry had said as we rode around the square. He always had seemed a little funny to me, but I just thought he was kind of backward and not real smart. Big Al had always said Strawberry was queer, even though he said he didn't know that for sure. If it was true, I figured Big Al would know the way he was always talking about getting his cock sucked. I just didn't believe there was real queers around, a feller that'd like sucking on somebody's cock and acting like a woman. I couldn't even figure that any halfway decent woman would like having an old cock in her mouth, let alone a man wanting one in his mouth.

By the time Strawberry got back with the beer, I'd decided that he probably wasn't a queer any more than anybody else was, that the whole idea of anybody doing perverted stuff like sucking cocks was what Miz Finley called "a figment of the imagination," something that somebody thought up but wasn't real. Maybe there was fellers that wanted it done to them, but I couldn't imagine anybody wanting to do it to somebody else.

My mouth was watering for the beer. Now that was something that was real, I thought. Truth was that I'd never had more than a sip or two at a time and could hardly believe that I was going to have a whole six pack to myself. Strawberry had got a six pack of his own and was already drinking one when he stopped in front of the school garage where we'd parked our bikes.

"I got me some of them Greisediecks, too," Strawberry said, laughing and giggling like a lunatic. "I like them old greazy dicks."

He laughed harder. Jerry and me looked at each other and laughed, too. I'd heard other fellers laugh about the name and figured everybody laughed at it. Old Joe Lewellyn, the feller that run the tavern down in Oblong, was telling somebody in the barbershop one day about him and a couple of other old boys from Southern Illinois ordering a Greisedieck in New York City when they was there on a pass before going overseas. Joe said the bartender thought they was trying to be smart and kicked them out of the place.

"Give me my Greisediecks, Strawberry," I said. "I'm ready to drink some of them old Greisediecks. Give me the church key, too."

He handed me the six pack and the opener. I took two cans out of the six pack and punched two triangular holes in the first one and handed it to Jerry.

"I better not drink one," he said. "Mom'll smell it on my breath, an' I'll catch hell."

"Oh, come on," I said. "The smell'll be gone long before you see her. Tell her it's her imagination, if she says anything."

Jerry took the beer, and I punched two holes in my can.

"Here's to you, boys," I said, raising my can to touch theirs and then taking a big swig. The beer had the same good old beer taste like Joe Marshall's Greisedieck did on the way home from Oblong, and I grinned great big and took another swig as a little beer dribbled out of my mouth and down my chin. I wiped it with the back of my hand and let out a war whoop.

I jumped in the back seat, leaving Jerry to ride up front with Strawberry. He nosed the car back out on the road and headed south out of town. Just a mile or so down the road, I drained the beer and tossed the can out the window. I could feel the warmth from the beer begin to spread over me as I opened the second can. Strawberry drove pretty slow down the gravel road. Somebody was talking all the time, but I don't remember a thing we said after we left town. We wound around the gravel roads for an hour or so and ended up at the cemetery. When we parked under the old hickory-nut tree, I started to get out of the car and go to Charlie's grave. But I'd had three more beers by that time and found that I could hardly walk.

"I reckon I'm gettin' drunk," I said, giggling a little and thinking how grown up I felt. "I can't hardly fuckin' walk."

I looked back at Strawberry and Jerry and saw them laughing. Their images would blur together when I looked at them. Closing one eye, I could see two of each of them; closing the other one, I could still see two of each of them, but they shifted a few feet to one side or the other.

That made me laugh. Then I started closing my eyes real fast and watched Jerry and Strawberry bounce back and forth in the front seat. After a minute, I got too dizzy to keep it up and just laughed and laughed.

"What's the matter with you, John Walter?" Jerry asked, a serious look on his face. "Are you drunk?"

"'Course I'm drunk, you fool. Don't I look like I'm drunk? An' you two fellers up there bouncin' back an' forth in front of me was funnier 'n hell. Fact of the matter is, they was two of each of you bouncin' back an' forth."

"What're you talkin' about?" Strawberry asked.

"I'm talkin' 'bout you an' Jerry, two of you old boys, floatin' back an' forth in front of my very eyes. Here they are, ladies an' gentlemen, the Bouncin' Bellairians. They walk, they talk, they bounce back an' forth in front of your very eyes while they double up an' keep on bouncin'. They go right along with the ladies here on my right. Today an' today only, you can see both of these shows for the price of one. Fifty cents, a half a dollar, takes you all the way.

"Step right up, ladies an' gentlemen," I said, sitting up on the edge of the seat and going into the pitch I'd heard the feller give for the girlie shows at the county fair in Oblong, "this show's for folks between the age of eighteen an' eighty. If you're under the age of eighteen, you wouldn't understand it; if you're over the age of eighty, you couldn't stand it. It's the kind of show your grandpa got slapped down at the table for goin' to see. It's red hot an' ready to go; it's the old burlesque show.

"That's little Cindy on my left. She walks, she talks, she crawls on her belly like a reptile. That's little Candy on my right. She does the Dance of the Seven Veils an' the Dance of Pandora's Box. She does things you've never seen done before. I'm goin' to take 'em back in two minutes, ladies an' gentlemen. Step right up, fifty cents, a half a dollar, takes you all the way back. An' you'll see the Bouncin' Bellairians bounce around before your very eyes while Cindy an' Candy do their dances to warm up for their show — an' warm you up for them. Ahhhhhaaa. ..."

I kept on talking, saying whatever came to my mind. Strawberry and Jerry kept laughing. I drank the last beer even quicker than I had the first four. The more I drank, the better the beer seemed to taste.

And I liked the good feeling, the warm glow that spread throughout my body. That feeling from the beer and a cigarette whenever I wanted one made me feel about as grown up as I ever had. I let out another yell to show how I felt. Then gagging on a drag on my Lucky, I got real dizzy all of a sudden and begin feeling sick to my stomach. I lurched out into the grass where I puked and puked until there was nothing left to puke. Through my watery eyes I could see Strawberry and Jerry standing off under the hickory tree, laughing and pointing at me.

"Fuck you, cocksuckers," I said between pukes when I could catch my breath. "Ain't nothin' funny that I can see here."

They laughed more. I didn't have any more to puke and started gagging and heaving until I thought I was going to die. For a few minutes, I even thought dying would be better than the way I felt. I wiped my mouth with the back of my hand and stumbled back to the car and fell through the open door into the back seat again.

"What're we goin' to do with you, John Walter?" Strawberry asked, standing with Jerry and looking at me through the door. "We're goin' to have to get out of here an' get you home. Big Mac's goin' to kill me sure as I'm standin' here."

"I'm the one that's dying, you silly sumabitch. Just take me out there an' dump me in a grave by old Charlie. That's what you can do with me. Tell 'em I just up an' died on you. I'm dyin' right now. Tell 'em I loved 'em, I loved 'em. ..."

Through my watery eyes, which I managed to open slightly, and the haze of the late summer afternoon sun, I could see the two of them standing outside the door looking in at me. I yawned and gasped for a breath of air before falling off to sleep.

When I woke sometime later, I was still laying in the back seat of the car. But I could tell we wasn't still at the cemetery. We was parked on the south side of the schoolhouse. It was real quiet, and I still felt sick. I could see Strawberry in the front seat but not Jerry.

"Where's Jerry?" I asked, sitting up real quick with that realization. "How'd we get here? What are we doin'?"

"You passed out," Strawberry said, giggling. "Jerry had to go home, an' I didn't know what else to do with you. I'm afraid I'm goin' to be in big trouble."

"You ain't in no trouble," I said, feeling sicker to my stomach when I thought about being alone and passed out with him. What if he tried to play with my cock, I wondered. That fucking Jerry Owens. Going off and leaving me with somebody who might try something really made me mad. I automatically reached down for my crotch to see if my fly was open. The zipper was about halfway down, but I wasn't sure that I'd zipped back up when I'd pissed the last time. Everything seemed to be okay, except the nagging feeling in the back of my mind that Strawberry had touched me. "You been fuckin' with me, Strawberry?"

"I just been tryin' to get you awake an' figure out what to do with you, John Walter. Jerry had to go home an' left me to take care of you. I sure don't want Big Mac to find out about me buyin' beer for you. He'd raise holy heck with me."

"Big ain't goin' to do shit," I said, holding my head and trying to decide what to do as I got out of the car and went to the porch. "'Cause he ain't goin' to find out. He'd probably kick your ass up between your shoulders so you'd have to take your hat off to shit, if he did, though. Mine, too. So you need to get out of here. You go on an' get out of here, an' I'll stay here until I get to feelin' like I got my right mind."

"You sure you'll be okay?"

"I got to be okay," I said, gagging a bit. My head felt like it was about to split wide open, and my mouth tasted like somebody had shit in it. "I feel like I've been shot at an' missed an' shit at an' hit. But I'll live, I think."

Strawberry laughed and said, "You won't tell your uncle?"

"Why the fuck would I tell him? Just get out of here before somebody comes along an' finds us here."

I fell back on the concrete porch and closed my eyes. Strawberry started the car and pulled out on the circle driveway, then backed up to where I was sitting on the porch.

"You all right, John Walter?" he asked.

"Hell no, I ain't all right. Do I look okay? I'm sicker 'n a fuckin' dog. Just get out of here before I get sicker 'n I already am an' die right before your very eyes. Then you'd have my body on your hands an' lots of explainin' to do."

He didn't say anything more and looked worried as he pulled away.

I stayed on the porch for a few minutes after he'd left and go up and walked over to the pump. The tin cup wasn't on the wire hanger like it was during the school day, so I put my hand down under the spigot and pumped so hard that water came up through the top of the pump. I drank my fill and got down on my knees and kept pumping with my head under the spigot. The cold water felt good pouring down on my head while I kept on pumping. When I finally quit, I felt some better, but my head was still splitting and I felt a bit sick to my stomach again. Before I could stand up, I began puking all the water I'd drunk and had more dry heaves.

I crawled over to the porch and collapsed on the step with my head on the porch. By then I really thought dying would be better than living and facing everybody at home. But I dozed off and slept for a few minutes. When I woke up, I was thirsty again and had a craving for salt. I got up and peeked around the corner of the schoolhouse to see if I could see a car or truck at the house.

With none there, I walked the quarter of a mile as fast as I could. Dad Garner was hoeing in the garden at the back of the house. I went directly to the salt shaker and shook a little in my hand and took the whole pile in one lick. Then I washed it down with a glass of water and went in on the daybed in the dining room and laid down. If I couldn't die, I wanted to sleep. And I did. I heard Aunt Helen and the girls come in sometime later.

"What's the matter with you, John Walter?" Aunt Helen asked as she walked to the kitchen. "You're white as a sheet."

"I don't know," I said, turning to the wall. "I don't feel good. I puked my guts up awhile ago."

"You haven't been smokin' again, have you?"

"No, I haven't been smokin' again. Must've been that baloney I ate for dinner. It tasted kind of old. But I was hungry an' ate two sandwiches of it an' three boiled eggs."

"The eggs'd be enough to make anybody sick."

She walked away, and I went back to sleep. After another nap, I woke up and felt good enough to get up and get out of the house until supper was ready. By then, I felt like I'd live after all and swore I wouldn't drink beer like that again.

The rest of the summer went by without me having any more beer to drink, but Ross Childers went on one of his famous, long drinking binges that he'd pull every so often. He'd start drinking and drink until his money ran out. That could be a week or a month. And everybody in town would be watching and listening to what Ross would do while he was drinking and carrying on. He was a salesman and a gambler and usually carried a big wad of money all the time. Richard and Jerry and me was sitting on the store porch early one rainy morning when Ross came stumbling across the road from his house. It was the biggest house in town and sat on a little hill catty-cornered from the store. Even during the summer, Ross dressed in a suit and tie with a Stetson hat on his head. But as the drinking binges went on, he'd shed the coat and tie and forget to shave every day. After a couple of days of not shaving, his dark black whiskers would begin to overshadow the scar on his lip where he'd had something cut out years before.

Back when Ross was just a kid in Prohibition times, Coony Pfeiffer told us Ross ran whiskey for the sheriff down in Robinson and had never worked at a regular job in his life. Coony said he'd helped out by keeping the whiskey and home brew in an old well back of his house to keep it out of sight and cool.

"Bellair was quite a place in them days," Coony told us one Sunday morning up at the store. "Some of the oil johnnies was still around, an' they liked to drink an' gamble. Ross was right there to give 'em what they wanted. Others'd come into town on Sunday mornin' from Robinson to buy their liquor an' then head down to Jake's place to drink an' play poker. Old Jake'd take a cut out've ever' hand, an' sell set ups for the drinks. He made more money on Sunday mornin' than he did for the rest of the week put together. An' old Ross was right there in the middle of things. Fellers sit out on the porch drinkin' an' cavortin' as the churchgoers went by to go to church just down the road. They was fit to be tied, but they wouldn't say nothin' or even look as they drove by. Clarence Hartmann's folks lived down there across from the Taggerts an' would drive clear around the square to go to church so they wouldn't have to drive past Jake's on the way. They'd be some pretty rough customers sittin' out there. A couple of them was drummers that traveled around the country sellin' stuff. Old Ross hooked up with one of 'em an' took to sellin' hisself.

That's where he met Velma. He was down there someplace in Kentucky. Her man got killed in a car wreck just after he come back from the war. She had a kid an' was up agin it. Ross up an' married her an' brought her an' her whole family to Bellair."

That's what came to mind as I watched Ross walk towards the store through the rain. He had a gabardine overcoat on over a wrinkled white shirt but no tie and looked like he'd been rode hard and put away wet when he walked across the street. His shirt had smudges of food over his belly that stuck out over his belt, and the buttons strained against the button holes.

"Goddamn, boys," he said, stopping by the steps to catch his breath and grinding out a Camel beneath his foot before he came on up on the porch, "I'm gettin' old. Too goddamn old to cut the mustard anymore. When you get that way, they might as well take you out an' shoot you like a fuckin' old horse."

He stopped in front of us and cackled like he always did.

"You boys want a drink? A Coke?"

We nodded.

"Well, come on in. I'm buyin'."

Inside, Ross sort of took over the store for the next half an hour or so. Carolyn Matthews was helping Mother while Horsey was off for his weekly trip to Terre Haute. And Carolyn's friend, Linda Springer, was there to see her.

"I'm buyin' these boys a bottle of pop, Lorene, if that's okay with you, my dear. An' I'll buy you one. Carolyn an' Linda, too. Get 'em a candy bar or whatever else they want."

"Thank you, Ross," Mother said, standing behind the cash register, "but I don't care for anything. The rest of them can have what they want."

Carolyn and Linda stood back, but Richard, Jerry and me ran to the pop case. I grabbed an RC and a package of peanuts. Ross started pulling money out of his pockets and tossing it on the counter. My eyes felt like they was popping out of my head when I saw all the crumpled green bills piling up. Looking around at the others, I saw that they was reacting the same way.

After he'd emptied every pocket of money, Ross looked over at Mother and said, "Take some an' leave some. I think you'll find enough there to cover my bill."

Mother reached over and took a dollar bill. "That'll be forty-five cents, Roscoe," she said.

"Would you girls count this money for me?" he asked, shifting to look at Carolyn and Linda who were standing farther down the counter, one on one side and one on the other. "I'll give you a five-spot, if you'll count it an' put it in a neat little pile. Velma says I don't have enough money to pay the bills."

The girls didn't say anything, but they started sorting the money by denomination and putting it in piles of ones, fives, tens, twenties, fifties and one hundreds.

I'd never seen a fifty or a hundred dollar bill before and could hardly believe my eyes. Ross looked around at us and grinned. His eyes was bloodshot but gleaming as he talked and watched the girls count the money.

"While these young ladies are countin' my money, let me give you a little advice about women that'll help you out in dealin' with 'em when you get older. Not that you'll pay a damn bit of attention to what I'm goin' to tell you. I wouldn't have. Didn't. But it'd have saved me a lot of misery an' a lot of money, if I would've just listened. But here you go: You can't get along with a woman no matter how hard you try, but you can't get along without 'em, either. They know that an' 'll take you to the cleaners, if you don't watch 'em real close."

Ross went on talking about women and laughing. Just as the girls finished counting, Ross said, "What I've just told you is advice that's worth every goddamn dollar these girls have counted. An' then some. You don't have to pay me, an' I'm goin' to throw in another bit about marryin' 'em that you better heed. I've been married five times an' have learned a lot about this marryin' business, but the main thing is this: Never marry for money, but let it make up your mind damn fast."

He laughed and his belly shook up and down like it always did when he was tickled at something he'd said. Taking the last drag off of a Camel, he tossed it in the coal bucket in front of the stove and laughed some more. I looked up and saw Mother frowning at me. The girls just stood behind the stacks of money and waited.

"Well, how much money have I got?" Ross asked them, walking over to the counter. "Am I in the poorfarm yet?"

"You've got $2,389, Ross," Carolyn said. "That's a lot of money to be carryin' around."

"That right? I couldn't spend it, if I didn't have it, though, could I? Here's a couple of dollars for you two fine young ladies for helpin' me count it an' stackin' it up so pretty. Don't that look pretty the way they got it all stacked up, boys?"

We had followed him to the counter and stood nearby, looking at the stack of money before him that was big enough to choke a horse. I was so shocked at seeing so much money that I couldn't say a word. Even when I'd watched Mother count the money in the cash register at the end of her day, I'd never seen so much money. And I didn't figure Richard and Jerry had ever laid eyes on that kind of money, either.

"Here, boys," Ross said turning to us, "here's a buck for each of you, too. And, by god, you remember what I said about gettin' married an' gettin' along with the women."

With that, he folded the wad of bills and turned to walk out the door. He stopped in front of Mother and smiled at her. She had sat down on the stool behind the counter and had a worried look on her face. She didn't look happy, and I was afraid she was going to be mad or make us give the money back to him.

"You look tired, Lorene," he said quiet like. "You're workin' too hard. Tell Howard you need some time off."

Mother never answered or said a word.

Ross peeled off a bill that I saw was a twenty and put it in front of her. She reached out and pushed it back toward him.

"I don't want your money, Roscoe," she said.

"I know you don't," he said. "Take it, anyway. You've had a rough row to hoe, Lorene, an' I'd just blow it on booze."

This time he stuck the wad of bills in his overcoat pocket and walked out the door. He was making a funny-sounding whistle through the cut-out place on his lip as he walked.

19

Over the next few months, Mother seemed to grow tired earlier each day. She never complained about anything, but I noticed she hugged me harder and more often than she had since I could remember. It got sort of embarrassing. I figured I was too old for my mother to hug me, anyway, let alone so hard and so often. Aunt Helen finally talked her into going to see Doc Bates to see why she was getting so tired so easy. He was the doctor over at The Corners that Grandma Mary Elizabeth said had been the McElligott family doctor since he'd set up practice there more than forty years earlier. He'd just started practicing when Daddy was born, she said, and had come out in his horse and buggy to deliver him. Ever since, anytime one of the family had a baby or got sick, Doc Bates was called or visited in his office.

When Aunt Helen took Mother to see him, he said her "iron was low" and gave her some pills to raise her iron level and told her to eat good and get plenty of rest. Besides taking the pills, I don't know that she changed anything about the way she ate or lived. But she never seemed to be much different. She got up and went to work at the store, came home and helped Aunt Helen with supper and went to bed by nine o'clock. More often than ever, I'd see her take out one of Daddy's letters and read it or hold the picture of them in her hands and stare at it for a long time. I always wondered what she was thinking. "I was just thinking about your daddy and me" was all she'd ever say when I asked her.

Big and Aunt Helen and Dad Garner all seemed to be worried about her. But Big had his own worries since he'd lost all the money on feeding cattle and just had the one truck to keep going. Most of the time, he was up and gone before I woke and got home long after supper. After he'd started farming Grandma's farm with the old H Farmall, another tractor and the tools he bought to get the crops planted and tended, during farming time he was there even less. I got to see him more, though, because I was in the field with him to fill the planter with seed and fertilizer or whatever else he had for me to do. One day I asked him why he worked so hard.

"Tryin' to get out of debt," he said, flipping a cigarette off in the field as he crawled back up on the tractor and threw his leg over the seat like he was getting on a horse. "I won't ever pay off my debts from feedin' them cattle an' keepin' too many trucks arunnin' too long. The fuckin' interest eats me up."

For only one of the few times since Barney Ford was buried, I walked over and picked up the cigarette as Big headed the old Farmall back down the field. Money was scarce, he hadn't smoked much of the cigarette and I thought I needed a smoke. While I smoked the long butt of the Pall Mall cigarette Big had changed to when they came out, I watched the tractor pull away. The corn rows he made was as straight as strings. He was proud of that. He said if something was worth doing, it was worth doing the best a feller could do and that other farmers always looked at how straight the rows was and how good the crops was tended to see how good a feller was at farming and what kind of a feller he was. Losing the money on the cattle seemed to bother him in the same way it would have if he'd planted corn in crooked rows.

Dad probably thought the same way. He'd been a farmer all his life. Now that he wasn't able to do much farming, he took over the garden and would spend hours putting it in and tending it. When I'd be mowing the yard, I'd watch him hoe away, up and down the rows, then stand at the end of the row, leaning on the hoe and looking at his work. He wore matching green twill pants and shirt, the kind that used to be worn by most farmers only on a Saturday afternoon trip to town. His shirt would be open three buttons down, the gray hair at the hollow of his neck mingling gently with the faded farmer tan — that burnt-bronze V at the neck from a thousand days under the summer sun. The straw hat would be pushed reluctantly to the back of his head while streams of sweat poured down his forehead. He'd dab at the sweat with a large, red bandanna and keep looking at his work.

Dad never said much or raised his voice about anything. On one of Sam's days off, he had stopped by to visit, ate dinner and ended up helping us load an old cow and a veal calf down at Joe Marshall's place.

Big was hurrying like he always did when he was going to Indianapolis with a load of stock. He'd left just enough room at the back of a
double deck load of hogs for the cow and calf. After he ran them up
the chute and into the stock rack, he set the chutes aside for some of us
to hang on the side of the truck and pulled the pin to let the gate drop.
A couple of hogs edged towards the back, and Dad shooed them back
in with his hand. The end gate, which was rimmed with wrought iron,
caught him hard on the way down and came crashing down on the
back of his hand with a thud. He never said a word while Big cussed
and hollered and raised the gate. Dad's hand was bloody and looked
kind of crushed.

"That looks pretty bad, Selva," Sam said. "We better take you to
Doc Bates to have him take a look at it."

"It'll be all right," Dad said and wrapped his handkerchief around
his hand. "Nothin' to bother a doctor with."

Then he ambled off towards his old Hudson and drove home. Big
wheeled the truck around the barn lot and headed up the road. Sam and
Joe looked at each other and just shook their heads. Joe shut the gate and
told Sam to come back again. Sam nodded as we walked to his car.

"Doc Bates or somebody ought to have a look at that hand," Sam
said. "He might've broke that hand."

"I don't 'xpect he'll go to the doctor," I said.

"I don't either. But he ought to."

Aunt Helen tried to get Dad to go to the doctor, too. When he
wouldn't, she tried to take care of Dad like she did everyone else. He
said he could take care of himself and rubbed some old Dr. LeGear's
horse liniment on his hand. Dad said it always worked with his horses,
and he reckoned if it worked on a wire cut or some other kind of hurt
on a horse that it'd work on him. For the next couple of weeks, he'd sit
in his chair in the front room and rub that smelly old stuff on his hand
and just rub it day after day until the scab was gone and there was no
scar left. I was kind of flabbergasted at the way he treated himself.

And I was kind of flabbergasted with the way Big was getting
along compared with the way Sam was now that he'd got the job at
the light plant. He said he just worked five eight-hour days and got
paid extra when he worked more than forty hours. I figured Big worked
six and seven days and twelve and fifteen hours a day most weeks.

"Why don't Big get a job like you've got?" I asked Sam at Grand-ma's one day.

"That's a good question, Sedwick. I told him here while back that they was goin' to hire another feller or two out in the yard, but he said he didn't think he'd like workin' for the other feller. Said he done that up at the lime quarry for a few months back in '37 or '38 just before him an' your dad started truckin'. He wants to run his own business."

With Big doing all the trucking and the farming and trying to pay off his debts, life around home wasn't always happy during the beginning of my high school years. Except for going to school through the week and to town on Saturday for Aunt Helen "to do some tradin'," as she called it, and to get a haircut every month or so, I stayed around Bellair and worked and roamed the country on my bicycle. On Sunday, we'd usually go up to Grandma's for dinner and visit with the rest of the McElligott family. Sam and Maggie came by on a Sunday now and then, but Sam didn't come by Bellair too often for me to talk with him like I used to.

Bart Finley and his wife Arlene had opened up a little restaurant across the street from the high school when I started my freshman year. So I spent as much time over there talking to Bart as I could. He wasn't Sam, but he was a good old boy that I like talking to every chance I got. We could smoke over there, too. Sometimes I could get over there for a cigarette before school, if I had any or if I could bum one. Bart wouldn't be there most mornings because he worked hoot owls over at the Ohio Oil Company refinery in Robinson. But he'd always be there by noon to help Arlene with the crowd of boys that poured in at noon. I liked the hamburgers they had better than the cafeteria food and went over every day.

Bart always kidded me about smoking. "Them cigarettes will stunt your growth," he told me one day when I'd slipped out of study hall halfway through the period and went over to the restaurant. "You won't be able to play basketball, if you smoke like you do."

"Is that the reason you're so short?" I asked him as he took a drag on a Winston. "Hell, I'm taller than you are right now, an' I don't want to play basketball. I want to join the Marines an' get away from here."

His eyes narrowed and the sparkle that was always in them left before I could take a drag on my Pall Mall. "You don't want to join the Marine Corps. You just think you do. That's what your daddy did an' look what happened to him."

"There ain't no war now, an' it's about my turn to serve the country like he did. An' like you an' all the others that was in the war."

"Let me tell you something, Sedwick, there was a helluva bunch of us that was in the service an' in that war you're talkin' about that didn't want to be there. We didn't have a choice like some of 'em, though. If we would've, I'll guarandamntee you that a lot of us wouldn't have been anywhere within ten thousand miles of where we ended up. But somebody had to go. It wasn't no picnic out there in the South Pacific or anywhere else where there was the fightin' goin' on."

We sat there smoking and talking until the rest of the kids started coming over for the lunch hour. From talking to him before, I knew Bart had been in the Army Air Corps and had been overseas for three years and away from home almost four. Most of the stories he told me was funny and sounded like he was having a good time. But he didn't think they was always so good.

"I did the same thing one time in trainin' here in the States to get out of it that you just did to get out of that study hall," he said, the glisten back in his eyes and the smile back on his face that I was used to seeing. "That was before I got in the Air Corps an' got shipped overseas. I got hooked up with an old boy from Mississippi named Joe Parsons who was always buggin' out. First time I noticed him much, we'd gone to the field for an exercise when the weather was cold, rainy an' miserable. He disappeared the first day. Never saw a thing of him for ten days. Then when we was hikin' in, here come old Parsons humpin' over a hill toward us. He was dirty, had ten days growth of beard an' looked like he was on his last legs. First Sergeant was goin' to run him up an' put him in the stockade. Parsons said he'd got lost an' had been wonderin' around the hills tryin' to find us. Everybody knew that was bullshit, but they couldn't prove a thing. He had some civvies stashed somewhere an' had sneaked off base for the whole time.

"Later, we was goin' out one mornin' on a long hike, an' old Parsons said he didn't need any marchin' an' dropped out. I followed him out of the formation at the edge of camp, an' we spent the day over at the slop chute. That evenin' when the company came marchin' back into camp, we slipped back into the formation. 'Course we got caught. By then we had orders for overseas an' didn't have time for the stockade. We spent the week before we left for California out in the field diggin' a hole. First Sergeant said he wanted it six feet wide, six feet long an' six feet deep.

"'Ought to bury you fuckin' malingers in that goddamn hole,' he said the first time we got one dug. 'That'd save everybody a lot of misery in the long run.' But then he'd look things over an' tell us that hole wouldn't do, to fill it up an' dig another one someplace else. That went on for a few days. Wasn't a bit of fun. That's when I asked for a transfer to the Air Corps an' got it."

I laughed and laughed while Bart was telling the story. It wasn't quite so funny after lunch. Old Harvey Pinther, the principal that I liked about as much as I did a bad cold, called me to his office and asked me where I'd been during study hall. When I told him that's where I'd been, he said I'd been marked absent. I told him I'd got sick and went to the toilet while the teacher had been talking to somebody at his desk. That was partly true. I had slipped out the south door of the auditorium while the teacher wasn't looking and had gone to the toilet. But then I'd gone over to the restaurant to talk to Bart. I didn't tell the principal that part of the story. Pinther smiled and gave me a week-long restriction to the school grounds and detention with him before school.

"Make sure you ask the study hall teacher the next time you have to use the toilet," he said. "That's the way things are done here."

"Yes, sir," I said, "I understand. I just didn't have time."

When I finally got back over to the restaurant the next week, Bart asked me where I'd been hiding. He had a big grin on his face, and I figured he knew what'd happened.

"I been diggin' holes," I said.

"That's just what I figured," he said, the big grin on his face spreading and getting bigger. "An' you want to join the Marines. You'd be diggin' holes all the time. I've got a better idea for you. I'm tryin' to get the company to adopt a plan to let the people they hire go on immediate retirement until they're thirty-five years old, then work until they die. That way you wouldn't have to waste the best years of your life workin' an' you wouldn't have to sit around on your ass with nothin' to do when you get old an' gray. That'd be better than goin' to the Marines."

"If the company takes you up on the idea an' they'll hire me right now," I said, going along with Bart, "I'll take it. But I'd still like to join the Marines first."

"That wouldn't be part of the deal."

Joining up wasn't something I talked with Mother about anymore. But I told Big one day when we was going someplace in the truck. He grunted and said I'd better stay away from the Marines.

"Better stay around here," he said. "By the time you're out of school, I should be in better shape an' have things lined up so you can farm with me the way your dad an' me planned to do back before the war. I think I'll be back on my feet enough by the time you're out of school that the bank'll go along with us. We can get some more ground an' make it pretty good."

I'd always thought about farming and trucking but not until I did my hitch in the Marines. It surprised me that Big had offered me the chance to work with him like him and Daddy was going to do. The idea had crossed my mind, although I'd never thought it'd be possible. I didn't know what to say. I knew it wouldn't bring Daddy back, but it'd make Big pretty happy to do something they'd planned to do a long time ago.

"That'd really be nice, Big," I finally said, almost choking up when I could talk. "It'd be just like you an' Daddy always planned, but I reckon I couldn't do it until I come back from the Marines myself. I'm afraid that if I'd say yes an' get started in figurin' on doin' that right after high school that I'd not be able to keep up with it. What if I'd get a wild hair an' take off an' leave you holdin' the bag after a while? That wouldn't be right. I want to get out an' see some other things before I settle down to farmin' an' livin' 'round here."

"You're just like Bill," Big said, a little smile on his face. I looked a little closer at him and saw that his eyes was watered up, not like he was going to cry but almost if he didn't hold back. "I hope you don't come back like he did."

"Don't worry about that, Big. I aim to come back an' farm with you, feed cattle an' drive trucks. That's all I ever wanted to do. Just like you an' Daddy planned on doin'."

"Maybe you'd better stay in the Marines," he said, smiling more now. "You've seen what feedin' cattle an' drivin' trucks does to a feller. Puts 'em in the poorhouse."

I knew we didn't have much money, but I never thought about us being in the poorhouse. We had plenty to eat and had a roof over our heads. The kids in town seemed to have more money than I did, but hardly any of them had cars of their own to drive. I wasn't old enough yet, but quite a few of the country kids had cars. Jim Wilson even had a new '54 Ford Victoria of his own. He was an only kid and raised his own hogs and had a little patch of his own to farm for his FFA project. I had a couple of hogs in a little lot in the back of the garden and would keep records on twenty acres of corn or beans for my project like the rest of the class would for the assignment, but Big had to have the money for the crops. They was mine only on paper.

Lots of things was like that. Like it was with me staying around Bellair and working and roaming the country on my bicycle. It was like the other boys and me owned the country for miles around because we went just about anyplace we wanted to go. And having all that didn't seem like we was poor.

Mother kept going to work at the store but started having days when she couldn't stay through the day. One Saturday when she was working to make up for missing a couple of afternoons, I stopped in about ten o'clock to see how she was getting along. She looked drawn and haggard but said she felt okay, just tired. I hung around for a few minutes and finally hopped on my bicycle and went up to Richard and Jerry's to see what they were doing. Aunt Helen had stopped to visit with Ruby, so they got their bikes out of the garage and rode off towards North Fork with me. We'd been riding down that way and going over to Madge's Old Mill and playing tag on the rafters. The one who was it would chase the others up the sides of the old building and all around and across the rafters until he caught everybody. Then the game would start over with the first one who got caught as it. Loose hay was scattered throughout the place, so when we ran the rafters and somebody got too close, we'd just jump or fall into the hay and scramble away. Madge was always afraid we'd get hurt playing there and didn't want us anywhere near the old building or anywhere on her place at all and had been told by somebody that we still went down there. At the path that led back to the Old Mill, I stopped and started to get my bike off of the road to hide and walk on back past the Old Bed to the Old Mill.

"Let's not go back there today, John Walter," Richard said. "Mom said Madge's been raisin' hell with her to keep us out of there. I promised Mom I wouldn't go back there anymore."

"What're we goin' to do then?" I asked. "Nobody's goin' to know we're back there. An' there ain't nothin' else to do today."

"Bub's right," Jerry said. "We promised Mom."

"We've all promised our mothers we wouldn't do a lot of things they don't want us to do," I said. "If we listened to them all the time, we'd never do anything fun. They want us to stay inside an' do housework like a bunch of fuckin' sissies."

"Let's go down to the bridge," Richard said, "an' see how high the crick is now. It was more 'n bank full after that rain last week."

The bridge always had been an attraction for us on that side of town, so I pulled my bike back out of the ditch and headed on down the hill with them. Bare-Ass Beach was a quarter of a mile north, but I never crossed the bridge but what I thought of the Halloween a couple of years ago that we stuffed an old pair of overalls and shirt with straw and lay it in the middle of the road where it curved in from the west to cross the bridge and tied a rope around the galluses and pulled it off in the ditch every time a car came along and slammed on its brakes when the driver saw the dummy in the road.

"'Member old Sterle Brandywine when he came along here drunk comin' home from Casey on that Halloween night?" I asked when we'd got there. Sterle'd lost an eye in a hunting accident after he'd come home from the war without a scratch and stopped by the tavern after work about every evening. He'd skidded his pickup right up to where the dummy lay and jumped out to see who he'd almost run over on the road. By the time he'd gotten to the front of his pickup, we'd pulled the dummy back in the ditch.

"Now goddamnit, boys," we'd heard him say and could hardly keep from laughing. We was only a few feet from him and thought he was talking to us. But Sterle always said boys when he was talking about anything. "I thought I saw somebody alayin' there in the goddamn road. An' I shore as hell didn't want to run over nobody an' kill 'em. But I don't see nobody. What the hell's agoin' on? I reckon I must be aseein' things again."

He rubbed his eyes and turned his head from side to side so he could see with his good right eye and then stopped to look under the pickup to see if he'd run over somebody, all the time mumbling about being afraid he'd run over somebody. I was beginning to feel bad about what we'd done and wished we hadn't. Sterle was a real good feller. He finally got back into his pickup and drove off real slow. That was the last time I played that trick but thought about it quite a bit. It was more dangerous than upsetting a toilet and wasn't the kind of trick that people around town laughed about and remembered the way they did about the time Coony Pfeiffer and his friends put Doc Ferguson's buggy up on the top of the store. I wished I had seen that. Coony told us about it one day but wouldn't admit to being one of the boys who'd done it. He'd just laugh when we asked if he was one of the boys. And he wouldn't tell us how anybody could get a buggy up on top of a two-story building.

"I 'member," Richard said about the Halloween trick we'd pulled on Sterle. "Wonder we didn't kill somebody the way they was slammin' on their brakes. Sometimes we ain't got no sense. Let's climb up the bridge. I've always wanted to climb to the top an' look around."

"Me, too," I said as we skidded to a stop in the gravel in front of the bridge and lay our bikes in the ditch by the edge of the road.

"Last one to the top is a nigger baby," Richard said.

The bridge had steel girders angling up to the top on both sides of the crick. Richard and me raced to the ones closest to us, leaving Jerry to cross the bridge to reach the one on the west side of the crick.

"This ain't fair, you fellers," Jerry said, running across the bridge in his slow, ambling gait that looked like an old plow horse who'd been turned out to pasture. "You got a head start."

Richard was wiry and quick. We reached the girders about the same time, but he was able to take ahold of the edge of the girder and stand with his rear end up in the air as he walked up to the top. I more or less scooted to the top on my knees with my toes curled to keep traction. He beat me by quite a bit, but Jerry couldn't get up either way and went over to the middle of the bridge to climb straight up on the upright girders, which had pieces of steel crisscrossing each other all the way to the top. We'd walked the length of the bridge standing up by the time he even got close to the top.

Looking down into the crick gave me a queasy feeling, but looking out through the trees into the bottom land made me feel like I was on top of the world. Richard was walking along the north side of the bridge like he was on the sidewalk that run most of the way around the square. He had his arms sticking straight out parallel to the crick for balance, a big grin on his face and a cigarette sticking out of the corner of his mouth with smoke curling up into his eyes as he walked along.

I wasn't quite so sure-footed and edged along in short steps, afraid I was going to fall any minute. About a quarter of the way back across the bridge, I saw Jerry stick his head up over the top straight ahead of me and climb up and stand on the girder. Richard turned and started across the cross beams that tied the bridge together at the top. They was more narrow than the side girders and wasn't something I'd try walking across. I figured I would fall right down on the floor of the bridge, if I did.

"Be careful, Jer," Richard said as Jerry started scooting his feet across the girder. "Don't look down. Just walk straight ahead an' take your time."

"I can't see where I'm goin', Bub," Jerry said, a whiny quiver in his voice. He'd gone three or four feet and suddenly stopped, frozen to the spot. "I'm scared. I'm goin' back."

"Stay put," Richard said. "I'll be right there."

He reached the south side of the bridge just as Jerry tried to turn around to go back, lost his balance and started falling. I sucked in air and watched him fall towards the crick, a long wailing scream following him all the way to the water below. He hit away from the bank on his side with his head slanted down and his left arm out in front of him. As he went under, I jumped off toward him and saw Richard out of the corner of my eye jump right behind me. Then I felt my feet hit the water and slam up against my legs and the rest of my body, and I went under. By the time I came up and got the water out of my eyes, I saw Jerry a few feet away, caught on some brush. The moving water of the crick pulled at his shirt, while his head laid still against the branches. Richard screamed out something I couldn't understand, and we both swam towards Jerry. I got to him first and saw a little blood trickling from his nose.

"Is he dead?" Richard asked shrilly, tears streaming from his eyes. "Please God, don't let my brother be dead."

"I don't know, but we got to get him out of the water an' worry about that later."

I don't remember much about the next few minutes. Richard was crying and praying and cussing all at the same time. We untangled Jerry from the brush and pulled him along downstream to a little sandbar where we could get him out of the water. I wasn't sure whether he was dead or just knocked out. I figured he was dead, but I wasn't going say so with the way Richard was acting. He kept crying and screaming after we'd pulled Jerry up on the sandbar and got him out of the water.

"Knock it off, Richard," I said. "That ain't helpin' nothin'. We need to get some help."

"It ain't your brother here!" he said, screaming at me. "Jerry's dead, an' you don't give a shit! We hadn't ought to have been up there on that damn bridge. We killed my little brother!"

"We didn't kill nobody," I said, thinking that he was the one who wanted to climb the bridge. "Just shut up."

Richard kept on hollering and crying until I finally backhanded him across the face with my right hand.

"Why, you sonuvabitch, you," he said. "You hit me."

"An' I'll hit you again, if you don't shut up. That fuckin' cryin' an' hollerin' ain't helpin' shit. Let's help Jerry. You stay here with him, an' I'll ride up to the store for help. Can you shut up an' stay with him while I'm gone?"

He nodded.

The slap to the face had stunned him enough that he had settled down and was just crying kind of quiet like. I started up the bank, slipped and fell back to the sandbar. When I got up, I picked my way up the bank and ran to the road. As I ran across the bridge to my bike, I stopped and looked down the crick to where Richard kneeled by Jerry.

"Don't worry, Richard, he's goin' to be okay. Don't move him anymore, an' I'll get some help."

On across the bridge, I jerked my bike from the ditch and headed back toward town, running along beside the bicycle until I was going as fast as I could run and then jumped on and rode up the hill. At the top, I saw the Chesty potato chip truck turn the corner from the store and head toward me. I slid to a stop and waited for the truck to reach me, waving wildly at Brad Irons.

"Hello, there, Young McElligott," he said, smiling. "I just asked your mother where you was."

"I need your help, Chesty. Jerry Owens fell off the bridge down yonder. We got him out of the water, but I don't know if he's dead or alive."

His eyes narrowed and he said, "Where is he?"

"Follow me," I said and turned my bike around and headed downhill. "I'll show you."

I raced across the bridge and turned in the little lane on the west side of the crick and saw Big's truck coming from the west with a load of lime from Casey. Chesty turned in the lane and flagged Big down. Both of them came running down the lane after me and skidded down the bank to where Richard sat stroking Jerry's face and crying softly.

"Please wake up, Jerry," he said. "Don't die, don't die."

Chesty put his big hand on the side of Jerry's neck and nodded to Big. "He's alive, Big," Chesty said. "Got a good pulse."

"He filled up with water?" Big asked, looking over at me.

"Don't think so," Chesty said. "The boys got him out of the water right away, but it looks like his collarbone is broke an' hard tellin' what else. I've got an old blanket in the truck we can use as a stretcher an' I've got some cardboard we can lay him on in my truck. I'll run him down to Oblong for Doc Bechtel to take a look at."

Chesty was up and running to his truck hardly before he'd finished talking. Big scooted around to get a better look and caught my eye.

"What 'n the devil was you fellers doin'?" Big said, growling like he did sometimes.

Richard kept his head down, still stroking his brother's face. I looked past Big's thick shoulders at Chesty hurrying back with an old Army blanket.

"We was walkin' up on the bridge," I said, nearly choking on my words. I knew they wasn't going to set well with Big.

"Clear up on top?"

I nodded.

"What 'n the Sam Hill was you doin' up there? Wonder all of you didn't fall in an' break your dang necks."

That got me to wondering if Jerry's neck might be broke. He hadn't moved since we drug him out of the water. I didn't even know if he was breathing until Chesty said he was. He slid down the bank, unfolded the blanket halfway and spread it out beside Jerry. Chesty kneeled down at Jerry's head.

"You get his feet an' legs, Big," Chesty said, putting Jerry's arms on his chest and then running a big hand under his head and shoulders. "We don't want to hurt him more than he already is, but we got to get him on the blanket."

Big nodded and slid his left arm under Jerry's back and right arm under his legs. Together the two men lifted Jerry and put him over on the blanket. He moaned just a little as they did, the first sound I'd heard from him since the awful scream he'd made falling from the bridge. Tears was still streaming down Richard's cheeks.

"Looks like there's a place down yonder a piece that's not quite so steep, Brad," Big said, pointing to an opening in the brush at the end of the sandbar. "We can get him out better down there an' not chance goin' up the bank here."

"Right," Chesty said. "He'll be okay as long as we don't drop him. I've got the back doors open an' the cardboard laid out to give him a little paddin'. Let's do it."

They lifted the blanket and started walking down the sandbar. Richard and me followed all the way and watched them lay Jerry in the truck.

"Can I come with you, Chesty?" Richard asked. "I want to be with my brother."

"Of course, you can come with me, Bud. We'll have to stop by an' get your mother, too. You can all go to the doctor with me."

Big motioned for me to get in the truck with him and told Chesty he'd go on ahead and tell Ruby. I started to ask about the bicycles, but Big already had the truck started and in gear before I could say anything. He had the truck and load of lime moving by the time I got the door closed. In the side mirror, I could see the Chesty truck back out of the lane and head toward us.

We all pulled to a stop in front of Richard and Jerry's house at the same time. I was glad of that. I knew Ruby'd want to be with Jerry, but I didn't want her not to see him right away, particularly with me there. I figured she'd go crazy when she found out what had happened. She was sitting in the porch swing smoking a cigarette when we stopped. Richard started bawling like a baby and hollering something about Jerry that I couldn't make out when he ran up the sidewalk toward her.

Ruby flipped her cigarette off in the yard and screamed, "Where's Jerry? Where's my baby? Oh, my god."

"Settle down, Ruby," Big said. "He's in the back of Brad's truck. The boys was climbin' on the bridge, an' Jerry fell. He's all right, but he's goin' to have to go to the doctor to see if he's got any broken bones an' what else might be wrong with 'im."

She let out another hoarse scream and ran to the truck. Chesty held the door so she could get in. Richard followed her. Both of them was crying pretty loud. I thought that'd bring Jerry around and wake him up, if anything would.

"Now don't move him, Ruby," Chesty said, looking in the back of the truck as Ruby bent over Jerry. "He's been knocked out an' it looks like his collarbone is broke. Maybe something else. But we got to let Doc figure that out. He's goin' to be okay."

I could still hear her crying and carrying on when Chesty shut the door and got in the truck. Chesty said something to Big that I didn't hear and started the truck.

"We'll tell Lorene an' then have Helen come to Bechtel's to get everybody or see what's goin' on," Big said as Chesty drove away. Then Big turned to me and said, "I don't know what 'n the devil you fellers was meanin' climbin' that fuckin' old bridge."

Nothing I could say would have made any difference, so I never said anything. We got in the truck and drove the rest of the way around the square to the store. I dreaded telling Mother what had happened as much as anything. She hadn't been feeling good the last few weeks, and I knew this was going to make her feel worse.

Aunt Helen, Nancy and Mary Beth was just getting out of the old Plymouth as Big rolled the truck to a stop at the side of the store. At least there'd be a crowd when Mother found out what had happened. I lagged behind everybody while we was walking into the store. Johnnie Larson, Ralph Crucell, Burns Larue and Ross Childers was back at the domino table playing forty-two. Ross was laughing and joking like he always did when he was playing. Johnnie and Ralph was partners, and they both cackled and laughed real loud when they played. Only Burns was quiet and seemed like he didn't know what was going on.

"Now, I'm goin' to bid forty-two, Burns," I heard Ross say while we filed down the aisle past the pop case to where Mother sit on a stool behind the cash register. "Are you goin' to help me or are you goin' to sit there an' let me go set?"

"Heeeeheeeehee," Ralph said, smoke from a Lucky Strike he held in the corner of his mouth drifting up into his eyes. "He's not agoin' to have much to do about that, Ross. Me an' Johnnie 're agoin' to see to it that you're agoin' set. Ain't that right, Johnnie?"

"That's right," Johnnie said between clenched teeth that held his old pipe and held his laugh to a little stuttering sound. "You ought t' know better than to try an' make forty-two agin me an' Ralph."

Ross laughed and slammed a domino down on the card table. "How 'bout that old double six?" he asked and flipped his engraved cigarette lighter open to light a Camel. "Can you beat it?"

"No," Ralph said, "but we only need one trick. An' I got a domino here for your loser sure as I'm sittin' here."

"If he don't, I do," Johnnie said, taking the pipe from his mouth. "You're set sure as the world."

Ross laughed. I could see him drag in the first trick and throw out the next domino as we stopped in front of Mother. Listening to the old men talk when they played forty-two was always real interesting to me, and I'd rather listen to them than do what I was going to have to do and listen to now.

While we walked up the aisle, Big had been telling Aunt Helen that Jerry had been hurt. He held back until I got to where he was and put his big hand on my shoulder, pulling me up to the counter in front of him.

"Tell your mother what happened," he said.

"Jerry got hurt," I said. "They're takin' him to the doctor."

Mother's face got whiter than it had been since she hadn't been feeling well. I just stood there. Big's grip tightened on my shoulder.

"Go on," he said. "Tell her what happened."

"Jerry fell off of the bridge."

"Oh, John Walter," Mother said. "How'd he do that? Is he hurt bad?"

"I don't know how bad he's hurt. But we was climbin' on the bridge, an' he lost his balance, I guess, an' fell into the water. We got him out, an' Chesty is takin' him to Doc Bechtel's office."

Ross must have heard what I was saying and came over to the counter in front of the pot-bellied stove that was always there in the middle of the store no matter what time of the year.

"Ruby know?" he asked. She was his half-sister, Mother had told me a long time ago.

"Her an' Richard went with Chesty."

"Game's over, boys," Ross said, hollering back at the forty-two table. "I'll go to Oblong an' see what's goin' on? Jerry hurt bad, Big?"

"I'm not sure. He was out cold an' Brad thinks he's got a broken collarbone, anyway. Maybe more. He fell clear from the top of that dang bridge, an' the boys drug him out. Hard to tell how bad he's hurt."

Mother's face turned even whiter, and she settled back on the stool. I went behind the counter and put my arms around her. She threw her arms around me and hugged me real tight.

"Oh, John Walter," she said. "Oh, John Walter. How could you boys be climbin' up on that old bridge? It's a wonder you didn't all fall off."

I felt her slump in my arms and her body go limp. That scared me. Big and Aunt Helen evidently saw what was happening because they both rushed around the counter and got on either side of Mother to make sure she didn't fall.

"Lorene," Aunt Helen said. "Lorene. Get back, John Walter. She's fainted, Bob. She's fainted. Let's get her over to one of the benches and get her head down between her legs."

I got back and let Aunt Helen and Big take Mother to the bench in front of the stove. Ross hurried on out the door and said he'd see about Jerry and Ruby and bring them back home. The fellers at the forty-two table got up and went out on the porch. Aunt Helen went to get a cold rag.

"Is she all right, Big?" I asked. "Is my mother all right?"

When he didn't answer, I thought the worst. He sat her down on the bench in front of the stove and let her back bend at the waist with her head resting on her knees. Aunt Helen said that and a cold rag on the back of her neck would bring her around. And it did after a while. I heard her groan and then she sat up.

"What happened?" she asked, looking like a punch-drunk fighter who'd had one too many blows to the head. Then she saw me standing before her at the stove. "Oh, John Walter. What if you'd been killed?"

"It was Jerry who fell," I said.

"Just calm down, Lorene," Big said. "John Walter's right here, an' Jerry's on his way to the doctor. Take a deep breath an' don't worry about what might've been. That don't do no good."

Aunt Helen was sitting on the other side of Mother on the bench, wiping her face with the wash rag and talking to her real soft.

Mother's face was nearly chalk white, and she looked like I'd never seen her look before.

"I think we'd better take you to the doctor, Lorene," Aunt Helen said. "Go get Arletta, John Walter, and tell her that we're taking your mother to the doctor right now and we need her to mind the store."

"I'm all right, Helen," Mother said. "I'm just tired."

"Something's making you tired. Let's find out what it is."

I ran all the way to Horsey and Arletta's house and told her to come to the store so Mother could go to the doctor. Arletta said she had a pie in the oven and couldn't come until the pie was done. But when I explained to her what had happened to Jerry and to Mother, Arletta said she'd take the pie out and be right there. Nancy and Mary Beth could stay with Cheryl, Arletta said as I was leaving. By the time I got back up to the store, they had Mother in the car ready to go. The girls was standing on the porch, looking kind of scared. Aunt Helen sat in the back seat of the old Plymouth with Mother, so I slipped in the front seat beside Big. Arletta and Cheryl was just rounding the corner, walking real fast, and met us as we passed the church. Big rolled the window down and told her we would be back from Doc Bechtel's when we could.

Mother laid with her head on the back of the seat and her eyes closed all the way to Oblong. I sat half turned in the seat and kept my eyes on her all the way to town. Nobody said a word until we pulled up in front of the doctor's office and parked beside Chesty's truck. I'd almost forgotten about Jerry until I saw the truck. Ross' shiny new Chrysler was parked on the other side.

Ross and Chesty was in the waiting room when we walked in. Both of them jumped up when they saw us. Aunt Helen took Mother on back to a room to wait for Doc Bechtel while Big talked to Ross and Chesty.

"I'm goin' to have to get on an' finish my route," Chesty said. "Jerry came around a little on the way down here. I think he's goin' to be okay. Looked to me like he had that collarbone broke an' maybe his arm. Doc brought a stretcher out to get him out of the truck, an' old Jerry hollered to beat the band when they loaded him up. That's a good sign."

About that time, old Doc Bechtel stuck his head out the door. He was a stocky, thick-shouldered feller who looked meaner than a old boar hog that was all riled up. Aunt Helen said Doc had a bedside manner that would scare anybody out of being sick. But then everybody said his bark was a lot worse than his bite. He had a thick mustache and a swarthy complexion that I thought made him look more like a Turkish warlord than an old country doctor.

Everybody had a story to tell about him. The one I liked best was about him being offered a job at the Johns Hopkins University Hospital someplace back East and him turning it down to be a country doctor who still made house calls. And everybody said he was sharper than a tack about real life things, too.

"What the hell's goin' on up there in Bellair?" he said gruffly. "Everybody gettin' hurt or sick all at once? The boy's pretty lucky he didn't break his goddamn neck. Broke his goddamn collarbone an' his right arm. Must've landed on that side. He's still a little squirrelly, but I think he's okay. Takes a lot to kill a kid. I'm goin' to keep him back there for a while an' see if there's any internal injury. He's goin' to be sore as hell for a while."

Just as quick as he'd opened the door, he shut it and was gone. After Chesty left, Big, Ross and me sat there for à long time before Doc came out again. This time, he wasn't quite so gruff and didn't talk so rough. Ruby and Richard followed him, pushing Jerry in a wheelchair.

"Boy's goin' to be okay," he said. "I've got the bones set an' he's not quite as goofy as he was before. Take him home an' put him to bed for a couple of days. I'm not quite so sure about Lorene. She's pretty sick, but I haven't figured out what's wrong with her. I'll send some blood off to the lab an' see what it looks like. Bring her back in a couple of days."

Doc left the waiting room without saying anything else. Ross took Jerry outside to the car and brought the wheelchair back inside the clinic. Just as he came back in, Aunt Helen brought Mother out. She was pale and seemed to need Aunt Helen to hold her up so she could keep walking. I hurried to her side and took her other arm. Together we walked to the car. I was scared like I'd never been scared before. We didn't talk much on the way home. Mother leaned over to me in the back seat. I put my arm around her and held her all the way to Bellair. Her being sick like she seemed to be scared me more than Jerry falling off the bridge.

20

Mother never went back to work at the store. For a while, Aunt Helen worked in her place and Dad Garner looked after Mother and the girls. But it wasn't long before Mother needed help getting around, stayed in bed most of the time and Arletta started working at the store so Aunt Helen could take care of Mother. She didn't eat much and lost so much weight that she was little more than skin and bones. Doc Bechtel couldn't find out what was wrong with her and sent her to a specialist in Terre Haute where they run more tests without ever finding out what was wrong.

"It's in the Lord's hands, I reckon," Mother told me one morning when I sat on her bed and talked to her before I caught the bus for school.

"He ain't takin' care of things very good, it don't look like to me," I said. Everybody was always saying things went according to God's plan. I never understood that. It seemed to me that a lot of it was just luck and chance like Sam always told me it was about how he made it through the war. A feller could do the best he could, he said, and from there on out it was just pure luck. Mother didn't go to church much, so I was a little surprised at what she said about things being in the Lord's hands. It looked more like bad luck to me.

"Whatever'll be, will be," she said. "That's what I always figured about what happened to your daddy."

"What if he hadn't joined the Marines?"

"Well, he was supposed to join the Marines."

"He decided that."

"That was supposed to be, I reckon."

That didn't make any sense to me, but I didn't say any more. By that way of thinking, I reckoned I would join the Marines or not join the Marines, according to whether it was supposed to be.

But everybody was always telling me not to join as though I could choose. And Jerry had only had a broken collarbone and arm besides being bruised up pretty much all over. That's the way he hit the water. If he'd have hit it some other way, he'd have got hurt in a different way, maybe even got killed. That was luck, I figured, pure luck, not a part of God's or somebody's plan. I kissed Mother and told her I hoped she got to feeling better.

"That's part of a plan I'd like to see work out," I said.

She smiled and told me she loved me as I went off to catch the bus for school. I saw through the window that it was coming around the corner and wished that it would just go on by. I'd really wanted to play football and basketball when I started to school, but when Mother got sick, I soon lost interest. In fact, I lost interest in anything connected with school after that and stayed home when I could. Maybe that was supposed to be, too, I thought. My grades was about as bad as they could get. For the first part of my freshman year, I was flunking English, history, algebra, even P.E. and just scrapping by with Ds in everything else. I flunked P.E. by getting kicked out of the class for fighting.

One day after Mother had been particularly sick but asked me to go to school, a big senior named Mike Young that I didn't like on my good days bumped into me in the locker room and elbowed me when I didn't get out of his way fast enough to suit him. I jumped across a bench and knocked him back into a locker and began hitting him wildly, mostly on the arms and shoulders. He was surprised at first, and I got in several blows before he was able to push me away and get up to start hitting back. By that time, Bill Smith, the football coach who taught the P.E. class, came running out of his office and broke us apart. After he got both sides of the story, he sent us to the office.

On the way, a couple of kids who'd been in the locker room walked along behind us and laughed at Mike. "Looks like old John Walter was about to kick your ass all over the place," one of them said. Both of them laughed real loud then.

"Come on across the street in the mornin' to see who kicks whose ass," Mike said. "If he ain't too much of a chickenshit to meet me over there in the mornin', I'm goin' to kick his skinny ass all over the place."

"Fuck you, Young," I said. "I'll be there. Don't worry about that.

We'll see who's goin' to kick whose ass. The only thing that's bad about you is your big fuckin' mouth."

We was at the principal's office by then, and Mike just glared at me. I was ready to go at it again.

Old Harvey Pinther made us stand in front of his desk and listen to his lecture about being good little boys, then he sent us to the study hall and told us to stay there for the rest of the week. I didn't mind P.E. class, but I liked the study hall better because it was in the library where I could sit at a table and read a western book or a war novel by sticking a paperback between the pages of some kind of school book and pretend to study. Sometimes I got caught and lost the book because the teachers didn't want me, or any student, reading paperbacks in school. I never understood that.

"I'll meet you across the street in the mornin' after the buses come in," Mike said on the way to study hall. "Then we can settle this off the school grounds. If you ain't a chickenshit."

"I told you I'll be there. You don't have to worry about that or about me bein' a chickenshit. You'll probably have your mommie call you in sick in the mornin' so you won't have to be there."

Mike glared at me again but didn't say anything as we walked into the study hall. Word spread around school the rest of the day about the fight that was going to take place between me and Mike over at the little store the next morning. I acted big and brave, but I was scared of what would happen. For the rest of the day and that night, all I could think about was fighting Mike Young. He was three years older and was bigger and stronger than me and outweighed me by thirty or forty pounds. I remembered old Jim Richards kicking Fred Campbell's ass over in the restaurant and pool hall in Porterville a long time ago and what Sam had told me about fighting that bully in his outfit back during the war. I figured I had to keep Mike away from me like Sam said he had to keep the feller from getting in a haymaker that'd knock anybody out and not let Mike get too close and get ahold of me. I knew I had to box, jab and punch like old Sugar Ray Robinson did with all the fellers he fought in the ring. I knew I wasn't Sugar Ray, but I knew how he fought and would try to fight the same way.

I was more quiet than usual at home that night. Big asked me if anything was wrong. I told him I was just tired and had things on my mind.

By the next morning, I was a bundle of nerves, but I had my plan down and went directly to the store after I got off of the bus. Young was already there, and there must have been twenty-five or thirty other kids there, waiting for the show.

"Well, there's the little chickenshit," Mike said when he saw me coming across the street. "I didn't think you'd show up, chickenshit. You ready to get your ass kicked?"

I didn't say anything. My heart was beating like a race horse on the back stretch in the Kentucky Derby, and I was afraid of what I'd say and how I'd sound, if I said anything. Wasn't anything to say, anyway. We walked to the north side of the little store and squared off. Young threw a wild punch at me. I stepped back a little, turned my head to the side to avoid his fist and jabbed a left hand toward his nose. It wasn't a hard punch, but it landed right square on the tip of his big hawk-like nose and brought tears to his eyes.

"Why, you little sonuvabitch," he said as a little blood trickled down his lip. "I oughta kill you."

I snapped another left jab out and caught him on the mouth that time. He swung wildly again with a haymaker, which I kept away from by turning my head and leaning back. Again, I threw a left jab and my fist smacked into his face right below his right eye. He'd swung wildly every time, and I'd have to step back or turn away to keep his swing from connecting. Kids was hollering and laughing as Young and me swung at each other. Blood was trickling from his nose and his lips was puffed up where I'd connected a couple of times already.

After I kept jabbing and hitting him but not getting hit myself, I began feeling a bit more confident and planned to catch him on the point of the chin with a right cross the next time he swung wildly. I saw the wild swing coming again and didn't turn as much or step back as much as I had at other times before I jabbed. But this time his wild left hand grazed my left eyebrow because I wasn't out of range. I felt his class ring cut into my eyebrow and felt the warm blood streaming down the side of my face.

"You sonuvabitch," I said, lowering my head and rushing toward him like a charging linebacker. I hit him about the belt buckle and drove him to the ground. Almost immediately, I realized my mistake. Young was much stronger than me, threw me off and was on top of me before

I knew what happened. I saw him draw back a fist to hit me in the face and rolled my head away from where I thought the punch would land. I knew I was in big trouble. But then I saw old Coach Smith reach down and grab the back of Mike's shirt and pull him off of me.

The coach took us both by the shirt collar and shoved and pulled us across the street toward the school and the principal's office. He took one look at us and told us we were out of school for three days.

"I'll call your parents to come an' pick you up," Pinther said. "John Walter, it looks like you'll have to go to the doctor to get that eye sewed up. I'll call your mother — "

"Leave my mother out of this," I said. "She ain't able to go no place."

"I'll call Bob then."

"He's in the field."

"Who do you want me to call then?"

"Don't call nobody."

"Somebody has to come an' get you an' take you to the doctor an' on home. You can't stay here."

"Put me in jail or do whatever you want to do. I don't care one way or the other," I said and stared at him as I took my handkerchief and pressed it against my eyebrow to help stop the bleeding. Pinther told us to sit down and wait in the outer office while he called our parents. Young glared at me as he wiped the blood from his nose and mouth but didn't say anything.

Twenty minutes later, Aunt Helen walked into the office.

"What in the world is goin' on?" she said.

I got up and walked toward her but didn't say anything. Young's mom and dad came in about the same time Aunt Helen got there. Young glared at me as he started telling them what had happened. I glared back and walked out through the door from Pinther's office, hoping I'd never have to come back to the school. But I knew I probably would for a while yet.

"Let me see that cut, John Walter," Aunt Helen said, taking my hand and my handkerchief away. "That looks awful. Your mother is beside herself wonderin' what's the matter with you."

"Ain't nothin' the matter with me. I just ain't goin' to let nobody push me around like old Mike Young thought he was goin' to do. Nobody. That ain't goin' to happen."

"You're so much like your daddy it ain't even funny."

"That's the best thing anybody's said about me for a hundred years. I'll bet he'd have done the same thing I did."

"Probably would have. Doc Wilhoit asked me one time after Lorene and me started going with your daddy and Bob if they was part of that fighting McElligott bunch down there by Moonshine. I didn't know what he was talking about then. But I reckon you're part of them."

Aunt Helen kept talking as we walked to the car and then as she drove the old Plymouth down through town and turned in at Doc Bechtel's office a few blocks away.

"What're we doin' here?" I asked.

"You've got to get that cut sewed up. It's spread open like a bad cut. You can see the bone."

I turned the rear-view mirror around so I could see. She was right. I saw what looked like bone through the open cut and felt queasy to my stomach. At the same time, I felt kind of proud that I was going to have a scar from fighting. I wondered if Daddy would be proud of me.

Aunt Helen told the receptionist what had happened, and we sat down in the waiting room. A few minutes later, Doc Bechtel stuck his head out the door and looked at me.

"Been fightin', I hear," he said, his eyes looking hard and big through the thick glasses. "Got your ass kicked."

"No, I didn't get my ass kicked. I was kickin' his when I got this. It was the only time he hit me. An' that was a lucky damn punch."

"Life's always a lucky punch. Get in here an' let's take a look at that goddamn thing."

Aunt Helen got up to come with me. I started to say something about her coming, but Doc Bechtel cut me off.

"You need somebody to nursemaid you," he said. "Come on in, Helen. You'll probably have to hold his hand."

"I don't need nobody to hold my hand."

Doc never said anything as he led us into a small room and shut the door behind us. I'd never been to see him for anything before, never even been inside a doctor's office except to old Doc Bates for an exam to go to school until Jerry fell off the bridge.

"Sit up there on the table an' let's get that thing sewed up," he said and started cleaning the cut with something that stung like anything. "Looks like he got you pretty good."

"He got me with a wild swing an' cut me with his class ring," I said, eyeing the needle and catgut thread he was going to use to sew the cut and feeling the burning, stinging sensation growing from whatever it was he was using to clean the cut. "Ain't you goin' to give me anything to numb me up there while you sew that up?"

"Why in the hell would I do that? You're tough enough to get in a goddamn fight; you ought to be tough enough to get sewed up without anything to numb your thick, goddamn head. That's numb, anyway. Number 'n anything."

"I just thought — "

"You don't think. That's your problem. Now just shut the hell up an' let me get this little cut sewed up before you start cryin' for your mommie like a little baby."

"You don't have to worry about that, Doc. Just get the sonuvabitch sewed up an' let me get out of here."

"That's enough, John Walter," Aunt Helen said. "Be quiet."

I couldn't see what Doc Bechtel was doing because I had my eyes closed, but I could feel him stick a needle of some kind through the skin on my eyebrow and pull the catgut thread through and tighten it, then come in from the other side.

"Looks like it'll take about five stitches," he said. "He got you pretty good for a lucky punch."

I felt a sting every time he stuck the needle in and more when he pulled the cut together and started over. But I just gritted my teeth. He was rough as he could be, I was sure, and he wasn't any different when I went back a week or so later and had the stitches taken out.

"There you are, Palooka," Doc said when he'd tied the catgut in a little knot and snipped off the end. "You'll have a nice little scar there for a while. Makes you look like a bad ass. You'd probably like that."

"Not particularly," I said. That wasn't exactly true, but I didn't see any benefit in being honest with him.

Aunt Helen went out to pay the bill, and Doc put his hand down on my shoulder when I started to get up and follow her. He told me to stay behind and closed the door. It wasn't noon yet, and I knew the waiting room had fellers waiting to see him.

"Don't worry about them," Doc said when I mentioned his other patients. "I want to talk to you. Nobody out there goin' to die right away. Least I don't think they are."

He sat down in the chair at his desk and opened his white jacket, exposing his protruding belly. His glasses was down on the end of his nose, and he peered out over them at me, thumbs hooked in his galluses. He pursed his lips, and the full dark mustache turned bottom out. I laughed and told him he was beginning to look like Albert Schweitzer.

"Wish I were as good as he is," Doc Bechtel said and put his hands behind his head. "But it's you I want to talk about, not some guy off in the African countryside. It's what's happenin' here that I'm concerned about, what's happenin' with you. You see, I had an instructor once who taught a deterministic philosophy, that you are what you are because of what you've been an' what you've done, an' there ain't a goddamn thing you can do about it. That's just your lot in life, your burden to bear. Now you've had a pretty rough hand dealt to you in life. But the philosophy of the Christian religion, which is the basis of our culture, is free will, that you have choices. I think the real answer lies somewhere between the two."

I wasn't sure what any of this had to do with me, but I sat still and listened. I was surprised to learn he'd been a Corsair pilot in the Marine Corps during the war and got shot down just off the coast of China just about the time the war was over. The Chinese had picked him up out of the ocean and took him to shore, where he was determined to stay.

"Now they tried to get me back to the ship," Doc said. "I told them I had no desire to get back to that goddamn ship, that I'd just get another plane an' have to fly more missions. I was only twenty-two years old but felt like I was a hundred. I didn't want to fly more missions. I'd had enough of that shit to last me a lifetime. An' they didn't take me back to the ship. I stayed there a couple of weeks an' when the war was over, I grabbed me a Jap soldier for a driver an' drove around the region in an old Plymouth convertible."

Doc stopped and laughed. Before he went on, he lit a cigarette. I started to ask him for one but stopped because I knew he wouldn't give it to me, and I didn't want him to have the chance to tell me no.

"I rode around the island to see what was goin' on for several days before the Americans got there. I'd stand up on the front seat, holdin' onto the windshield an' wavin' my .45 around like that fuckin' Patton. The Japs an' the Chinese both thought I was crazy. An' I probably was. Point is I chose to not go back aboard ship because I'd had enough of war. That war or any war. It was my choice, but I made that choice because of what I was an' where I'd been. An' that's what I wanted to bring to your attention regardin' your behavior."

"What do you mean? My behav — "

"Your behavior is a result of your own choices but also because of what you are an' where you've been, somewhere between that deterministic philosophy my old instructor taught an' the free will Christianity teaches. Your father's death before you remember is an' was a terrible thing. An' now your mother's health the way it is compounds that. Your actin' out by fightin' an' gettin' into trouble at school won't help a thing. If you keep it up, it'll just get worse an' you'll end up in more trouble than you can handle. Don't get me wrong. I'm not suggestin' that school is what it's cracked up to be at all, because I don't think it is. It's more babysittin' than anything. But you have to live an' get by where you happen to be right now."

"I'm goin' to join the Marines."

"Oh, that's a good choice. That's just what I've been tellin' you. You make the choices, but the choices are the result of the hand you got dealt. You think joinin' the Marine Corps will make everything okay when it'll only get you in deeper shit."

I slouched back in the chair and frowned at Doc. What he was saying was interesting, but I didn't see what any of it had to do with me. I didn't start the fight, and I didn't have anything to do with my daddy getting killed or my mother dying of some strange disease. All I was trying to do was just get by the best way I could in a world I didn't understand.

"Nothin' you say makes any sense about me," I said, looking at the door and wanting to get out, "if that's what you're tryin' to do. It's easy for you to sit there an' talk; it ain't so easy to have to live my life. You don't know nothin' about it."

Doc looked at me for a full minute before he spoke, his lips pursed and his mustache turned bottom out again. And before he said anything, he put his hands together in front of his face and looked at them while he pressed his fingers together.

"Well, let me put things another way," he said. "When I didn't know for sure whether I was going into medicine or law — an' I didn't decide on medicine until after the war, an' I saw what a fix the world was in — I took a course in English constitutional history. There were two or three hundred hangin' offenses at the time. One of them was pick-pocketin'. They executed people publicly, an' people came for miles around for the festive occasion, sort of like a carnival or a county fair.

"At the hangin' of the pickpocket, a lot of people got their goddamn pockets picked. Now that ought to tell a man something. I think that man hasn't changed, basically, since the day he shot craps for Christ's clothes. An' I don't think he's going to change. If Christ came back here today, they'd put him in a fuckin' electric chair instead of puttin' him up on a cross. An' then when we venerated him, we'd put an electric chair on the churches instead of a cross. I'd wear a little miniature electric chair around my neck instead of a little cross."

"What in the world does Jesus Christ gettin' electrocuted have to do with me? I ain't even Catholic an' don't wear no danged cross."

"I'll get to that," Doc said, smiling a little. "I think man is inherently defective; I think he's inherently selfish; I think he's inherently power hungry an' rebellious. A combination of those things cause some people to be anti-social, whether it's a violation of the law or not. With your background, you've got the right elements to go along with the basic imperfections of man to find trouble. More trouble than you'll want. But whether it materializes in you, I think you'll find the same criminal personality also commits other anti-social acts. I think there's some common threads runnin' through there that have been in every civilization. I don't know of a single civilization that has ever, ever, ever erased crime. Or poverty. Or war."

Pausing for a minute, Doc took his glasses off and rubbed his eyes. He told me that he'd read once about a bank robber on the way to rob a bank had stopped and helped an old lady across a street. He said he believed that people who commit crimes see themselves as just people, that they have some rationale for why they committed a particular crime.

"You aren't a criminal, but you've committed an infraction in the school that you've rationalized about, an' that behavior leads to more infractions an' criminal behavior. But you know, I've always had trouble with the definition of criminal. I don't have trouble with it, but I find that my definition isn't always the same as other people's. Are you a criminal if you commit a criminal act? Are you a criminal if you're caught? Are you a criminal if you're caught an' convicted? Or are you a criminal if you're caught an' convicted an' incarcerated?

"Now some people will draw a line between all of them. Philosophically, I think a criminal is a person who has committed a crime. If that's the case, show me a person who isn't a criminal. Show me who ought to carry the key."

The phone buzzed. Doc picked it up. "Yes," he said. "I'm with a patient now. Check with me later." He hung the phone back on the cradle and started talking again.

"But you know you get into white-collar crime, or group crime — like war is a group crime, in my opinion. I think merchants who are guilty of consumer fraud are just as bad as a guy who holds you up. You go buy something that's represented as one thing, an' it turns out to be a whole lot less than that. Isn't that deception? An' isn't deception a crime? The trouble is that I see crimes around me all the time. Yet no one is ever prosecuted for them. An' they're not labeled as criminals. As a matter of fact, in our materialistic society we encourage people to get things. An' we really don't care by what means. When we exalt a man because he has a million dollars an' everybody looks up to him because he has money, I think we're punchin' an' pickin' at that festerin' sore even more. An' I think there is a criminal personality in mankind. Now I haven't read research that supports that or found a book on the subject, but I think you'll find certain things that run through most of these personalities."

I still didn't see how anything he was saying applied to me, so I asked him to tell me what those "certain things" happened to be. I wondered if I had them or if he thought I had them.

"Rebellion against authority at early ages is one of the most common traits," he said, hesitating and looking me straight in the eyes as he spoke. "Incorrigibility, risk-taking, livin' off life rather than in it. Having the need for attention an' that sort of thing. We all have some of these traits, but it's a matter of degree. It's a big problem, though. I don't know the answers. The more I know, the more I know I don't know anything an' nobody else does. I hate to toss in the sponge an' give up.

I want to read research on the criminal personality an' find whether the research supports what I kind of believe.

"Right now, though, I just wanted to talk with you an' tell you that I hope you think about these things as you go through your life. As I said, you've had a rough go of it so far. But that's just the beginning. I hope you don't think you're the only one; I hope you try to get along an' not fall by the wayside. I knew your father; he was a good man, a helluva good man, but he ain't here; I know your mother; she is a good woman, but she may not be here long. That's the way it is; that's where you come from. But where you go from here is up to you. That's your choice, I think, by an' large, anyway. Not totally, but by an' large. Now I've got some patients to attend to. Go an' get the hell out of here. Just take care of yourself an' watch out."

Doc shook hands with me, patted me on the back and shoved me out the door. He'd given me a lot to think about. Aunt Helen was waiting for me, and we headed home. I tuned her out as she drove up the wide gravel toward Grandma Mary Elizabeth's house and didn't think about where she was going until she stopped at the Sycamore, a forty-acre field Big said was called that because of the old sycamore tree standing back near the west edge. Big was disking corn stalks, getting the field ready for plowing.

"What the devil's wrong now?" he asked after he'd shut off the tractor and came over to the edge of the road. "What's that cut over your eye?"

I told him.

"How's the other feller look? He have to have any stitches?"

"No, but I bloodied his nose an' lip. He got in a lucky punch. Just hit me once."

"Looks like one was all he needed. That's what luck'll do for you. Next time you get in a fight, you better have some luck 'r you'll wish you had when you get home. Get the ax out of the truck an' get the sprouts cut down there on the west side of the field. An' throw the limbs from the old sycamore up under the tree. I think there's another pair of gloves there on the floorboard of the truck. Now get. I ain't got time for this kind of shit."

I left him talking to Aunt Helen. I knew there was no use to argue with him. My head was throbbing as I got the ax, put it over my shoulder like a rifle and marched off toward the west fence row. I cut sprouts for the three days I was out of school and never got to sleep in or stay up late like I thought I would.

"I've cut a lot of fence rows an' know how much a feller can cut in a day," Big said the first morning at six o'clock when he woke me and told me Aunt Helen had a dinner pail and a Thermos jug ready for me. "An' if you don't do the job, you're not goin' to like it a bit when I pick you up at quittin' time."

I was always tired at quitting time and was happy to see him coming to take a look at how much brush I'd cut and piled each day. Big never told me I'd cut enough or said that I'd done a good job. But he never said anything else, either, and never said another word to me about the fight. That was good enough for me.

Mother didn't say much about the fight, either. But I could tell from the look in her eyes that she was hurt. She was in bed most of the time now. Doc Bechtel or none of the doctors still knew what to do with her except keep her in bed.

"Please be a good boy for me, John Walter," she said every time I went to her bedside to tell her goodbye. "That'll be some help to me."

I'd tell her I'd be good, then I'd go off and not keep my promise and get in trouble or do something stupid. Big and Aunt Helen didn't know what to do with me and talked until they was blue in the face, as Big said. He thought keeping me working would help. And I suppose it did some, but I still acted up.

Big put me out working with Dad Garner anytime it was possible. From the time I could remember, he'd told me the story about how he had come to see me on the morning I'd been born. It'd been raining that morning, he said, had been for two days, one of those spring rains that starts with a big thunderstorm and smooths out into a steady rain after a while. We lived on a dirt road, a quarter of a mile off of the gravel road, and back up a lane. When Dad told me the story anymore, it seemed as though there was a tinge of remorse in his voice, as though he was sorry for having made the trip to see his first grandson at all.

Dad was more than eighty years old now and the labors of eighty summers under the boiling sun had made his hands and face tanned and weathered like old shoe leather. Beneath his gartered sleeves, his arms was milk-white like the rest of his body.

Leaning on his hoe one day the spring before when we was replanting corn where the planter had skipped, Dad said, "Aaawwwww, boy,
you don't sow corn; you drop a kernel or two every eight to ten inches.
I'm just makin' a row here so we can replant what didn't come up.

"It don't make no difference," I said and skipped up and down the
rows of growing corn while Dad leaned on the hoe. "It won't come
up, anyway. If it does, we can just chop it out."

"What do you think Robert had us go to the trouble of replantin'
this corn for? He wants it done right."

"How do you know what Big wants?"

"He told me," Dad said.

"What'd he tell you?"

"He told me — "

"What was it like when you was a boy, Dad? What did you want
to be when you growed up?" I asked, interrupting him and trotting
ahead in a slight crouch, stringing corn in a row made by Dad's hoe.
When I reached the end of the row, I jumped over to the next row and
started back in the other direction, stringing the corn behind me to get
rid of what I had.

"It was a good deal different than it is now, I can tell you that. My
pa would have set me on my backend, if I even thought of actin' like
you do."

Dad bent over and slowly and methodically drug the extra kernels
out, leaving them in the middle of the rows where they would wither
and die. He covered only a kernel or two at a time in the row, spacing
the hills eight to ten inches apart.

"You won't ever amount to a hill of beans, I'm afraid," Dad said,
still working while I looked on. He didn't like to have to do needless
work, but I knew he was proud that he could still do a day's work at
his age. "When I was ten years old, younger than you by three or four
years, anyway, I was shuckin' corn, cuttin' wood, threshin' an' I don't
know what all for fifty cents a day. You can't even drop corn like I tell
you to. You might as well go back to the truck an' let me finish this."

"I'm done," I said. "See? The sack is empty."

"Yeah, you're done all right. But I've got to drag all the wasted
corn out an' that takes longer than it would have taken me to do it
myself in the first place."

"You don't want me to help you, I won't," I said and threw the empty sack to the ground and stomped off to the pickup.

"Whoa, dynamite, whoa there," Dad said, leaning on the hoe again and looking into the setting sun. He took his hat off and wiped the sweat from his forehead before he spoke again. "It just beats the life out of me why I ever walked out in the rain an' mud to see you. If I'd have known you was goin' to turn out like a wild man, I'd have stayed home. Can't tell you a thing."

I kept walking back to the pickup and never answered. It wasn't that I didn't like Dad. I liked him very much. It was that I didn't like to work much anymore. Not like I used to, anyway. I couldn't understand how anyone liked to work. And I got as tired of hearing about it as I did of doing it.

Dad didn't seem that way. When he no longer worked in the field all day, he worked in the garden or helped out any way he could, like replanting the skips in the corn. Then he began making peach-seed baskets. He collected the seeds, dried them and carved the upper half of the hard outer shell of the seed away. It was a slow process, and it took a sharp knife. Dad had the time and worked at it for hours on end. When the shell was carved away, he took the seed from the shell. But he still wasn't done. He carved more, taking a bit from here and there, until it suited him. After that, he sanded the shell and polished the outside with a cloth until it had a dull shine to it. On others, he applied a coat or two of varnish. Anybody who came to visit Dad got a peach-seed basket. He enjoyed making the baskets and giving them away, telling everyone he hoped they enjoyed receiving them and would keep them.

I knew fellers took notice of the kind of work anybody did. But I had a hard time understanding why Dad'd spend all that time working on the baskets and then give them away. Then Garvey Charles braked his old Allis Chalmers to a stop in front of the house and squinted into the afternoon sun late one day not long after Dad and me had replanted the corn and helped me understand again about how a feller could like his work and be proud of it.

"Hi, Garvey," I said. "How're you?"

Garvey didn't say anything for a minute. He cocked one leg up on the left back tire and reached for his papers. A can of Prince Albert was already in his right hand. He slipped a paper out of the package with a work-thickened thumb and forefinger before tucking it back in his pocket. As he fashioned a paper with his left, Garvey flipped open the top of the Prince Albert can and run another thick finger into the can to loosen the tobacco.

I watched the old man as he rolled the cigarette. A pile of tobacco lay heaped in the middle of the paper. Garvey closed the lid and put the can back in his hip pocket. He leveled the pile of tobacco and twisted the cigarette between his old thumb and forefinger.

"You want a job, boy?" he asked, looking up from the cigarette before licking the paper to seal the smoke.

"Yeah — "

"Now, by god, I mean a job," Garvey said and licked the paper with a quick flick of his protruding pink tongue. "I don't mean nothin' else."

"What kind of a job?" I asked.

Garvey looked down at me again, then flashed a box match out of his overalls and scratched a gnarled thumbnail over it. He held the match to the cigarette between his lips.

"A hard job," he finally said, blowing the rich blue smoke out of one side of his mouth. He rubbed the three-day-old growth of graying beard with a callused hand and then rubbed his hand back through his short dark hair, hat in his hand. "Viola wants a well dug down there on her place. I'm goin' to dig it. But I need you to help me haul the mud out. Pay you five bucks a day an' get you your dinner as long as you can stand the work an' take it."

"I can take it," I said.

"You make damn sure you can. I don't want a bucket of that mud on my head. When you can't pull it up the side anymore, we'll get a block an' tackle; when you can't pull it up that way anymore, we'll hitch this old tractor to it. We'll start 'bout half past seven in the mornin'."

He moved his foot away from the tire and flipped his cigarette away, exhaling his last drag as he did. Garvey hit the starter, and the tractor jerked away. I watched until he turned the corner about a hundred yards away before turning to the porch.

Five bucks a day was good money, and I felt good that somebody wanted me and thought I could do the job. That made the work much more appealing.

I was waiting when Garvey drove down the road on the old Allis Chalmers the next morning. He braked the tractor to a stop, and I jumped up on the drawbar.

"Now you hang on there, boy," he said.

"I will," I said and watched the front wheels of the tractor turn right and felt the sway of the turn and held on tighter. Two minutes later, Garvey stopped at the foot of the hill below Viola Childers' house.

"Where you goin' to dig her, Garvey?" I asked.

"Up there behind the house unless she tells me to dig somewhere else. That's where we're goin' to take my spade an' shovel."

Some people had already gathered in the backyard. A feller I didn't know had a forked limb off of a peach tree he was using to witch for the water. That was supposed to tell where there was a water vein. I'd heard about finding water that way, but I couldn't understand how a limb turning down could tell anybody where to find water. But that's what everybody seemed to believe. Several of the people there had tried it already and pointed to places where the water had forced their limbs down. I saw the limbs turn down when they walked along.

"Where you goin' to dig her, Garvey?" Old Burns Larue asked, the peach limb now in his hands and pointing down. "They's water right here. Looks like it's comin' off that vein from Harry's place up yonder across the hill there."

Garvey looked at Viola, the little gray-haired woman standing in the back doorway of her house. She looked at Madge standing beside her. She shrugged her shoulders. Viola looked at Garvey.

"What do you think, Garvey?" she asked.

He pointed the spade a few feet in front of her.

"Then dig her there," she said.

By the time the first spadeful was dug, only Garvey and me was left. And there wasn't much for me to do while Garvey could still throw dirt out of the hole. He was only about five foot, three or four inches tall, but he threw the dirt out over his shoulder until I couldn't see his head for a long time.

"Your last name Garvis, Garvey?" I asked to kill time. "Or Charles?"

"Charles."

I tried to think of other things to get him to talk, but he'd grunt or give one-word answers and keep on digging. The day passed pretty slow.

But he was down far enough by the next morning that I began pulling a five-gallon bucket attached to a thick rope and full of clay from the hole to the top and dumping it on the pile Garvey and me had made a few feet away. As Garvey dug deeper, he began to shield his head from the bucket with a stubby hand.

The deeper the well got, the heavier the mud got. And it took Garvey longer to fill the bucket. I was glad of that because I got to rest a little while he worked. He kept the walls straight and rarely rested. He came out of the hole at noon and at quitting time. Other than that, he worked at a steady pace all day.

When the mud got so heavy I was afraid I was going to drop a bucket on Garvey's head, I told him. He had me tie the rope to a stake he'd pounded in the ground and used the rope to climb the wall to the top. He tied three poles in teepee fashion and hung a block and tackle from it for me to use in pulling up the mud. Back in the hole the same way he'd come out, he went back to digging and quit looking up.

"How you makin' it, boy?" he asked in the early afternoon.

"Okay," I said, quiet like and proud of how I was doing. But then as I pulled the bucket to the edge of the well and pulled it back real quick and sat it on the ground, I said, "I think we'd better use the tractor tomorrow, Garvey. Maybe not right off, but tomorrow sometime."

"Okay. Whatever you say. I don't want a bucket on my head."

I hated to give up and use the tractor, but I didn't want to drop a bucket, either. The next morning, I felt stronger and told Garvey we didn't have to use the tractor yet. He nodded and rode the bucket down the hole as I held the rope and let it down easy. Just before noon, my arms was burning by the time I pulled a bucket of mud to the top and told him I couldn't do it anymore. Then we hooked the tractor to the rope. Garvey would fill the bucket, hold it over to the center of the well, and I'd pull the tractor forward, stop it and go back and swing the bucket out from the well and dump it before backing the tractor back toward the edge of the well.

Four feet deeper, Garvey hit water. I pulled him out of the well, and he sat on the edge in his muddy overalls and boots, smoking a Prince Albert cigarette he'd rolled as soon as he scooted to the edge of the hole.

"You done good, boy," he said. "I thought you never would give up. Now, you want to help me brick the wall? I'll need somebody to hand bricks down to me."

I smiled and nodded. I liked working. I felt good and understood a little more what Dad liked about working and showing some pride in it.

Mother didn't feel good most of the time and didn't seem to be getting any better. I'd seen other people stay in bed, but they was old like Granddad McElligott and Mom Garner. They seemed ready to die and just lay there waiting to go. It wasn't that way with Mother. She was still young, and I needed her to live. Sometimes I'd take a chair in from the dining room and sit beside her bed. She'd hold my hand, and we'd talk more than we usually did. I could tell from the sad look in her eyes and things she'd say that she was going to die. That scared me. I knew Big and Aunt Helen would let me stay with them as long as I needed a place to stay. They was family. But not having a mother or a father either one was weighing heavy on my mind.

"You'll start gettin' better soon, Mother," I said one afternoon. "It won't be long before you're back up to the store an' bein' your old self."

"I don't think so, John Walter," she said, taking my hand with both of hers. "I know this is hard on you, never knowing your daddy and about to lose your mother. I'm real sorry how things have been for you. Bill and me never meant for it to be this way. We'd sit out there under the stars up home or down to his folks and talk about how he'd come back from the Marines and farm with Bob and raise a family. We was going to have a whole houseful of kids and make a go of farming like him and Bob had planned to since they was just kids. Then that damn war broke out with him right over there in the middle of things, getting killed and not coming home."

I was surprised to hear Mother talking so openly. And I'd never heard her swear before and was sort of shocked to hear it. I put both my hands in hers, then buried my head on her shoulder to keep from crying where she could see me.

"You're goin' to be all right, Mother," I said, holding her real tight and wiping my tears on her dress. "Daddy didn't have no choice about what happened to him after the war broke out, an' he was already in the Marines. You just get better."

"I can't, John Walter. This thing has got ahold of me, whatever it is, and it won't let go. Nothing the doctors have done has made one bit of difference in how I feel or has made me any better. And it don't look like they'll be able to do anything. They don't even know what's wrong with me. I want to get better and be here for you, but it's not for me to be, I don't think. Your daddy always said we had to meet things head on and be honest with each other. That's what I'm trying to do with you now. I want you to grow up to be a good man that your daddy and me would be proud of. We'll be looking down on you even if we ain't here in this world to be with you. Promise me you'll be a good boy, John Walter. Will you promise that for me?"

"Yes, Mother, I'll promise," I said, tears starting to stream down my cheeks again and agreeing to anything to make her happy. "But don't leave me, Mother. Don't leave me."

She just squeezed my hand tighter and looked at me out of the saddest-looking eyes I'd ever seen and have never seen since. She wasn't crying like I was, but the tears rolled down her cheeks as we looked into each other's eyes for a long time before I got down on my knees at the side of the bed and put my head on her shoulder again. I felt so helpless.

Although we never talked like that again, what we said that day and how things was was always there when I was in the room with her. She seemed to just waste away before our eyes. Her appetite was gone, and she had to force herself to eat anything. By Christmas of my sophomore year of high school, she was little more than skin and bones, and everybody knew it wouldn't be long before she was gone. She was only thirty-six years old. Sometime not long after midnight on New Year's Day, Mother started to sit up and fell back. Aunt Helen and me was sitting up with her in the dim flickering light of a coal oil lamp Mother had asked us to use so the bright ceiling light wouldn't hurt her eyes. I knew she had died. I felt her hand go limp in mine and saw the relaxed look on her face. Aunt Helen started crying, but I couldn't cry anymore and never could when they had the visitation at the funeral home in Martinsville or the funeral down at the old Wesley Chapel where they buried her next to Daddy in the McElligott burying place in the cemetery.

I was numb, I guess, like Doc Bechtel had said. Big and Aunt Helen and the girls didn't know what to say to me. Neither did Dad. But them just being there helped me along. A long line of people came through the funeral home, all of them taking my hand and telling me how sorry they was that my mother had died. I'd nod and mumble thanks and wait for the next one. Sam and Maggie came by early in the day. He took my hand in his and looked at me a long time before he said anything.

Then he said, "Hang in there, Sedwick. Sometimes that's all you can do in this life."

"I reckon so," I said, nodding and glad to see him. "But sometimes that's hard to do. Real hard."

"I know," he said, his face twisting up and his eyes kind of glazed over. "But you do what you've got to do. I'm real sorry about your mother. She was a fine lady an' a good mother."

I looked away, not able to say anything, and Sam stepped on over to Dad. He sat in a chair and hardly said a word, either. I reckoned it was about as hard on him to lose his daughter as it was for me to lose a mother. And crying wasn't his way of handling things in life. Aunt Helen was different. She cried more tears than I ever knew a person could cry and not dry up.

She kept on crying at the funeral the next day, too. I sat there not being able to cry and not hearing what the preacher was saying and looking straight at Mother's casket setting in front of us. I reckoned that's the way things are done when people die. But I hadn't liked my mother laying there with us all staring at her before they closed the casket and the sermon started. I sort of come out of it when Cletis Bonham sang *Amazing Grace*. He had a deep voice and sang Mother's favorite gospel song in an old-fashioned, down-home style that she always liked to hear. I felt a couple of little tears roll down my cheeks as the last word of the song faded away and then died out.

After the funeral was over and the casket was resting on the outfit they used to lower it down in the ground and everybody had left, I stayed behind a few minutes. Big had nodded and touched me on the shoulder when I told him I wanted to stay behind for a minute. I could see the grave diggers standing off next to the road, waiting for me to leave so they could lower Mother in the ground and cover her with dirt.

They'll have to wait, I thought. I wanted to be alone to say my last goodbye to both Mother and Daddy.

I didn't know much about Daddy. He was that hole in everybody's life that we all felt all the time. It was pretty strange for me to think that both Daddy and Mother would now be buried out in the family part of the cemetery, and that they'd go on with the rest of the family that'd been buried there and forgotten as time passed. About all I really knew about any of them was the name on the tombstone and a little about how I was related to them. And the farther back the relationship went, the less I knew about them. The only bridge from one of them to the other was the love in the family that was passed down. I figured that was kept alive as long as there was any of the family still alive.

In Mother's case, that love and that memory was alive in my mind real strong. She'd been taking care of me for my whole danged life. Big and Aunt Helen helped with letting us live with them and by just being there. I couldn't imagine what I'd do without them. But Mother, well, Mother would have taken care of me no matter who was there. After Daddy got killed, she didn't do much else in her life except to see that we was taken care of and keep that love going between her and me and the three of us.

Daddy's life had been stopped; Mother's had been interrupted and never took off again. Their love and their plans was never realized or fulfilled. Yet she was never bitter or showed that she was. Her life went on, and she tried to pick up the broken pieces and do the best she could. I'd heard that time heals all wounds. But at least in her case, I didn't see it that way. She lived on memories and for me. I know she must have thought how life might have been, if only. ...

She never seemed to be a real part of life after Daddy got killed. Maybe she was wounded in the war, too, I thought, and it just took her this long to die. That was as good an explanation as any I'd heard or thought about.

"Goodbye," I said, wanting to say so much more but only managing that one final word when it came down to it. There wasn't anything else to say. I was alone.

21

Nothing much mattered to me after Mother died. I went through the motions at school and flunked everything. Big and Aunt Helen tried to be understanding and kind, but I could tell that they was both losing their patience with me. Big more so than Aunt Helen. I was disking corn stalks one Saturday in late spring just after I'd turned sixteen, and we was eating dinner in the truck when he first talked to me about the way I'd been doing.

"What're we goin' to do with you, Sedwick?" he said, taking a big bite of his tenderloin sandwich. "You're old enough to know better than to act the way you been actin'."

I didn't say anything and just listened while Big went on talking about all the things I'd been doing that wasn't right. Besides flunking my classes, I'd gotten in a couple more fights and sent to the principal's office for cutting class and going over to talk to Bart at the little restaurant. He told me to quit coming over during school and wouldn't let me smoke when I did.

"You ain't ever goin' to amount to a hill of beans, if you don't straighten up," Big said. "I know it's hard on you not havin' a daddy all these years, an' losin' your mom like you did. But there ain't nothin' you can do about it. Nobody has an easy way to go in this life. You have to take what comes an' deal with it the best you can. An' you ain't dealin' with things atall. I don't know what you mean, actin' like you do."

"I don't mean nothin'," I said. "I want to join the Marines."

"Actin' the way you do around here, you'd last about as long as it'd take you to get there. Maybe that's just what you need, though, somebody who won't put up with none of your shit."

"I just need to get away from here. Ain't nothin' here for me no more. I need to get away an' get on with the rest of my life."

Big looked out across the field and said, "Gettin' away won't change a thing, Sedwick. You're the only boy I ever had. I wish you'd just stay here an' finish your schoolin' an' then try farmin' with me. But finish your schoolin' first. Your daddy an' me an' the rest of us never had a chance to go to high school."

"High school is stupid," I said. "They treat you like little kids. They don't teach you to think an' figure things out for yourself. I can't even read a book I want to at that stupid place. When I read something I want to an' I do behave, the stupid teachers take books away from me 'cause they ain't the ones they say I should be readin'. Them teachers don't know nothin' about what I should be readin' or what I should be doin'. I just want to join the Marines an' get away from here an' that school."

"You ain't old enough for that, Sedwick, an' you know it. You ain't even dry behind the years yet."

"Maybe not, but I'm goin' to join as soon as I can," I said, thinking about the plan I had for that after school was out for the summer. After Mother had died, I took her room and looked through all the pictures and stuff that was mine that she'd kept in a drawer. I found my original birth certificate, which I'd never seen before, stuck in the pages of her old Bible. The birth certificate was just a regular old form that had been filled out by the doctor at the time he'd delivered me out on the farm. Everything was completed except he hadn't written in the year I'd been born. Since I was turning sixteen before school was out, I figured I'd make myself eighteen by writing in that I'd been born two years earlier and get my driver's license and run away from home and join up. I didn't write the year in right away because I wanted to be sure that nobody could tell I'd written in the year. So I got a black ink pen and practiced until I didn't think you could tell the difference in my writing and that of old Doc Bates.

"I'd like to be a little mouse in your pocket when you do," Big said and smiled. "They ain't goin' to put up with the kind of shit in there like your aunt an' me have since your mom's been gone. They'll kick it all out of you."

I figured he was right about that but knew I'd get along. It was getting along at home that was hard for me to do. I kept getting in trouble, and Big started taking me with him every time he could. He worked my butt off and talked to me, he said, until he was "blue in the face."

And he showed me about life like they never did in school or like it never did in any of the books the teachers wanted me to read. I didn't have as much time to look for trouble when I was with him.

"You want to see what it's like to be a soldier or a Marine," Big said one afternoon when we'd just hauled a load of registered Angus cattle from a place down on the Wabash River across from Vincennes to a farmer up south of Danville. "Chris is in the VA Hospital just up the road here. While we're s' close, we'll go see him. He ain't worth a nickel. Havin' a purty bad time of it. He's 'bout done, I imagine."

I'd never been to the veteran's hospital and had almost forgot that Uncle Chris had been taken there. He'd had a little stroke and his leg and hip that he got hurt over in France during World War I had been giving him problems for quite a spell. It got so Aunt Catherine couldn't take care of him at home anymore.

Big turned the truck into the hospital grounds. They was kept so neat and clean I couldn't believe it. I'd never seen anything like it. The first buildings looked almost stately, I reckon you'd call them. As the road followed the curve of the ground off to the east, the old-style buildings gave way to some that looked a bit more modern. The more stately looking two-story buildings stopped and a bunch of one-story, sprawling buildings started stretching out on either side of the winding road and the fresh-mowed grass.

A robin hopped along the grass, looking for something to eat. Across the street, a young squirrel ran between two buildings. In one place, two men lay in the grass listening to a radio. In another, men sat in wheelchairs in the warm afternoon sun. Some of the men was missing legs, others arms. Some was smoking, others talking, a few just staring off.

"These fellers went away to the war, Sedwick," Big said as he parked the truck in a parking lot. "Ask them about joinin' the Marines. Or the Army. Or joinin' anything."

"What's the matter with them?" I asked. "They don't look good. Was they all hurt in the war?"

"Some of 'em, I 'magine. Not all of 'em. Some of 'em are just old an' sick."

Allen's Sanitarium in Robinson was the only hospital I'd ever been in to see anybody. And that was only once when Aunt Helen had her appendix taken out. I'd sure never seen so many men in a hospital and didn't know what to say. We walked into one of the buildings, and Big stuck his head into a nurse's station and said he was looking for Chris Bryan, his brother-in-law. The nurse nodded toward the sitting room where more old men, soldiers of another time, sat in wheelchairs, nodding off to sleep.

"Wait in the room around the corner from you," the nurse said. "I'll bring him in there."

In the visiting room, we sat in one of the imitation leather chairs that was set between couches around the room. The nurse wheeled in a frail, white-headed man who looked real old. I hardly recognized Chris. His hair had always been coal black, and he was always tanned and had a big, booming laugh. This Chris was all hunched over and looked only about half the size I remembered him. He looked at us out of the wheelchair slump.

"Who are you?" he asked, his eyes glinting in the afternoon sun and showing no sign of recognition.

"Bob," Big said. "An' this is John Walter, Bill's boy."

"Oh, hell yes," he said, the recognition showing in his eyes as he smiled and held out his hand to shake ours. "I know who you are now. How the hell are you?"

"Pretty fair, I reckon," Big said and shook Chris' hand.

I shook his hand next. The handshake was feeble, the voice shaky. Chris' hand was still large and thick. But now it was baby soft and the grip was weak, not like the fingers that used to pinch us and the hands that used to be work-hardened and strong.

"You haven't been to see me for a long time, have you?" he asked, his eyes moving from Big to me and then back again. "Not since I've been sick, anyway."

Big told him we hadn't been to see him since he'd been in the veterans' hospital. Chris said some words to Big that I didn't understand, laughed a little and snapped his mouth shut to hold his false teeth in place.

"I thought you quit chewin'," Big said. "That's what you said the last time I talked to you."

"Oh, yeah," Chris said, smiling. "I've still got two packs, though. Tried one this morning, an' it made me about half sick so I threw it away. I didn't throw the package away, just the chew. Want one?"

"Me?" I asked when I saw he was talking to me. "No, I can't chew that stuff. I tried an' it more 'n makes me half sick. It makes me sick all the way."

Chris laughed but didn't say anything. His bony frame was covered by floppy skin, and his crippled leg was back against the side of the wheelchair the way I'd always seen him sit. I saw that there was a bar across his lap in the wheelchair so he couldn't get out. It was just a fragile, plastic-looking little cover over a rod held in place by a little screw and stuffed through a couple of flimsy pieces of plastic on the sides of the wheelchair. When he was strong and healthy, he would have been able to rip it off with one hand. Now it kept him in place.

"I'd like to get this damn thing off," he said, seeing me look at the bar. "Swiped a screw driver a couple of times to get it off, but they found it an' took it away from me."

The three of us laughed. I was kind of glad that he wanted out of the chair bad enough to try to steal screwdrivers. But from the looks of him, I knew that it'd take more than that.

"But, now by god, I'll tell you," Chris said, shifting his crippled leg and pulling it more to the front of the chair, "tell 'em you gotta shit, an' they let you out in a hurry. I used that a couple of times. It works, too."

We laughed again. Then he looked over his shoulder at the door, hunching his shoulders slightly and scrunching his neck down a little. His eyes had some fear in them, but he began talking about other things. He talked first to Big, then to me, skipping from subject to subject with little connection between them.

"Aw, hell, I don't know," he finally said. "Tried to starve myself to death here while back. 'Bout made it."

That surprised me at first. But I remembered what a big, strong man Chris used to be and sort of admired his courage in a crazy kind of way. I knew I wouldn't want to live like he was living then. Who would? I wondered.

"What'd you want to do somethin' like that for?" Big asked. "That ain't right."

Chris laughed and said, "Ain't right? What ain't right? I ain't got nothin' to live for. Not a goddamn thing. Just thought I'd starve myself to death an' get it over with."

Under the circumstances, I thought I understood. Big didn't seem to feel comfortable with what Chris was saying. I shrugged and knew there was nothing I could do about it. But a helpless feeling settled over me, thinking about all the people I knew that had died or was dying. That didn't make me feel good.

The more he talked, the more I could see Chris was getting tired. He jumped from subject to subject more and more and kept forgetting what he was talking about more often. Big asked him if he hadn't been home not long before and if he hadn't enjoyed that.

"Oh, I don't know when it's been since I was home," Chris said. "I just couldn't tell you. But you can't tell a damn thing about what I say, 'cause I'll say one thing an' mean somethin' else. I don't know nothin'."

"Didn't you go home for Easter?" the nurse asked, sticking her head in the doorway.

"What'd you say?" Chris asked, turning to her and putting his hand to his ear.

She repeated the question, raising her voice.

"Did I call home?"

"You went home," the nurse said louder this time.

"Leave home?"

"Went."

"Went home? A couple of days after Easter?"

"Right."

"That's too far back," Chris finally said and laughed. "I don't remember that far back."

"You remember when you got your leg hurt, don't you, Chris?" Big asked. "You remember that far back, don't you?"

"Oh, you're goddamn right I do," Chris said, his eyes narrowing and clearing up. "Don't think I'll ever forgot that mornin'. War was 'bout over. Still some shooting goin' on. We was still gettin' wounded, an' we was takin' one back to a field hospital. That sonuvabitchin' Jackson was drivin' an' tried to beat a train. He didn't make it. If he'd 've paid attention to what he was doin', we'd 've missed that goddamn train. The wounded feller was killed, I was crippled an' that goddamn Jackson never got a scratch. Ought to 've killed 'im deader 'n hell."

The nurse nodded her head at us. "That's the way he is," she said, lowering her voice now and acting like he wasn't even there. "Sometimes he remembers pretty well back then; at other times, he can't remember anything. Not even five minutes ago."

"I know," Big said. "An' I know he was back home awhile back. We went up an' visited with him."

"Then I must've been there then, if you say so, Bill," Chris said. "You're Bill, ain't you?"

My heart raced. He thought Big was Daddy now.

"No, I'm Bob," Big said. "But this is Bill's boy."

"Aw, hell, 'course you're Bob," Chris said. "Big. But I don't know a goddamn thing. Can't even jack off anymore. My old pecker won't get hard like it used to. What the hell's the use in livin'?"

My face turned red as I stole a look at the nurse. She acted like she never heard what he said and turned away while Big and Chris went on and talked about the weather and farming. Chris asked about a couple of people by name that I didn't know, and I wasn't even sure which one he was asking about. Big didn't seem to be, either, and asked which one he meant.

"Either one," Chris said. "Don't make no difference."

Big told him where the two men was and what they was doing. For a minute then, Chris didn't seem to know the men at all, even though he'd asked about them. When Big told him they were relatives on the Bryan side of the family, Chris shook his head.

"I don't remember nothin'," he said. "Not a damn thing. I'm in a helluva shape. My memory is gone. Can't remember nothin'. Damn, I don't know. I ain't worth a damn for nothin'. Oughta died a long time ago."

Chris looked at us and then out the window for a while.

"What the hell?" he finally said. "When you get to a place where you don't get nothin' out of life, you might as well die. An' life don't mean nothin' to me. Not a goddamn thing."

I wasn't used to hearing talk like that and didn't know what to say. Big had kept quiet most of the time, but he asked Chris if he hadn't had a good life.

"Yeah, I admit that," Chris said. "An' I appreciate it. Catherine's been good to me. Her whole damn family. I've got some good kids, too. But, Jesus, I feel bad now. My head's achin'."

He looked at the door the nurse had left by. Big started to get up. I figured he was going for the nurse, and Chris must have thought the same thing.

"No, uh-uh, don't call the nurse. She won't give me nothin'. They don't know nothin'. Don't know a fuckin' thing."

We sat quietly for a minute. Chris' eyes was filled with pain. The look made my head hurt, too.

"The headaches generally don't last long," he said, starting to fiddle with the locks on the wheelchair. "They come an' leave. But, boy, I'm in a bad way now—I want to lock these damn wheels. There. Got that one."

Big reached over and locked the other one.

"I thought I wanted to get up," Chris said. "I don't know now. Well, I think I'll go over there an' lay down on the couch."

"Wouldn't it be better to go back to your bed an' take a nap?" Big asked. "That'd help the headache go away."

"A nap might help," Chris said. "But I don't want to go to bed. The couch is fine, if the nurse'll take this damn bar off."

Big went for the nurse this time. When she came in, she took the bar off and helped Chris stand and guided him to the couch. He still limped quite a bit, and he drug the bad leg along much more than I remembered.

"Come back, boys," he said after he'd stretched out on the couch. "I like company, just not too much of it. I'm not worth a damn for nothin' no more."

He took Big's hand and pulled him slightly toward the couch, holding Big's hand longer than usual. Big held his hand and told him we had to go now but that we'd visit with him later. I wondered if Chris would still be there when we came back.

"You're comin' back today?" Chris asked.

"No," Big said, "but sometime."

No time in particular, I thought, just when we're on our way somewhere. Sometime we'd come back. More 'n likely we'll be going to his funeral before we get around to coming back, though, I thought. I said goodbye and squeezed Chris' bony arm, the muscle all gone. Big and me walked down the air-conditioned halls on the shiny floors. Everything seemed so cold and unfriendly. It was a helluva place to be, I thought, a helluva place to die.

Outside in the warm afternoon sun, we walked back to the truck. I thought about growing old, getting sick and staying in a place like Chris was in. I wondered what it'd be like, if I made it to an old age like him and if I'd end up like him. I hoped I wouldn't and thought of the song I'd heard about living fast, loving hard and leaving a beautiful memory.

After I got all the way grown up, I hoped I didn't have to spend any time anyplace outside of my own choosing. Doc Bechtel's words about free will or doing what you did because of where you'd been and what you'd done crossed my mind. I liked the idea of having free will, and I hoped I'd never end up in a place like Chris was where the nurses talked to me like I was a kid, speaking to me in a louder voice to make me hear, whether I was hard of hearing or not, and allowing an edge of looking down their noses at me to creep into their voice until everyone talked to me in the same kind of snotty way.

Seeing Chris in the shape he was in really made me think about spending my last days away from my friends and relatives. That'd be a rough way to go, I thought. As Big drove away, he didn't say anything. I think he just wanted me to think about Chris and what we'd seen at the veterans' hospital. Which I did.

On Memorial Day a few days later, I halfway listened to the Indianapolis 500 car race like I had for the last few years. But I didn't even hear who won and didn't care. The radio was still on when Big came rolling in in the old Dodge and came in with a real sad look on his face. I knew something bad had happened just as soon as I saw him. So did Aunt Helen.

"What's the matter, Bob?" she asked, bringing her hands together at her mouth. "What is it this time?"

"That dang Matthews kid come flyin' up the 'Napolis Road from Porterville like a bat out of hell late this afternoon," Big said, tossing his hat over on the floor in the hall before going on in a cold, hard voice, "an' come down over that hill by that little crick bridge down there a couple of miles south an' hit Sam an' Maggie head-on. Threw her up against the windshield an' broke her neck an' busted her head all up. Sam dang near broke the steerin' wheel but hung on an' jammed his neck hard up against the roof of the car."

Big sat down in his chair in the front room and lay back like he was all tired out. For a minute, he just sat there real quiet and stared out the window. Then he went on in the same tone of voice, but I noticed his hands shaking a little as he talked.

"Albert was throwed clear out of the car an' out in the field. He was a mess, all bloody an' mangled but still livin'. Don't know how he's goin' to make it. It was a bad one. Wonder anybody is livin'. I was up to Charlie's at the garage there when somebody called in about a wreck. I went down with him in the wrecker. Sam was still out when we first got there, but by the time the ambulance came he was conscious an' knowed Maggie was dead an' started hollerin' an' cussin' like he did that time when we was spreadin' lime an' he fell off the back end of the spreader.

"I got him settled down after a while," Big said, his voice dropping to a softer tone, "an' they took him to the hospital in Terre Haute. I'm goin' over in the mornin' an' see how he is. I know he'll want to come home, if he can atall, an' take care of arrangements for Maggie. They'll have to bury her in the next couple of days, I reckon."

Both Aunt Helen and me just stood there like we was in shock. Which I reckon we was. Nancy and Mary Beth hung back and listened. Dad sat over in the corner and moved his thumbs around in circles, first one way, then the other, the way he often did.

"Is Sam goin' to be all right?" I asked.

"I 'magine he'll come through okay," Big said. "He was up an' walkin' around, but he's pretty bunged up. Couldn't turn his head much either way."

"What about Big Al?"

"He might live, might not. I don't know. He looked awful. Bad as any feller in a wreck that I've ever seen. They done as much as they could for him there an' then took them on to the hospital. He's goin' to have a rough way to go, if he does live."

I hope the sonuvabitch dies, I thought. That's what I hope. Sonuvabitch deserved to die a long time ago for what he'd done. Then I figured that wasn't right. He was an asshole for sure and had just killed Maggie, but I didn't reckon I really wanted him to die.

When we heard later he would live, I figured that'd be better than dying because he'd have to live with what he'd done.

Big and me went over to Terre Haute the next morning and brought Sam back to The Corners with us. The doctors wouldn't let him go at first, but he said he was going whether they let him go and whether Big would give him a ride or whether he had to take a cab or whether he had to walk in the hospital gown he was wearing. It didn't make no difference to him one way or the other, he said.

"You fellers might as well get it in your heads that I'm goin' home," Sam said to Big and the doctors, a glazed, half-crazed look in his eyes that I'd never seen before, and he started walking out the door. "Ain't no reason for me to stay in here when they's things to be done. I aim to get over home an' get 'em done."

So Sam got his clothes and personal things, and Big let him ride back home with us. He looked awful. He had a neck brace on that kept his head stretched up like an old goose strutting around the barnyard, both eyes was black, and he had cuts and bruises all over his face and arms from the broken glass. Big wanted to go with him to make the funeral arrangements, but Sam said he'd take care of that himself. Nobody said much on the way back from Terre Haute. Sam just said a quick thanks when we stopped at his house, and he walked up the driveway.

Two days later, we all went to Maggie's funeral over at Wesley Chapel. I hadn't been over there since Mother's funeral and was beginning to lose any connection to the tombstones with my family's names on them. They was just stones and there wasn't nothing but the tombstone and caskets down in the ground with old moldy, decayed bodies in them that used to be my mother and daddy. Dust to dust, ashes to ashes and all that crap, I thought, as I stood back away from the graveside where they was saying a prayer.

I went over to Sam after everybody had shook hands and told him how sorry they was again and headed for their cars at the roadside. He looked at me when I walked up to him, then back out across the field. I saw the tears in his eyes and felt kind of awkward. I didn't know what to do or say.

"I'm might sorry, Sam," I said, tears running down my cheeks, too. "You an' Maggie seemed like you was so happy. It just don't seem fair."

"Nobody said life had to be fair, Sedwick," Sam said, looking down into my eyes. "Hardly ever is so's I can tell. I wouldn't be here, if it was."

We stood facing each other, neither of us knowing what to say. It was real awkward for me to even look at him.

"Well, I'm goin'," I finally said, kind of lame-like, and shook his hand again. "I'll see you sometime, I reckon."

"I reckon you will, Sedwick," Sam said. "Maybe. Just don't take no wooden nickels. You can't spend the damn things."

Big and me did see Sam again three days later when we stopped by Sam's house on the way home that evening from the field where Big'd been planting corn. Sam was out behind the house at a fifty-gallon oil drum he used as a trash-burning barrel. As we walked up, flames shot up every little bit when Sam tossed some waded-up papers in the barrel. He stopped and took a long drink from a bottle in his hand before he seemed to notice that we was there.

"That don't help nothin', Sam," Big said, motioning to the bottle. "Just makes things worse."

"Makes the pain go away sometimes, Big. An' I've got a helluva lot of pain right now. Makes you think it's not so goddamn bad to be left behind when everybody else goes on an' leaves you behind to face another fuckin' day."

"Somebody's always got to be left behind, Sam," Big said. "That's the way it is. Some make it an' some don't."

"I reckon," Sam said, taking another drink. "I always wanted to make it. Sometimes when we'd been through hell back in the war an' lost a lot of men, old boys I'd been with for a couple of years or more, I'd look at them an' think, 'You sonsabitches got it made now. You don't have to ever go through this shit again. You lucked out an' got the easy way out. Lucky bastards. But you left me here all alone.' That's about how I'm feelin' about things right now. Wherever we go after this has got to be better than this shit. If it ain't, there ain't nothin' to it."

I didn't know what to think and felt like I was kind of invisible to Sam and Big. They was close to the same age, and for a long time I'd thought they was more like brothers than any of Big's real brothers, except Daddy. And he hardly counted because he'd been gone for so long.

"Don't talk like that, Sam," Big said, taking a long drag on the Pall Mall he'd just lit and then flipping it off into the burn barrel. "Don't do nobody no good. You're still here, an' you don't go until your time comes."

"You can make your time come."

"I reckon you can do anything you want to. Lots of fellers get by somehow, though. Look at Grandma. You can remember how she had it, can't you? She lived fifty years or better after Granddad died there right at the end of the War Between the States."

"I ain't lots of people, an' I don't aim to get by for no fifty years. That'd make me a helluva lot older that I ever want to be. I never figured I'd live to be an old man, no how."

"What you doin' now?"

"Gettin' rid of lots of old papers an' things I don't need no more," Sam said, taking another drink. "Should've got rid of 'em a long time ago. Just this, that an' one thing an' another."

Big talked with Sam a bit longer, and then we went on to Bellair. It scared me the way Sam was talking. I'd never heard him talk that way in all the time I'd spent riding with him. And for the first time I could remember, I wasn't able to sleep. I'd been spending a lot of time on Sunday mornings when we didn't work in the field going through pictures of Daddy and Mother and other things she had kept that was special to her and our family. So I turned on the light after tossing and turning for a while and started sorting through what Mother had left me of our family memories and mementos. All together they might have filled a grocery sack or two. There was an album that had pictures from the time Mother and Daddy'd started going out, when they got married, some of Daddy in the Marine Corps, a few of the three of us and then some of Mother and me down through the years. There was several letters from Daddy all tied up in a neat little bow. I felt funny about reading them and had left them all where they was except the one on top. It was postmarked October 12, 1942, a few days before Daddy got killed. I looked at it for a long time before finally pulling the letter out to read it. It was a one-page letter, dated October 2, 1942, in handwriting that looked much like mine:

"Dear Lorene,

"I haven't had much time to write lately but think of you and John Walter every day. Sometimes those thoughts are all that keep me going. I don't know how much longer I'll be out here. But I can't wait to get this war over with and get back with the two of you and everybody back home. That can't happen soon enough for me.

"How are you and him getting along? I'll bet he's growing like a weed and getting into everything. That probably keeps you hopping. Please give him a big old hug from his daddy and tell him I love him very much. More than I can tell you.

"I love you, too, Lorene. You probably don't know how much, either. I'd just like to hold you in my arms one more time. I'd give anything to be able to do that. Those little dimples in your cheeks when you smile make me feel like a million dollars. I can still see them real clear all the time.

"Hold onto things and take care of yourself and John Walter until I make it back. And tell Mom and Pop and Brother Bob and Helen and the rest of the family hello for me. We all just got to keep on keeping on.

"With love,

"Bill"

I sat there on the bed with the letter in my hand for a long time. The letter itself didn't say much. It did tell me that Daddy loved me and knew me. That was sometimes hard to know because I only knew him through pictures and stories. But the letter was the last word Mother had had from him, and he said he did. It wasn't much to have to hold onto. Yet that was it and was about all I had. One day he was there, writing a letter, thinking about Mother and me and when he was coming home; a little more than three weeks later he was gone for good. Even though they'd sent what was left of him back, he'd stayed there forever on a far-away island that was only a name to me. What was left of him would probably only fill a grocery sack now, too, I thought. Big said it was hard telling whether it was even him in the casket. I finally put the letter back in the envelope and put everything back in the drawer and was able to get to sleep for the rest of the night.

After going back to bed, I slept late the next morning. It was half past eight when I woke up and Big came home with more bad news. I wasn't ready for it on top of everything else.

"Sam killed himself this mornin'," Big said, his voice cracking up a bit. "He'd got that old German rifle he brought back from the war back from Billie here while back."

I shuddered and remembered the rifle.

"He spent all day yesterday goin' through his things an' burnin' papers like he was when John Walter an' me was there in the evenin'.

I should've knowed what he was goin' to do an' tried to stop 'im. But I never even thought about him doin' somethin' like this."

Big stopped talking for a minute and kind of sobbed. Me and Aunt Helen was both crying, too, but I'd never seen Big so upset that he'd cry like he was doing. He'd always been there like a rock when everybody else fell apart and needed somebody to lean on. And we'd all leaned on him from time to time.

It was a while before he could talk again.

"You can't blame yourself, Bob," Aunt Helen said, putting her arms around him. "Whatever will be, will be."

"I'm not so sure about that anymore, Helen. Gil was there later last night an' said Sam was cleanin' that old rifle an' oilin' it up. I've always been able to talk to him when other fellers couldn't. I should've been able to see what he was goin' to do an' done something to stop him. Wes Davis said he should've seen what was goin' on an' talked to him, too. He thought he might've been able to help him because they was together so long durin' the war. But I've been around Sam all my life an' knowed him as well as anybody. I should've stopped him.

"He told Gil that old rifle almost got him one time, that it was too bad it didn't. Gil tried to take the rifle away from him before goin' home, but Sam told him to go on home an' mind his own business. Gil said he was his brother an' was mindin' his business. But Sam pushed him out the door an' shut the door in his face. Told him to get the hell on out of there an' leave him alone. Wasn't much else Gil could do, I reckon.

"But he must've been the last one to see Sam alive. Somebody called Gil early this mornin', said they'd heard a shot over at Sam's. When Gil got there, he saw Sam layin' on the ground just off the back porch. He'd stuck the rifle in his mouth an' fired the only round he still had for that old rifle an' blew his head off."

"That's enough, Bob," Aunt Helen said, her voice cracking. "These kids don't have to know everything. They've heard enough."

My life was already filled with gory details. A few more wasn't going to hurt anything. Big stopped, though, and said again how he should've been able to stop Sam. I figured if Sam wanted to kill himself, there wasn't much anybody, even Big, could have done to stop it.

Gil and Sam's other brother and sisters made the funeral arrangements. Like all the rest of the funerals I'd been to, Sam's was pretty simple.

The visitation at the funeral home was the night before the funeral. The next day, men wore American Legion and VFW caps with their suits and saluted as the honor guard fired a gun salute at the end of the graveside ceremony. Wes Davis stood off to the side by himself with a faraway look in his eyes. Three of Sam's other buddies he'd served with in the war saluted the casket and stepped back as the rifle shots faded away and echoed through the countryside.

"Goodbye, Mac," one of them said real quiet like. "You picked a helluva day to die."

And I reckon he had. He'd picked June 6, twelve years to the day after he'd landed on Omaha Beach on D-Day. The day he'd picked wasn't just a coincidence, I was sure. I figured the Invasion was what was going through his mind when he pulled the trigger. He'd told me once that the war and that day would be the last things he thought about before he died. Nobody else said anything about it, though. The newspaper story about Sam killing himself never even mentioned his time in the Army or where he'd been and what he'd done. The head- line over the story just said, "Annapolis man takes own life."

The June 6 date was the start of a time Sam always said he wouldn't live over for a million dollars but also a time that he wouldn't take a million dollars for; it was the date he got married, and it was the date he did no telling what else that mattered to him. It'd been the most important day of the year to Sam, just like he'd been real important to me. He was the brother that I'd never had, the daddy that I never knew and the cousin and the friend that I always knew meant the world to me. He was just as much a part of my life as Mother and Big and Aunt Helen. That he was gone now was about more than I could take. I felt the tears well up in my eyes and looked around to see if anybody had noticed. Wasn't no goddamn sense in letting anybody see me cry.

Big knew I was hurting. After supper that evening, he asked me to come out on the porch. He lit a Pall Mall and didn't say anything until after he'd smoked it and flipped the butt off in the grass.

"I reckon you've had about as rough a life as Sam an' some of the boys who went away to the war, John Walter," Big finally said as the setting sun brought the twilight of the evening. "You're just sixteen years old, an' you've already lost your daddy an' your mom. She had a rough row to hoe, too. An' now Sam's gone.

"None of us is promised a dang thing in this life, except a chance to live. The war comin' along an' the way things are achangin' in this old world didn't leave things very promisin' for us. Things might have been a lot different for me, if I'd have gone to the Army. But I stayed here an' tried to keep everything goin' with them dang old trucks.

"Now the truckin' business is about dried up, an' I'm too old to get out an' get a job that amounts to anything. So I'm tryin' to keep one truck runnin' an' farmin' Mom's ground an' what other ground I can get an' take care of things here. Life's a devil of a sight different than your dad an' me thought it'd be back before he went to the Marines. We thought we'd have the world by the tail in a downhill drag after he come home, an' we'd truck an' raise cattle an' hogs an' have things goin' our way."

Big's voice sort of trailed off, and he lit another cigarette. He didn't say anything for a long time, and I didn't know what to say. Long after he'd finished the cigarette and the twilight was fading, Big reached over and put his hand on my shoulder before he stood up.

"Ain't nothin' to do but keep on keepin' on, Sedwick," he said real soft. "That's all any of us can do. No matter what happens."

I just nodded and remembered Daddy's letter but didn't say anything. Big walked across the porch and on into the house. I kept looking at the door after he closed it behind him. I wasn't ready to go in yet myself. So I turned back to watch the moon slowly rise higher in the eastern sky and to think some more about what Big'd been saying.

Keep on keepin' on, he'd said, no matter what. And that's what Big knew how to do better than anybody I'd ever known. He'd hung in there for a long time — when he had to stay home during the war and take care of us all and handle everything that happened as everybody around him tried as best they could to figure it out. Some of them couldn't, I guess. And through it all, Big'd done as good a job as a feller could do. I reckoned he'd have been a pretty good soldier, if he'd had the chance. I wanted to be there for him like he was there for me. And yet, I figured I wasn't anything like Big; I never would be. My chance to see who I was really meant to be was still out there, I knew, somewhere other than Bellair, waiting for me to find it.

✳

Acknowledgments

This novel is a work of fiction that springs from a lifetime of breathing Midwest. The people there are the salt of the Earth. My heartfelt thanks goes out to my father and mother and all of those whose lives have touched mine and somehow provided material for this story.

Every World War II combat veteran I ever met or read about has contributed to my knowledge of the war and its effects. From Bruce Elliott, Ben Correll, Norm Ulrey, Art Farley, Stormy Napier, Bill Ridgeway, Cleon Matheny, Merv Beil, Leonard McCrory and many others on through to Gunny Brickman and Mac McManus, veterans of Guadalcanal and other South Pacific campaigns with whom I served in the Philippines, I am deeply indebted. And I'm indebted to the veterans I talked with during the writing of the novel: John Dart, Dick Lewis, Bob Brigham, Bob Steele and Colonel Mike Barszcz spoke openly about their war experiences and life afterward. Betty Frye made invaluable contributions to my knowledge of the experiences of and the effects on the women who were left behind. Thanks to them all.

A special thanks is due to my wife Vanessa Faurie for being there every step of the writing and publishing process. Her contributions have been monumental. Thanks, too, to designer Carlton Bruett for the cover concept that captures the essence of the novel so well.

Readers have helped shape the content. Vanessa read the manuscript long before it was ready. George Hendrick wasn't far behind. Their input and encouragement are much appreciated. Thanks also to Miles Harvey, Teri Hallowell, Walt Harrington, Don Sackrider, Jack Scovill, Mable Elliott and John Bowers for their insightful comments. Each of them brought a unique perspective that was most helpful.

Without these many contributions, there would be no novel.